Hope's Corner

CHRIS KENISTON

USA TODAY BESTSELLING AUTHOR

Indie House Publishing

Indie House Publishing

BOOKS BY CHRIS KENISTON

Champagne Sisterhood
The Homecoming
Hopes Corner, Texas

The Honeymoon Series
Honeymoon for One
Honeymoon for Three

Aloha Series
Shell Game
Aloha Texas
Almost Paradise
Mai Tai Marriage
Dive Into You
The Look of Love
Love By Design
Love Walks In

ACKNOWLEDGEMENTS

There are always so many people to thank when a book comes together and *Hope's Corner* is no exception.

As always to Molly Cannon for sticking by me no matter how many deadlines loom. To Vicki Batman for reading this thing over and over and over. To Linda Steinberg for finding the spring point. To Liz Lipperman, Karen Chetty, and Cheryl Lucas for taking on yet another book. And To Mary and Kathy Sullivan for the constant support.

A special thank you to Regina and her hubby, Steve. No matter what time, day, or personal crisis, you walked me through the police procedures so as not to embarrass myself. Any and all mistakes are mine and no reflection on your patient efforts.

And to my publishing coordinater, Dallas Hodge, for sticking with me despite the growing demands in the publishing business.

CHAPTER ONE

*H*urry. The crumpled brown grocery bag slipped an inch farther down her hip; sweat trickled along her brow. If only her hands would stop shaking. Blinking quickly, she willed back the tears. She would not cry.

A heavy weight brushed against her pant leg. Fear surged and her grip tightened. The ragged edge of a key sliced into her palm. Then she heard it; not the thump of human footsteps but a soft mewl. Peaches, the calico she'd rescued from a local shelter, had jumped from the porch railing and now circled her feet. Her forehead hit the cool glass window of the old wooden door. "Damn."

This was ridiculous. No one pressed behind her. No stale hot breath bathed her neck. No icy fingers restrained her. Nothing chased her but her own fear. Her mind knew all this, and yet, she couldn't stop the rising panic, the growing sense of danger any more than she could stop Peaches from leaping onto the porch.

She'd moved home to Hope's Corner, hoping, praying it would put an end to the daily torment. While she no longer suffered from nightly terrors, the occasional nightmare left her nervous, on edge, and downright petrified of her own shadow.

"Are you okay?" A distant baritone voice carried up to her.

The ebbing panic rose again, licking at her racing heart.

"Do you need some help?" The voice, a very masculine voice, moved closer. With his every step, the wooden porch groaned under his weight. When the heaviness of the bag she'd clutched to her side lifted away, she bolted back as though stung by a live wire.

"I noticed you seem to be having a little trouble with the lock." The words were spoken softly, slowly. He'd taken a half step back. The corners of his mouth tilted in what he no doubt meant to be a disarming smile, but his piercing eyes studied the way she now pressed herself against the wall with an intensity that set her every hair on end. Still smiling, his hand stretched hesitantly forward. "May I try?"

Her grip tightened on the keys in her hand. The sharp stinging pain shot up her arm. She almost tripped over the cat now preening at her feet. The polite stranger, who had been casually holding her groceries and patiently extending his hand, wrapped his strong fingers around her arm to steady her.

"Careful." His voice came out in a near whisper, the look in his eyes softer.

Irrational fear and panic in control—her throat tightened, she couldn't speak, couldn't find words. Keys still clenched in her hand, she raised her arm to him. As he pried her fingers open to retrieve them, she kept her attention on his face, watching every shadow, every nuance. Shock flickered momentarily in his eyes when he saw her grip had been tight enough to draw blood.

It was his grimace that brought her a slip of calm. She'd seen the pain in his eyes as he'd pulled the keys away and stared at her bleeding palm. Nearly numb from head to toe, she watched him slide the key into the lock, turn the latch, and shove open the door.

Grateful she was able to make her mouth move, she mumbled, "Thank you", yanked the keys from the lock, and hurrying inside, slammed the door shut behind her. Her back pressed to the door, she dragged in deep ragged breaths. Another surge of panic rushed through her. He still held her groceries.

***

Now what? He looked from the closed door to the bag in his arms and back again. He didn't need a psych degree to know something had spooked that woman badly, and his offer to help her had done anything but.

"Jefferson Davis Parker, what are you doing growing roots on Pamela Sue's porch?"

Good question. "She seemed to—"

"I thought I told you to be here at four? It's only three o'clock. You're early." Etta Mae Parker stomped up her neighbor's porch steps and snatched the bag from her son's arms, cutting off his reply.

"A smart boy should be able to tell time," she muttered, nudging him toward the porch steps. "You go on back next door. There's fresh banana bread on the counter. I'll be there in a minute."

A smart *man* knew when to stand his ground and when to do as his mother told him. No one in Hope's Corner could say Etta Mae had raised a fool. He was halfway across Pamela Sue's front lawn before he heard his mother rap softly on the door.

"Pamela Sue. It's me, Etta Mae. I've got your groceries for you, honey."

The door inched open slowly. From his mother's walkway he could barely see wisps of long blond hair peeking through the narrow space as his mom handed over the bag.

Images of an angelic face with button-round bright blue eyes gripped in terror flashed through his mind. Possibilities of what put that fear there in the first place raised his hackles.

He wasn't a violent man. It wasn't part of his job description. But his fists clenched shut with wanting to beat sense into whoever had put that fear in those angelic eyes. One more reason why he knew it was time for a new career.

***

"Here you go, sweetie."

"Oh, Etta." Pam took a deep breath. Had Etta witnessed the entire scene? Once again she'd made a fool of herself. She'd thought it would be different here, better, easier. "I'm so sorry."

"Nonsense, dear. I made some banana bread. Why don't you put your groceries away, and join Jefferson and me for some coffee."

"Jefferson?" Oh no. "That wasn't—"

"Yes. Nice boy when he's not scaring the bejesus out of my new next-door neighbor."

Oh, God, she'd just acted like a first-class nutcase and slammed the door on Etta's son—Pastor Jeff. "I don't think this is a good time, Etta."

"Of course it is. You take all the time you need. I'll go make sure he leaves us some bread." With a wave of her hand, Etta smiled and scurried across the lawn to her own house.

"All the time I need," Pam muttered as she sank to the floor beside the closed front door. "And just how much time is that, Etta? How much time?"

As if saying, "Enough already," Peaches stepped onto her lap and, with precise aim, flicked her tail, clipping Pam square in the nose.

A heartfelt burst of laughter escaped. "Right." Scooping the cat into her arms, she nuzzled her chin across the soft silken fur and took a deep breath. "I can do this." She set Peaches back down, picked up the grocery bag, and pushed to her feet.

Peaches trotted ahead, her tail held high like a parade flag. Following her cat's example, Pam squared her shoulders, lifted her chin, and marched into the kitchen. A few minutes to put away the groceries and she'd be ready.

She wouldn't let that bastard win.

***

"Is your father still napping?" Etta Mae breezed through the front doorway.

"Yeah. He got up to use the bathroom, but decided to go back to bed."

"I was afraid the two of you would have eaten all the banana bread. I wanted to give Mrs. McCarthy across the street a loaf too."

"I'm not hungry, Ma." Staring out the window, Jeff could see his mother's young neighbor moving about her kitchen, putting away the contents of the brown sack he'd held.

His hands still fisted at his sides, he hadn't noticed the painful way his nails bit into his palms until his mother walked up beside him and patted his arm.

"She'll be all right."

"What happened to her?" Flexing his fingers, he continued

watching through the window.

"I don't know." Etta Mae picked up a large knife and slowly sliced the still warm banana bread. "The day she moved in, she was all friendly and smiles. I never noticed her acting skittish. She seemed just fine. Her brothers brought a huge crowd of folks to help. You remember Jake and Bo Wharton?"

"She's big Jake's sister?" He dragged his eyes away from the window long enough to see his mom's grin grow wide as she placed the slices on the blue-and-yellow platter his sister had made for her in fifth grade ceramics class.

"Grown up some, hasn't she?"

"That Pamela Sue is little Pammy Sue Wharton?"

"One and the same. Only now she's Pamela Sue Dawson."

It couldn't be. The last time he had seen her, he and Jake were seniors in high school and little Pammy Sue was a twelve-year-old tomboy. When the rest of the girls her age, including his sister Carol Ann, were discovering makeup, boys, and padded bras, Pammy Sue was still wearing ball caps, T-shirts, and blue jeans, looking like any other middle school baseball player.

The kid was a regular hellion. No one with any sense would dare say a word against her siblings while she was within earshot. Pammy's mouth was a lethal weapon, and for a little pipsqueak, she had a nasty right cross. Once when another player had been teasing Jake for dropping an easy-out fly ball in left field and then falling flat on his face, little Pammy Sue had torn into the dugout and thrown a punch that left the outfielder with a black eye for a week. Her brother Jake laughed it off. He'd snagged Pammy's baseball cap, mussed the top of her short boyish hair as though she were still a toddler, and said, "Way to go, sport."

That fall Jeff had gone off to college in Austin and never gave little Pammy Sue another thought. He certainly never expected the scrawny kid to blossom into his mother's beautiful next-door neighbor. He also wouldn't have expected her to be so horribly afraid of her own shadow.

"I first noticed something wasn't right a few days later." Etta set the plate on the table, then turned to the refrigerator, and pulled out a large pitcher of sweet tea. "I'd taken her some blueberry muffins. Got carried away again. Made too much batter. Figured she could use a little meat on those skinny bones more than your father or me. Anyhow, she was pulling a plate out of the cupboard when I put my hand on hers and asked if I could help. She nearly shot through the ceiling."

Without asking, Etta poured her son a glass of tea and placed it beside him on the counter. "I just wrote it off to her bein' one of those jittery people."

"So what changed your mind?" He'd turned his attention back to the neighbor's house. Pammy Sue had finished puttering in her kitchen, but his gaze lingered on the empty room.

"I was working in the vegetable garden, pulling those infernal weeds. Pamela Sue was reading a book on one of them lounge chairs—the kind you use when you want to get a tan. Anyhow, she must have fallen asleep, because the next thing I know the poor girl was thrashing about and shouting. By the time I was able to get around the fence and into her backyard, she'd let out a bloodcurdling scream, bolted upright, and cried like a baby. She apologized from here to next Tuesday, tried to brush it off as a bad dream. Said something about what she'd eaten for lunch not sitting right with her. But I haven't been a preacher's wife for nearly forty years without knowing when to recognize a soul is hurting. Whatever is haunting that girl, it has nothing to do with bad Chinese food."

He wasn't any good at this. Once again, his fingers curled into fists at his side. Something, or more likely someone, had broken that beautiful spirit. And this time, more than anything, he wanted to be the person to teach that someone a lesson. A lesson he'd never forget.

***

Pam put everything away in the kitchen, arranged the cookies on a pretty plate, then stopped herself from wasting more time cleaning countertops that weren't dirty. Feeling the need to look more presentable, she hurried up the stairs to her room. "I did it again, Travis. I promised myself I wouldn't let that happen anymore, but I freaked out—again. And in front of Etta Mae—again."

Her hands finally a bit more steady, she took a seat at her vanity, touched up her lipstick, and ran a quick brush through her hair. Maybe, she thought for the hundredth time, she was ready to get it cut. Something cute and easy to manage.

"Or not." Turning to the framed photo of her wedding day, she waved her hairbrush at the picture. "Travis Dawson, if you didn't love long hair so much, I could chop it all off and have a nice wash-and-run hairstyle. But I just can't bring myself to do it."

Pam set down the hairbrush and pushed back the small vanity stool. A drop of blood from the cut on her palm had stained the front of her shirt. She needed to change before going to Etta Mae's. "I still remember so clearly the first time I realized you liked girls with long hair…" She walked to the closet. "Jeanne Browne. Remember her? There you were standing in the hall, in front of God and the rest of us, with your tongue on the floor as usual. That's when Jeanne batted those mascara-laden eyes at you, patted the back of her head, and drawled, 'I've been thinking it's time for a change. Maybe I'll cut my hair.'"

Undoing the buttons on her blouse, Pam tossed it into the nearby hamper. "Jeanne might as well have told you that she was going to slit her wrists. You practically lunged at her, begging her not to cut her hair."

The light blue shirt, she wondered. No. The pretty pink top she'd bought online from Talbots would be better. Help her mood. Bright, cheery, not too modest, but conservative enough for a visit with Etta Mae. It would be perfect. "I thought my hair would never grow out, and then when it grew past my shoulders, I still couldn't get your attention. Finally, halfway through your senior year you asked me out. I thought I was going to melt into a puddle right there on the spot."

She slid the shirt over her shoulders and chuckled at the memory. "The first time you ran your fingers through my hair and mumbled something about how beautiful I was, I knew I'd never have short hair again. Of course back then you hadn't told me the truth about the math book yet.

"I remember that night after dinner when you finally confessed what it was about me that first caught your attention." The memory of Travis blushing at the kitchen counter, hemming and hawing made her smile. "You said I was leaving school, about to cross the street to walk home, when I dropped my math book. You just happened to look in my direction as I bent over to pick it up, and then you watched me walking away until I was out of your line of sight."

Buttoning the blouse, looking up at the ceiling, feeling much better, she laughed a little louder. "I thought growing my hair long had gotten your attention but no. My ass. You finally spotted my ass. Good thing Mama knew what she was talking about. She'd said having rounded hips would come in handy someday.

"Of course, I just thought I had a fat backside. Figures Mama was right." Pam's smile faded, she shook her head, sighed, and blinked back the water pooling in her eyes. "You know it made me love you even more that you told me."

Taking a deep breath, she glanced at her reflection in the mirror, then squeezed her eyes shut. "God, Travis. I miss you so much. I'm scared, and I want you here to tell me not to be. To hold me in your arms and tell me I'm beautiful. Tell me I'm the only girl in the world for you, the way you always did. I want everything to be all right again. I need you to make it all right again."

***

"Etta Mae, this is the most delicious banana bread I've ever had." Since moving next door to Etta, Pam had finally resigned herself to the idea of growing old, round, and fat in Hope's Corner. She could no more resist Etta's baked goods than Peaches could turn up her nose at a bowl of fresh cream.

"None of us ever had a shortage of friends," Jeff sat at the kitchen table across from Pam, grabbing at his mother's apron and pulling her close. "Growing up, it was chocolate chip cookies, cupcakes, and blueberry sour cream pie. Every kid in the county wanted to be friends with us, just so they could have a taste of mom's homemade bread."

"Well, that explains why my brothers spent almost as much time here as at home. My mom tried baking bread once. We used it for a doorstop." Pam chuckled, took another bite of banana bread, and swallowed the urge to moan with delight. Yep, she could definitely feel the inches spreading across her hips, but this was so worth it.

"You two cut it out, or you're gonna give me a swelled head." Etta leaned over and kissed the top of her son's head. "How's the hunt going to find a fill-in for Ellen while she's on maternity leave?"

Jeff's smile slipped. "It's not."

"Oh, that is a shame. What seems to be the difficulty?" Etta took a seat across the table from her son, then lifted the teapot designed to look like an ice cream sundae, and poured herself a cup.

"It's proving to be a bit more challenging than we'd expected to find a temporary secretary who knows both her alphabet and how to answer a phone."

"Yes, I heard about the episode with Mrs. Del Rio."

Pam wasn't sure but she thought she noticed Jeff give his mom a quick disapproving glance.

"Mrs. Del Rio?" Pam ventured to ask.

"It was nothing," Jeff said.

This time Pam was sure. He definitely shot his mom a stern warning. Only if Etta noticed, she paid no attention to it and kept right on talking.

"Poor Mrs. Del Rio. Whenever she gets confused, she forgets herself and starts speaking to people in her native Spanish. Your father had hoped that wouldn't pose a problem, but John Haskell told him what happened the other day." Etta turned to Pam. "The head of the finance committee called the church office asking for a copy of last quarter's fiscal report. It took over three hours before the poor woman would speak English again."

"Ma-ah." Jeff drawled the word making it sound like two syllables rather than one.

"I know. I know." She patted Jeff's hand. "No need to get your feathers ruffled. I'm not gossiping, just explaining the facts to Pamela Sue." Etta nudged the dish toward Pam. "Have another slice. You're looking too thin."

Pam almost laughed. It felt good to be mothered. Her mom had died from lung cancer three years ago. Though her mom and Etta Mae were polar opposites in many ways, they had two things in common. They loved their kids and never missed an opportunity to show it. "No, thank you. I couldn't eat another bite."

"What about you, Jefferson?" Etta inched the plate toward her son.

"Thanks, Ma, but I don't have time." The previous difference of opinion quickly forgotten, he gave his mother an appreciative grin, pushed his chair from the table and carried his empty plate to the kitchen sink. "I have to be getting back to the church. Tomorrow is Jennifer Buckner's funeral."

The solemn expression that took over his face stabbed unexpectedly at Pam's heart, reminding her of her own sorrow. She couldn't help but wonder if his pain was merely that of a pastor for a parishioner, or if there was something more personal about the sadness she saw in his eyes.

Knowing how he'd reacted to her bloodied palm earlier this afternoon, it shouldn't have surprised Pam to see him hurting over the death of someone in his church. And yet the way his shoulders seemed to deflate at the mention of Jennifer's name led her to think this death was more personal for him.

Just who was this woman to Pastor Jeff Parker? The name didn't sound familiar. Maybe Jennifer had moved to town in more recent years. So many things had changed since they were all kids. Especially Jeff Parker. The handsome man who'd come to her rescue on her porch looked nothing like the gangly teen who she remembered playing baseball with her brother.

Jeff's youthful sun-bleached blond hair was now a darker sandy color, but the way errant locks occasionally dipped over his brow only served to accentuate the deep sea-green of his eyes. Even in a suit, Pam could see his muscles pressing against the fold of fabric with every graceful movement. He definitely had the strong lean build of a man who worked out on a regular basis or maybe still played sports. She would be willing to wager there wasn't an ounce of fat anywhere on him. With his good looks, he should have a string of anxious single women falling at his feet.

"Don't you agree, dear?"

What? Pam felt heat rush up her neck and flush her cheeks at being caught pondering the personal life of Pastor Jefferson Parker. Not that it was possible for Etta Mae to read Pam's mind. "I'm sorry. I was thinking about something else. What did you say?"

"That you're the perfect answer to Jefferson's problem." Etta Mae grinned with pride. She had the same smile plastered on her face in the nearby photo of her taking the blue ribbon for one of her pies at the county fair.

"Excuse me?" Stunned, Pam was sure all the color that had risen to her cheeks a few moments ago had just drained away. She wasn't the answer to Jeff's problems. She wasn't the answer to anyone's problems. She had too many of her own demons to face.

"The church needs a secretary, and you're looking for work. You won't mind a temporary job until Ellen comes back from maternity leave, will you?"

A secretary. Etta Mae was talking about a job. Relief washed through her followed by a rushing wave of embarrassment. That's what this little tea party of hers was all about. Of course. How stupid, stupid, stupid to think Etta had read her mind and was playing matchmaker. She felt so foolish—again. "I, uh, I don't know."

"Nonsense. You told me the other day that you're havin' a hard time finding work. We all know Hope's Corner isn't a mecca of employment opportunities." Etta Mae shook her head. "I'm sure, if you go to the church tomorrow afternoon, Jefferson can make time for a proper interview."

For the first time since her mind had wandered off contemplating Jeff's personal life, she dared to look over at him. He appeared as dismayed as she felt. She had a feeling this wasn't the first time Etta had blindsided him with unexpected plans. And the small sigh she thought she heard escape from him told her that he didn't expect this to be the last.

"Thank you, Etta, but I don't know anything about working at a church."

"It can't be any different than working for a bunch of lawyers. Last I looked, phones worked the same all over. Instead of clients wanting to sue, parishioners'll be asking for prayers. You'll do just fine."

Pam looked to Jeff for guidance or maybe salvation. He smiled, hitched a shoulder, and made a lost-cause gesture with his hands. If he wasn't going to challenge his mother, then there was no reason for her to. In the past three weeks, if she'd learned one thing living next door to Etta Mae Parker, it was that there was no point in disagreeing with her. The woman had more grit than Rooster Cogburn.

Besides, Pam couldn't very well argue that Etta Mae didn't have a point—Pam did need a job. She glanced in Jeff's direction. *Oh, what the heck.* How hard could working at a church be anyway?

CHAPTER TWO

This was the day from hell. One of the worst of Jeff's life. Second only to the day the nurse at Mercy Hospital had called to tell him Jennifer Buckner had not survived.

Funerals weren't his favorite thing. This funeral was a damn nightmare.

"Ashes to ashes, dust to dust."

A concept he'd learned early in life. From the moment he'd understood most things were finite, his parents had drummed into him the idea of the circle of life. For everything a time, a place under heaven. And in all of that, the unwavering faith in the wisdom of God. Where was that wisdom today?

Jennifer was only a year behind him in school. Smart and friendly, she was just like any of the hundreds of others who had passed through the halls of the local high school. Like everyone else in town, he'd danced at her wedding to Frank Buckner. As far as brides go, Jenny had been among the prettiest he'd ever seen. It wasn't right.

Across from him, Jenny's mother sat stoically staring at the simple white coffin. She'd chosen to bury her only daughter beside Jenny's dad in what should have been her own grave.

He worried about Mrs. Harris. Through everything he hadn't seen her shed a single tear. Jeff's father, Senior Pastor Harlon Parker, had come out of his sickbed to officiate the service. Despite being on medical leave to recover from a triple bypass, Jeff's dad had done his best to offer the grieving woman comfort. But not even the beloved Harlon Parker could soothe the bleeding wound that Frank Buckner had inflicted on Jennifer's mother. He'd cut into her heart as cleanly as if he'd sliced her with the same knife he'd used to slit her daughter's throat.

Jeff wanted to go to her, tell her all would be well, not to despair. But how could he do that? Him of all people.

Jenny had come to him, trusted him, no one else. Not his father, the experienced pastor, the man with the knowledge and history to have handled things…differently. His father would have found a way to stop her from returning time after time to an abusive husband. Harlon Parker wouldn't have let her down. Now Jeff stood among a crowd of so many at Jenny's funeral. He'd failed.

Tomorrow at St Joseph's, Frank Buckner's parents would hold a simple memorial service for the son who had also turned the deadly knife on himself. Half the town would be there. The other half who couldn't understand, couldn't forgive, would not. Jeff needed to attend. It was his job to encourage forgiveness, to help the congregation heal.

He had no right. How could he lead the way to forgiveness when, if given the chance, if it would bring Jenny back and help clear his conscience, he would gladly put Frank Buckner in the grave again with Jeff's bare hands.

Considering the circumstances, his father was holding up well. Soon he'd be able to return to his duties at the church. Only part-time at first, but it wouldn't be long until the congregation would once again be fully under his gentle guidance and protection. Then it would be time. Jeff had already faced the truth. He wasn't cut out to be a pastor. He should have stayed in the corporate world. Maybe if he had, Jenny would still be alive.

As soon as his father was well enough to return to work, Jeff would tell his parents. They'd be upset. Tell him that he was being rash, turning away from his calling. He'd expect that, be prepared, but he couldn't go on living a lie. He knew now he would never fill his father's shoes. Senior Pastor Harlon Parker would never have let Jenny Buckner die.

***

In all the years growing up that she'd attended services at Hope's Corner Community Church, Pam had never been inside the pastoral offices. For some inexplicable reason, the thought of working there now, even temporarily, scared the heck out of her.

It made no sense. This would be a great place to work. The lovely old building was perched on the edge of a creek-side lot. Large plate-glass windows ran the length of the rear wall behind the pulpit, across the main lobby, and all the way back to the offices. As a child during Sunday services, looking out the window behind Pastor Harlon at the trees and grass, and especially the spring flowers, had always made Pam feel a little closer to God. Sometimes even more than his sermon.

Maybe it was the waiting that was making her feel so edgy? It had been over half an hour since she'd first arrived. Jeff had been on the phone. With a few gestures, she had motioned to him that she would wait in the lobby. Now, sitting in one of the lobby's wingback chairs, Pam stared steadily at a blue jay building a nest and wondered what had her feeling so skittish.

For just a moment she glanced up at the ceiling mural, studied the fluffy white painted clouds and pastel blue sky. The chubby cherubs in angel's wings made her think of Travis.

"I don't know. Maybe this isn't such a good idea, after all. For heaven's sake, I'm a paralegal. You of all people know how hard I worked to be a paralegal. It doesn't seem right to give that up now." She turned her attention back to the busy bird.

As if disturbed by her complaints, the bird seemed to look in her direction and then flew away, leaving Pam with an absurd feeling of emptiness. "Oh, Travis, I know I shouldn't let it upset me. It's only a bird. Birds are supposed to fly away."

She let her eyes fall closed, then opened them, tilting her head heavenward, and focused on the cute little dark-haired cherub on the far corner of the ceiling. "Do you think, if we'd had children, they would have looked like that?" With a casual gesture, she raised one hand and pointed at the ceiling.

"I'd always thought someday we'd have a family. You'd have been a wonderful father." She shook her head and blew out a heavy sigh. "I'm sorry, Travis. Forget I said anything. I don't know why I'm being so gloomy. I'm sure, if Jeff offers me the position, working here would be just fine. Ellen only has ten more weeks of maternity leave, and then I can go back to real job hunting. I mean, somewhere in this town there has to be a lawyer in need of a good paralegal. Right?"

Just then she heard the door to Jeff's office squeak open, his shoes slapping on the linoleum, followed by his gentle voice. "Sorry to keep you waiting. Some days the phone never stops ringing."

After a quick smile, a handshake, and gathering up her purse, she followed him into his office.

"It was nice of you to come." He gestured toward one of two vacant chairs in front of his desk. "When my mother makes up her mind, there's no stopping her. You don't have to put yourself through this, if you don't want to."

Something wasn't right. He was smiling, talking, saying all the right things, but something was terribly wrong. What little flicker of light she'd seen in his eyes the day before was no longer there. "Is everything all right?"

"Excuse me?" He squared his shoulders.

"I'm sorry. I don't mean to be rude, but you look...upset." Oh, God. *Open mouth, insert foot.* "I'm so sorry. I forgot. You had to go to a funeral this morning. Please forgive me."

"Nothing to forgive. Losing Jenny was hard for everyone." Picking up a nearby pen, he began tapping it softly against the blotter. "Last week was her thirty-third birthday. You might remember her as Jenny Harris. She was a year behind Jake and me in school. Married Frank Buckner a little over two years ago."

Pam shook her head. "Can't say I remember her. Jake's six years older than me, Bo's three. If she wasn't in either of their classes, it's unlikely I'd have known her. After Travis and I moved to Dallas, Mom would share every detail, and I mean *every* detail of the weddings and births in Hope's Corner, but it sounds like Jenny got married after Mom died. I'm sorry.

"No, I'm the one who's sorry." He set down the pen and forced a smile. "Let's get to the reason you're here—a job."

"Yes." She wasn't sure if smiling at him was the right thing to do. What she really felt like doing was to run behind the desk, pull him into a big old bear hug, and whisper in his ear that soon it wouldn't hurt so much. She still wasn't convinced the pain ever went away altogether, but at least after time she knew it wouldn't hurt quite as much.

"The work is Monday through Friday—"

Interrupted by the ringing of the phone, he lifted a finger at her and took the call. "Community Church. Yes, Mr. Haskell, it's a lovely day…mmm-hmm…mmm-hmm… Excuse me, but I have someone in the office now. Can I get back to you in a bit? Great, thank you." He disconnected the call and turned his attention back to Pam.

"Where were we? He flashed her a sincere smile. Not the strained imitation he'd worn since she had first arrived, but an honest, twinkle-in-his-eyes smile. Praise God she'd already been sitting down. For the first time since Travis, she felt her knees go weak.

He went over the salary, the hours, and explained his schedule. Sometimes he might need her to accompany him on certain home visits of the elderly, but the majority of what he said wasn't registering. She was nearly mesmerized by the bright sparkle that had returned to his eyes. What was the matter with her? She didn't notice men. Not since she was six years old and had fallen in love with Travis.

No. She wasn't going to do that ever again. This job was not a good idea. There was only one man in her life, and he was gone. That was it.

"Excuse me," a delicate voice interrupted.

"Yes, how may I help you?" Jeff pushed to his feet and stepped around the desk to stand next to the short, dark-haired, and very pregnant woman.

"I'm on my way to my doctor's office."

A flicker of panic flashed across Jeff's eyes. The sight so reminded Pam of an old sitcom that she almost laughed out loud.

"Shall I call an ambulance?" he asked in a rush.

"Naw, nothin' like that. It's just my regular checkup, but my car started riding funny. I pulled into your lot here and realized I have a flat."

"Oh, I see." He looked so relieved, Pam had to cover her mouth with her hand to hide her smile.

"Anyhow, I found the jack but can't figure out where it goes. I'm not exactly built for crawling underneath a car and looking for the spot in the manual's diagram."

"Good heavens, no. If you have a spare, I'll be happy to change the tire for you. It'll only take a minute."

"Oh, I don't mean to put you to any trouble."

"It'll be my pleasure, ma'am." He flashed the petite woman a broad grin. When she batted her lashes and blushed in response, Pam wondered how many broken hearts were scattered around Hope's Corner. The man's smile was lethal.

Still smiling, he turned to Pam. "Would you mind waiting? This won't take long."

"Not at all."

"Great, be back in a minute." Without a second glance in Pam's direction, he collected the soon-to-be-mommy's keys and escorted her to the front door.

Outside the Texas afternoon heat slapped Jeff in the face like a cast iron skillet primed to fry an egg. "If you'd please pop the trunk," he asked the woman waddling at his side. "I'll get the spare, and we'll have this taken care of in no time."

Settling the jack under the side of the car, he loosened the nuts to the flat tire and cranked the handle on the jack. Watching the tire lift off the ground, he thought about Pamela Sue. She didn't seem to be the least bit upset that he'd kept her waiting for so long. One of the parishioners, Mrs. Trumble, was refusing to take her medicine again. The only person who could calm her quickly was his dad, so the frustrated daughter would always call the church when her mother was being ornery. Unlike his dad, it could take Jeff close to an hour to get the old woman to cooperate. With Pammy Sue waiting for him, he was lucky today had taken little more than half that time.

The car in the air, he removed the loosened lug nuts. He had to admit, he didn't know what to make of Pammy Sue. The woman sitting politely in his mother's kitchen and in the church lobby couldn't have been the terrified person he'd found on her front porch. Could she?

Easing off the tire, he rolled it to the back and tossed it into the trunk. When he'd approached Pammy Sue in the church lobby, he'd feared he might startle her, but there was no sign of the jumpy woman his mother had described. He simply didn't know what to make of it.

Pushing the spare tire in place, he lightly screwed on the lug nuts. He could use the help in the office, but he wasn't the man to deal with a broken, and he suspected, battered woman.

He grabbed the jack handle, lowered the car, and tightened the lug nuts. Maybe her reaction on the porch was the result of some seldom-triggered phobia. Or maybe he was thinking too much and should just get back to the interview. Heaven knew, with at least three or four more weeks till his dad could return to work, and Ellen on bed rest till her baby arrived, he desperately needed some help.

"All set." He wiped his hands on an old rag he'd found in the trunk.

"Thank you very much. My husband worries about me so when he's out of town, but I tell him not to. God always provides."

"Yes. Yes, He does." Waving good-bye as she slid awkwardly behind the wheel and drove off, he thought of the woman waiting for him in his office and turned toward the building.

"Yes… I'll make sure he calls if there's a problem… No, it was no trouble at all, Mrs. Cahill… Yes, I'll see you on Sunday." With her back to the door, Pam dropped the phone into the cradle.

"Making yourself at home?" he teased.

"Oh." She jumped up from his chair, and stepped out of the way. "Sorry about that, but it kept ringing."

"It does that." She was cute when she was embarrassed. This was a side of her she didn't show as a kid, or maybe he just didn't remember seeing it. Either way, he preferred a blushing assistant to the young girl who would take a swing at anyone who dared malign her or her family.

"Mrs. Trumble's daughter called again," she continued. "Mrs. Trumble took all her medicines without a single complaint. Mr. Beauchamp faxed you the scholarship names. He needs you to sign them ASAP and fax them back." She paused to hand him the two messages and the page from the fax machine.

He looked down at the papers in his hand then back at her. Still holding more messages in her hand, she hadn't noticed him staring at her.

"Your mom called. She wanted to know how the interview went. I told her it isn't over. You were called to more important things. She didn't take that very well, until I explained that a woman who looked to be eleven- or twelve-months pregnant was about to attempt to change her own tire. You might like to know, your mom thinks you're a good boy."

Biting her lower lip, she stifled a small laugh and looked at the next piece of paper in her hand. "And last but not least, Theresa Cahill wanted to know which weekend you have available for her granddaughter's baptism." She glanced up at him through the longest lashes he'd ever seen. "I took the liberty of looking at your calendar and mentioned the weekend of the 21st or 28th of next month looks best, but I'd have you call her back if I was mistaken."

"Was I gone that long?"

"Apparently." She smiled, looking rather proud of herself.

Shaking his head, his gaze locked on hers. "You're hired."

***

"So how's my favorite girl?"

"Greg, when are you going to get a woman of your own?" Pam laughed into the phone. "You should find yourself a new law partner with a nice single sister. Or better yet, find yourself a new single female partner."

"Now why would I want to do that when I have you?"

"That's just it. You don't *have* me."

From the first time she'd met her husband's future business partner, he'd teased Travis that he'd married the last good woman on earth. Of course that hadn't stopped Greg from test-driving every breathing female within a fifty-mile radius.

For more than two years now, he'd upped the ante on the playfulness. She figured it was some macho, take-care-of-the-little-woman-left-behind thing, and she was fine with that. Talking to Greg made her feel closer to Travis. Not that she'd ever forget Travis, but some days she felt so alone, and he felt so…gone.

She blew out a tired breath and forced a smile, hoping it showed in her voice. "I found a job."

"What law firm?"

"Hope's Corner Community Church."

"Churches practice law in Hope's Corner?"

"Comedian. I'm the temporary replacement for the church secretary. She's on maternity leave."

"Are you serious?"

"Yep. Today was only my third day, but so far I'm really liking it. It's a nice change of pace having a stress-free job." Or maybe it was just nice having a good night's sleep. Either way she was counting her blessings.

"One should never underestimate the value of blood-pumping stress in life." He chuckled softly. "Anyhow, I called to apologize for not making it out there the other day. When we spoke, I was sure there'd be enough time after my meeting to take a little detour and come visit my prettiest girl."

"You are incorrigible, but I understand. It would have been nice. I'm dying to show you the house I rented. It's a great old prairie-style. I've got a porch with a swing. The front room has a huge working stone fireplace—"

"Fireplace? If memory serves me correctly, Hope's Corner's average temperature in January is fifty-five."

"Details." She laughed. "It looks nice. Besides, that's the average daytime temperature. The nights can get pretty cold around here."

"If you'd move back to Dallas, you might actually get to use a fireplace in the winter."

She closed her eyes. "I can't, Greg. I tried. You know I tried. It's too hard for me there. It was time to come home."

"At least tell me the nightmares are getting better." The playfulness in his voice was gone.

"They are. I've only had a few since I moved in."

"Well, I suppose that's something. Listen, I've got someone waiting on me, so I need to cut this short."

"Blonde or brunette?"

Greg chuckled on the other end of the line. "If you must know, she's a redhead. She's also got four legs and a tail. Not my type, but what can I do?"

"So you're buying another filly?" When Greg had first started investing in racehorses, she and Travis had thought he'd lost his mind. Who'd have guessed the city slicker knew how to pick the winners?

"This time I'm looking at her for a friend."

"Ah, now I see. Blonde or brunette?" If she leaned back on the sofa and closed her eyes, she could almost hear Travis chiming in to tease his best friend.

"Blonde, and I'm taking the fifth. I'm already late and in serious danger of ruining any chances for a sensually delicious breakfast."

"Okay—too much information. Have a good night, and—"

"I know, be careful driving home. Good night, Pam."

"Night."

Just a few more minutes. Relaxing on the sofa, if she kept her eyes closed, she could see Travis, almost feel him. Time hadn't passed. Nothing had really changed. She could see the three of them so clearly, drinking champagne, toasting a win for an important client. Another minute and just she and Travis would be dancing in the kitchen to their own music, waiting for the oven timer to ring, burning the dinner when they finished their dance in the bedroom. With her eyes closed, nothing had changed…

It's so dark. Where was she? In a cave, a tunnel, so dark. Yellow lines. A road. The streetlights are burned out. Need the high beams to see. But it's late. Too late.

Oh, the bright light is so pretty. Her dress is red satin. Folds of fabric draped across her chest. Travis looks so handsome in his tuxedo. Even the red cummerbund looks sharp, matches her dress. Like My Fair Lady, she could dance all night. Travis her knight in shining armor.

The music is so sweet. "I'll always love you," she whispered into his ear. Together forever.

It's dark again. Someone's blocking the light. Why is her dress torn, and where's Travis? "Travis?"

She has to find him. The music is still playing. He promised they could dance all night. "Travis!"

The dress is too tight. Can't breathe. Makes her ribs hurt. So much pain. "Travis, make it stop."

Thunder. A storm. The thunder is so loud. We need to hurry home. "Travis." Where did he go? "Travis, I don't see you. Answer me. We have to go home. Lightning is dangerous."

She stepped on her dress, tripped, fell. It's too hard to get up. She has to find Travis. Where is he?

Everything is all wet. Rain, the storm. No, not water. Blood. So much blood.

"No!" The scream ripped from her throat. She couldn't breathe. Springing upright on the couch, her hand pressed to her chest, she looked around. It was so cold. "Breathe. Have to breathe."

Still shaking, she pushed to her feet and stumbled across the dark room, searching for the switch. Groping the walls, struggling to inhale, finally she found her prize and flipped on the lights.

"It's okay. I'm okay. It's just a dream." Another nightmare. Then why could she still feel cold fingers wrapped tightly around her neck? The pressure so hard.

Peaches circled her feet.

"I'm okay, girl." She bent over and lifted the cat from the floor. "It's only a dream," she told herself, but just the same, carrying the cat cradled in her arms like a life preserver, Pam checked the locks on both doors. Bolted. It was just another dream.

Leaning against the kitchen door, she sank to the floor. She couldn't take it anymore. She had to make it stop. But, dear Lord, how?

CHAPTER THREE

Something was definitely rotten in the country of Denmark. Or at least in Hope's Corner. For three days everything at work had gone as smoothly as cool water rolling over white-washed river rock, but today, Jeff felt as though he were once again dealing with the frightened woman he'd first met last week on her front porch.

"Here's the fax we've been waiting for." Pammy Sue, or Pam, as she'd told him she preferred to be called, set the paper on Jeff's desk without ever looking up.

Jeff reached for the page.

"Oh, no. Wait. Wrong paper. This is the right one." With a shaky hand she pulled a sheet from the top of a stack she'd been juggling in her arms, and all the pages slipped from her grasp and fell to the floor.

For a split second Jeff thought she was going to break into tears. Crouching down on the floor to help her retrieve the spilled documents, his heart sank to his stomach at the sight of her. Her normally rosy complexion was pasty and pale, and the dark circles under her eyes made her look older, worn out, broken.

Images of Jennifer standing lost and battered at his doorstep raced through his mind. No. This isn't Jennifer. This is Pammy Sue, Pam, and he wasn't the one to help her. He wasn't the one to help anyone. But still…

"Want to talk about it?" The words seemed to slip from his mouth. He hadn't meant to ask, but he'd been acting pastor for the last three months since his father's heart attack, and before that, deacon.

In one capacity or another Jeff had been part of the pastoral staff since the day he had completed his masters of theology at seminary. Uncovering what troubled his parishioners was almost second nature to him now. Unfortunately he'd learned the hard way, helping them was an entirely different gift. One he didn't have and the reason why he had no business prying into Pam's life.

Her mouth turned at one corner in a feeble attempt at a smile. "I guess I'm just all butterfingers today."

Let it ride. Don't go there. He couldn't help her, but he knew he had to do something. "Not sleeping well?"

Her hands froze on the last few pages still splayed on the floor. "I, uh…" She looked up at him, and for a few fleeting seconds, he could see the anguish bottled inside her before the curtain of self-preservation descended.

"I'm a good listener." Why was he insisting? Hadn't he learned his lesson?

"Thank you, but I'm fine. Really. Besides, Mr. Haskell is waiting for this report, and if I don't get it back in order and messengered over by the end of the day, he may have me run out of town on a rail."

Forcing a smile, Jeff nodded and picked up the last piece of paper from the floor. "I certainly wouldn't want to be the cause of you facing the board of director's wrath."

Shoulders slumped and head down, Pam scurried out of the office. What the heck had happened to her since yesterday?

***

"Have a little more." Etta Mae scooped up another spoonful of goulash.

"Ma, if I eat anymore, you'll have to roll me out of here in a wheelbarrow."

"Nonsense. I worry about you. You're losing weight. You're too old to be living alone on frozen dinners and takeout. Look at your brother Danny. He's three years younger than you, and he's happily married with two children and one more on the way. A man needs a woman to look after him. You should find yourself a nice wife."

"I am not losing weight. If anything, by eating all that takeout, I should be putting on weight. And when I meet the right woman, I promise you'll be the first to know."

"What about that nice nurse? The one who started coming to church a few weeks ago. What's her name?"

"Sandra Quinn." Jeff didn't like the twinkle that suddenly sparkled in his mother's eye. "Ma, don't look at me like that."

"What? A mother can't look at her son?"

"You know what I mean. Please don't start scheming up ways to put the two of us together."

With a hand flat against her chest, Etta Mae managed to look truly brokenhearted at her son's words. "Would I do such a thing?"

"Yes."

"Jefferson."

"Does the name Barbara Lynn ring any bells?"

"That was different." At least his mother had the decency to look flustered at the reminder.

"No. It wasn't. Barbara was a very nice lady who was gracious enough to volunteer with the infant care during Sunday school."

Etta's expression morphed from remorse to indignation at the speed of light. "An excellent quality for a pastor's wife."

"Maybe so, but that didn't give my mother the right to invite her out for lunch only to put the poor woman through an inquisition about her past. And then, to make matters worse, you asked Barbara if she'd ever considered a calling as a pastor's wife. Not very subtle of you."

"I was simply being hospitable."

"Right. And I suppose offering to give Barbara cooking lessons was also just being hospitable?"

Etta flicked at some nonexistent lint on her blouse. "Every woman should know her way around a kitchen."

"And Pop sitting down with her after services to tell her all about you and how rewarding a life it is to be a preacher's wife— what do you call that?"

"He loves me."

"Yes, well, we all know he does. Unfortunately, with the

pressure this family put on Barbara, it wouldn't have made any difference if I was interested or not. She hightailed it out of town as fast as her car could drive."

"Her transfer had nothing to do with our hospitality."

"Mother, she took a job in Anchorage."

"The pay was better."

"Why are you in such an all-fired rush to marry me off? Why not pick on Carol Ann or Kenny?"

"They're babies."

"I think Carol Ann would take issue with being called a baby at twenty-six. And Kenny is twenty-two and graduating this year. He's the same age as Danny was when he and Terri got engaged."

"My point exactly. You're behind the curve."

"Ma…"

"You're my firstborn. I only want what's best for you."

Why did he bother arguing with his mother? "Just promise me one thing."

"What would that be?"

"Please don't let the family be too hospitable with Sandra. The choir sounds so much better with her in it. I'd hate to see her move to Fiji."

"If you at least went on a date or two, your family wouldn't feel the need to step in. We love you."

When his mother put on that wounded-puppy-dog expression, if she'd asked for the moon, he'd probably find a way to give it to her. "I love you too, Ma."

Patting him on the shoulder, Etta stepped away from the table. "I just want to see all my children happy."

"I know." There was no point in explaining to his mother that loneliness had nothing to do with what was eating at his soul.

"Tell me, how is Pamela Sue working out?" his mother asked.

"She's great. Reminds me of Ephesians 3:20. She's better than anything I thought of or could have asked for." Except for today.

"I'm only sorry I didn't think to suggest her for the job sooner." Etta stood at the sink, rinsing off the lunch dishes.

"I seem to remember her moving away to marry that Dawson boy. What was his name?"

"Travis. Such a shame."

"What happened?" He didn't remember much about the Dawson kids, but the family seemed to be nice people. It was hard to imagine that any of them could have grown up into the kind of man that would put such fear in a woman's heart.

"He died. I think it was a car accident. Don't remember the details. Your father had just had his first heart attack back then. I wasn't keeping up much with the comings and goings of the townsfolk. I did hear Pamela Sue was having a hard time of it. She loved that boy with everything in her."

Jeff had spent his vacation time in Hope's Corner the summer Pammy Sue and Travis had run off to get married. The elopement was all the town had talked about. One thing he clearly remembered was everyone saying, if any two people were meant for each other, it was Pammy Sue and Travis. "Must have been hard on her."

"I'd have thought with her being sick and all, she'd have come home sooner, but she wanted to stay in Dallas."

"Sick?"

"Don't know exactly what ailed her. Just know that her sister, Valerie, took a leave from her job to stay with her."

Pam's sister was anything but a city girl. Hope's Corner was just the right size for her. Here she was a big fish, even if it was in a little pond. What could have been so wrong with Pam to make Valerie grace the big city? And could whatever it was be the same thing that had turned friendly, competent Pam into a basket case today?

***

Something had to give.

Pam sat slumped over the steering wheel, her head resting against her arms. She hadn't taken long to reorganize the report and drive it over to Mr. Haskell's office. That had just been an excuse to get away. A little fresh air.

In Dallas she'd used her makeup skills to hide the dark circles. In a busy law office, no one took time to notice if she was or wasn't getting enough sleep. But things were different in a small town. Jeff had picked up on her mood as soon as she'd come to work. His concerned tone was almost enough to make her tell him everything. About the hurt, the pain, the loneliness, the guilt, and the paralyzing fear that lingered through the day after the terrifying nightmares had ended.

The nightmares had been a constant in her life ever since Travis had died. At first she'd tried to keep them a secret, but Greg eventually noticed her increased anxiety. Every day he would take time from his busy schedule to check on her. Sometimes it was only a phone call, sometimes a dinner out. Always he'd ask if she felt any better. Occasionally she could pretend all was well, but she couldn't hide the truth from him completely.

Desperation helped her make the decision for a clean break. She'd been happy in Dallas, but everywhere she went was a reminder of the life taken away from her. The life she had lost that night. The night her nightmares wouldn't let her forget.

Sitting up, she leaned heavily against the seat, letting her head fall back. There was a small tear in the roof of the car. Probably from trying to shove lengths of metal lawn edging into a vehicle designed to carry rounded people not long sharp objects. "Oh, Travis. I thought moving home would make the difference."

Now what? She couldn't very well spend the rest of the afternoon sitting in the church parking lot, staring at the torn ceiling and talking to her dead husband. She needed to return to work. But she was so tired of the fight, the pretense. The day after a nightmare sent her back to the dark, terrifying place she'd been after that fateful night. Tomorrow would be better. Almost normal. As long as she didn't dream.

"What am I going to do? I could always count on you for sound advice. Val says I need to stop. She thinks hanging on to you like this is part of the problem. How could she think that? You were everything good in my life.

"Those first few days after moving home, I thought I'd made the right choice. I slept clear through the night. Didn't remember a single dream, good or bad. By the third day I was convinced I hadn't made a mistake. And then…wham, another nightmare."

Pam unfastened her seat belt, reached across the seat for her purse, and dragged it onto her lap. "You remember. The next day Etta Mae brought me muffins. I'd forgotten Pastor Parker and his family lived next door when I had rented the house. I was real happy to see her, but damned if I didn't jump halfway to Kansas when she came up behind me in the kitchen and tapped me on the arm.

"I was terrified to close my eyes that night." She shook her head and opened the car door, but didn't turn. Instead, she stared out the windshield at the church. "When I finally dosed off, I slept till noon. And the day after that, and the day after that. I even came to think the nightmare had been a fluke."

She clutched her purse more tightly against her chest. "And then it happened again. Only this time Etta Mae saw the whole thing. Do you think things would be different if I'd gone to a therapist? The police tried to tell me I needed counseling, a support group. Maybe I should have listened, but I couldn't face it. I thought with time things would get better. I'd be okay. But it's not getting better, and I'm not okay."

Her eyes focused on a blooming magnolia off in the distance. It was as if some deep part of her expected an answer, a sign. Something, anything to tell her what to do. "Val is right. I need to stop this. But I can't let you go. I just can't."

***

So Travis Dawson is dead. Pamela Sue Wharton Dawson is a widow. And on any random day she morphs into a woman who's scared to death of something, or someone. But what?

Jeff had spent most of the evening chatting with his mom and dad, and knew little more about Pam than he had after working with her this week. "Such a nice girl," his mom had said. "Always the smart one in the family," his dad added with a proud smile. Jeff's dad often gloated over the successes of his flock as though he'd fathered every one of them himself.

If Jeff wanted to know more, short of asking Pam directly and possibly stirring up more trouble than either of them could handle, Jeff was simply going to have to find another source.

Turning left off the main road, he pulled into the parking lot of the Last Chance Café. Every time he drove by, he wondered why Redding Foster had saddled the town restaurant with such a ridiculous name. Most of his life the café had been known as the Hope's Corner Café. Three years ago Redding had decided the restaurant needed some panache and had come up with what Jeff thought was the hokiest name. If they had lived in a dime-store novel or a film noir, the name worked perfectly. But in small-town Texas, it was just plain clichéd.

"How's it going, Pastor?" Redding flung the white dishrag over his shoulder and hurried to the door to greet Jeff, handing him one of the gold-trimmed plastic menus. Another of Redding's ideas meant to add flare to the ordinary country restaurant. It might have worked had he used a photo of the actual café for the cover. But the detailed drawing of a modern glass structure perched precariously on the edge of a cliff as the surf crashed against the rocky shore below seemed absurdly out of place in landlocked East Texas.

"Had a hankering for some of your sweet potato pie."

"Now that's quite a compliment, seeing as how your mama makes the best sweet potato pie in the county."

Jeff offered a broad smile and followed Redding to a nearby table. "Does the men's baseball team still come in after the games?"

"Yep. Should be here any minute." Redding eyed him curiously, furrowed his brows, then shrugged a shoulder, and smiled. "You thinking about going back to the game?"

"Nah, just wondering is all. How about a little extra whipped cream on that pie?"

"You got it. Coffee too?"

"Please."

"Coming right up."

Jeff looked out the window at the main road. He remembered, when he was a boy, Hope's Corner had only one traffic light. In college, whenever someone joked their hometown was so small you'd miss it if you blinked, his mind would always wander home. Now storefronts spanned Main Street from one side of town to the other, and the street boasted a whopping three traffic lights.

With a push of people moving farther out to the country to escape big city suburban sprawl, the population of Hope's Corner had grown from close to four hundred, when he was a kid, to over two thousand. There was a time when he knew every one of the eighty or so families living in or around town. Now he didn't even know how many families lived in Hope's Corner. He wasn't sure how it had happened, but the outside world was slowly closing in on their little corner of the world.

His dad always said, "If you're not growing, you're dying." That probably applied to towns too. But at least some things didn't change. The men's baseball league still played ball every Thursday night, and Pam's brothers, Bo and Jake, were still on the team.

By the time Redding brought Jeff his pie and coffee, the first of the players were laughing their way through the front door and bumping past each other to a group of tables in the back. Miscellaneous nods and greetings were directed Jeff's way as each man crossed the room. Some stopping to chat longer than others. He'd played ball for years with half the team. Even played on the adult league the summer between college and grad school.

Billy Ray Edwards flopped in the seat across from Jeff. "Hey, man. Long time no see."

"I'm at the same place every Sunday morning."

"Yeah, well." Billy stuck his little finger in his ear, closed one eye and maneuvered his pinkie as though he were digging for gold instead of searching for something to say. "You know how it is."

"I gather from the mood the team won?"

"You bet!" The gold in his ear forgotten, Billy lit up.

"Hey, Jeff!" Jake Wharton bellowed from the doorway. Pam's brother Jake stood six foot three, weighed 250 pounds, and was as bald as a cue ball. Even in a soiled baseball uniform, the guy looked more like an out-of-place biker than a banker. Wearing a grin as wide as Main Street, he strode in Jeff's direction.

"You should have seen us. Billy here hit a line drive straight between old Hooter's legs." Jake's beefy hand smacked Billy on the back with such force, Jeff was surprised their friend hadn't flown across the room. "Three runs came home while they were doing the Keystone Kops routine in left field. Man, you shoulda been there."

"Sorry I missed it."

"Enough to play again? There's nothing in the Good Book that says you can't join us next week."

"It's been too long. Last thing I want is to be the one in left field dropping the ball."

Jake laughed louder and slapped Billy on the back again. "You gotta catch it before you can drop it. At least join us in the back for a drink. You know most of the guys."

"Thanks, I think I will." With a cup of coffee in one hand and pie in the other, he tried not to drop anything as the players moved about, pushing tables and pulling chairs and slapping him on the back, as though they hadn't all lived in the same town almost their entire lives. His mom was right; he needed to get out more often.

Now his only problem was how to steal Jake or Bo away long enough to find out more about Pam. He probably should have waited to visit Jake at home or called him on the phone. Coming here to casually bump into Pam's brothers seemed like a great idea when he was pulling out of his mother's driveway. At the time he hadn't given any thought to the fifteen other guys who'd be hovering within earshot.

"Pammy seems real happy working at the church," Jake said after a few minutes.

Jeff wasn't sure, but the way Jake looked at his beer instead of at him gave Jeff the impression that Jake had been looking for a way to talk about Pammy as much as Jeff had. The two high school buddies didn't see each other very often anymore, but back in school, Jeff could always tell when Jake had something on his mind, and tonight didn't seem any different.

"She's an answer to prayer. I was seriously thinking of talking old lady Ballard out of retirement."

Jake let out another deep, rolling laugh. "That woman has to be a hundred if she's a day."

"Exactly."

Jake pulled a chair from an empty table. Turning away from the boisterous crowd, he flung a leg over the seat, straddled the chair, and with his arms hanging over the wooden back, he lowered his voice. "I'm kinda glad she took that job. We've been worried about her."

Nodding his head, Jeff strained to hear over the raucous crowd beside them.

"She's had a real rough time of it since Travis died."

This was exactly the sort of conversation Jeff had been hoping for. Jake nodded toward an empty table a few feet away. His half-eaten pie forgotten, Jeff grabbed the cup of coffee and followed.

"Life for Pammy hasn't been easy these last couple of years." Jake looked across at the men laughing and joking. "Remember when she used to look more like my kid brother than a sister?"

Jeff smiled and nodded.

"Spitfire, she was. Never thought I'd see that die." Jake turned his attention back to Jeff. "You know much about what happened to Travis?"

He shook his head. "I was still at seminary. All I remember hearing is her husband died in some kind of accident."

"Hmm. That's the story Mrs. Dawson told. None of us saw fit

to contradict her, but it wasn't exactly an accident. He was killed."

"Killed…" Jeff wanted to say something more profound, comforting, but the inside of his mouth had turned to cotton.

Jake lowered his voice. "Carjacking,"

Carjackings and murders weren't the sort of thing the people of Hope's Corner dealt with. Even with the town's growth, until Frank Buckner, the worst crime spree Jeff had known of was when the Hansen boys and a few misguided friends thought painting the statue of the town founder, Archibald Perry, green, gold, and purple in honor of Mardi Gras would be a good idea. They'd barely had time to start on the second statue of his wife, Hope, who the town was named for, when they were spotted by Billy Ray as he drove around trying to put his colicky twins back to sleep.

No, a carjacking was the sort of gossip that would keep a town like Hope's Corner gabbing for months, maybe years. In time Travis would be remembered more for how he died rather than how he lived. He couldn't blame Mrs. Dawson for keeping quiet that part of her son's death. "What happened?"

"Don't know all the details. According to the police, Travis was dead by the time the cops arrived. Pammy was barely hanging on."

"Shot?"

"I wish. Some bastard beat her to within an inch of her life. They said it was a blessing Pammy didn't remember what happened. We'd hoped, since she didn't remember the attack, that meant she'd been unconscious for most of the brutality. But when she started mumbling in her sleep, pleading out loud, we knew, even if she didn't remember, she'd been conscious for some of it."

The anger Jeff had felt on the front lawn days ago returned full force. Needing something to do with his hands rather than punch the nearest wall, he reached for the coffee cup. "Where were they when it happened?"

"Their garage."

Jeff almost spilled the cup he'd been toying with. No wonder the woman was scared to death. If you're not safe in your own home… "Was it that bad a neighborhood?"

"Nope. The police think the guy saw them someplace and followed them. Slipped into the garage behind them." Jake lifted his drink, hesitated, then set it back down. "I know the world is full of sickos who get their jollies beating up on other people, but you don't expect one of your own to ever cross paths with them."

"Was she… assaulted?" Assaulted. Some professional he was. Couldn't even use the word *rape*. Not when it was someone he knew.

Jake raised a shoulder in a slow shrug. "At the time Pammy said no. So many damn laws nowadays. Without her permission, no one would give us any details. Not the cops, not the doctors. Really pissed Dad off, but there was nothing any of us could do. She was conscious and lucid."

"Exactly what did she tell you?"

"Nothing. She barely spoke to the police. She refused counseling. She wouldn't talk about that night to anyone. Still doesn't."

Well, that certainly shed a little light on Pam's jitters. If she didn't seek out professional counseling, fear could grow deep roots. "Did they ever catch the guy?"

"Nope. Car probably made its way to a chop shop. There was no physical evidence left behind to give the police a solid lead. The creep might have been a mean son of a bitch, but he knew what he was doing."

"And Pam hasn't been to a counselor since?"

Jake shook his head again.

Damn. The woman needed help. Real help. Not the pretentious trappings of assistance he wore. He'd already been responsible for the death of one woman. He didn't need the responsibility of another. Even if Pam's life wasn't in physical danger anymore—if she didn't get real help and soon—eventually she would lose her life as surely as if the carjacker had left her dead on the cold concrete slab of her garage.

"We were hoping moving home would be enough." Jake's words broke through Jeff's thoughts. "You know, the safety of the bosom of your family and all that. She doesn't like us fussing over her, says she doesn't need nursemaids. After Mom died, Bo, Val, and I made a habit of having Friday night dinners at Dad's. Now that Pammy's back home, she comes too. It gives us a chance to see for ourselves how she's doing, without her feeling we're checking up on her. For the most part she seems to be looking better, but a couple of times something dragged her back to the way she looked when she still lived in Dallas."

"How was that?"

"Old." Jake looked up, his eyes settling on Jeff's. "Dark circles under her eyes, pale, tired, and scared. I know it has to do with those nightmares."

"Nightmares?"

Jake nodded. "After she got out of the hospital, Val went up to Dallas to stay with her. Every night Pam would wake up screaming and then refuse to go back to sleep. She wouldn't tell Val what the dreams were. Said she didn't remember them once she woke up."

"When did they stop?"

"Don't know that they ever did. We think that's why she finally agreed to move home."

The two men stared at each other in silence for a long few minutes. Jeff had known by the way Pam spooked that there was something ugly in her background, but he hadn't been prepared for this.

"Has she said anything to you?" Jake asked. "Confided in you?"

Jeff shook his head.

Jake sighed and leaned back in his seat. "I'd thought, maybe, you being a pastor and all, she'd tell you what's too horrible to tell the rest of us."

"I know a couple of good trauma counselors in Poplar Springs. If you'd like me to give you their names—"

"Maybe if you… I mean, well…she might listen to you since she hasn't seen fit to pay any attention to what we think. Something happened that night besides Travis dying, and someone needs to get to the bottom of it."

"I see." Whether he liked it or not, he was in the middle of this situation. And from the looks of it, he was about to dig in even deeper. "I'll see what I can do."

CHAPTER FOUR

"You must be the new secretary?" A woman with huge blue eyes and dark brown hair in a short bob, smiled down at Pam.

"Yes, Pam Dawson." With a smile Pam pushed from her seat and stuck out her hand as she got to her feet.

"Sandra Quinn. Is the pastor in? I mean, if he's not busy or anything."

"I'm sure he can spare a few minutes. If you'll have a seat, I'll be right back."

The intercom portion of the phone system wasn't working, but it was just as well. Pam had too much energy today to sit still. Despite her fears, she'd slept through the night without even a hint of a bad dream. By morning the sun was shining bright and she felt as though the birds were singing just for her.

She'd made a decision. One she should have made long ago. It was time to deal with these nightmares and the stifling fear that lingered in their wake. She'd hid her head in the sand long enough. For God's sakes, last night the irrational fear kept her from climbing a lousy flight of stairs to her room! If she'd listened to the police in the first place and gone to a therapist, or a support group, she wouldn't have lost the last the two years of her life.

There was something wonderful about being on the verge of a new beginning. An exciting sense of freedom that reminded her of springtime, fresh flowers, and falling in love.

"Excuse me." She tapped on Jeff's door.

"Yes?" He glanced up from his desk. A pencil rested behind his ear and the top of a pen peeked out from a clenched fist. The fingers of his other hand raked through his hair, the palm supporting the weight of his head. The way the hair on one side of his head stood straight up, he looked like a punk rocker.

"Fund-raiser plans?" she asked pointing with her chin at the expanse of papers littering his desk.

"Hmm," he mumbled, tossing the pen on the desk and sitting up.

"You have a visitor. Sandra Quinn."

Jeff's brows rose high on his forehead. She couldn't quite make out if it was a look of surprise, confusion, anticipation, or dread. But the way he straightened his hair, his shirt, and smiled, she figured it couldn't have been too unpleasant a surprise.

Instead of waiting in his office, Jeff sprang from his seat and followed her out to where the attractive woman sat waiting.

"Miss Quinn." He extended his hand.

"Pastor. I'm sorry to just pop in like this."

"Not at all. You're welcome anytime."

"Thank you. Recently I signed up for one of those new alternate shift programs at the hospital. For three days I work twelve hours on, twelve hours off, then I have three days off in a row. It's working out even better than I thought."

"I'm very happy to hear that. Is there something you need us to help with?"

"Actually." She dipped her chin and a pale pink hue flushed her cheeks as her eyes met his. "I was thinking I could help you."

Pam had a great view of the scene playing out before her, and with little effort, she could hear almost every word.

"You see," Sandra continued, "I seem to have more time off than I know what to do with. At choir practice I overheard one of the ladies mention the church's program for visiting the elderly shut-ins was shorthanded. Could you use a nurse?"

"Could we!" Whatever had been bothering him moments before fell by the wayside. His face beamed as he slipped a hand behind Sandra and guided her toward his office. "Do you have some time this afternoon?"

Sandra bobbed her head with a little more enthusiasm than Pam would have expected from someone who had just volunteered to spend her free time with the sick and elderly.

"I've been worried about a few of our old folks who don't

have any family," Jeff explained as he eased Sandra down the hall. "I'm not convinced they're getting the proper medical care, but one in particular, Mrs. Perkins, has me especially worried at the moment. She's been losing weight steadily, and yet I know she's getting enough to eat. The woman in charge of the Meals on Wheels has taken to sitting with Mrs. Perkins while she eats. I've been wondering what to do. Let me tell you, you're an answer to prayer."

If the bright grin on Sandra's face was any indicator, Pam was willing to bet a week's salary that Jeff was an answer to Sandra's prayers too.

***

"How'd the visit go?" Pam looked up from her desk as Jeff came through the lobby doors.

"Great. Sandra sat with Mrs. Perkins's cat on her lap, asked her about her friends, and what Hope's Corner was like when she was growing up. It was amazing. The woman opened up like a morning glory at sunrise. The conversation shifted to the trials of losing hair and dealing with dry skin. The next thing I knew Sandra was feeling Mrs. Perkins's throat and suggesting she make an appointment with an endocrinologist she knows at the hospital. Sandra thinks Mrs. Perkins is having thyroid problems."

"Looks like you were right."

Jeff cocked a brow at her. "About what?"

"That Miss Quinn's an answer to prayer."

"Oh. Yes. I suppose she is." In his enthusiasm to resolve his concerns over his parishioner's failing health, Jeff had bestowed the often-used phrase on Sandra as easily as he might wish someone a good morning. When he'd said she was an answer to prayer, he hadn't taken the time to remember he'd stopped believing God answered his prayers. Or at least he thought he had.

"Isn't it wonderful?" Pam beamed.

"Excuse me?"

"When you don't know what to do and God drops the answer right on your doorstep."

"Sandra?"

"That's right. She's going to help with your visiting the elderly program, she figured out what's wrong with Mrs. Perkins, and if I'm not overstepping my job description, I think she might be sweet on you."

"What?" Surely he didn't have another meddling female in his life. No, God wouldn't do that to him.

"Never mind. Sometimes I let my good mood get the better of me. You go on and get back to the fund-raising budget and forget I said anything." She waved him off with one hand and, still smiling, turned to the work on her own desk.

In a few long strides, he was crossing the threshold into his office and sinking into his chair. Mrs. Perkins was taken care of. Sandra offered to call the doctor for her, and even offered to pick her up and drive her to her appointment.

Whether or not Sandra had any personal interest in him wasn't even a consideration at the moment. And how to make sure Pam didn't become a member of his family's *Jeff Needs a Wife Club* could also wait for another day.

What he needed was to stop stalling and find a way to bring up Pam's need for therapy. But how do you approach a woman who looks to be on top of the world and tell her she needs to seek counseling?

Last he heard, accusing a woman of being schizophrenic didn't win a man any brownie points. He didn't want to scare her off. He needed her. This office had never run so smoothly. Pam had a way of knowing what to do before anyone realized it even needed to be done.

After talking last night to her brother Jake, Jeff had no doubt someone had to step in and convince her to go to counseling. But Jake had made it clear her family wanted that someone to be him.

He'd taken the first step and called his friend Caleb in Poplar Springs. Jeff hadn't wanted to invade Pam's privacy by revealing too much information. Not that he knew all that much. And Caleb wasn't willing to say much without seeing Pam first, but he did agree, from the little information Jeff had shared, the lady needed to talk to someone. Soon.

What neither man had anticipated was that the sullen woman who had spent the better part of yesterday counting the dust bunnies on the floor rather than look Jeff in the eyes would be all sunshine and smiles today. She didn't seem to have a care in the world. What the heck had happened between yesterday and today?

Even though he'd seen this abrupt change before on the first day they'd met, for some reason seeing her so happy today caught him off guard.

Who was he kidding? He simply didn't want to be the one to rob her of her good mood. There was something about her smile that made him smile too. Even if he'd had the day from hell, her smile touched something deep down inside that made him want to smile back. He'd missed that yesterday. He'd missed her yesterday.

Maybe Caleb would consider making a house call. A discreet, incognito evaluation. After all, back in college they were pretty good at covering each other's backs.

A pale slim hand, Pam's delicate hand, slid a cup of coffee across his desk. "You look like you just lost your best friend. Is there something wrong with Mrs. Perkins that you're not telling me?"

"No, no she's fine." *But you need professional help.* "I've got a lot on my mind."

"Then my special blend of vanilla almond coffee should be just what the doctor ordered. Guaranteed to cure whatever ails you."

He hadn't lied. Her sweet smile made him want to smile back, but it was going to take a lot more than a cup of coffee to cure what ailed either of them.

***

"Psychoanalysis." Pam ran her finger down the page. "Stress, love, marriage. I don't know, Travis. Sounds more like a fortune teller."

As soon as she'd gotten home from work, Pam had pulled out

the phone directory, reading each and every name, carefully noting every little advertisement. "Now here's something a little different. Play therapy. What do you suppose that means?"

She was pretty sure, whatever it was, she was better off moving down the page. "Sexual addiction. Spiritual wellness. You'd think there'd be at least one ordinary old counselor who treats ordinary old nightmares."

All right. So her nightmares probably weren't ordinary, and she definitely needed a specialist, but a specialist in what? Certainly not *play therapy*.

Slamming the yellow pages closed, she drummed her fingers against the thick book and stared out the kitchen window. Etta Mae was baking again. Of all the women she'd known growing up, none had an affinity for baking like Etta Mae Parker. "The woman should go into business."

Peaches hopped from the floor, to the chair, to the tabletop and sauntered over to Pam, nuzzling her hand before gracefully sprawling across the closed book.

"What? You didn't want to be here in time to lay across the open book?" Pam scratched behind the cat's ears.

"Okay, so, if I don't pick a counselor from the book—where do I go?"

Still petting the cat, Pam stared at the ceiling, almost as though waiting for the heavens to open up, and Travis to come take a seat next to her at the table and answer her question.

"I know what you're thinking. Ask the church. Jeff could probably recommend someone."

Peaches stretched herself taut, pressing her exposed chin even closer to Pam's moving fingers.

"I don't think I can do that." Jeff probably already thought she was crazy. She couldn't bring herself to come straight out and ask him to recommend a therapist, and prove him right. No. There had to be someone else who could help her. But who?

***

"Two nights in a row. Got another hankering for my pie?"

Redding grinned at Jeff.

"Maybe I do." Jeff smiled and followed behind Redding to the same table he'd occupied the night before.

Normally he loved the peace and quiet of his small apartment, but lately the walls seemed more like a prison than a refuge. Usually when he felt the need for company, he'd find his way to his mom and dad's house, but tonight, much like another night not so long ago, he wasn't ready to bare his soul to his all-too-intuitive parents.

Growing up, Jeff never could simply hang around and sulk. Whether it was a bad test grade, a rejection from a pretty girl, or one of those baseball games when what should have been an easy out for him turned into a winning clip for *America's Funniest Home Videos*, going home always meant facing Pastor Harlon Parker and his wife.

Sure, when he was four years old with a freshly skinned knee, curled up on his mother's lap, all he knew was Mom made the hurt feel better. But by the time he was close to ten, he'd come to understand Etta Mae Parker had a different way of mothering than his friends' moms. By high school he'd realized that Etta Mae was first and foremost a pastor's wife. When all he needed was first aid for his physical ailments, Etta Mae was sure to add first aid for the injured soul.

Chatting with his dad wasn't much different. Somehow Jeff always felt like he was on the wrong end of a counseling session. The senior pastor had an easy way of making you re-examine your goals and motives, and the next thing you knew, you'd walk away with more questions than answers.

Tonight he didn't want to face his motives and goals. He wasn't ready to let his parents know just how badly he had failed, and there would be no way to bring up his doubts and struggles with how best to help Pam, without exposing how he'd failed the parishioners, his father, and most of all, Jenny Buckner.

The day the congregation voted unanimously not to hire a temporary pastor to replace Harlon in his absence, but to let Jeff step up to the role, Jeff thought his dad's face would freeze in a permanent smile.

Not even when he'd told his father that he'd decided to give up his career with the bank to attend divinity school did Harlon Parker beam so proudly. And he'd glowed and grinned pretty good for weeks after that particular announcement. Seemed he'd always known his son had the calling to follow in his footsteps. He'd only been waiting for Jeff to stop sowing his oats and figure it out for himself. It had taken Jeff a few years longer than his father had hoped, but much like a father with his own prodigal son, that only made Jeff's decision all the sweeter for his dad.

"Just here for dessert, or are you going to have some of Mabel's meat loaf?"

"Did she make her special gravy?"

"Does a prickly pear make sweet jam?"

Jeff had to smile. Redding wasn't a poet, but he certainly knew how to get his point across. "Meat loaf with extra gravy."

He'd almost finished his meal when Redding slid into the seat across from him. "Church keeping ya busy?"

"Pretty much." He nodded and passed the last forkful of potatoes into his mouth.

"Except for last night, we haven't seen ya in here much. Not since that horrible business with Jenny Buckner." Redding shook his head and clicked his tongue making that same *tsk-tsk* sound every person in town made when Jenny's name came up. "Such a tragedy that one. Right under our noses. You'd think with all the busybodies makin' everyone else's lives their business, someone would have seen this coming."

Yeah. Someone. Except the only person Jenny had confided in was him. And now she was gone. Jeff could barely nod, hoping Redding wouldn't push the subject further.

"Heard little Pammy Sue Wharton is back in town and working at the church."

"Thank the Lord." Despite his worries, and except for yesterday's appearance of Pam's alternate personality, she had been nothing less than a godsend. "With Ellen on maternity leave and Dad still recovering from surgery, I'm not too humble to admit, the load was getting a little heavy."

"Well, if Pammy Sue's the reason behind two visits in two nights, I'm obliged to her." Redding leaned forward, looking quickly to either side as though ensuring their privacy before divulging classified information. "Never hurts business none when the Lord's representative graces your establishment. Especially with us serving, you know, spirits and all."

"Anytime," Jeff whispered back in the same conspiratorial tone.

"I'll get you some of Mabel's pie. Blackberry. On the house."

Jeff nodded and watched his former Little League baseball coach saunter off. The mention of Jenny's name took his mind back to that awful night. He'd been having dinner here at the café when the news had rushed through town like a flash fire in a drought-ridden forest. Jenny had been found by her neighbor. She'd managed to crawl about ten feet into her yard before blacking out. From what the police had pieced together, she'd probably been baking in the hot Texas sun for hours before her neighbor spotted her body heaped on her front walkway.

He'd rushed to the hospital. Sat by Jenny's and Mrs. Harris' side for two days straight. He'd finally broken away to go home, freshen up, and get a little shut-eye with every intention of returning shortly.

He never had the chance. He'd been home less than fifteen minutes when the phone rang. Jenny had arrested. They couldn't revive her. It was over.

Freshening up didn't seem very important anymore. He'd hurried back to be with Mrs. Harris, but the hospital room was empty. According to the nurse, when she'd informed Jenny's mother she could stay as long as she needed with her daughter, the woman had quietly explained she'd already said her good-byes, and then asked the nurse to relay a message. "Tell Jeff, Pastor Parker, I appreciate all he did for my baby. I'll forever be grateful, but I'd like to be alone for a while."

Unable to drown his sorrow in a bottle of whiskey, he'd left the hospital and come straight to the diner to wallow in Mabel's homemade pies with extra cream. He couldn't face his mother and father. The hurt was too raw. The truth too painful. They'd have seen his failure before he'd passed through their door. He didn't want to see the disappointment in their eyes. Didn't want them to ever know his part in the death of Jenny Buckner. So he'd come to sit with the closest thing to a father a boy raised in Hope's Corner could have—his baseball coach.

Now here he sat, troubled yet again, in the company of his long-ago mentor and Mabel's soothing home cooking. If only he could find, buried in the blackberry pie with extra cream, the answer for what to do about the two sides of Pamela Sue Wharton Dawson.

CHAPTER FIVE

Visiting with Abigail Clarke was one of Jeff's never-miss appointments. Lunch at noon with Miss Abigail was penciled in on every Thursday square on every calendar in his office. Pam turned up the old country road and glanced at the clock on her dashboard. Eleven forty-five, fifteen minutes early.

It was obvious to anyone with eyes how much he hated canceling at the last minute. Volunteering to take his place just seemed like the right thing to do. She could only hope Mrs. Clarke was as pleased with the idea as Jeff had been.

Pulling into the gravel parking lot, the three-story yellow Victorian house reminded her of an elaborate gingerbread creation. A wraparound porch trimmed in curlicue wisps of decorative white wrought iron invited passersby to stop and take notice. The rocking chairs swaying ever-so-slightly in the breeze called for folks to come up and sit a spell. All in all, if it was necessary to spend what was left of your golden years in a nursing home, the old Keller estate appeared to be the place to spend them.

The slate path wound gracefully from the surrounding white picket fence, past the colorful blooms, green lawns, and hundred-year-old trees to the charming old house. Inside, the Keller Nursing Home held even more surprises. Passing through the front door was like stepping back in time. The last of the Keller family had died off in 1978 and had left the house, the surrounding land, and all the furnishings to the city under the stipulation that the home always be used to care for the elderly. If the condition of the turn of the century furniture and the fine shine on all the intricate wood trim was any indication of patient care, it explained why Mrs. Clarke was still alive and well at ninety-seven.

"May I help you?" Sitting in a tall, straight-backed dark wood chair covered in plush red velvet, the gray-haired woman playing solitaire at the oversized desk reminded Pam of a small child seated in a king's throne.

"I'm looking for Mrs. Clarke. Pastor Parker sent me."

"Oh. Is he going to be late?" The woman's smile faltered for only a moment.

"I'm afraid not. He was needed at the hospital."

"Oh, dear. Nothing serious I hope?" Pushing to her feet, the woman stood in front of the ornate chair. She couldn't be more than four-foot-and-a-wish tall. She was also considerably older than Pam's first impression.

"We hope not."

"Good. I'll add young Jeff's ailing parishioner to my prayer list tonight." The woman moved around the desk and took hold of Pam's hand.

Pam had no idea which surprised her more, that the woman had taken hold of her hand and was leading her down the hall as if she were a lost little girl, or that this petite card-playing receptionist was the ninety-seven-year-old woman Jeff was worried about.

"You're Mrs. Clarke?"

The old woman chuckled. "Don't look so surprised, dearie. Think of me as French cheese. Not really old, just ripe."

It was Pam's turn to laugh. The old girl had a sense of humor.

Stopping a short distance down the hall, the woman gestured at a narrow doorway. "This is my room. Why don't you have a seat?"

Pam moved in the direction the aged finger seemed to be pointing and sank into an overstuffed easy chair. The modern comfort seemed somehow out of place among the other antiques in the room, including Mrs. Abigail Clarke.

"Every boudoir needs a good reading chair," Mrs. Clarke explained. "I don't read as much anymore, but that's no reason to give up the most comfortable seat in the house."

Pam paused to take in her surroundings. The rosebud-covered wallpaper, marble-topped dresser, and bedside tables seemed to suit the petite woman who had now taken a seat across from Pam in a traditional woman's Victorian sewing chair.

"This is a lovely room."

"Thank you. I've seen a lot of changes in home decorating in my time, but this era is still my favorite." Abigail shifted her gaze from the velvet-draped window to Pam and smiled. "So tell me, dear. How can I help you?"

***

Oh, good grief. Surely his eyes were playing tricks on him.

Jeff made a U-turn at the corner and pulled into the café parking lot. There was no missing his mother's pristine 1976 Chevy Impala nestled among the array of beat-up old pickups. "Okay, so it was my mother and probably Carol Ann." But that didn't mean the third woman in the bunch was Sandra Quinn.

He glanced at his watch. Almost one o'clock. He wouldn't mind some of Mabel's cooking about now. He'd missed his weekly lunch with Miss Abigail. Little Benjamin Palmer's crisis had come and gone with a whimper. When the boy's mother had discovered an empty bottle of aspirin on the floor, and her precocious three-year-old blithely informed her he had eaten them, she'd panicked and raced him to the hospital. Not until much later did everyone learn, after eating only one, the aspirin had tasted so yucky that Benjamin had thrown the remainder of the pills in the toilet.

Looking up at the restaurant's large paned windows, Jeff shook his head. If that was Sandra he'd seen entering the café with his mother and sister, then it was his duty to save her from whatever scheme they had conjured up this time. Heaving out a deep sigh, he turned to the door and marched up the front steps and across the large room to his mother's table.

"Why, Jefferson, dear, what a nice surprise." Etta Mae smiled up at her son with all the poise of the most innocent of Southern ladies.

"Hey, handsome," his sister said with a broad smile. "Gonna join us? We just sat down."

"I know. I was heading back to the church when I spotted Ma's car and saw y'all walking in here."

Carol Ann patted the seat beside her. Sandra and his mother were already sitting side by side across the table from her. For a split second he was tempted to shout at Sandra, "Run for your life."

Visions played before him of her driving out of town and not stopping until she reached Anchorage like the last woman his mother and sister had tried to set him up with. The sound of the choir singing off-key as it had before the blessed addition of Sandra's strong melodic voice screeched painfully in his head. He couldn't let that happen. With a nod he slid in beside his sister. "Thanks. I'm starved."

"You know Sandra here, don't you, dear?" Etta Mae waved a hand at the woman seated beside her.

"Of course he does, Ma." Carol Ann rolled her eyes at her mother, and Jeff wondered if he'd underestimated his sister all these years. Perhaps she wasn't in cahoots with their mother's matchmaking. Maybe, like debris in a tornado, she was just sucked in. He'd certainly learned a long time ago, when his mom set her mind on something, there was no point wasting his breath trying to talk her out of it.

"Nice to see you again, Pastor." Sandra nodded politely.

"Oh, call him Jeff. Everyone does," his mother suggested sweetly.

Time for him to take control of the conversation. "Sandra will be working with the church elderly program. Yesterday she went with me to visit Mrs. Perkins." He shifted his attention from his mom to Sandra. "Mrs. Perkins called me this morning. She's very taken with you. She tells me that you've already got her scheduled to see someone about her thyroid?"

Sandra smiled. "I've made an appointment with Dr. Sanderson. It took a little finagling. Fortunately his nurse and I go back a long way. She squeezed us in on Monday."

"How nice of you, dear. Isn't that nice of her, Jeff?"

"It is most definitely a blessing to have Sandra helping out. I'm sure Mrs. Perkins especially is thankful Sandra chose to move here to Hope's Corner and not some other place." He paused to look his mother square in the eye. "Like, say, Alaska."

***

"Oh, my. Just look at the time." Abigail Clarke stared up at the large digital clock on the dining room wall. "Young Jeff must be wondering what I've done with you."

Much to her surprise, Pam found herself wishing it wasn't so late. She hadn't expected Miss Abigail to be such an entertaining storyteller. Even though Pam had grown up in Hope's Corner, she'd simply taken for granted that things in town had always been the way she had remembered them. She'd never thought back to what it was like when the town was too small for a beauty parlor, café, or post office. "Would it be all right if I came back some time for another visit?"

"Why heavens, child. Of course it would be all right. It would be my utmost pleasure to have your company again."

"Thank you."

"It's me who should be thanking you. Jeff's a sweet young man, but his eyes tend to glaze over just a bit if I spend too much time talking about Haddie and her dresses."

"Haddie?"

"Did I not mention Haddie?"

Pam shook her head.

Abigail smiled. "We threw such a grand opening when she opened her dress shop. It was a bit strange, her being a colored woman and all, but she'd saved her money working back East for one of them fancy stores with fancy labels.

"Her plan had been to go farther west. She was going to go to Fort Worth. Haddie'd heard about the government opening up Camp Bowie, and that colored people could buy a home there, though not in the nicer part of town, mind you. Back then there weren't many places where colored folk could buy their own place."

"How did she wind up in Hope's Corner?" For three hours Pam had listened to Miss Abigail talk about her hometown. She needed to get back to work but couldn't resist just one more story.

"I don't rightly know. If anyone asked her, she'd shrug and say, 'The hand of God.' At first she hired on as cook right here at the old Keller place." Abigail chuckled. "Even when I was a girl, this was the old Keller place."

"It has been around a long time."

"Nearly sixty years before I was even born."

"So Haddie worked for the Kellers?"

"Why, yes, yes she did. She was here a while. Can't remember exactly how long. I was just a little thing at the time. None of us knew then that she had a way with a needle and thread. One day this strapping man as dark as night in the woods came knocking. I remember it so well. I was playing in the front yard with Gracie Keller. We'd never seen anyone so big. Scared us half to death until he smiled. Those big white teeth in that dark face was a shock, but his smile was one of those smiles that goes clear up to a man's eyes." Abigail giggled. "Would you believe his name was Tiny?

"Haddie had sent for him. She'd bought a little piece of land on the edge of town. Not that it was much of a town then. Most men could spit from one end to the other. Anyhow, Tiny, turns out he was Haddie's brother. He built her a little shop.

"The womenfolk were so happy not to have to go all the way to Poplar Springs for a new dress that Haddie's business took off right away." Abigail's gleeful expression slipped. "Few years later Tiny succumbed to the influenza. Such a strong man killed by a little old germ."

Pam could see the pain of a little girl in her new friend's face. She felt tears well in her eyes.

"Now don't you go starting the waterworks." Abigail leaned over and patted Pam on the leg. "Tiny was a good man. A good friend. And I know someday soon, I'll be seeing him again."

With a nod of her head, Abigail put on a bright smile and

stood up. "I think I'd best be letting you get back to young Jeff, or he may not let you come visit again."

"Yes." Pam pushed to her feet. "Although I don't think Jeff would ever want to stop me from visiting, but I really do have work to do."

After a long hug and a short wave, Pam slid into the front seat of her car and drove off. Miss Abigail stood on the porch waving until the house was out of sight.

"Have you ever met anyone so interesting?" Pam glanced up before turning onto the main road to town. "She reminds me some of your Grandma Raven. Don't ya think? She liked to tell stories too. First time you took me to Hunters Ridge was after your grandmother's story about how the street Lovers Lane in Dallas really used to be a lovers' lane."

Stopped at a light, Pam looked up at the feathery clouds inching their way across the sky. "Oh, Travis. Do you know how much I miss you?"

A horn tooted. The woman in the sedan behind her waved. Pam recognized the high school principal and waved back, smiling into the rearview mirror as though there were some chance the nearsighted old teacher might actually see her remorseful grin.

"You were a good man, Travis Dawson. A good friend, husband, and lover, and Miss Abigail's right. I will see you again."

***

"Whose side are you on?"

"Yours." Carol Ann flopped in the chair across from Jeff's desk. "But it wasn't that bad. Trust me. Ma was much worse with Barbara Lynn."

"I find that hard to believe. I'm thirty-four. Why is Mom carrying around a photo of me when I was six months old? And for Pete's sakes, on a bearskin rug. Real people don't do that!"

"You were a cute baby."

"Yes. I know. And bound to produce more cute babies. I think Mom got that point across to Sandra loud and clear."

Carol Ann muffled a giggle. "Sandra didn't seem to know

which way to turn, but all in all, I think she handled it very well. Much better than Barbara."

"Yeah, well, I certainly hope so. Besides the fact that the choir doesn't sound…painful anymore, having a volunteer nurse working with the church means a great deal to me, and I don't want to lose her."

"Excuse me." Pam walked into Jeff's office and waved at Carol Ann. "I'm back if you need me. And don't want to lose who?"

"Sandra Quinn." Carol Ann waved back. "Mom invited her to lunch today."

"After she *accidentally* bumped into her at the grocery store." Jeff turned to his sister. "What did Mom do? Sit in her car until the woman showed up, then accost her in the frozen foods aisle?"

Pam covered her mouth with her hand to hide the chuckle.

"She's not *that* bad." Carol Ann defended their mother, trying and failing to hide her own amusement.

"Okay, let's say I believe Mom and Sandra just happened to bump into each other at the market. Why can't Mom leave my love life alone?"

"Because you don't have one." Carol Ann turned to Pam again. "Isn't he good-looking?"

"Uh." Pam looked from Carol Ann to Jeff. She shrugged apologetically, then glanced back at his sister. "Yeah."

"See. I rest my case. Good-looking guys should have girlfriends."

"If you don't need me here, I think I'll go back to work." Pam took two steps back before Carol Ann sprang from her seat, blocking Pam's exit.

"Oh, no you don't. I need help." Carol Ann reached for Pam's arm. "He's right. Our mother gets a little overly gung ho sometimes, but she's not totally wrong. What we need is another voice of reason. Help me convince big brother here there's more to life than his work." She turned Pam so they were both facing her brother.

"I'm not so sure I'm the voice of anything," Pam said softly.

"Nonsense."

"Carol Ann—" Jeff started.

"I'm serious. You don't have to get married. Get out, have a little fun. Ask someone, anyone, to a movie, dinner, something." Carol Ann raised her palms upward, silently pleading with her brother.

"Okay. Fine. I'll ask someone to dinner. Happy?"

"Yes. Who?"

"Who?"

"Too many words for ya, big brother? Who are you going to ask out?"

"I don't know, but I promise to let you know as soon as I do."

"Ah, ah." Carol Ann shook her head. "Not going to work this time. You want Mom off your back? Pick a woman of your own. It doesn't have to be serious."

"You've said that already."

Carol Ann spun around to face Pam. "What are you doing for dinner tonight?"

Pam raised her hand to her chest, pointing to herself. "Me?"

Carol Ann nodded.

"Probably stop at the café."

"And you?" Carol Ann turned to Jeff.

"Carol Ann," he drawled out, clearly frustrated.

"Answer me."

"I don't know."

"Fine. Have dinner at the café. And since you're having dinner there, and Pam's having dinner there, why don't the two of you share a booth?"

"Carol Ann." Jeff's tone rose an octave.

"I'm not fixing you up. I'm being practical. You both have to eat. You're both unattached, and it will keep Mom from siccing Sandra Quinn on you. You do want Mom to stop playing matchmaker don't you?"

"You're as bad as Mom." Jeff pushed back his chair and

stood up. "Sorry, Pam. Insanity seems to run on the female side of my family."

Relieved that Jeff wasn't taking Carol Ann seriously, Pam managed a small smile. "Don't be too hard on them. They both love you, but I really do have to get back to work."

Pam couldn't get out of Jeff's office fast enough. She knew he didn't have any interest in her, but just the same, the thought of having dinner alone with another man, any man, felt too much like cheating on Travis. Someplace deep in the back of her mind she knew it made no sense, but that didn't change a thing.

She'd had all of ten minutes to sort through the stack of files on her desk when Carol Ann plopped herself on the corner of Pam's desk. "You've got to help me out here."

"Me?"

"Just a gentle suggestion here or there. Maybe point out when a nice single woman is paying attention to him."

"Like Sandra."

"Sandra pays attention to him?" Carol Ann perked up like a pedigree dog on point.

"Let's just say I don't think she'd say no if he asked her out to dinner."

"Oh, really?"

Pam could almost see the plans forming in the woman's head.

"I think Mom was disappointed with Sandra at lunch today, as if she didn't quite pass the checklist. But if Sandra already has the hots for big brother, maybe—"

"Pam, the copy machine is jammed again. Could you call…" Jeff stopped short at the sight of Carol Ann sitting on the edge of Pam's desk "I was just leaving, big brother." Carol Ann walked over, leaned in, gave her brother a kiss on the cheek, and looking rather pleased with herself, strolled out the door.

Jeff moved over to Pam's side. "I really am sorry if she embarrassed you."

"I'm fine. I'll give Fred a call about the copy machine."

"Yes, please. I can't seem to find his number in my father's

Rolodex."

"No problem." Pam reached for the phone.

"Also." Jeff shifted from one foot to the other. "She is right about one thing."

"Only one?" Pam chuckled. She probably shouldn't have said anything about Sandra to Carol Ann, but maybe it would work out.

"We do have to eat."

Pam felt her shoulders stiffen.

"The Thursday night special at the café is always chicken fried steak. Don't tell my mother I said this, but the only things her cooking can't compete with is Mabel's blueberry pie and her chicken fried steak."

"I won't say a word." Pam swallowed the lump in her throat and tried to smile.

"Good." Jeff smiled. "Then you'll join me for dinner at the café?"

CHAPTER SIX

inner? Oh, God. Dinner? Like a date? A dinner date? Pam's lungs seized while her heart raced. Was that even physically possible? *Breathe!*

She didn't want to go on a date. Not with Valerie's neighbor the architect who had everything except the right woman. Not with Mrs. Cahill's son Peter who really can't be blamed for his two divorces. And most especially not with her boss, Pastor Jeff, whose smile could make any woman go weak in the knees. *Breathe!*

But wait. Carol Ann had suggested "share a booth." Nothing about a date. Only a step to stop his mother from meddling. Air filled her lungs. "We do have to eat" wouldn't qualify in anyone's broadest imagination as an invitation to a romantic dinner for two. Another breath.

Jeff slipped his hands into his pockets, his expression blank except for the slight dip in his brow. *Oh, great.* Now he was probably once again thinking she was a nutcase and planning his fastest getaway. A boss asks his secretary to a simple meal, and she reacts like Count Dracula has just invited her to his castle. She wouldn't be surprised if he turned and ran for the door without looking back.

Her sister was right. She needed to get out more. Make new friends. Have dinner out. When Travis worked late, night after night, on a big case, Pam would go out with friends. It was time she did it again. Just friends. So what if he was a man?

***

Jeff was getting a kick out of watching Pam eat her dinner. The way she savored every bite, anyone would think she'd been eating at a five-star Parisian restaurant.

When he had first asked her to join him for dinner, he swore he saw all the color drain from her face, and was convinced she was going to tell him that she'd forgotten she wanted to stay home and clean out the refrigerator. He came within inches of backpedaling and rescinding the invitation, but until that moment, he hadn't realized just how much he had wanted her to say yes.

After Carol Ann had left his office, it had occurred to him that a casual dinner at the café would be just the right place to chat a bit with Pam about her situation. Mention Caleb, his old college friend the psychologist, and subtly introduce the idea of therapy. But as soon as the dinner invitation was out of his mouth, and her smile had slipped, he hadn't cared about therapy or counselors. He'd only wanted to see her smile again. And he'd very much wanted to see that smile over dinner, even if *that* gave him one more thing to worry about.

"Hmm. You were so right." Pam speared another small piece of meat. "This is the best chicken fried steak I've ever eaten. Ever."

"Only one person on the planet cooks nearly as good as my mother. And not even Mom makes a better chicken fried steak than Mabel."

"I loved my mother to death, but cooking wasn't one of her gifts in life. I'm not sure if Dad really liked cooking the way he claimed or if it was just self-preservation."

Jeff laughed. "That bad?"

"Mom? Oh, yeah. I once caught her holding a Butterball turkey up on its legs. When I asked her what she was doing, she answered, 'Trying to see which way it walks.' I had no clue what she was talking about, so I asked her why. Seems she was having a hard time telling which side was the breast on the perfectly round twenty-pound turkey."

"Did she figure it out?"

Pam shook her head. "That was the year Dad started cooking Thanksgiving dinner."

"Then how is it your dad never brought the family to the café to taste Mabel's cooking?"

Pam tipped her head in thought. "I honestly don't know."

"What about you? Do you like to cook?"

Pam shrugged a shoulder. "I don't think I'd say I *like* to cook, but I don't mind it. It's sort of like laundry or housecleaning. It has to be done." She put down her fork and let out a soft chuckle. "But at least I know which side of a turkey is up." Delicately she dabbed the corners of her mouth with her napkin. "What about you?"

"We all cook." Jeff watched Pam finish off her last piece of steak. "Even though Ma's the queen of her kitchen, she made sure all her kids knew their way around one. But I don't see much point to cooking for only me."

"So you eat here a lot?"

"Not as much as I used to. Sometimes I go home for dinner. More often I just eat frozen or takeout."

"I know what you mean." Pam dabbed the corners of her mouth again. A small drop of gravy remained to one side of her mouth.

"You missed a spot." To his surprise, he very much wanted to reach out and wipe the drop away. Maybe his sister and mother were right. He needed to spend more time in the company of women. It had been much too long since he'd felt a woman's soft skin under his fingertips.

Not that he'd done that much touching since his carousing days at college. But even the feel of a woman's smaller hand in his was a comfort. A comfort he missed more than he'd been willing to admit, and heaven help him, right now he very much wanted to find that comfort in the feel of Pam's hand in his.

"Contemplating the immortality of the crab?"

"Excuse me?"

"Something my grandmother used to say when she was lost in thought. I got the feeling you were someplace else for a few minutes there. Anything interesting?"

What was he doing? He shouldn't be thinking about wiping away droplets or holding hands. He needed to focus. She needed help. Real help. And this time he would do his job right and see that she got professional help from someone qualified to make a difference. "Not really."

"Then why are you blushing?"

"Was I blushing?" Sometimes having inherited his mom's pale Irish complexion was a real pain.

"Oh, yeah." Pam flashed a broad grin, the kind that made him want to grin back.

He gave himself another mental kick. The fact that Pam's smile warmed his insides wasn't important. And maybe if he repeated that often enough, he might just believe it. "It's just my naturally ruddy complexion."

"Right." She laughed. "And Mabel's a natural redhead."

"If it means that much to you, my mind wandered back to when I was in college. My friends." At least it had briefly—between thoughts of her.

"Did she mean a lot to you?" An impish grin spread across Pam's face.

"Actually, *he's* the best. Caleb Young. We were roommates at UT. Couldn't have asked for a better friend. Only downside was our food bill senior year when we had our own apartment. The guy ate like a linebacker."

Pam put the roll she held in her hand back on her dish. "And I remind you of him?"

"Oh, no." *Great move, Pastor Jeff. Why not just tell the woman she eats like two hundred pound football player.* "It was the dinner that made me think of him. Chicken fried steak was his favorite. One summer he spent a few weeks here in town, and I think he ate Mabel's chicken fried steak three times a day."

Pam picked the roll back up. "So tell me more about this friend."

A flash of school days' antics made him smile. "Back in college I had no intention of ever following in my father's footsteps. I'd had enough of the disciplined godly life. The day I walked onto campus, I was free and ready to start living. You might say Caleb and I majored in girls, parties, and baseball. Not exactly a stellar background for a future pastor."

Marybeth Houlihan sprang suddenly to Jeff's mind. He'd dated her for almost six months his sophomore year. They'd continued sleeping together off and on for another six months after that. Over the course of four years in Austin, he and Caleb had sown enough wild oats for several NCAA Division 1 Baseball teams. The details were forever sealed in a pledge of silence between Caleb and him.

He waited for Pam's reaction to his admission of a wild past, but she merely smiled at him. A sweet smile that silently said we all had college days like that, though he couldn't picture it. There was no way the woman sitting across from him had ever partied hard.

Gesturing with his hands, he signaled for Redding to bring them some coffee. "My first year of college I was convinced I had the stuff to be a pro ball player."

"Really?" Pam pushed aside her empty plate. "What changed?"

"It started with minor nerve surgery on my pitching arm." He lifted his arm and showed her the thin line across the inside of his elbow. "By the end of sophomore year I'd blown out my rotator cuff and accepted that I'd never pitch at a major league ballpark."

"I'm sorry." Pam stretched her fingers forward slightly, brushed her hand against his, and then, as though shocked by the touch, quickly dropped her hand to her side. "I remember how much you loved to play ball. Jake too. Baseball was more important to him than anything. Even girls."

Thoughts of Marybeth popped back up, and Jeff felt the rising heat in his neck. He really needed to get out more. "Yeah, well. Since there was no way I wanted to be a stodgy pastor like my father, I buckled down and walked away with a degree in economics."

"Really? So what changed your mind? About being a pastor I mean."

"In a nutshell, I discovered I didn't have the heart to do whatever it took to climb the corporate ladder. Apparently all those years of doing right in the face of the Lord were more ingrained in me than I'd thought."

"So what you're telling me is that you can take the boy out of the church, but you can't take the church out of the boy."

A grin teased the corners of his mouth. "Yeah, that pretty much covers it. I found myself doing what was best for everyone rather than what was needed to make money."

"Doesn't surprise me. You're really good with people. Some pastors come off as pious and pretentious, but it's obvious to anyone with eyes you're the real deal."

"Real deal?"

"Yeah. Like the way you worried about Mrs. Perkins until Sandra came along. This isn't just a job with a pretty title to you. You're a pastor in every sense of the word. You really care and it shows."

The real deal. Focusing on a spoon he now spun between his fingers, Jeff thought of Jenny. The real deal would have been able to save her. "Sometimes caring isn't enough."

"Sometimes caring is all you can do."

Lifting his gaze to meet Pam's, he wondered what she'd say if she knew the one time his choices were a matter of life and death—he'd made the wrong one.

Pam reached out, her fingertips gently stilling the hand fiddling with the spoon. For a long moment the silence spoke volumes. When Pam withdrew her touch, he was tempted to snatch back her hand. Now more than ever he wanted the comfort of holding her smaller hand in his. But good sense won out. He kept his hands at his sides and forced a smile to his lips.

"Anyway, I went from partying-wannabe-ballplayer, to bad businessman, and now here I am."

"What about your roommate? Did he make it in baseball?"

Jeff shook his head, thankful for a chance to redirect the conversation. "Somewhere along the way Caleb managed to fit in a degree in psychology."

"Oh." Pam straightened in her seat.

The stiffened response wasn't the reaction he'd expected. He'd thought to use his friend as a casual lead into discussing the need for therapy. But Pam's tense body language gave him a moment's pause. "Anyhow, five years later I found myself in divinity school ready to follow in my father's footsteps, and by then, Caleb was well on his way to a promising career as a clinical psychologist."

"Clinical psychologist?"

"Mmm." He nodded, wondering briefly how far to push the conversation. "In Poplar Springs—"

"Here you go," Redding interrupted, setting two cups of coffee on the table. "Ready for dessert? Today's special is pecan pie." He hesitated a moment before adding, "Fresh from the oven."

"Oh, my." Pam licked her lips. "I don't think I could eat another bite."

"You sure?" Redding glanced from Pam to Jeff and back. The way Pam was nibbling on the corner of her mouth, anyone could see it wouldn't take much convincing for her to change her mind.

"What if we split a piece?" Jeff suggested.

"I don't know." Pam stared at the empty plates Redding held in his hand. "I don't usually eat this much."

"Then what harm will a little more do? One piece of pecan pie with two forks coming right up." Redding gave Jeff a wink, and turned about, whistling on his way to the kitchen.

"Wonder what came over him?" Pam watched Redding until he disappeared through a rear doorway. "I mean, why would agreeing to a piece of pie make a man so happy?"

"I don't think it was the pie. I think it was the two forks."

"Two forks?" She turned her attention back to Jeff. He knew the minute recognition dawned. Her eyes grew round as silver dollars, and her chin nearly hit the table. "Uh-oh. You don't mean…"

He nodded. "I should have anticipated someone might misconstrue the situation. Tomorrow morning I'll call Mrs. Cahill to confirm the date of her granddaughter's baptism. I'll find a way to mention dinner tonight was simply the church's way of thanking you for doing such a great job filling in for Ellen." That wasn't far from the truth. Once Ellen returned from maternity leave, the church would want to do something nice for Pam. Maybe he'd ask Mrs. Cahill to be in charge of the thank-you committee. Then there'd be no doubt left in Mrs. Cahill's mind that this wasn't a social dinner. "By lunchtime she'll have single handedly informed the whole town this wasn't a real date."

"You may want to practice on Redding." Pam tilted her head toward the older man walking their way with a plate of pie, two forks, and the biggest grin this side of the Pecos.

Jeff cast a quick glance at Redding, then back to Pam. "Maybe I'd better call Mrs. Cahill tonight."

CHAPTER SEVEN

Caleb Young in Poplar Springs. At least now Pam had the name of a psychologist, a good one according to Jeff.

No advertisement in the yellow pages, just his name, address, and phone number. No wonder she hadn't noticed him before. Pulling a pen out of the kitchen junk drawer, she scribbled his number on a piece of paper. With careful precision, she folded the page in half. Making sure the ends aligned perfectly, she ran her finger along the crease and then halved it again so it would fit in her wallet.

"Wonder what Caleb Young would say about this. Folding from corner to corner, pleating the sides not once, but twice, before folding again. Always matching the corners precisely. Think he'd consider me compulsive?" Pam laughed at the piece of paper in her hand. "Maybe my problems have nothing to do with you being dead and everything to do with me being crazy."

She slipped the paper into her billfold and placed her purse on the kitchen counter by the bag from the café. Somehow Redding had talked her into bringing home a piece of Mabel's pecan pie and a tub of cream. She'd put the cream in the fridge, but the pie still sat on the counter, and she'd almost be willing to swear under oath it was calling her name.

"Oh, heck. What's a few more calories?" She was going to need the fortitude anyway. If Jeff didn't reach Mrs. Cahill tonight, Pam should expect a deluge of parishioners calling first thing in the morning to get the latest scoop on him and her.

The way Redding, with his broad grin intact, kept nodding at Jeff, as he explained about the working dinner, told Pam that Redding didn't believe a word Jeff had said. Even though there wasn't a single thing to indicate they were anything more than employer and employee, Redding was perfectly content to put his own spin on dinner.

How could she blame the man for jumping to conclusions, when it had taken her a very long couple of minutes to convince *herself* that Jeff wasn't asking her for a date. And even then it wasn't until her first bite of chicken fried steak that she'd truly relaxed enough to enjoy Jeff's company.

She'd barely had enough time to put her first forkful of pie into her mouth when the phone rang.

"Dang." Juggling the plate in one hand, Pam grabbed the phone. "Hello."

"Is it true?"

"Valerie?"

"Is it really true?" Val's eagerness was coming through the phone line loud and clear.

"Is what true?"

"You and Jeff Parker?"

"Oh, for heaven's sake." Pam set the plate on the end table and looked at her watch. Home less than half an hour and already news had spread to her sister. "I work for the man."

"And had a nice intimate supper at the café."

"Intimate? At the Last Chance? Are you completely out of your mind?" Good grief this was worse than she'd expected.

"Two people alone in a booth is about as intimate as you're going to get without driving all the way to Poplar Springs."

"It was nothing more than sharing a simple meal. We were both going to the café after work, so it made perfect sense to share a table. That was it. Nothing more. Pastor and receptionist. Period."

"Uh-huh."

"Don't you 'uh-huh' me. Where'd you hear we were out for an intimate dinner?"

"So now it's not just a meal, it's an intimate dinner?"

"Whatever! Who told you?"

"So it is true! You're seeing Jeff Parker."

"No, it's not true, but I need you to do some damage control before this gets back to Mrs. Parker."

"Too late."

"Why?"

"Who do you think called me?"

Pam sank into the nearest chair. "Mrs. Parker?"

"Yeah, but I'd already heard the news from Theresa Cahill. She heard it from Sally Norton, who heard it from Jan Evans, whose sister Beverly stopped by the café to pick up one of Mabel's pies for a special dinner for her daughter Margaret and her new husband. I hear the husband's kinda cute, but don't worry, Jeff's cuter."

What a miserable mess. "Is there anyone in town who doesn't think I had a date with my boss?"

"Uh, probably not. So what gives? Why all the secrecy?"

"Nothing gives. That's the whole point. There was no date. No intimate dinner. Nothing."

"Nothing?"

"Nada."

"Really?"

"Why would I lie?" Val hesitated a little longer than Pam would have liked. "Val?"

"You wouldn't." All the earlier eagerness in Val's voice was gone. "It's just—Travis has been gone two years."

"Don't you think I know that?" Pam snapped. She hadn't meant to, but how could she forget that two years, three months, and twenty-four days had passed since that horrible night?

"I'm sorry, of course you do, but you're only twenty-eight years old. It's time you get a real life again."

"I have a life."

"That's not what I mean. You're too young to be alone all the time. You need people to talk to besides your family. Like friends, guys. And talking to a dead husband doesn't count. You should be dating live men."

A dull steady pain began tapping at Pam's temples. What was it today with sisters and dating? First Carol Ann wants Jeff to see more women, and now Valerie wants Pam to get a life. "Val, I don't need this right now, and for the record, I don't want to date. I've already had the best. What I need is for you to stop lecturing me and help me put out some fires."

"There really isn't any chance for you and Jeff?"

"If there's a chance for anyone having a relationship with Jeff, my money's on Sandra Quinn."

"That doesn't make me feel any better. Jeff's a nice guy. You deserve nice."

"I had nice." Pam's voice faltered. She cleared her throat and spoke a little louder. "Will you help me put a stop to the rumors or not?"

***

Some days, like Dorothy in *The Wizard of Oz*, Jeff simply knew there was no place like home.

It was only Sunday afternoon, and already this had been the longest weekend of his life. There was no other way to describe it. He'd spent most of Friday and Saturday dodging bullets from half the parishioners, and this morning after services, he'd gotten an earful from the remainder who hadn't caught up with him during the days before.

He'd expected the gossip-hungry citizens to sink their teeth into the juicy news of the pastor's new girlfriend and did his best to dispel the rumors. What he hadn't expected was the backlash from the more serious side of the congregation. It had started Friday morning. He'd barely gotten out of bed when his phone rang. John Haskell, on behalf of the church board of directors, had wanted to know if there was any truth to Jeff "taking an interest" in his new secretary.

"Mind you, it's not that we have anything against her," Haskell had said. "She's a lovely woman. Shame about losing her husband so young and all, but you're her boss, Jeff."

"Yes, sir." What more could he have said?

"Then you understand why this doesn't reflect well on the church?" He didn't wait for Jeff to respond. "In this era of potential sexual harassment and media mania, to some folk, dating a subordinate is inappropriate, no exceptions. As our representative you have to be held above reproach. Of course, all of us on the board know your intentions are honorable, but it may not look that way to everyone. Especially outsiders."

And so his weekend had begun.

"What time is dinner?" Jeff watched his mom flip on the oven light and peek through the tinted glass to the made-from-scratch rolls baking inside.

"For heaven's sake." Etta Mae grinned. "What's the hurry?"

Stepping up behind her, Jeff looped his arms around his mom's waist and lightly rested his chin on her head. "Would you rather I didn't look forward to your cooking?"

"I'd rather you told me what's really eating at you."

Jeff kissed his mother's head and retook his seat at the kitchen table. "Just a long few days."

Etta untied her apron, tossed it on the counter, and settled in the seat beside her son. "Your father told me about Haskell. John couldn't wait to phone Harlon as soon as he was done talking to you."

"Hmm." Jeff fiddled with the edge of the place mat. Every one of Mrs. Henry's first grade classes had taken family photos and made place mats as Christmas gifts for their parents. He and his three siblings were no exception. What surprised him was that his mother still used them to this day.

"That old coot…" Etta continued, "…has been giving your father grief since the first day he was named to the board of directors."

Jeff glanced at his mother. He couldn't imagine anyone finding fault with his father. In everyone's eyes Pastor Harlon Parker was the next best thing to having the Lord Himself preach.

"Which old coot is that?" Harlon Parker sauntered into the room, sniffed the air, and smiled at his wife, his eyes twinkling like a sparkler on the Fourth of July. "Smells like dinnertime."

Jeff had never thought twice about how much his father loved and respected his mother. When he was a little kid, he'd thought that's the way everyone's parents were. As he grew older, he realized his folks had something special. It amazed him that after almost forty years of marriage his parents still lit up like candles when the other walked into the room.

"John Haskell," Etta answered her husband.

His dad's eyes narrowed as they studied his wife. "Etta."

"I know. It just irritates me to think that man has nothing better to do than spend his days finding fault with our boy."

"John Haskell is a good man." Harlon patted his son on the shoulder. "And Jefferson is a good pastor. He's done a remarkable job taking over. I don't believe I would have done nearly as well handling everything without Ellen."

"Pop, you would have done just fine without Ellen, and you know it. And I haven't taken over. Just trying to keep up till you get back. The church needs you." *Especially Pam. Someone has to help her find her way, and I'm not that man.*

"You've done more than keep up." Harlon turned to his wife and kissed her square on the mouth for just a second longer than Jeff was comfortable watching, then took the seat beside her. "So, Haskell called to fuss at you about dinner the other night with Pamela Sue."

Jeff nodded.

"You got any untoward intentions with the lady?"

There was no need for a mirror. Jeff knew his eyes had opened as big and round as a spotted owl's. "Of course not."

"That's what I thought. You pay no mind to John."

"And what about the rest of the board?"

"*Hmph.* You listen to your old man and your own conscience. If you spend your ministry trying to cater to the whims of the board, you'll find yourself all twisted up like an old phone cord. You do what you know is right in the sight of God, and you'll do fine." At that the doorbell rang, and his dad patted his wife's knee and pushed to his feet. "I'll get that."

Though they were still waiting on his brother Danny and his family, and his sister Carol Ann, neither of them would have rung the bell.

"You expecting company?" Jeff asked.

From the way his mom's eyes darted over to the stove and back, and the rush with which she popped out of her seat, grabbed her apron, and said, "Could be," he knew.

"Oh, Ma. You didn't?"

"And why shouldn't I? Pamela Sue is a very nice young woman. And if you haven't noticed…" Etta squared her shoulders. "…a very attractive woman at that."

"Ma-ah." Leaning on the table with his elbows, he let his head rest in the palms of his hand. He should have realized, if his mother thought he'd taken an interest in anyone, she'd home in like a missile on heat. "What were you thinking? If word gets out about this—a family dinner with Pam—it's going to fuel all the gossip I've spent three days trying to squelch."

"Nonsense. Pam isn't the first neighbor I've invited over for a meal, and she won't be the last."

"Yes, but this is different…" Expecting Pam and his father, Jeff was caught off guard at the sound of pounding feet running in his direction.

"Uncle Jeff" sounded through the room moments before a projectile hit him full force in the chest.

"Hey, buddy." His three-year-old nephew Gavin was his biggest fan. "What ya got there?"

Clutched in the little boy's grip was a fistful of somewhat bent dandelions. "Oh, I forgots." He hopped off his uncle's lap and, flashing a toothy grin, thrust his hand at his grandmother. "These are for you, Gram. I picked them."

Grandmother and grandson stood side by side, beaming at each other with so much love and pride, that Jeff's heart warmed, melting away all the irritation he'd felt for his mother only moments before.

His brother Danny's pregnant wife, Terri, came waddling through the doorway and settled into the nearest chair with unexpected ease for a woman of her girth. "Help your gram put those in water."

When Jeff pushed back his seat to stand, his sister-in-law waved him off. "Don't get up on my account." Then she smiled. "Great sermon today. You outdid yourself. Made me want to go out and join the Peace Corps or something."

"Yeah, well, I think you're needed more here." Jeff grinned.

"Seriously, what you say really resonates with us of the younger generations."

Just then Jeff spotted Pam standing to one side of the door with his one-year-old niece, Emily, perched on her hip. Pam whispered conspiratorially as the little girl cooed with delight.

Whatever he'd meant to respond to his sister-in-law was quickly forgotten. He couldn't explain it, but his eyes were riveted to the sight. Michelangelo couldn't have had a better subject for mother and child.

"We nearly collided at the front door." Terri splayed both hands across her well-rounded tummy. "Emily usually doesn't take to strangers." Terri flashed an impish grin. "I don't suppose you babysit?"

"Anytime," Pam shot back without hesitation.

One by one they took a seat around the old oak harvest table that was big enough to seat the Walton family and then some. Danny stood behind his wife rubbing her shoulders, while Terri and his dad rehashed, almost word for word, Jeff's sermon.

His sister, Carol Ann, always bursting with energy, practically flew into the room mumbling, "Sorry I'm late," as she made her way greeting everyone around the table.

"You hurry up and take your place," Etta instructed. "Supper's almost ready."

Emily clapped her hands and kicked her feet at her grandma's announcement.

Pam pointed at a box of Cheerios Etta always kept handy on the kitchen counter for when her youngest grandbaby came to visit. "Will it hurt her appetite to have some of those?"

Terri glanced behind her at the cereal and shook her head.

"Nah."

Pam made her way across the kitchen, never stopping her conversation with Emily. After pouring the bowl of Cheerios, she and the baby took a seat at the table. Anyone watching would never have guessed she was only the next door neighbor. Pam fit in as though she'd been raised in this house with the rest of them.

As the sound decibel grew around the table, Jeff kept his eyes on Pam and his niece. Emily focused intently on the round pieces of oats, painstakingly maneuvering her little fingers to lift each one to her mouth. Holding the child on her lap, Pam kept a firm arm around her middle. Since the day Emily had taken her first step two months ago, the child had been like a whirling dervish. Sitting still was not on her list of favorite things to do. Judging from the way Terri and Danny would cast a sideways glance in Pam's direction, her gift at settling an active child hadn't gone unnoticed. Apparently there was more to Pamela Sue Dawson than a friendly smile and an ability to keep him organized. A lot more.

***

Pam watched Etta Mae loading leftovers into plastic containers. "I couldn't possibly eat all this food by myself."

"Better you than Harlon and me. We don't need any more padding. Oh, Jefferson," Etta called to her son, chatting with his brother in the living room. "Come here a minute, please."

"Sure Ma, just a sec."

Etta smiled and nodded, as if her son could see her through the wall. Then one by one, she placed the leftovers into a brown paper shopping bag.

As much as Pam loved Friday nights with her family, dinner with the Parkers was so different, so…normal.

Compared to dinner with her dad and three siblings, dining with six adults and two children definitely made the evening a bit louder, a bit more chaotic, and occasionally, a bit overwhelming. But not once did anyone treat her like a fragile vase that might shatter without warning. Oh, she and her family teased and laughed and argued just like they had done growing up, but eventually someone would say or do something to remind them why Pam had moved home from Dallas, and nothing could reverse the heavy mood that would settle on the rest of the evening.

"I can't thank you enough for inviting me." She handed Etta a nearby container.

"You're welcome anytime. There's always room at our table and no need to wait for an invitation." Etta Mae patted Pam's hand before turning to the cabinet for another bag.

And to think Pam almost hadn't come. As much as she'd enjoyed her dinner with Jeff the other night, she didn't think having Sunday dinner with his entire family on the heels of the gossip fest was such a good idea. Jeff didn't need any more aggravation. But Etta Mae wouldn't take *No, thank you* for an answer, and Pam was really glad she hadn't. Playing with the children, conversing over dinner, and helping Etta Mae with the dishes, reminded her so much of what life had been like before. Of what she wanted it to be again.

Of course, without Travis, she'd always be aunt Pam. But she wanted to be this happy aunt Pam 365 days a year. She didn't want to be at the mercy of nightmares, stable and normal one day, and a crazed neurotic the next, never knowing when she'd wake up afraid of her own shadow.

Her glance drifted over to her purse and the phone number she knew was tucked away safely inside her wallet.

***

Smiling, Jeff sidled up beside his mother. "What's up?"

Holding two oversized shopping bags, Etta Mae held them out to Jeff. "They're a little heavy, so you go on and help Pam take these home."

"Oh, that won't be necessary." Pam reached for the first bag. "I can manage."

"Nonsense. What good is a man if he can't help you carry the load?"

Jeff had a very distinct feeling his mother wasn't talking about leftover meat loaf, but Pam's appreciative smile gave no indication she'd caught the implication.

They covered the short distance to her house in only a couple of minutes. Standing on her porch, waiting as she unlocked the door, an odd sense of loss took root inside him. He'd really enjoyed dinner at home. Some time with his family was just the escape from reality he'd needed, but having Pam there somehow managed to make it even better. And much to his surprise, he realized now, he didn't want the evening to end yet. "Shall I put these in the kitchen for you?"

"Yes, please." Pam shoved open the door and pointed to the back of the house. "Straight ahead."

Jeff deposited the bags on the counter. Then, like a bellboy at a hotel waiting for his tip, he stood aimlessly in the middle of the room, not wanting to leave, not sure what else to say.

"Would you like some coffee before you go? Maybe help me polish off a little of your mom's apple pie? I noticed you didn't have any after dinner."

She had? He'd been so at peace relaxing for the first time in days that he was content to simply sit back and watch everyone else. "Sounds delicious. Thanks."

The sound of dishes clattering as she pulled two from the cupboard filled the room. "Whipped cream?" she asked.

"Nope. Straight up."

"Got it." Pam laughed, a full rolling laugh that warmed him deep inside, and then she turned back to face the counter. "One slice of apple pie, straight up."

"I hope having dinner with the entire clan wasn't too much for you."

"Are you kidding?" Pam set the two plates of pie on the table. "My family does dinner every Friday night. Put us all at the same table and we make yours look like *The Brady Bunch*. Too well adjusted to be real."

"Your family seems as well adjusted as the rest of us."

"You think?" Her voice dripped with sarcasm. "Did your sister ever die her hair pink?"

Jeff swallowed a grin. "No, can't say that she did."

"And what about Danny? I don't suppose he ever went through a stage where all his girlfriends wore combat boots?"

"Combat boots?" He felt his brows arch high on his forehead. "Which brother?"

"Bo."

"You're kidding! How did I miss that?"

"You weren't around much then." She poured two cups of coffee. "You'd gone to college at UT. Bo went to community college here for two years before transferring to Tech."

"Combat boots." Jeff shook his head. At least when he was going a little crazy in college, all the girls he hooked up with would have been suitable enough to take home to mother. Well, most of them anyhow.

"Then we have your brother Kenny. He looks like the poster child for the all-American boy. If my brother Jake ever gave up banking, the Hells Angels would take him without hesitation." Pam slid into her seat, waving a finger at him. "And when was the last time you and one of your brothers arm wrestled over who got the first slice of pie?"

"Actually, I was fifteen, and it was the *last* slice of pie. I sort of broke Danny's finger."

"Sort of?"

Jeff hitched a shoulder. "It was an accident."

"Okay. So maybe your family isn't perfect." She gave him one of those sweet smiles he'd grown so accustomed to and couldn't resist returning. "But I'm still glad your mom invited me to come for supper after church today."

"I think Emily was glad she invited you too. I've never seen that child so quietly content."

"She's a sweet little thing."

"You'll make a great mom someday."

Pam's smile faded. "I'll be happy as aunt Pam."

"You don't want children of your own?"

She toyed with the handle of her coffee mug. "I used to."

"Used to?"

"We…Travis and I…always thought there'd be plenty of time to start a family." She didn't look up at Jeff but kept her eyes focused on the warm liquid in front of her. "I can't imagine having anyone else's children."

"I see." That would be such an awful waste. Anyone could see how great she was with children. His niece didn't warm up to just anybody. Heck, his own sister-in-law had been surprised at how easily Pam seemed to entertain his normally exhausting niece. "You're still pretty young. With time, maybe someday—"

"No." Pam raised her eyes to meet his. "I don't want to ever do that again."

"That?"

"Love a man with everything you have, everything you are, only to lose him."

"Losing someone you love is a horrible hurt." He'd never been in love with Jenny Buckner, but her death, so young, so tragic, ate at him like a cancer. He couldn't even begin to fathom the pain Pam must have suffered. Especially if she'd seen her husband murdered. "It doesn't have to be that way." He reached out to touch her hand and thought better of it, letting his hand fall back to his side. "Just because Travis died doesn't mean—"

"It doesn't matter," she cut him off. "When Travis died, I felt like crawling into a hole and never coming out. No one expects to be widow at my age, to face that soul-shattering loss. I don't ever want to hurt that much again. I can't. I won't. Besides, even if replacing Travis didn't seem utterly obscene, I've already had the love of my life. A girl just doesn't get that lucky twice in a lifetime." As if she'd declared something as benign as "The weather seems to have turned cold," she pushed her seat away from the table and grabbed the coffeepot. "Another cup?"

"Sure." What the heck? He didn't need to sleep tonight.

"What about you?" Back in her seat, Pam stirred a spoonful of sugar into her coffee.

"What about me?"

"Your nephew seems to think you could hang the moon."

"I don't make him eat his peas," he said with a smile.

"There's more to it than that. He never strayed more than a couple of feet from your side all night and not once did you make him feel unwelcome."

"Making people feel welcome is part of my job description." Or it will be for a little longer.

"Bull."

"Excuse me?"

"You heard me. That's a load of crapola if ever I heard some."

Suddenly Jeff felt like a teenager back in high school, and the fiery Pammy Sue who would clock anyone who spoke ill of the folks she cared about was sitting across from him. It was a nice sight to see.

"Well?"

"Sorry." He took a slow sip of coffee. "I was just thinking about when I played ball with your brother."

"How'd we go from you're good with kids and should have some of your own to my brother and baseball?"

"The mind is a funny thing." He shrugged. "And why does everyone suddenly feel compelled to marry me off?"

Laughing, Pam dribbled coffee down her chin and stuck out her tongue to lick up the errant drops. The simple action punched him hard in the gut, sending an unexpected pool of warmth southward.

It took a few deep breaths to squelch the unexpected rise in his libido. For heaven's sake, this was Pammy Sue. Jake's kid sister. His mom's next-door neighbor. An employee at the church. Technically, his employee. Sure she was a pretty woman. Okay, a beautiful woman. And men reacted to beautiful women. It was genetic. Not his fault. But still, he wasn't just any man, and she wasn't just any woman.

Thankfully, she gave up on using her tongue to clean her face and grabbed a paper towel from the counter behind her. "I didn't say you should be married. Just that you're good with kids."

"Yeah, well." He shifted in his seat and took another deep breath. "It's sort of a requirement in my line of work to have a wife before you start making babies."

He was going to have to stop thinking of the church as his line of work. Once he returned to the corporate world, no one would give a rat's behind about who he had dinner with, did or didn't sleep with, and whether or not he was married or making babies.

The room grew loudly quiet. He could hear Pam take a sip of her coffee. Knew she was watching him. Could feel her gaze on him as surely as he could feel a warm woolen blanket.

"Penny for your thoughts?" she whispered across the table.

"Not worth that much." He made the mistake of looking into her eyes. Narrowed with concern, they drilled into him with laserlike precision. If she couldn't read his thoughts, he was sure she could at least see into his soul.

"I don't believe that for a minute," she finally said.

Peaches chose that moment to land with a thud on the table, flick her tail in Jeff's face, and strut over to her mistress. He'd have almost been willing to swear the cat turned to give him a warning glare before stepping down onto her lap and curling up in a fuzzy ball.

"I can hear her purring from here." Despite the cat's dirty look, he was most definitely grateful to Peaches for the distraction.

He'd come within inches of baring his soul. Telling Pam everything: his crazy college escapades, his final acceptance of a higher calling, and the devastating consequences of his failure with Jenny Buckner. All his futile efforts to get Jenny to leave her animal of a husband, go to a woman's shelter, anywhere safe. His arrogant mistake that had cost her her life. And no longer being able to deny the truth, he had no business trying to fill his father's shoes.

But he had no business unloading his burdens on Pam, either. She had enough troubles to deal with. Leaving the church, probably leaving Hope's Corner, and making a new life for himself was something for him to do—alone. Pushing away from the table, he stood. "I'd better be going."

"Oh. Yes. Well. I guess it is getting late."

For just a second he thought he saw disappointment in her eyes as she lifted Peaches from her lap and placed the kitty on the floor. He shouldn't let his imagination get the better of him. Whatever she felt, it certainly had nothing to do with his leaving.

Pam pushed away from the table and lifted from her seat. Her skirt rose slightly, exposing just enough shapely white thigh to send his libido soaring again.

"I'm sorry," he muttered in a rush. "I really need to go."

Door closed behind him, standing on Pam's porch, Jeff closed his eyes and took in a deep breath. What was happening to him tonight?

***

Pam wasn't sure how long she'd stood at the window. She'd watched Jeff walk back to his parent's house, and was still looking through the glass when he came out, got into his car, and drove off.

"I hadn't realized how much I missed having someone answer me when I talk." Her fingers loosened the firm grip they held on the edge of the curtains. Slowly she backed away, finally turning toward the kitchen. "I never realized how quiet this house is at night."

Standing over the sink, she rinsed off the dirty pie plates and noticed Etta working across the way in her own kitchen. "They have a really nice family. Don't you think?" Her hold on the last dirty dish tightened painfully.

The silent stillness of the room surrounded her. She was sure, if she'd dropped the proverbial pin, she could have heard it bounce off the floor.

There would be no reply to her question. No conversation. Travis wouldn't, couldn't, answer her. All her incessant chatter would never break the silence. She was alone. All alone.

CHAPTER EIGHT

"Yes, Mrs. Cahill." Jeff moved the phone to his other ear. "I'm glad you see it that way… Yes, I think a ladies' luncheon is a wonderful idea." He smiled into the phone hoping he didn't sound as exasperated as he felt.

His sister had called first thing that morning, supposedly to talk about plans for their mother's birthday more than a month away, but instead spent more than twenty minutes carrying on about what a delightful dinner guest Pam had been.

Then his sister-in-law had phoned him to sing Pam's praises and inquire if he thought she might seriously consider babysitting. The question was absurd. His mother would be cold in the grave before she'd let anyone else babysit her grandbabies, and Terri knew it as well as he did.

At least Theresa Cahill had taken to the idea of a Thank-You Committee like a starving cat to caviar. If she'd garnered any romantic notions about him and Pam after Thursday's dinner, she was perfectly happy to set them aside for the title of committee chair. He didn't want to think what would happen to the rumor mill if the woman got wind of his mother inviting Pam to Sunday supper.

When Theresa Cahill finally ran out of steam and let him hang up, he was sorely tempted to take his phone off the hook and turn off his cell. But the last thing he needed was for someone to have an emergency and not be able to find the acting pastor. No, he'd stay home today, keep busy. By tomorrow when he had to return to his office, most of the dust from the storm of gossip would have settled, and everyone would have forgotten his dinner with Pam at the café. And with the grace of God, Sunday supper with his family wouldn't become the next fodder for the town gossips.

Now sitting on the sofa, matching clean socks, he had a

different problem to sort out. *He* didn't want to forget about either dinner with Pam. What he wanted was to see her smile, watch her play with his niece, hear her voice, listen to her tell him some silly story about her mom's bad cooking, or her sister's crazy boyfriends.

She'd be at the church office alone today. He wondered if she was okay, or had she also been on the receiving end of concerned parishioners' *friendly* comments? He certainly didn't want her to retreat into her shell because of local gossip. Maybe he should call and check in with her? Or maybe not. Yesterday she'd seemed untouched by the gossip.

While still battling with himself, the phone rang, and he glanced at the caller ID, not sure he was recharged enough to deal with more *helpful* comments. The relief, then the rush of warmth, that washed over him when he read the church name on his phone stopped him cold. What was happening to him? He couldn't do this. This was no time in his life to fall for a woman. Especially this woman. As soon as his father was back to work, Jeff's world would be turned upside down. Leaving the church to start over with a new career would be hard enough. The responsibility of a wife was the last thing he needed.

He froze with the telephone in hand, hanging in midair. *Wife*? Where the hell had that come from?

"Pastor?" A muffled sound wafted toward him.

He stared wide-eyed at the receiver as though it were some newfangled discovery.

"Hello?" A soft voice laced with confusion filled the air. "Jeff? Are you there?"

"Sorry, yes." He had to get a grip. He didn't know when he'd gone from thinking of her as a temporary replacement for Ellen to a potential wife, but he needed to put it out of his mind.

"Sandra Quinn called. She said to tell you the appointment for Mrs. Perkins is at eleven this morning."

"Right. Good to know."

"She seemed to hedge a bit. I'm not sure, but I think she was hoping you might want to go with them."

"Uh, yes, that might be a good idea. Thanks for letting me know."

"Anytime." Pam hesitated a moment. "Is anything wrong?"

"Wrong? No. Why do you ask?" Yes, something was wrong. A simple telephone conversation relaying a phone message had his heart pounding at twice its normal rate.

"You sound funny."

He took a deep calming breath. "I'm fine. But I'd better call Sandra, and, Pam…"

"Yes?"

"Anything else happening over there?"

"No. Just another Monday. Not much happens around here on the pastor's day off."

"Good." Better than good. He didn't want her upset by some well-meaning parishioner.

"Also, if you don't mind, I'd like to have lunch with Miss Abigail today. Is that all right with you?"

"Yes, yes, of course it is. She's a great lady, isn't she?"

"Yeah, she is."

He could hear the smile in Pam's voice. "Take all the time you want. Like you said, it's a slow Monday."

"I can't take too long. The copy machine is on the fritz again, and Fred said he could probably squeeze me in between two and three o'clock."

"If the fund-raising goes well, maybe we can spring for a new copy machine. In the meantime, tell Miss Abbie I'll see her Thursday." He'd barely had time to let go of the handset when the phone rang again. "Hello."

"How's my favorite up-and-coming pastor?" The sound of his mother's voice did little to help his mood.

"Morning, Ma."

"Did you sleep well, dear?"

Perfectly fine once he'd stopped tossing and turning, trying not to think about how long it had been since he'd really been with a woman. "Like a baby."

"Good. I'm glad you didn't let John Haskell's phone call lose you any sleep."

He could honestly report he hadn't once thought of the president of the church board of directors all night. "Nope."

"Oh, I got some wonderful news this morning. You remember Carol Ann's friend Margie?"

"Works over at the Shop and Save?"

"That's the one. Well, you know she and her husband have been trying for years to have a baby."

"No." He didn't like the sound of this. "I didn't."

"Well, they have. She's had a dickens of a time of it. But you can't really be surprised. Infertility is a growing problem in this country with everyone waiting till they're older to start a family. Waiting till you're in your thirties before conceiving simply isn't part of God's plan."

"Maybe so, but what did you want to tell me about Carol Ann's friend?"

"Oh. She's pregnant. She did those fertility treatments and multiple births was a real concern, but it looks like she's carrying only one little baby."

"That is wonderful news, Ma. I'll make sure to send them a little note of congratulations on behalf of the church."

"There's nothing like bringing a baby into the world."

Here it comes.

"Your own flesh and blood. A little person who depends solely on you. Pammy Sue did really well with Emily yesterday, don't ya think?"

"Ma."

"There's something so gentle about her. I just knew she'd be good with children. She should have a passel of her own. And she's not getting any younger. I mean, look at poor Margie."

"Ma. I have to get back to the fund-raising report." There was no way he was getting into a conversation about families, babies *and* Pam with his mother.

"Just this past Saturday morning all the ladies in my bridge club agreed you and Pam make a lovely couple. You know I love you, Jeff, but you're not getting any younger either."

"I love you too, Ma. But I really need to get going."

After disconnecting the call and staring at the phone for a full five minutes, Jeff knew what he had to do. The gossip about him and Pam had to stop. Flipping through the new church directory, he found Sandra's number.

***

"My, that was a hot summer." Ninety-seven-year-old Abigail Clarke fanned herself at the memories. "I thought, if I drank one more glass of Haddie's lemonade, I'd turn into a lemon."

"I can't imagine what it must have been like without air-conditioning." Pam's throat was parched from just listening to Miss Abigail talk about the heat wave of 1939. She couldn't fathom surviving a hot Texas summer unable to don a pair of shorts and a cool T-shirt with only a few fans and Haddie's lemonade to ease the misery.

"Oh, it was more than the weather that had me overheated." The grin that swept across Miss Abigail's face was bright enough to light up all of East Texas. "That's the summer I met my Edgar. It was scandalous." The older woman rolled her eyes heavenward, and her shoulders shifted with glee. "Me being an old maid and all. He was so handsome in his uniform. I was smitten the moment I laid eyes on him."

Miss Abigail stared silently out the window. Her gaze focused on some unknown point on the other side of the tinted window. Then her expression softened, replaced by the sweet reflection of a woman in love.

It wasn't hard for Pam to picture this older frail woman when she was young, beautiful, and desperately in love with a soldier.

"I was twenty-nine years old. Almost thirty. Not that old by today's standards, but back then I was an old maid in everyone's eyes. Edgar was older than me by six years." Abigail kept her focus straight ahead. "The war in Europe hadn't truly started yet, but there were those carrying on about war being inevitable and our needing to be a part of it." Miss Abigail turned to Pam. "That's what brought my Edgar this way. He was doing a recruiting tour. Looking for good men."

Pam inched forward in her seat, hanging on Miss Abigail's every word.

"At first he'd come to speak with my brother Henry, but I knew from the start there was more to it. Edgar only called on the young men of Hope's Corner once. My brother had many talents, but when Edgar came to our house calling every evening, it was pretty clear he was looking for more than good men to fight a war no one here really believed would happen.

"It wasn't proper for us to be left alone. Either Henry or my little brother George had to stay in the room with us." She sat back and waved a hand at Pam. "Oh, I know the times had changed in most places, but not Hope's Corner. We hung on to the old ways as long as we could." The mischievous twinkle returned to her eye. "Except maybe when it came to my Edgar. If Henry and my father had known what we'd done in the old root cellar, they'd have polished their shotguns."

"Oh, dear." Pam said softly.

"It didn't matter none to me, but Edgar was a good man. He wanted to make an honest woman of me, but we couldn't ask my father's permission. You see, Edgar was Jewish." Abigail pushed to her feet and rummaged through a drawer in her nightstand.

Pam waited, watching Miss Abigail's back, wondering what the old woman was looking for. Wondering what it must have been like to be in love with a man who society said you couldn't have. Wondering what she would have done if she couldn't have married Travis.

The two years Travis went away to college and Pam stayed behind, waiting to graduate and turn eighteen so they could be married, were the longest and loneliest two years of her life. As soon as Travis came home, she'd been so desperate to be with him, they'd run off and gotten married without telling anyone.

Neither of them could bear waiting months for her mom to plan a proper wedding. She could almost feel the heartache Miss Abigail must have endured knowing she and Edgar would never be together.

Aged unsteady hands presented Pam with a small silver-framed photograph. The edges of the picture were torn. A single crease ran down the length of one side, but she could still see the image of a man in uniform smiling up at her.

"This is Edgar?" she asked.

Miss Abigail nodded.

It wasn't hard for Pam to see why Miss Abigail had fallen for him. In the small black and white photograph, she could see a confident, handsome man who probably got anything he wanted when he flashed that winning smile. "He's very good-looking."

"He was more than good-looking. He was strong, and kind, and generous."

Pam handed the photograph back to her new friend. Miss Abigail ran her finger across the monochromatic image. Pam saw the old woman's eyes grow moist before she blinked back the threatening tears and returned to her seat, keeping her eyes on the cherished frame in her lap.

"He didn't like the idea people might think he was toying with my affections. As the summer passed, it bothered him more and more that folks might find out about our relationship, and I'd be branded a trollop.

"That September when Hitler invaded Poland and England declared war on Germany, Edgar was called back to camp. He had only two days to report for duty. I always knew he'd have to leave one day, but when the time came, I couldn't stand it. Suddenly I didn't care what Father, Henry, George, or anyone else in town thought. I wanted to be Edgar's wife.

"We went to Poplar Springs to be married by the Justice of the Peace. Didn't dare go to Judge Bernie here in town."

Miss Abigail stopped talking, and Pam held her tongue until she couldn't stand the wait any longer. "So you were married in

Poplar Springs?"

"Didn't make it that far." Abigail tightened her grip on the old photo and closed her eyes. Blowing out a deep breath, she stood, slowly made her way back to the nightstand, and gently placed the frame inside the drawer. "I was waiting at the drugstore, having a soda, while Edgar went alone to make arrangements. I heard the screech and I knew. I just knew.

"They said he wasn't looking where he was going. Just skipped onto the street like he owned it. The truck tried to stop, but it was no use. By the time I got outside, the crowd was so thick I almost couldn't get through to him. Someone must have gone for the local doctor 'cause a man with a black bag was leaning over Edgar, murmuring something. I couldn't hear. People were talking to me, and I couldn't hear a word any of them said. All I saw was my Edgar, bent and bleeding, still clutching our marriage license in his hand."

Pam's heart stopped. Air seemed to seize in her lungs. She felt Abigail's pain. Knew it intimately. The raw, stabbing agony of having your heart torn out.

Not wanting to cry, she blinked back her tears, wondering if this would be her in sixty years—old and alone and still grieving over the one love of her life.

***

"I can't tell you how much I appreciate what you've done for Mrs. Perkins." Jeff held open the door to the café as Sandra stepped inside.

"It was my pleasure. She's such a sweet woman. It's a shame her children don't live closer."

"Pastor. What a pleasant surprise." Redding Foster's broad grin froze as his gaze slid over to Sandra.

The way his eyes momentarily seemed to bulge from their sockets made Jeff glance at Sandra to see if maybe she'd lost her skirt on the way up the front steps.

"Table for two?" Redding asked, his smile more relaxed and natural. "Or are we waiting for Pammy Sue to join you?"

Bingo. "Just the two of us for lunch, Redding." Maybe now the town would believe there was nothing romantic about his and Pam's relationship.

Placing his hand along the small of Sandra's back, he gently turned her to follow Redding. When they reached the table, Redding pulled out a chair for Sandra, and his gaze zeroed in on Jeff's hand still casually guiding Sandra along.

Settled at a small table near the kitchen, Jeff ignored the way Redding kept watch on them and instead focused on the menu the café owner was so proud of. "I'm so hungry I can't make up my mind. Everything looks good."

Sandra nodded. "The few times I've eaten here it's always been delicious."

"Mabel's got a way in a kitchen. Have you tried her blueberry pie yet?"

"No, but her sweet potato pie was to die for."

"Blueberry's even better." Jeff looked over the specials for the day again, his mind drifting to Pam and Miss Abigail's lunch. The two women were probably chatting up a storm at this very minute.

"Ready to order?" Redding reappeared at the table, stiff, reserved.

"I think I'll try the pot roast." Sandra set her menu to the side.

"Same for me."

Redding scribbled down their choice of dressing for salad, beverages, and with barely a nod, collected the menus and turned toward the kitchen.

"I love a good roast," Sandra said, "but it's no fun cooking for one."

"Hmm. I know what you mean." She was right. Living alone, you learned to cook single items, a pork chop, a chicken breast, a steak, a boxed frozen dinner. Maybe the next time his mom cooked a roast, she could invite Pam again. She probably got just as tired as he did of eating the single man's diet.

Sandra unrolled her silverware from the napkin. "You know,

I'm actually pretty good in the kitchen myself. How about you?"

"I get by. Mom made sure all of her kids could survive in a kitchen."

"Your mother is a lovely woman. I really enjoyed our lunch the other day."

"Everyone loves Mom." Probably because it was so obvious to everyone how much his mother cared about them. Look at how she'd taken to Pam. Quietly nurturing what she knew was a tortured soul.

"Your sister's very nice too."

"Yes." Carol Ann. It was all her fault. She was the one with the bright idea of having dinner with Pam. *You both have to eat*, she'd said. Troublemaker. Though he couldn't really blame her. After all, he was the one who had actually asked Pam to join him. He'd caved in to the inexplicable need to stay by her side, to see her smile again.

"Your family seems very close."

"Oh, yes. I suppose." If you didn't consider the four years he had run amok at college and kept his distance from his family. Looking back now, he could admit it was a guilty conscience over partying hard that had stopped him from visiting home, but not then. He didn't usually share that information with people. A blood-brother pact of silence. Except with Pam. Talking to her had been easy.

"To be honest"—Sandra picked up her fork, twirling it between her fingers—"I envy you."

"Me?"

"It was just my mom and me growing up. No grandparents, aunts, or uncles. Just the two of us. I'd always thought it would be nice to have lots of brothers and sisters. Especially around Christmas and Thanksgiving."

"I can agree with you now, but growing up, there were plenty of days when I would have been just as glad to have Mom and Dad sell my brothers and sister to the gypsies."

"Really?" Sandra laughed. "I don't believe it."

He nodded. "Believe it."

Redding reappeared with a small tray. Silently he set the two drinks on the table, then the salads. "Pot roast will be out in another minute."

Jeff watched the man walk away. Redding's behavior reminded him of the days when he had played Little League. As a coach Redding had always been warm and encouraging, like a father to the boys. When they'd disappointed him, Redding became distant, reserved. Whatever the player had done wrong, whether it had been breaking curfew, or getting caught with chewing tobacco, he didn't do it again.

The man's quiet reproof settled uncomfortably over Jeff like a sweltering day in August. This was a mistake. He was physically sitting here with Sandra, but his thoughts were with Pam. What had Pam and Miss Abigail eaten for lunch? Did they have a nice time? Would she be back at work soon? Did he dare stop at the church and check on her?

What the heck was he doing here? What had he been thinking?

And there was the problem. He wasn't thinking clearly. When it came to Pam, everything became a jumble of confusion. He was her pastor. Her boss. She had issues. Serious issues. The kind he wasn't able to fix. Shouldn't try to fix. But Lord help him, he wanted to. He wanted to be her knight in shining armor. He wanted to protect her, take care of her, just be there.

No woman had ever made him feel this way. He'd wanted to help Jenny Buckner, save her. Like Jenny, Pam needed help, too. But never once had he thought about Jenny the way he thought of Pam. But then again he'd never been in love with Jenny.

In love? His insides suddenly felt as though a flock of angry geese had descended and were wildly flapping their wings. He couldn't be in love with Pam. Could he?

CHAPTER NINE

Once it had struck Jeff that he might be in love with Pammy Sue, it was all he could do to eat his lunch and keep up his end of the conversation.

Thankfully Sandra didn't seem to have any trouble finding things to talk about, and bless her, she didn't seem to mind a bit when all Jeff could manage was to nod his head or mumble his assent. She'd smile sweetly at him and keep right on talking.

By the time he'd gotten home, Pammy Sue was all he could think about. No matter how much he tried to put her out of his mind, she wouldn't leave. Her warm smile, her bright blue eyes, the slight sway to her step, the enticing tone of her voice, it all followed him.

Over and over he told himself he couldn't possibly be in love with her. At lunch he'd allowed his imagination—his lonely, celibate imagination—to run away with him. The entire idea was impossible. He and Pam barely knew each other.

Going over the numbers on the fund-raiser budget he'd brought home with him had been a total waste of time. He moved on to busywork: put away laundry, vacuumed the living room. Trying everything to distract himself, he actually gave in and scrubbed at the scummy buildup in his shower that hadn't bothered him until today.

No matter what he did, the walls of his tiny apartment seemed to close in on him. He was not in love with Pam. He wasn't ready for that. His career, his life, was about to undergo some drastic changes. He didn't have time for a woman. Wasn't looking for a woman. And certainly not this woman, who didn't want a relationship, not with him, not with anyone.

But he couldn't stand it any longer. He needed to know. To be sure. So here he was, pulling into the church parking lot on his day off, unable to wait until tomorrow to see Pam face-to-face.

Only now that he was here, he was almost embarrassed to admit that he'd let himself, even for a brief moment, think he could be in love with her. Hitting the key fob to lock the car door, he walked slowly, deliberately, to the office entrance. It was almost laughable to think he'd fallen in love.

He'd just about convinced himself it was a waste of time to be here at all when he reached for the front doors. Locked. "Why would she keep the doors locked?"

It took a few seconds to find the right key. He'd unlocked this door every morning for almost four months, and now his fingers were suddenly all thumbs.

"Pam?" He called the moment he pushed open the door. "Why's the door locked?"

No answer. With every step he took, another of those wild geese returned with wings flapping. Not sure what he'd find, he quickened his pace until he was almost running to Pam's office. Locked. His eyes darted to the clock at the end of the hall. Almost three o'clock. She was supposed to meet the repairman at two. "Where could she be?"

An accident. There were a few nasty curves between the old Keller place and town. If she'd missed any of the turns, she could have gone off the road, and no one would know she was there. Maybe hurt, maybe dying. What little air was left in his lungs whooshed out in a panicked rush as he pulled out his phone and punched the familiar numbers.

"Sheriff's office," a scratchy voice that sounded too young to shave answered.

"Hey, Drew, it's Jeff Parker," he announced, feigning a calm he didn't feel. "Is the sheriff in?"

Jeff drew in a deep breath and waited for Billy Ray to pick up the line.

"Billy Ray here."

"Hey, Billy. Sorry to bother you, but I was wondering if there's been any calls for an accident on Old Town Road?"

"Nope. Nothing's come in today. Why?"

"It's probably nothing." He hadn't noticed he was pacing the lobby until he heard the glass door swing open behind him.

It took a few seconds for his eyes to adjust to the streaming sunlight flooding the room. But there was no mistaking the golden locks reflected in the bright light. Like an angelic halo, the ray of sunshine framed her. She was beautiful.

"Jeff? You still there?"

"Yeah, sorry." His eyes remained riveted on her as she closed the door behind her. "Never mind, Billy. Everything's fine."

"You sure?"

"Yeah. I'm sure. Thanks."

***

The drive back to work had been unsettling. Visions of herself at the old Keller place, retired and alone with nothing but memories to keep her company, and maybe a visit or two from a thoughtful church associate, peppered Pam's thoughts.

Fumbling for the keys in her purse, she thought of the psychologist's number neatly folded in her wallet. Life had been calm, steady, this past week. No more nightmares. She could wait to make that call, but one thing had nothing to do with the other. Even if the nightmares never returned, if her mind had finally managed to put that night to sleep forever, she was a widow now and that would never change.

Sliding the key into place and rotating her wrist to the left, the latch didn't turn. The door wasn't locked. How could she have forgotten to lock the door? As anxious as she'd been for her lunch with Miss Abigail, that was no excuse for being careless.

Crime wasn't a real concern in Hope's Corner, but still she had a responsibility. Jeff trusted her alone with… "Oh!"

"I didn't mean to startle you." Jeff stood across the lobby, his back to the plate glass window. His right hand clutching his cell phone, his hair mussed from where his fingers had raked a ragged path, he seemed rigid with tension.

"Is something wrong? Did something happen?" Dropping her purse on a nearby counter, she scurried across the room. "It's not

Pastor Harlon, is it?"

Without any thought, she laid her hand on his arm, waiting for an answer. Jeff's gaze dropped to her hand, and his silence lasted so long she thought something absolutely terrible must have happened while she was off having a fun lunch. "Oh, Jeff."

"No." He looked up and deep green eyes, filled with what she thought was fear, locked on hers. "Nothing's wrong."

In a few fleeting seconds she had seen a myriad of emotions play out in his eyes, and she hadn't a hope of deciphering any of them. And yet there was something in those eyes she'd never seen before, an intensity in the green depths that made her nervous. He watched her as though he were trying to glimpse into her soul.

Uncomfortable with his lingering gaze, she took a quick step back and reached for her bag. "I'm sorry I'm so late. Fred called and said he was running behind, and I guess time just got away from me."

"It's easy to lose track of time when you're with Miss Abigail. I gather y'all had a nice lunch?" Jeff's gaze remained fixed on her.

"Oh, yes." She fumbled with the strap of her purse, then took a single step toward the hall, not sure why she was feeling so self-conscious. "Miss Abigail's so full of wonderful stories. Did you know she was once in love with a soldier?"

Jeff nodded. "Edgar."

"That's right." She let out a small sigh and resisted the urge to take another step. "Such a tragic story."

As though he'd just realized he'd been staring at her, Jeff blinked, then glanced down at the phone he still clutched in his hand before slipping it into the holder on his belt. "Are you doing okay?"

"Me? Yeah, I'm fine." The way he looked over her shoulder, avoiding her gaze after having focused so intently on her, she realized he seemed somehow—unsettled. "Are you sure there isn't something you're not telling me?"

Shifting his weight from one foot to the other, his eyes darted back and forth across the room before taking a sudden interest in the floor. When he finally glanced up at her again, his eyes held that familiar sparkle. "Nothing important."

"You sure?"

"Sure."

"Then why are you here on your day off?"

"I, uh, needed some papers from my desk. Since everything is under control here, I'm going to head back to the apartment and see if I can't finish up the fund-raising numbers for John Haskell."

"That man is a slave driver. But if you tell him I said so, I'll swear you're lying."

The comment hit its intended mark and made Jeff chuckle. "Yeah, well. He's *my* slave driver, so I'd better get moving. Let me know if anything important comes up." Jeff headed for the door. Stopping short beside her, he reached over and touched her hand. "I'm glad you're okay."

Before she could say anything in response, he was out the door—empty-handed.

Glancing down at her hand, she could still feel the warmth of his touch. "What the heck just happened here?"

***

This changed everything. Jeff wasn't sure how long he sat in his car, unable to look at anything but the church building. There was no denying it. No talking himself out of it. Somehow he'd fallen in love with Pamela Sue.

Staring at the door, as though answers would appear from heaven like the Ten Commandments on stone tablets, wasn't getting him anywhere. He needed to get away, to think.

A short drive on open road had always done wonders for clearing his mind. But there wasn't enough time. He'd promised Haskell the stupid reports by morning.

Turning the ignition, he dragged his gaze away from the church and took a deep breath. He longed for the comfort of his childhood home, and his mother's smiley-face chocolate chip cookies. But that wasn't an option either. The last thing he needed now was to face his insightful mother and have to explain something he didn't fully understand himself.

His insides churned with confusion, doubt, and fear. Should he ignore his feelings? Move on with his plans? Forget Pammy Sue had ever walked into his life?

Or did he dare take on a new life with this woman at his side? From his time with Pam, he was fully aware she was still in love with her husband, or at least the memory of her husband. Could Jeff find a way to bring her to love him as much? And if he couldn't? What would it be like to live with a hole in his heart? To carry on from day to day having given a piece of himself to someone who didn't want it?

Pictures of a life somewhere else, without Pam, alone and busy, a repetition of the last few years played grimly through his mind. The vision left him cold.

On some sort of subconscious autopilot, with no recollection of traveling down the small town streets, he'd driven to his apartment. He didn't want to be alone. Not now. Climbing the stairs, a brighter image flashed through his mind: Pam, sitting on a twin bed in a pastel painted room, wearing jeans that hugged her curves just enough to make him look twice. A blonde curly-haired little girl snuggled on her lap. Jeff beside her, one arm draped possessively around his wife, reading from a colorful picture book.

Warmth filled his senses, made his nerves tingle. He wanted this. More than he'd ever wanted anything in his life, he wanted her.

He could hear the phone in his apartment ringing from down the hall. Hurrying, he unlocked the front door and practically lunged across the sofa, grabbing the handset just as his answering machine kicked on. "Hello."

"Jeff?"

Who else did this person expect to answer his phone? "Yes."

"John Haskell here."

"Oh, Mr. Haskell." He didn't want to deal with this man. He had more important things to work out. "I'm almost done with those numbers for you."

"With the growth we've seen in Hope's Corner this past year, fund-raising is the key to keeping up with the needs of the community."

Pam had it right. The man was a slave driver. "I understand. I'm almost finished. I should have them for you by morning as promised."

"Good, but that's not what I'm calling about."

Jeff didn't care for the righteous tone Haskell had taken. He wasn't up for another lecture. Not now.

"Tried your cell phone. Went straight to voice mail. Not good for a pastor to be out of reach of his parishioners."

Flipping his phone open, Jeff quickly scanned the incoming calls. John Haskell at 3:22 and 3:31. How did he miss those? "Sorry, I must have accidentally turned down the ringer."

"I heard you had lunch today with Sandra Quinn."

"Yes." He took a short deep breath in an effort to control his tone, hide his exasperation with the board member. "She's volunteering with the elderly program. Today we took Mrs. Perkins to see an endocrinologist."

"Jeff, you've done a good solid job of stepping into your father's position. Until this week, not a day had gone by that anyone on the board regretted their decision to not bring in outside help."

Please Lord, not now.

"While I'm sure your intentions were honorable—"

Jeff's patience was running thin. He wondered if the old man would drop on the spot if he interrupted him and said no, he was looking for a quick roll in the hay?

"I thought we made it clear," the man continued, "that a single man such as yourself, especially at your age—"

At my age?

"Needs to be more thoughtful of how he spends his spare time. None of us see any harm in your wanting to court a woman—"

Court? It was lunch! And the wrong woman.

"But it doesn't look right so fast on the heels of your dinner date Thursday night."

A soft word turneth away wrath. He knew that and at the moment didn't care. "No, sir. I can see where, to someone with impure thoughts, the situation could be misinterpreted."

"Uhm, yes, well. I realize that young folks don't see the need to worry about appearances, but we need to hold ourselves to a higher standard."

"Yes, sir. Of course we do. And I think Sandra's giving back to the community by sharing her special skills as a nurse sets an excellent example for the church."

"It's not Miss Quinn's behavior that is casting shadows on our community, Jeff. We can't have it appear that our pastor is taking advantage of the single women in the congregation. Perhaps you should consider inviting someone along, a chaperone of sorts, next time you want to thank a female parishioner with a meal."

Taking advantage? A chaperone? How had he not previously noticed the board had such an archaic mind-set? Not that it mattered. Soon the board would no longer be his problem. And with a little time and patience, hopefully he wouldn't remain a single a man. "Yes, sir."

"Now I realize the board has yet to meet regarding your father's permanent replacement—"

"What?" Permanent? Surely they weren't going to fire his father because of his heart condition? The church was his father's life. Jeff had done his level best to fill in for his dad. Except for the Jenny debacle, he'd thought things had gone well. It was only a few more weeks till the doctor would allow his father to return to work part-time, and then soon he would be senior pastor again. Couldn't they wait a little longer? "I don't understand."

Haskell cleared his throat. "I'm sorry. I thought your father had discussed this with you."

"Discussed what?"

"Your father's decided it's time to retire. Turned in a letter of resignation."

"He can't do that," Jeff muttered softly. This congregation needed his father, and Jeff needed to move on.

"We thought you knew. Son, he's recommended you to replace him."

CHAPTER TEN

"You don't have to worry about feeding me, Etta. With all the leftovers from yesterday, I could eat like a queen for a month." Pam helped Emily pick out a different colored marker.

"Believe you me when I say you're a blessing from heaven." Etta Mae pulled a jar from the refrigerator. "I couldn't get a thing done with the princess running about on full throttle. Harlon has to have his dinner at exactly five-thirty, or he goes into grizzly mode."

"I don't believe for a single minute that such a sweet man has even one grouchy bone in his body."

Etta's hand froze over the pot of homemade spaghetti sauce. "Dear, everyone has a grouchy bone. The trick is making sure they forget where it is."

Laughter erupted unexpectedly from someplace so deep inside Pam, she'd forgotten she knew how. And it felt good. Etta Mae brought out the best in everyone. The woman was an eternal optimist. "Well, I'm glad I could help out."

"I'm just thankful little Emily is so taken with you. When I heard your car door slam shut in the drive, I knew you were the answer to prayer."

Pam had a hard time thinking of herself as the answer to anyone's prayers. But she was glad after she'd gotten home from work to see Etta Mae scurrying up her walk holding Emily in one arm and waving with the other.

Today's visit with Miss Abigail had left Pam thinking all day of the love she once had, would never have again. She was dreading walking into her empty house. A little time with the Parkers was a welcome reprieve.

"If you don't mind dear, could you set the table?"

"Sure."

"Set it for four. I have a high chair for Emily."

"Four?" Nothing ever rattled Etta, but for just a few seconds, Pam would have sworn Etta seemed flustered by the question, but why?

"Yes." Etta quickly recovered. "We might as well set an extra place in case my Jeff comes by."

"Four it is." Pam shrugged off her curiosity, and settled Emily in the high chair with a small plastic bowl and some Cheerios. Satisfied the little girl was suitably entertained, she pulled four sets of silverware from the drawer.

"I know I shouldn't." Etta lifted the lid on the boiling pot of water. "But I worry about that boy."

Pam glanced over her shoulder at Etta. "Worry?"

"He should be dating, looking for a wife, planning a family."

"Jeff had lunch with Sandra Quinn today."

"Oh?"

"I think she's sweet on him."

Etta measured out several handfuls of spaghetti and fanned them into the pot. "Hmm. Yes, I got the same impression."

"Maybe she'll be *the one*."

The odd, almost pained expression on Etta's face surprised Pam. This wasn't good. That little bit of information should have made Etta happy. "I think they'd make a nice couple."

"Why, yes, of course." Etta flashed a strained smile. "Sandra's a lovely lady."

Walking around the table, Pam set a knife and fork at the first place setting and wondered what to make of Etta's odd behavior.

"But," Etta paused and blew at a spoonful of sauce. "Jefferson needs a different kind of woman than Sandra. Someone who shares in his roots in the community. With a strong sense of family."

Pam stared at the silverware in her hand. *Just in case Jeff stops by.* A queasy feeling settled in the pit of her stomach. Surely Etta didn't have some misguided delusion that Jeff and she could somehow… She stole a quick glance in Etta's direction. *Uh-oh.*

Etta tasted the sauce in the large wooden spoon. "I got a chance to visit with Sandra at lunch the other day. Did you know she's an only child? Raised by her mother. No father figure."

"No. No, I didn't." Pam put down another knife and fork, and took a deep breath, wondering where Etta was going with this. "Her mother must be very proud of her. It couldn't have been easy raising a daughter alone."

Her brows drawn together, "Hmm," was all Etta Mae said.

If Etta was not only discounting Sandra as a potential wife for her son but thinking of playing matchmaker for Pam and Jeff instead, she needed to set the woman straight—and fast. "You know, Etta Mae, if I were in the market for a man, which I'm not, I'd hate to have his family judge me by my crazy family. Maybe you should give Sandra a chance?"

"Do you think I made enough?" Etta sprinkled another condiment into the simmering pot.

Apparently, for now, the topic was closed. As much as she'd like to think otherwise, Pam was willing to bet big bucks the crinkle still set in Etta's brow had nothing to do with the sauce. Unsure if she'd made her point or not, Pam glanced at the huge stockpot. There was enough sauce to feed the entire Dallas Cowboys' cheerleading squad. "I'm sure there's plenty."

"Mother," Jeff's voice boomed from the other end of the hall. "Where is he?"

Etta wiped her hands on her apron and squared her shoulders. Her grin frozen in place. "Jeff, dear, how fortunate we set the table for one more."

"I'm not here for dinner." His heavy steps stomped toward the kitchen. "I'm looking for…" His words trailed off the moment he crossed the threshold and spotted Pam by the table.

"We have company for dinner," his mom said. "Pam is such an angel. I was overwhelmed with Emily and trying to fix supper for your father. She's a treasure to keep the baby busy for me."

With the speed of a pinball machine, his eyes darted from his mother, to his niece, to Pam, and back. The stern set of his mouth told Pam whatever he was thinking, it probably wasn't meant for mixed company.

"I should really be getting home. I have some laundry to catch up on." Pam walked over to Emily and ran her fingers gingerly over the baby-fine hair. She should be the one thanking Etta. It was wonderful sharing time with such a sweet baby. Another thing she'd never have of her own.

"Nonsense." With a definitive nod that said, *Don't argue with me,* Etta resumed her position stirring the sauce. "Dinner's almost ready."

"I'm sure mother's made enough food to feed an army." Jeff blew out a deep breath, and the starch in his stance seemed to evaporate. "Can't the laundry wait?"

"Of course it can wait." Etta didn't give Pam a chance to say no. "I'll go get your father."

"No." Jeff took another step into the kitchen. "I'll go get him. Is he in his study?"

Etta hesitated a moment. Pam was convinced she was going to voice an objection, but instead she gave a quick nod, and turned to the butter and garlic spread sitting in a bowl on the counter. "Everyone will have to eat at least one piece of garlic bread, or there'll be no kissing tonight."

***

Jeff almost swallowed his tongue. His mother was going to be death of him yet. Although his father was running in close competition.

What was his father thinking? Retiring so young. He wasn't even sixty-five yet. No preacher of his dad's caliber ever stepped down before he was too old and frail to stand and thump a Bible. Heck, he'd even seen some men preach sitting down rather than give up their congregation.

Jeff's steps drew to a halt at the sight of his father sound asleep in the well-worn leather wingback chair. Before the heart attack Harlon Parker had seemed invincible. Now he looked every one of his sixty-three years and maybe a few more.

"Pop?" He approached his father's favorite reading spot quietly. When the old man didn't stir, a single spark of panic shot up his spine. "Pop?" he called a little louder.

Nothing. By the time he reached the chair, Jeff's heart was racing like a metronome on speed. "Pop?" He lightly touched his father's arm.

"Nott. Noww."

The disgruntled mumble was like music to his ears. "Supper's almost ready."

Barely turning his head, his father began sniffing at the air. A slow, steady grin eased across his face. "Smells good," he mumbled more clearly without opening his eyes.

"Yeah, it does." Jeff ran a nervous hand through his hair and snuck a glance out the window. Where to begin? "Can we talk a few minutes?"

Sitting up straighter in his seat, Harlon Parker reached for his glasses. Jeff could see the slight change in his countenance, the one Jeff had come to recognize as the arrival of Pastor Harlon.

"Sure, son. Whatcha got on your mind?"

"I think you know."

"John Haskell call you already?"

Jeff nodded.

"I thought he might. I know I probably should've said something to you before I called him, but once I made up my mind, I saw no need in putting off the inevitable."

"Why, Pop?"

"It's time."

"No, it's not. These people need you. Your relationship with them is irreplaceable, your experience invaluable."

"I listened to you yesterday morning in rapt attention. I actually forgot you were my son. Forgot that used to be my job. You're good. A little young but that helps the younger folks relate to you. I could see them intent on your every word the way I never saw them listen to me. When even the elders of the congregation nodded and whispered amen, I knew it was time to step aside. It's your turn now, Jeff."

"It's not my turn." He hesitated a moment, searching, praying for the right words. "I'm not called to lead these people. As soon as you're well enough, I'm moving on."

The flash of white across his father's knuckles as his fingers tightened on the arms of the chair sent another spark of concern skittering through Jeff. Only when his dad released the viselike grip and took in a deep breath did Jeff feel some of the fear for his father slip away. Some.

"This is your home," his dad said softly, so softly Jeff could barely hear him. "You've known some of these folks as long as you've been alive. That's precious when you're called to lead. It won't be easy starting over some place new."

"I won't be starting over at a new church." He spun about, picked up Kenny's brass baby shoe paperweight from his father's desk, unable to face him and still say the words. "Thought I might go back to Austin, put my MBA to good use." Jeff glanced over at his dad. "Banking is a solid career."

Most of the color drained from Harlon's face. "You can't mean that."

Jeff actually heard the chair groan under his father's tight grip. "I'm afraid so. I'm only fooling myself. These people need you, not me."

"I beg to differ with you. I'm not saying it was God's will I be incapacitated with a bad heart. But as sure as I'm here living and breathing today, I know it was God's plan to have a strong man of God ready to step into my place. You've done well, son. Why would you throw it all away?"

His gaze veered out the window. *Why?* How could he tell his father how badly he'd failed? He hadn't saved Jenny. He couldn't take the chance of losing someone else. Pam's family expected him to help her. But they were wrong. His father would know how to save her from her past. Not him. "There's nothing to throw away."

The unexpected silence drew his attention away from the

window. "Pop?"

***

"That's wonderful news. I knew you'd trample all over those people if you actually got them in court. But, I'm afraid I've got my hands full at the moment." Pam juggled her cell phone with one shoulder while mixing some sauce into a bowl of macaroni for Emily. "Can I call you later?"

"Well that depends, beautiful. I'll be out for dinner celebrating in about an hour and will be turning off my phone."

Part of her was thankful Greg hadn't been on a date the night Travis died. If he had been, he wouldn't have stopped by their house unexpectedly, and he wouldn't have found her in time to call 911 and save her life. But her heart resented that he hadn't shown up soon enough to save them both. It was hard to stay thankful for being alive with Travis gone.

"Well…." Pam caught the way Etta slanted a glance at her then quickly averted her eyes. "You go enjoy your dinner and don't worry about me. I'm in good hands."

"Then everything is going well?" Greg asked.

"I'm feeding my neighbor's grandbaby, about to have homemade spaghetti sauce with dinner, and haven't had a…" she lowered her voice, whispering into the phone, *"you know* in a while."

"Good! Must be all that home cooking. You were right going home. Even if things aren't the same around here without you."

"Flatterer." She couldn't help but smile, even though the phone beeped in her ear every time she'd pinch her shoulder too tightly, and her favorite blouse was painted with imprints of Emily's sauce-covered fingers. "I really have to go now."

"Be good, sweets."

Pam slipped the phone into her pocket and wiped some of the excess sauce from her clothes. "Sorry about that."

"No problem." Etta pulled the garlic bread from the oven. "A special friend?"

Pam nodded, and reached for a rag to wipe the excess sauce

from her blouse. "My husband's best friend."

"You and he are close, are you?"

There was no missing the concerned tone of Etta's voice. The fear that Pam already had a man in her life was etched in Etta's prim expression. This wasn't good. Obviously Etta was still thinking in terms of her and Jeff. She didn't want Etta building false hope, but it wasn't fair to let her think Greg was more than a good friend. There would never be another man in her life. Somehow she'd have to make Etta understand. "Greg feels responsible for me. He wasn't convinced my moving home was a good idea. I'm sure he feels he owes it to Travis to keep an eye on me. In a way, I've become some sort of best friend by proxy."

"I see." Etta flashed a fragile smile, then looked up at the clock on the wall. "If my husband and son don't get out here soon, we're going to be eating soggy pasta." Sifting a strand of spaghetti out with a fork, she nibbled on a small piece and scrunched her face. "Would you please go see what's taking those two so long? I'm going to pour out the water. Better to have cold spaghetti than mushy spaghetti."

"I'll check on what's keeping the men."

Pastor Parker's study was the first door on the left, down the hall from the kitchen. Jeff's voice easily carried out of the room. "There's nothing to throw away… Pop?… Pop!"

His frantic cry brought Pam running into the room. Pastor Harlon sat slumped in the chair with Jeff curled around him, an ear pressed to his father's chest, his face pale as chalk.

Dear God, not again. Grabbing her phone, she dialed 911.

CHAPTER ELEVEN

In less than an hour word had spread quickly through town. Prayer chains had been started. The church doors had been unlocked. As they'd done earlier in the year when Jeff's father had his heart attack and emergency surgery, folks would take turns at church ensuring twenty-four hours of prayer.

To Jeff, the short while they'd been in the bright blue and white waiting room had felt like an eternity. Unable to reach Kenny on his cell, Jeff had left a brief voice mail simply asking the youngest Parker to call. With every second that passed, he prayed by the time Kenny got the message there would be good news, and they wouldn't have to tell their youngest sibling to fly home like the wind. Danny and his wife, Terri, huddled in one corner. Carol Ann and his mom sat across from them, side by side, holding hands.

Seated at the small wooden children's table in the opposite corner, Pam managed to keep Emily and Gavin entertained with an array of puzzles, crayons, and a new version of Go Fish.

Fueled with worry, and guilt, Jeff couldn't seem to stay still. He'd paced the small room from the moment they'd brought his father in. He should have known better than to confront his father. This wasn't the time to tell his father his plans. Jeff had known that. Not until pastor Harlon was back to work full-time would he have been ready to hear the news. But his father wasn't coming back to work. Not full-time, not part-time. Jeff had to say something. He'd had no choice. Damn. "You'd think by now someone would have some information for us."

"I'd like to think no news is good news." His mom blew out a heavy breath. She hadn't said much. Jeff knew she'd been silently praying for the man she'd devoted most of her adult life to.

"Mrs. Parker." Dressed in her nurse's scrubs, Sandra Quinn walked through the doorway.

Etta Mae smiled politely. "How nice of you to come, dear."

"I just heard what happened. I'm not scheduled to go on duty for another hour, but I thought I might be able to help."

Letting go of her mother's hand, Carol Ann stood and stepped up to Sandra. "Can you find out how my father's doing? No one is telling us anything."

"I've already been inside." Sandra smiled at Carol Ann and walked over to where Etta Mae was still seated. "Pastor Parker is stable and asking for you. If you'll come with me?" She extended her hand to Jeff's mom and addressed the rest of the group. "There was a nasty accident on Old Town Road. It's a little harried back there, but the doctor should be out soon to update everyone."

"Then he's okay?" Anticipation caught in Jeff's throat. His father had to be all right. He just had to.

"The doctor will have to fill you in. Try not to worry." Sandra flashed a reassuring smile in Jeff's direction, but it didn't help. He needed to see his father for himself.

Even after Sandra and Etta Mae walked down the hall and out of sight, no one moved. Jeff glanced back at the children's table. Pam stood and inched her way forward with Emily perched on her hip.

"Was it another heart attack?" she asked.

"I don't know," Jeff answered, fighting the urge to reach out and pull her and Emily into his arms. Not sure if he wanted to offer comfort or be comforted. "The doctor should be out soon. Thanks to Sandra at least now we know Dad is stable."

"Thank God," Pam said softly. At the same moment, heavy with relief, Carol Ann fell into the chair beside them, and Terri burst into tears.

"Honey, stable is a good thing. If they were prepping him for emergency surgery like last time, they wouldn't let Mom in to see him." Danny soothed his wife and glanced up at Jeff. "I think it would be best if I took Terri and the kids home."

"I don't want to leave. Not yet. Not till we know more." Terri wiped a tear with the back of her hand and rubbed her tummy with the other.

"I know. Neither do I, but at least we know Dad's stable, and you and the kids need to rest. Jeff will call us if there's more news."

Terri glanced at her son still coloring at the back of the room, then slid her gaze to Pam and Emily. Without a word she nodded her head and eased out of the chair. "But I want to know right away if anything changes."

Jeff and Carol Ann nodded.

In a few minutes Danny had all the children's paraphernalia tucked away neatly on the shelves and his family ready to go.

For the first time ever, as Jeff watched his brother walk down the hall with his own family, a heavy sense of longing settled over him. Watching Terri lean against her husband, his arm around her waist, each holding a child, reminded him how empty his life had become.

"Is it all right if I stay a little longer?" Pam stood beside him, her hand on his arm.

It had been Pam who called for an ambulance. Before he could reach for his phone, she had dialed 911, comforted his mother, and managed to care for Emily as well. She'd been amazing. "Please."

"Would you like something to drink? Coffee, cola, tea?"

"No. Thank you. I just want to hear what the doctor has to say."

"Carol Ann? How about you? Can I get you something to drink? You didn't have time for dinner. I'm sure I can find a snack machine."

"Thanks, Pam, but I'm with Jeff. What's keeping the doctor?"

"I don't know." Jeff looked down the hall.

"Your father's a strong man." Pam linked her arm in Jeff's and guided him over to the chairs. "He'll be just fine. I know it."

The next thing Jeff knew, he was seated in a middle row of chairs, and Pam was handing him a hot cup of steaming tea. He hadn't even noticed when she'd walked away. "What's taking so long?"

Before anyone could comment, the doctor walked into the room. "I'm sorry I couldn't come speak to you sooner." He gestured to the seats along the wall, and after a brief moment of shuffling about, everyone was seated around the doctor. "We're shorthanded tonight, and an accident came in just after your father arrived."

Carol Ann nodded. "Sandra Quinn told us."

"Yes. I noticed her with your mother and father. Well." He slapped his hands on his thighs. "The good news is all the tests are normal. Your father didn't have a heart attack."

"Thank God." Jeff blew out a deep sigh of relief. "Then why did he pass out?"

"Most likely his blood pressure medicine needs to be adjusted. Until we know for certain, he'll need to stay overnight for observation. We'll move him shortly, and the nurse will be able to tell you the room number at that time."

"Thank you," three voices echoed.

"There." Pam flashed a timid smile. "Everything's going to be fine."

"Hmm." Jeff focused on the long empty hallway. His father may not have had a heart attack, but from where he stood, everything was far from fine.

***

The plastic-covered seats in the waiting area had gone from uncomfortable to borderline torture. No matter how Pam shifted, the kink in her lower back was there to stay. She probably should have headed home hours ago, but she couldn't bring herself to leave. It was long past the end of visiting hours, and Etta Mae was still sitting by Pastor Harlon's bed. The thought made Pam smile. She doubted a team of Navy SEALs could have moved that woman from her husband's side. It was certainly beyond the nursing staff's skills.

One by one they'd explained to the determined woman that

she couldn't stay past visiting hours. And one by one, each of the nurses had walked out of the room shaking their heads mumbling words like *fiddle-faddle, poppycock,* and *hogwash.* Two hours later Etta Mae was still glued to her husband's side, and Pam couldn't blame her. Had there been a glimmer of hope for Travis, had her presence contributed one iota to his recovery, she would have risked eternity in hell to stay holding his hand.

Of course, she never got the chance. Travis was gone before help arrived. There was nothing anyone could do. Not Greg, not the police, not the paramedics. At least that's what everyone had said. She'd passed out during the attack. Couldn't remember a thing, only what she'd been told. A blessing everyone insisted.

But she wasn't convinced. Especially now, waiting here with Jeff and Carol Ann as each took turns keeping their mother company, Pam desperately wanted those last minutes with her husband. She didn't care how badly either of them had been hurt, she wanted those few minutes to tell him one last time how much she loved him, to hold him in her arms, and when all hope was lost, say one last good-bye.

"I don't think there's any convincing my mother to leave." Pam's chair shifted as Jeff took a seat beside her. "We've all tried," he said, shaking his head. "When I left the room, Carol Ann was on full throttle. Quietly yelling through clenched teeth, her arms flailing about like a flagman at NASCAR, but Mom's attention is riveted on Dad. She's hunkered down for the night."

"Can't they at least find her an empty bed or something, so she can lie down and get some rest?"

"She won't move. The nurses have finally caved, and they're going to see if they can't find her a more comfortable chair. One of them is off now hunting for an empty recliner in one of the family rooms."

"What about you and Carol Ann?"

"Carol Ann's going to stay and make sure Mom's okay."

"And you're going to stay and make sure Carol Ann's okay?"

"No. I'm taking you home. It's late, and there's no reason for you to lose a good night's sleep too."

"Oh, no. I can call one of my brothers to take me back to the house. It's not too late."

"Yes, it is. Mom would never forgive me, if I didn't see you home safely."

Pam smiled at visions of Etta Mae waving a wooden spoon at Jeff, telling him that she had raised her sons better than to let a woman find her own way home. "I suppose you're right."

By the time Pam slipped into Pastor Harlon's room for a quick good-bye, a nurse had already confiscated a somewhat more comfortable chair, and Etta Mae was leaning back, eyes half closed, her hand outstretched, tightly gripping her husband's. A vise squeezed Pam's heart. Resentment at having her last moments with Travis stolen from her gurgled to the surface. Once again she shoved it back into a dark buried corner of her mind. "Jeff's taking me home. I'll keep the whole family in my prayers."

"Thank you, dear. For everything." Etta glanced at Jeff for a brief second then looked back to Pam. "You're a treasure."

The car had barely turned the corner out of the parking lot when Pam found herself fighting the urge to nod off. It had been a long day. She hadn't done much physically, but mentally she was drained dry.

If she weren't so tired, she'd indulge in a long hot soak in the old bathtub; except the way she felt, she'd probably fall asleep and drown. No, tonight it was straight to bed. Or maybe the couch would be closer to the door. "Oh, fish." She turned to Jeff with only one eye open. "Do you have keys to your mom's house? I left my purse in the living room."

"Yeah, I do."

"Good." She closed her other eye. Just a few minutes to rest her eyelids. One of those power naps. Forty seconds.

Such a beautiful sunny day. She loved picnics in the park. Even though they could afford nice restaurants, it was more fun to bring a basket of fried chicken with homemade potato salad and a bottle of white wine. Even in the middle of the big city, it always felt like she and Travis were the only two people in the world.

Travis? Where'd he go? He was right here beside her. "Travis?" Why would he wander off? The sun was setting. It was late, growing cold. "Travis." So hard to breathe. The air was hot and thick. She tried to get up, get away, look for Travis, but she couldn't move. Her arms frozen. Sharp pains stabbed at her side. "Travis, help me."

So hard to move. Her fingers swirled at her side. The wine spilled. Not white wine. Red wine. Red blood. Her blood. Travis? Where was Travis? God, the pain. The lights. Hands, big hands, holding her, pinning her down, hurting her, strangling her.

He'd pulled up to his mother's house just as Pam started muttering to herself. It didn't take a genius to recognize this was the onset of a nightmare.

Hurrying, he came around the front of the car to her side. There'd barely been enough time to open the door and lean inside in an attempt to soothe her awake, when Pam sprang up screaming, "NO!", and clocked Jeff with an unexpected right cross.

Her fists beat against his chest. The tighter he tried to hold her, the harder she pounded him. "Pam, honey. It's okay. It's me. No one is going to hurt you. Please."

Drenched in sweat and shaking with fear, her gaze locked on his, focused. The sheer terror that had been in her eyes moments before seemed to dim as the light of awareness grew stronger. "Oh, God," she whispered, then collapsed into his arms.

Without the slightest hint of what she'd dreamed, the shrill of her cries and the depth of fear in her eyes had his body on high alert. His heart raced in a frantic rhythm as he fumbled to undo her seat belt. He needed to get her inside and calmed down.

In a move that would have surprised him had he taken the time to think about it, he swept her out of the car, into his arms, and carried her up the walkway to his parent's home. He was pretty sure in all the hurry to get to the hospital, no one had thought to stop and lock the door behind them. At least he hoped not. The way Pam clung to him, her body racked with gasping sobs, there was no way he was putting her down to unlock the front door.

"I'm sorry," Pam mumbled into his shirt, her arms still in a stranglehold around his neck.

"Nothing to be sorry about." He managed to turn the knob with one hand and shoved the door open with his foot. Halfway to the sofa he tripped over one of Gavin's toy trucks and stumbled the rest of the distance, falling unceremoniously onto the sofa with Pam still firmly in his arms.

Gently, he lifted one hand from behind her back and raked his fingers through her hair, the way he might soothe Emily when something made her cry. Only this wasn't the short-lived whimpers of an upset toddler. This was Pam.

Oh, Lord, now what do I do?

CHAPTER TWELVE

Pam's gulping breaths filled her lungs with air. Heat surrounded her. Warm, comforting, safe, so safe.

Another deep breath and she found the courage to loosen her hold on Jeff's neck, bringing one hand down to wipe away the dampness on her cheek. "I'm sorry."

His fingers slid away from her hair and drew wide lazy circles along her back. The gentle rhythm slowed her racing heart. She knew she should pull away from his arms, get out of his lap and move to her own seat. But she couldn't. If only for a few minutes, she needed someone else to be strong for her.

"Want to talk about it?" he asked, his voice as gentle as his touch.

She shook her head and swallowed the urge to start crying all over again. "I'm sorry."

"You keep saying that."

With another deep breath, she straightened her shoulders and shifted off his lap onto the sofa beside him. "Now your shirt's all wet."

"It'll dry."

Calmer now and breathing more easily, her fear took a backseat to embarrassment. She couldn't bring herself to look at him. Not only had she fallen apart and cried like a frightened child, she'd hauled off and slugged him.

Jeff shifted slightly then pushed to his feet. "If I made some tea, would you drink a cup?"

Closing her eyes, she summoned her courage. She had to do this. Face him. Eyes open, she lifted her chin and let her gaze meet his. He looked almost as lost as she felt. The pain and concern she saw etched in his furrowed brow took her from merely being embarrassed to totally mortified. "No, thank you. I…I'm fine now. I…"

More words wouldn't come. The way he watched her, she couldn't think straight. His eyes studied, scrutinized. She knew he had to be debating if she was only slightly off her rocker or completely certifiable. Looking around, she spotted her purse on a nearby chair.

"I should go home and let you get back to the hospital." On wobbly legs, she stood, missed a step, then righted herself and grabbed her bag. "I—I'm okay."

"The hell you are." He ran an impatient hand through his hair, turned to walk away, then spun back around, and stepped beside her. "Now I'm the one who's sorry. It's been a long day. Our nerves are rubbed pretty raw. Let me make us both a cup of tea."

"You don't have to—"

"Hey, it's either the tea or I rustle up some scrambled eggs, and I can do a lot more damage to my mother's kitchen with eggs than with a cup of boiled water."

The hint of a smile at the edge of his lips took her by surprise. So maybe he'd concluded she wasn't totally insane. Or at least, no longer a danger to him, even if she had used him as a punching bag. Besides, she really didn't want to be alone.

She managed a feeble nod, and the other side of his mouth tipped into a full-fledged smile.

"It'll just take a minute." He disappeared down the hall.

If only life were that simple. A cup of tea and all would be well with the world. Yeah, right. Not in her world. Never again in her world.

***

It had taken every ounce of self-discipline Jeff could muster not to pull Pam back into his arms and promise he'd make everything right.

Standing in the kitchen pouring water into a kettle, he had to laugh at himself. Whether he liked it or not, he was turning into his mother. Cup of tea? What he really needed was a stiff drink.

And who wouldn't after a day like today? First he finds out

the church board expects him to take over as head pastor of the congregation. That is, of course, if he agrees to stop leading the single females astray. Then he practically shoves his father over a cliff into a heart attack by announcing his plans to leave the ministry and rejoin the corporate world. And if that wasn't enough to turn any sane man to the bottle, he'd gotten a ringside seat to the horrific depths of Pam's nightmares.

"Can I help?" Pam stood in the doorway, her arms wrapped tightly around her middle, as if that was all that held her together.

"Not much to do." Leaning against the counter, he waved an arm toward the simmering kettle. When Pam jerked back a step as though he were about to hit her, an angry fist tightened around his heart.

Flashing a dim smile and pretending his sudden movement hadn't frightened her, she inched back into the doorway. "You know what they say"—her eyes scanned the room as she spoke—"a watched pot never boils."

"So they say." He didn't dare move a muscle. Couldn't, wouldn't risk adding to her fears. As it was, hugging herself, unable to look him in the eye, she reminded him of a jittery junkie in desperate need of her next fix. The way her eyes darted from the kitchen door to the windows and back may have bordered on paranoia, but it was enough to make him want to double check the locks for himself.

"I, uh… I guess I could…"

Her eyes fixed on the back door.

"Shall I make sure it's locked?"

Her gaze swung from the door to him. "Would you mind?"

The desperation in her eyes tripped over the relief in her voice. Both sucker punching him in the gut.

"No problem." Except of course for how did he move from the sink to the back door without startling her out of her skin again? Slowly he lifted his right arm along the cabinet until it was high enough to point to the door. "I'm just going to step over there."

She nodded, tightened the hold on her waist and shimmied sideways along the wall. From the corner of his eye, he watched as she eased her way farther into the kitchen, and away from the back door. *My God, what happened in her dreams?* "All locked up. Nice and tight," he said with more enthusiasm than necessary.

"I, uh…thank you."

"What are friends for?"

The abrupt whistle of the teakettle snapped the brittle tension-filled air. He bolted forward to ease the sharp siren while Pam opened a nearby cabinet and retrieved two mugs.

She'd spent enough time in his mother's kitchen to be as familiar with the layout as one of the family, yet her movements were slow and deliberate. He wondered if she was silently talking her way through every action. *Take two steps to the sugar bowl. Open the silverware drawer. The milk is in the refrigerator.* He watched as she briefly paused, her gaze surveying each target before proceeding with the next step.

Despite her obvious unease, her painstaking efforts produced an old ceramic pot warmed under the traditional mantle of a silver cozy, two Tweety Bird mugs, a creamer of milk, a bowl of sugar, and two spoons on a large Shaker-style wooden tray.

His uncle Bob had made the tray for his mother years ago. It was her favorite and it didn't surprise him that Pam had chosen that particular tray over the others in the cabinet. But all her efforts at normalcy couldn't mask the nightmare's aftereffects. Her hands still shook with a palsied rhythm. Even tightening her grip until her knuckles whitened with pressure wasn't enough to raise the tray with a steady hand.

"Let me." He reached over to help. Too swift in his movements, he brushed his arm against hers and silently cursed himself when she dropped the tray to the counter with a rattle. "I'm sorry."

"No. I'm the one who—who should apologize. This isn't a good idea. Your family needs you. You should be with them. I should go home." She closed her eyes, blew out a short breath, then met his gaze with a determination borne of sheer will. "I'll be fine."

"The tea is already steeping. I can't drink that whole pot by myself, and besides, Mom's couch beats the waiting room sofa for comfort hands-down." Not waiting for a reply, he lifted the tray and walked out of the room, leaving her no choice but to follow.

"Has anyone ever told you you're a very stubborn man?"

Jeff was pleased to see her arms hanging loosely at her side. Perhaps getting her dander up was the best way to chase away her nerves. "Nope, not a one. Do you like milk in your tea?"

She shook her head. A narrow crease formed between her brows.

Taking a seat on the sofa, he reached for the pot and began to pour. "One lump or two?" he asked without looking up.

"One." She lowered herself onto the sofa beside him. "I really can take care of myself, you know?"

"Mmm." He nodded, scooping a spoonful of sugar. "I prefer mine like the English." He handed her the mug before pouring a bit of milk into his own. "I don't know why, but the tea always tastes best if you pour the milk first."

"And exactly how does an East Texas boy know how the English drink their tea?" Holding the cup to her lips, she blew gently over the steaming liquid.

"I dated a girl from Suffolk for a few months in college." He was pleased to see Pam's hand less shaky. "Not only did she pour the milk first, but teabags were sacrilege."

Pam's nose crinkled and her head tipped to one side. "Why the heck would someone from England want to go to school in the middle of Texas?"

"Why wouldn't they?"

With a casual shrug, she set her cup on the end table. "I don't know. I think if I had a chance to study in a foreign country, I'd pick someplace more exciting."

"You mean like New York or Los Angeles?"

"Yeah, I guess. Or Chicago or San Francisco. It's a big

country."

"True, but Austin is growing in popularity, and UT is rated one of the fifty best universities in the world. Besides, the cost of living in Austin is a heck of a lot cheaper than living in New York or California."

"Maybe." She picked up her tea and took a sip.

The haunted look in her eyes had faded, and a steady hand held her mug. Jeff wondered if now was a good time to ask about the nightmares, or if he should count his blessings that she wasn't cowering in a corner and leave well enough alone. For now.

***

Maybe she was still dreaming. Maybe the nightmares had taken an odd turn and she wasn't really sitting in Etta Mae's living room chatting with her boss about the cost of living in Texas but was actually sound asleep in her own room and would wake up any minute. Maybe this was a new way for her subconscious to stop the insanity that messed with her head and her life. Or maybe she really had woken up swinging, and Jeff was the only thing tethering her to what was left of her sanity.

Silence grew thick as they sipped their tea. Jeff sat back, looking relaxed. His ankle perched on his thigh while one hand balanced the mug on his knee. The other arm draped casually along the edge of the sofa, his fingers inches away from her shoulder.

He kept his gaze on the nearly empty mug. A few more sips and it would be time for her to go home. Then as always, in the empty house, she'd be all alone.

"Would it be—?" she asked.

"Pam, I think—" he started at the same time.

"Sorry," they echoed.

Jeff shifted, unfolding his leg, to place his drink on the table. "You first."

"I was going to ask if I could have another cup."

He hesitated a moment. "Of course. I'll be right back."

It only took a few moments for him to fill their cups and

return beside her. Now that she had him for the duration of another cup of tea, she wasn't so sure she wanted to hear what he was about to say. Maybe if she didn't ask, he'd sip his drink and leave well enough alone.

"What happened?" he asked, never lifting his gaze from the mug held tightly in his hands.

So much for that idea. She pushed to her feet and took a few steps around the large square coffee table. "I wonder if your mom still has some of those peanut butter cookies she baked the other day."

"Pam?" He stood and stepped beside her, placing his hands on her arms.

She tried, she really tried not to jump at his touch, but she couldn't stop the shivers that rushed up her spine, or the rock that settled in her throat and clogged her airway. Her heart beat double time, and her feet sprinted of their own volition.

Clasping at her neck with both hands she struggled to breathe. If only he hadn't touched her. She could still feel the pressure on her neck. Just like in her dreams. So much pain.

"Pam?" Jeff almost vaulted over the table to reach her.

"Don't." She held out one hand. "Please."

"What the hell happened?"

It was all she could do to shake her head. "Please. I…I should go."

"No. I won't touch you. I promise I won't touch you, if you don't want me to, but you're not leaving."

This was ridiculous, silly, absurd, childish. A hundred words ran through her mind. Like a little kid, she was scared of the boogeyman. Only Jeff wasn't a threat, and she knew it. And yet when he'd grabbed her arms, even though his touch was as tender as a mother cradling her newborn babe, the fear, the terror, surged through her veins unbidden, the way oxygen filled her lungs. She had no control to stop it. "I'm sorry."

"Stop apologizing and talk to me. Just talk to me." He eased back a few steps giving her room, but for what? To breathe? To think? To speak?

God how she hated feeling this way.

"Pam?" He took a seat on the love seat closest to her. "Can you sit down?"

She looked around the room. What she really wanted was to go to him. Have him wrap her up in the same warmth that had calmed her when she had first woke up, but she didn't dare move, never mind sit beside him.

"I can't," she mumbled.

"Sure you can." He gently coaxed her the way someone might speak to a frightened child or an injured animal. "One step at a time."

One step at a time. Travis's voice flowed through her thoughts. "My husband would say that to me all the time. It's how I get through things without him. One step at a time. One day at a time."

"You loved him very much."

It wasn't really a question, but she nodded anyway.

"High school sweethearts, right?"

"Sort of." She hitched a shoulder. "We started dating his senior year. So I guess, maybe, but not all through high school."

"I didn't really know him. Knew his family. He has an older brother Larry?"

She nodded.

"Heck of a football player."

"Yeah, he was." She felt the tension ease from her shoulders. "He lives in New York now. Got a hotshot job out of college and is happily traveling the world."

"Not bad for a kid from Hope's Corner."

"He always had a bit of wanderlust. As soon as he and Travis had saved up for a car, Larry talked Travis into traipsing all over. Dallas, Houston, Austin, San Antonio." She didn't know how it happened, but she'd moved a few feet closer to where Jeff held out his hand to ease her into the seat beside him.

"You ever go with them?" he asked.

"No. I think Travis wanted to make as many memories with his brother as he could. We all knew, once Larry left Hope's Corner, it would be for good."

"I thought it would be like that for me too, but as you can see, I came back."

"Hometown boy after all?"

"Let's just say sowing my oats wasn't all it was cracked up to be."

"You mentioned something about that the night we had dinner at the café."

Jeff rolled his eyes and actually squirmed. A hint of red crept up his neck and made her laugh. The sound of her own voice startled her. So did the realization that her heart was beating a normal rhythm, her breathing was easy, and her hands weren't shaking.

***

They'd talked for hours. Even though every time Pam mentioned Travis' name a soft look filled her eyes and he'd felt a chisel prick at his heart, he still encouraged her to keep talking. With each story, she relaxed a bit more. Soon she was leaning against him, and he was rubbing her shoulders. By the time she got to Travis' law school graduation, she was sprawled out on the small sofa, her head in his lap, and he was raking his fingers through long strands of hair the color of sunlight.

With a lazy effort to hide a yawn, she'd mumbled something about Pammie's Luck winning by a nose. Then she lost her battle with the sandman, and her eyes fell shut. Little by little the broken and shattered look that had covered her earlier in the night had slipped away. Now he looked down at the sweet, self-assured woman he'd grown to love.

A woman who was clearly still in love with her dead husband.

Not that it mattered. He had no business loving Pam. His life was about to take a major detour. Starting a new career from scratch at his age wasn't going to be fast or easy, and Pam was in no condition to tag along for the bumpy ride.

If he'd had any sliver of doubt that she needed professional help, watching her react to a nightmare up close and personal was more than enough to convince him that she couldn't go on this way. The question at hand was still the same. What to do? What should *he* do?

Turning his wrist, he glanced at his watch. Two forty-five in the morning. She looked so peaceful, he hated to disturb her, but tomorrow was going to be another long day. Neither of them was going to get a very good night's rest squished on the small love seat.

"Pam," he said softly. "Time for bed."

"Mmm, bed." One leg slid off the couch and landed with a thud. And then nothing. Once again, she was sound asleep.

"Okay, sleepyhead. I guess we're going to have to do this the hard way." He slid his arms under her and pushed to his feet. "Good thing you don't weigh much more than that sack of groceries."

Now his newest dilemma. Where to? She didn't weigh much, but there was no way he was carrying her back to her house. And absolutely no way was he fumbling through her purse in search of her house keys.

"One thing about grown-up children is lots of spare bedrooms," he said, even though sound asleep, she couldn't hear him.

For a moment he thought he saw her open a sleepy eye and look at him, but by the time he'd made his way around the obstacle course left behind by his nephew and down the hall, she was again fast asleep.

"Figured you'd like the frilly girl colors." He stepped into what used to be his sister's room. Putting one knee on the mattress, he stretched his arms and eased her onto the double bed.

Immediately she turned onto her side, slid her hands under her cheek and snuggled into the pillow.

"Good night, Sleeping Beauty."

She really did look like a fairy-tale princess. How he wished a simple kiss could break the curse she lived under. Asleep on the white comforter speckled with little pink rosebuds, no one would guess the fear and terror that plagued her.

As unfortunate as it was, people were robbed, mugged, and beaten probably every second of the day somewhere in the country, but did they suffer from these debilitating nightmares? Could it be Jake was wrong? Or had Pam lied to her family? Had she been raped? Tonight his touch seemed to exacerbate her fears. That would fit the profile for a rape victim. But he'd touched her lots of times. A hand on her back as they had walked along or a pat of encouragement, and she hadn't reacted like this.

If she'd been raped, the aversion to touch, the fear, the insecurity would be her constant companion, not appear and disappear at the whim of a fitful nightmare. Maybe it wasn't rape, but something happened, something so awful that not even in her dreams could she deal with it.

According to Jake the nightmares started in the hospital after her attack. "What did that man do to you? What could be so horrible, so unbearable, you can't face it?"

Wanting to stay by her side, to protect her, to ward off her fears, he grudgingly turned on his heel. He needed to get some sleep, even though he knew, tonight, it wouldn't come easy.

"I don't know."

The sound of her voice was so soft, so quiet Jeff wasn't sure he hadn't imagined it. Spinning around, with only the dim ray of the streetlight shining through the window, he saw.

Eyes open, a single tear trickled down her cheek, and then she said it again, "I don't know."

CHAPTER THIRTEEN

She'd been sleeping on a cloud. A soft fluffy cloud. She was a princess. He'd said so. She heard him. But then the cloud shifted, the voice went away, and now she'd be alone—again.

She didn't want to be alone. Not anymore. Her lids were so heavy, but she forced them open, focused. A glimmer of light shined on a bear. A stuffed bear. Winnie the Pooh. She loved Winnie the Pooh.

Then he spoke again, the voice, her prince. "What did that man do to you? What could be so horrible, so unbearable, you can't face it?"

Tears filled her eyes. One slipped down her face. There was no cloud, no prince. Only questions with no answers. "I don't know."

Too long, so very tired. She wanted answers, she wanted help. She could see the face now. The face with the voice. Jeff. He'd asked.

"I don't know," she repeated. Pushing on her hands she lifted herself up, swung her legs over the side of the bed. Feet flat on the floor she glanced out the window. "Sometimes I remember snatches of what happened. Like flipping fast through a photo album. I know I blacked out before help arrived. My family, the doctors, they all said it was for the best." A few leaves flickered with the breeze. Scattered clouds hid the stars. Neighbors most likely slept comfortably in their beds. Hands gripping the edge of the mattress, she turned to face Jeff.

He hadn't moved. "I thought you were asleep."

"I was."

"I didn't mean to wake you." He swung the door fully open. Light from the hall flooded the room.

Standing in the dark with a backdrop of bright light gave Jeff the appearance of an angel, an avenging angel.

"It wasn't you. I don't usually sleep well after a nightmare."

"I'm not surprised." Letting go of the doorknob, he rubbed one side of his face, dropped his hand awkwardly to his side. "Wanna talk about it?"

"No. Yes… I don't know." Her gaze shifted out the window to the rustling leaves. "I don't know if I can. I've…never really tried." She shrugged one shoulder. "Why try to remember something my mind wants to forget? Knowing all that happened wouldn't bring Travis back. So why fight it?"

"Maybe that's the problem." He took a step closer to her.

"Maybe." She shifted, stood, and walked to the door. "Or maybe this is just my punishment."

"Punishment?" Jeff followed her out of the room and downstairs. "Punishment for what?"

Her purse sat on the floor by the sofa. She snatched it up, clutching it firmly against her chest, but didn't turn to look at him. "For being alive. For surviving. For not dying like…"

"Like your husband?"

Silent, she nodded, then walked to the front door.

"That's the most absurd thing I've ever heard."

Her hand froze on the doorknob. "Is it?"

"You know it is." He didn't dare take another step closer for fear she'd walk out the door, and then they'd have this conversation out on the street for every neighbor to hear and gossip about for days, maybe weeks or months to come. "Talk to me."

"I told you. I don't have any answers." She still hadn't turned to face him, but she hadn't walked away yet either.

In the recesses of his mind, the part that processed words before his mouth spoke, he knew what he shouldn't say. But his gut, the part of him way down deep that didn't care how badly he'd screwed up before, because he desperately wanted to make things right now, that part spoke up loud and clear. "Maybe together we can find some answers."

"Maybe. But not now. I can't. I need to go home." Her hand remained on the knob. Either unable or unwilling to open the door.

"Okay. Not tonight." He agreed, waiting a beat, wondering if he should ask her to stay or let her go. And if he asked her to stay, then what? "I'll walk you home."

Still frozen in place she dipped her chin in silent agreement, but made no move to turn the knob and open the door.

"Would you like me to keep you company until you fall asleep?"

"No, thank you. I've kept you awake long enough." Shoulders stiff, head held high, she yanked open the door.

For a long moment Jeff didn't think she was going to leave. Pam lingered in the open doorway, her fingers curled tightly around her purse straps. Just when he was about to suggest she stay, she crossed the threshold.

He eased himself beside her and pulled the door shut. At the sound of the latch clicking into place, Pam turned with a start.

"Sorry." He wanted to reach for her, soothe her, but if he'd learned anything in the last few hours, it was how easily she spooked after a nightmare. Now her erratic behavior made so much more sense. "Shall I go first?"

Clutching her purse to her chest, Pam nodded. "Yes. Yes."

Slowly he inched his way across the yard. Pam fell into step beside him, but not so close as to risk accidental contact.

Fearful of a repeat of the first time they'd met, Jeff's breath caught while he waited for her to rummage through her purse for the keys. Despite tension hovering over them, nothing seemed out of place. She took no extra time, the key slid easily into the lock, the front door opened, and with a soft thank-you, she slipped quietly inside.

Stepping off the front porch, Jeff paused, waiting for a light to come on inside. Nothing. Minutes ticked by. All the while visions of her huddled in a dark corner shaking with fear flashed through his mind in a never-ending loop. Just as he lost patience with the wait, primed to storm the house and rescue her from herself, the light in an upstairs window came on.

She was fine. Safe. She'd gone straight upstairs without turning on a light. A few moments later her bedroom fell into darkness. She'd probably only taken the time to kick off her shoes and collapse on the bed fully clothed. There was no way he would let his mind contemplate how long she would have needed to strip out of her clothes or slip into a nightgown. No. Definitely not going there.

***

Carol Ann folded her arms and leaned back in the chair at the foot of her father's bed. "Well, don't you look like something the cat dragged in."

"We don't have a cat," Jeff said flatly, his gaze fixed on his sleeping father.

"Details. I know none of us slept well worrying about Dad, but you could've at least shaved."

His fingers rubbed the length of his stubbled jaw. After staring at the dark windows of Pam's house until the sun blinked on the horizon, he'd done well changing into a clean shirt. Maneuvering a sharp blade against his skin hadn't seemed like the best idea. He lifted his roughened chin toward his dad. "How's he doing?"

"Good. He just fell asleep a few minutes ago. Mrs. McCarthy from across the street came by bright and early. She took Mom to the cafeteria for something to eat." Carol Ann's gaze shifted to her father, then to the empty chair where her mother had spent the night and back to Jeff. "I'm glad he goes home today. Another night in that chair and Mom would need the bed beside him."

"When will they release him?"

"We're waiting for the doctor to make his rounds. If all is well, Dad'll be in his own bed by dinnertime."

"Good." Jeff dropped into the empty chair nearest his father.

"So." Carol Ann tipped her head, staring at him as though searching for some secondary picture within a picture. "What the heck happened to you last night?"

"You mean besides pacing the halls of the waiting room waiting to find out if our father would live or die?" *Or if I'd killed him.*

"That part I know. I also know it's not like you to walk out the door looking like a boxcar hobo. What gives?"

One of his sister's more endearing qualities was her ability to see past the facade and know when something was troubling a member of the family. It was also her most annoying trait. Especially this morning.

"You already said it. I didn't get much sleep last night. Decided if I was going to spend the morning pacing, I might as well pace here."

"Hmm." She closed one eye, and he felt as though she could see past the morning stubble and tired eyes into his thoughts.

"You look pretty beat yourself," he said, hoping to turn the conversation away from him. "You should go home and get some sleep. Pam's covering the office. I can stay till they release Dad. Take him and Mom home."

"I'm okay. After you left, Danny came back and sat with Mom for a while. I got a few winks on one of the loungers in the family room."

"A few *winks* isn't a good night's sleep."

"Pot calling the kettle black?"

"I've always thought it would be fun to have a sibling to share things with," Sandra Quinn said from the doorway. "Even if it is name-calling." She grinned at Jeff and Carol Ann, then stepped into the room.

Jeff pushed to his feet. "Morning, Sandra."

"Morning." She nodded. "Your father's color looks good."

"He should be able to go home today." Jeff stepped aside giving Sandra space by the bedside.

"I'm glad. I wanted to check on him sooner, but the ER was a madhouse all night. I'd swear there was a full moon."

"I thought that was just an old wives' tale," Carol Ann said.

"Yeah, well. There's a reason these old wives' tales have

been around so long. I doubt there's an ER nurse in the country who doesn't cringe working the night shift on a full moon."

"You folks don't believe in letting an old man sleep. Do ya?" Harlon opened one eye at his guests. The right side of his mouth tipped into a teasing grin.

"Sorry, Pop." Carol Ann jumped up from her seat.

The smile on Sandra's face slipped. "It's my fault, sir."

"Nonsense. There'll be time enough for sleeping when I'm dead." Harlon lifted his arm and wiggled his fingers.

Carol Ann immediately reached for her father's hand and squeezed. "I don't like it when you talk that way."

"Everything has its season. Death is not something to fear."

"I know, but that doesn't mean we have to talk about it. Especially not now." Carol Ann lowered their joined hands to the bed and brought her other hand to rest on top.

"Well. I suppose now that I've seen for myself how fine you're doing, I should be going. My shift ended twenty minutes ago, and I'm dead on my feet."

"I heard you had a busy night," Harlon said.

"Understatement of the year. Right now all I want is a big breakfast, then bed." Sandra turned to Jeff. "I don't suppose I can entice you to join me?"

Jeff knew his face must have flustered a bright shade of red at the implication of the invitation.

The way Sandra's eyes flew open wide, she no doubt had just realized how her words sounded. "I—I, uh…" Sandra stuttered momentarily. "I mean for breakfast. Join me for breakfast."

"Thank you." He cleared his throat. "Maybe another time."

"Another time." She nodded with a nervous quickness, then patted his father's hand. "Glad to see you looking so well, Pastor." Lifting her hand in a brief wave, she turned and hurried out the door.

"That was nice of her to stop by. She was an answer to prayer last night. I'd been asking for your mother for so long I was beginning to think not a blasted person on duty could hear worth spit. Then Sandra came in to visit, and next thing I knew, she'd escorted your mother past all those by-the-book nurses and brought her straight to me."

Carol Ann patted her dad's hand. "It was sweet of her to help."

"Did I miss something?" Etta Mae stood in the doorway. "I just saw Sandra Quinn rushing down the hall like a cat with its tail on fire."

"End of shift," Jeff answered. "She's probably just anxious to head home." And a bit flustered, he thought.

"Hmm." Etta Mae leaned back far enough to peek down the hall. "Hmm," she repeated.

He wasn't all too sure what his mother's huffing was all about, but at the moment, he had bigger things to concern himself with. Like talking his father into staying on as senior pastor and getting to the bottom of Pam's nightmares.

And while he was at it, maybe he could end famine in Africa and bring peace to the Middle East.

***

"Why, dear, you look like you've lost your best friend. Whatever is the matter, child?" Abigail Clarke set aside her daily crossword puzzle.

Still awake and counting cracks in the ceiling at the break of dawn, Pam had dragged herself out of bed and gone through the motions of the day. A cup of tea and peanut butter toast for breakfast, a shower, a few minutes at the computer to check her email, and then off to work. Except both numb with exhaustion and hyperaware with nerves, she was ready to crawl out of her skin.

When the leaves from the trees brushed against the office window with the breeze, she'd lifted off her seat. Each time the phone rang, her heart took off racing like a greyhound after a rabbit. By eleven o'clock she knew it was time to stop stalling and call Jeff's friend in Poplar Springs. When she reached for her purse, instead of pulling out the phone number she'd kept safely tucked away, she decided to call it a day and headed for the old Keller place.

Now that she was standing in front of Mrs. Clarke, she had no idea what to say.

"Is it young Jeff?" the old woman asked.

Pam shook her head, and jerked awkwardly when Ms. Abigail touched her arm.

"Oh, my." Abigail Clarke stepped back, carefully eyeing her. The seconds ticked by, feeling like hours, before the woman spoke again. "Did I ever tell you my daddy raised some of the finest horses this part of the country had ever seen?"

Again she shook her head. Without words Ms. Abigail sank into her favorite reading chair and rummaged in the basket beside her for her needlework. It had amazed Pam that with the gnarled and arthritic fingers of a ninety-seven-year-old woman, Ms. Abbie could still crochet such delicate doilies.

"He did. Folks came from near and far for one of my daddy's yearlings. Brought him their sick and troubled horses too." She glanced up over her wire-rimmed glasses just as Pam took a seat in the velvet parlor chair. "Daddy had a way with horses. He'd watch and listen. When the horse was ready, he'd tell Daddy what was wrong.

"Some folks even said Daddy had a magic touch." Abigail chuckled. "No magic to it. Patience. Can't rush a good horse. Daddy always waited for the horse to come to him. Too many trainers, bad trainers, would impose their will on a horse before the horse was ready. Daddy never liked the word 'breaking' for a horse. Always called it 'gentling.'

"See." Abigail pulled the string hanging to the side, then counted a few stitches. "The trick is patience. A patient man could learn to understand the horse's language. If he puts back one ear or two, what he means when he moves his lips like he's chewing, or lowers his head. Daddy understood the language of horses. I wish now I'd paid more attention, but it was my brothers who learned Daddy's way. Of course it's been ages since the family's been in the horse business. Must be nearly thirty years since we sold the stables. My nephew, Peter, George's boy, moved to California right after graduating college. Started working with computers before most of us knew what a computer was. My brother Henry and his wife never did have any children."

As always Pam sat fascinated as Ms. Abigail spun her story. Listening to the old woman tell her tales of life in Texas decades ago, it was easy for Pam to forget her own troubles. Her own pain.

"We were getting on in years. Selling out was the only sensible thing, but it nearly broke George's heart."

"And you?" Pam asked.

Ms. Abigail's fingers stilled. "Life's about moving on. It was time to move on."

Pam sat watching Ms. Abigail wield the crotchet hook, looping the string, pushing through, pulling back, patiently creating a lovely pattern.

"Yes, sirree," Abigail said, tying off the string on the small patch and starting over. "Patience works with so many things. Take this tablecloth. I've been working on it since last Christmas. I make my little patches, keep them in that basket over there. When I have enough, I'll crochet them together. No point assembling it all before I have enough pieces to work with.

"It was the same way with the horses. No point in teaching them to race if something inside was broken. Mind you, I'm not talking about a bone or an organ. I mean the spirit that drives a horse to shine, to be the best."

Pam wondered if Abigail was working with her the way Abigail's daddy had worked with horses. Except for the moment when she'd sat and Ms. Abigail had briefly looked up, the woman hadn't taken her eyes off the work in her hands.

Between thoughts, the old woman focused on her tablecloth. It was almost as if Pam wasn't in the room. Then when Pam was convinced Ms. Abigail had forgotten Pam was there, Ms. Abigail would start talking about her daddy's horses again.

"Sea Wind was one of my favorites. That horse had a

bloodline worth its weight in gold. But he was plumb loco. Almost killed his trainer. The owner was told to put him down, but he didn't have the heart. Out of sheer desperation they drove Sea Wind to my daddy all the way from Kentucky.

"I was just a little thing, maybe six or seven. First time I saw the horse, he was up on his hind legs, batting his forelegs like a lethal weapon. Sheer madness shone in his eyes, but he was a beautiful animal. His coat a lustrous black like fine ebony. Strong muscles. When he finally stood on all fours, any fool could see the horse was something special. Day after day I'd sit near the corral and watch Daddy work. To me it looked like every time the horse came near, Daddy would shoo him away. I didn't understand. Then one day, I'd come back from town with my mother, and Daddy was leading the horse around. I couldn't believe the horse was following him, tame as can be.

"Daddy said the horse had to trust him first. Only then could they work together. Yep, patience and trust." Closing off the last stitch, she put her crocheting into the basket and stood. "You must be hungry. Let's see what's being served for lunch today."

Like a faithful dog, Pam followed after Ms. Abigail. The formal dining room of the old mansion had been converted to a quaint dining area. Square tables with white linens, fresh floral centerpieces, and seating for four were scattered about the room.

Miss Abigail led the way to a quiet table in the far corner of the room and took a seat with her back to the window leaving Pam with a view of the lovely gardens. On each table was a half sheet of colored paper with the specials of the day.

"I think I'll just have the soup," Abigail said, delicately placing her napkin on her lap.

The soup of the day was broccoli and cheese, one of Pam's favorites and probably about all her nervous stomach could handle.

"Yes. I think I will too." Pam lifted the fork and inspected it for no good reason. Setting it back down on the table, she flipped the fork over and back, considering the story she'd heard. The words *patience* and *trust* rolled around in her head. She fidgeted a moment with the knife. But people weren't like horses. Were they?

Her eyes shifted from the silverware to Abigail Clarke. So consumed in her own thoughts, only now did she realize the old woman had been watching her. Wisdom shone in Abigail's eyes much like madness must have shone in Sea Wind's—or maybe even her own. "Was the horse okay?" She let go of the knife and dropped her hands into her lap. "I mean did he stay…sane?"

"Oh, heavens, yes." Abigail paused a moment. "I never did find out exactly what happened to make him loco in the first place. Though Daddy said he wasn't really crazy, just scared. I suppose in many ways animals are like people. Fear festers in cold dark places. Once it's brought out into the light of day, it dies. I heard Daddy say something to the owner on the phone one day about the jockey's riding crop and damn fool trainers and their idiotic notions. Not sure what it was all about, but the owner must have understood, because Sea Wind went on to set all sorts of racing records. A fine horse he was, yes, mighty fine."

Yes, well, Pam picked up the fork again. If only Abigail's father were still alive, and if only Pam were a horse. But there was no arguing the truth in the old woman's words. Fear festers, and if Pam wanted to conquer the fear, it was time to bring it into the light of day. No, it was way past time to bring it into the light of day.

CHAPTER FOURTEEN

"Woman, will you stop your fussin'."

Jeff watched his mother flitter around her husband like a moth unable to ignore the flame. Seeing his father propped in his favorite recliner blustering at his mother's attention only two days after spending the night in the hospital was almost enough to lift the heaviness that had settled in Jeff's heart a few nights before.

"Don't you take that tone with me." Etta Mae gave one more tug on the quilt she'd placed across her husband's lap.

His father looked to the ceiling, probably praying for patience, and Jeff covered his mouth to conceal his amusement.

"Ma," Carol Ann called from the kitchen. "Mrs. Cahill is on the phone. Shall I tell her to call back later?"

"No. I'll be right there." One more time, Etta Mae fluffed the pillows, tugged on the blanket, and shifted the half-empty glass of lemonade forward on the table. "As soon as I'm done with Mrs. Cahill, I'll bring you a fresh glass."

Not waiting for a response, his mom turned on her heel and marched off to the kitchen. It was a nice feeling knowing some things would never change. Whether it was a twenty-four-hour bug or a massive heart attack, Etta Mae Parker would mother you until you weren't so sure which was worse, the disease or the cure. But he wouldn't have it any other way. Neither would his dad.

"Before your mother comes back, I want to talk to you." Harlon Parker flung the heavy quilt to one side and leaned forward. "I want you to think about what you're doing."

"Pop." Jeff grabbed the blanket and spread it out over his father's legs. "Now isn't the time. You just got out of the hospital. If Mom walks in on anything other than a conversation on baseball stats, she'll skin me alive."

"This is important. Your whole future is at stake."

"I'm more worried about you. We almost lost you the other night. The whole town's been praying for you."

"No one almost lost anything. Except maybe you and your senses. The doc fixed my medication."

"Yes, and he also said to take it easy and avoid stress."

"You think not talking about this is going to make it any less stressful for me?" His father glowered at him with the same laserlike gaze that could make a lifelong sinner repent.

Jeff raked his fingers through his hair and carefully considered his options. Lying to his father wasn't something he'd made a practice of growing up, and he didn't want to start now. On the other hand, all through college he'd been guilty, and then some, of what the Catholics called a sin of omission.

But he wasn't in college anymore, and like it or not, there would be no convincing his father of anything if he didn't talk to the man. Jeff simply didn't want to talk *now*.

Maybe this time, though, God was on Jeff's side. The sound of the door chime rang through the house. He was literally saved by the bell. He could almost laugh at the timing.

"Oh, dear." Etta Mae stepped into the hall. Unconsciously she swept a hand at a loose strand of hair laying limp across her cheek, then wiped her hands on the front of her apron. "Looks like we're going to start receiving company."

"I'll get it, Ma." Jeff sprang up. Anything to escape having *the* talk with his father—again.

"I hope I'm not intruding?" Mrs. Meechum, a longtime parishioner, stood on the front porch with a covered casserole in her hands. "I spoke with Pamela Sue at the church. She said Pastor Harlon was doing well enough to have visitors. I can't tell you how relieved we all are at the good news. I know Mrs. Cahill is organizing meals, but I thought Miss Etta wouldn't mind if I went ahead and brought over a little something myself."

"That's very sweet of you, Mrs. Meechum." Jeff waved her into the house, relieved to have someone else for his father to focus on. "I'm sure my mother'll be real happy to see you." He certainly was.

"I meant to bring it by sooner, but my Joshua was having a hard day."

"Oh, look at that." Etta hurried in from the kitchen and beamed at the woman still standing in the front entry. "Now isn't this a blessing."

Mrs. Meechum's cheeks spotted with a tinge of pink. "It's my beef stew. Heats up real easy. Freezes even easier."

"Please come in." Etta relieved the woman of the dish. "I'll take this into the kitchen. May I get you something to drink? I just made some fresh lemonade for Harlon."

"No need to put yourself to any trouble."

"No trouble at all. Two glasses of lemonade coming right up."

Forty minutes later Jeff wondered if someone had shot off a starting pistol. Every ten minutes the doorbell rang, and another concerned parishioner came bearing gifts. So far his favorite was Mrs. Bixby's offering of double chocolate chip cookies. On days like today he thought perhaps the Lord might have had Mrs. B's cookies in mind when He said man did not live by bread alone.

Five women, two with husbands, two more with children in tow, sat scattered around the living room chatting up a storm. For all the fright his father had given the family the other night, this afternoon he looked to be healthy as a horse. One that had just won the Triple Crown and was reveling in the post-race attention.

His father was definitely in his element. So why couldn't the man see he was too young to retire? How could he not recognize how much he was loved and how badly he was needed? But more importantly, how could Jeff make his father understand he, not his son, was the one born to pastor the church?

"My, look at the time." Mrs. Bixby stood. "I'd best be heading home. I've got another batch of cookies waiting to go in the oven." When his mom moved to stand up, Mrs. Bixby waved her off. "Don't get up. I can see myself out. Let me know if you need anything. We have to get Pastor Harlon back in that pulpit.

No one delivers a sermon the way he does."

Bless you, Mrs. Bixby. Before Jeff could get down on bended knees and worship at the older woman's feet, her eyes popped open wide, a rush of bright red flooded to her cheeks and she gawked at Jeff, stumbling over her own words. "Oh, dear. I didn't mean, that is, well, I meant no offense."

"None taken." He smiled. If his father wouldn't believe him, maybe he'd believe someone else.

"I'm not so sure about that, but it's nice to hear anyway." His dad smiled sweetly, and Jeff's momentary euphoria evaporated.

He'd seen that grin too often at church board meetings. It was the one that said *Thank you for your valued opinion. Now get out of my way while I do what I want.*

It didn't take long for the parade of well-wishers to follow Mrs. Bixby's lead. As the last person made her way down the walk lugging her overeager three-year-old beside her, Pam pulled into her driveway, grabbed her purse, and dashed across both yards.

"Afternoon, Miss Etta."

"Don't you look pretty as a picture." Etta held open the front door.

"Is this a good time to visit?"

"Absolutely. I was just getting ready to serve supper."

"Oh." Pam paused on the porch. "I can come back a little later."

"Pamela Sue Wharton, don't make me mad. I've got my hands full with one curmudgeonly old man. I don't have time to straighten you out too." She waved Pam into the living room. The twinkle in her eye trumped any attempt at a stern expression. "You keep the men company while I go fetch Harlon's supper."

"No." His dad shoved the blanket aside with gusto and pushed easily to his feet. "I'm eating dinner at the table with the rest of the family."

His mother dropped her hands on her hips. Her elbows sticking out like chicken wings, she rolled her eyes and blew out an exasperated sigh. But there was no missing the relief glittering in her eyes. She wasn't going to lose the man she loved. Not yet.

***

"Wasn't it nice of Pam to come by?" Etta Mae ran the brass-handled brush through her hair one more time before setting it down on the mirrored tray her grandmother had given her as a child. She treasured all the memories of her grandmother. Sitting at the vanity after doing the dinner dishes, rubbing cream into her hands. The same vanity she sat at now. She didn't understand how folks with no history, no roots, no family found the strength to push through their days.

"She's a nice girl." Harlon nodded without looking up. "Jeff says she's been a blessing with Ellen gone."

Etta's mouth turned up in a knowing smile. "Did you also notice the way Jeff watched her at dinner?"

"Now, Etta. Don't go getting any of those harebrained matchmaking ideas. Jeff's got a lot on his plate right now. John Haskell is already champing at the bit to make something of the rumors about town. Your son doesn't need you complicating things."

"I'm just saying how nicely she fits in with the family is all. And you know as well as I do there's something more to the way he kept his eyes on her tonight than just being pastorly."

"Mmm." Harlon closed the Bible he'd been reading and set it on the nightstand. "Maybe." He folded his glasses and placed them atop the Bible. "I've been thinking. Jo Beth Meechum's worried about her boy Joshua."

"What's Joshua got to do with Jeff and Pamela Sue?"

"I'm not talking about Pamela Sue. You know Bert's passing wasn't easy on any of the Meechum boys, but it had to be hardest on young Josh, him being so much younger than the others."

Etta nodded. Listening, she spread some lotion on her hands the way her grandma had taught her.

"Seems he's a bit awkward. Not real social like the rest of the family. Tends to keep to himself. Jo Beth's at a loss about what to do to make things better. David and Andrew had each other.

"And their dad." Etta made her way across the bedroom. "I seem to remember Bert and those boys always off fishin' or camping or something."

"Yeah, but Joshua being a later-in-life baby, Bert didn't have much time to do any of those things with him. And by the time Josh was old enough to learn from his brothers, they were taking off for college."

Etta slipped under the covers beside her husband. "All right. I'll bite. Where are you heading with this?"

"Jo Beth says the boy seems to have some interest in baseball, but not a lot of talent."

"Harlon?"

"Jeff's real good at baseball. Always was. Could be the boy just needs someone to toss the ball around a bit with him. Show him some pointers, seeing as how his daddy never got the chance."

"Harlon."

"It would be good for Jeff to work with the young boy. Help Joshua build his confidence, self-esteem, bring him out of his shell a bit. Sports are a good thing for young men."

"Harlon Parker. Why don't you quit beating around the bush and just sit down and talk to Jeff?"

"Are you telling me you don't think sports would be a good thing for little Joshua?"

"Of course not." She waved a finger at her husband. "I'm saying maybe it's time to tell Jeff that you know what's botherin' him and just talk to him instead of using little Joshua Meechum as a means to show Jeff his value to the community. Talk to Jeff. Remind him of all the good he's done for this church. Let him know what things were really like for you when you first started out. Make him see Jenny Buckner's dying wasn't his fault."

"I wish it were that easy. I tried to talk to him earlier, but a man like Jeff has to come to the truth in his own time, his own way." Harlon shifted sideways to face his wife. "He told me yesterday he's planning on leaving the church, going back to a business career."

Etta's hand flew to her mouth.

"See why it's time to take some action? I need to make him see for himself. Talking to Jeff would just be words. His whole life we knew this was his gift. Tried to bring him up prepared for it. And yet he chose to run loose in the world for more years than I'd have expected before accepting what he should have known all along—the church was his true calling. This is where he belongs. Words weren't enough then. They won't be enough now. But there isn't the time I thought."

"Oh, Harlon. He's older. More mature. Maybe now, if you try again, someplace quiet, tell him how hard it was for you. Tell him why you know what he's feeling—"

Harlon shook his head. "The hurt is too deep. The guilt of Jenny's death too strong. I see it in his eyes every time he looks at me. Words won't work, but maybe, maybe Joshua Meechum is the Lord's answer to my prayers."

Her gaze wandered a moment to her husband's Bible, then settled on his dark eyes, laden with concern. "Well." She took his hand and gave it a tight squeeze, then smiled. "I suppose it won't be the first time the Lord knows better than I do."

***

"You didn't have to see me home." Pam unlocked her front door.

"What kind of example would I set, if I let a nice girl like you walk home alone in the dark at this time of night?" Jeff teased.

Shoving open the door, she didn't know why she was protesting. The truth was her house had seemed a football field away. The thought of traversing the small distance alone only agitated her already frazzled nerves. Not even an afternoon with Miss Abigail or dinner with the Parkers could quash the irrational fear that lingered after a nightmare, robbing her of the courage to face the dark.

Standing in the doorway, his hands in his pockets, Jeff shifted from one foot to another. He looked the picture of the hormonal teenage boy fumbling his way through that awkward moment at the end of a first date. If only it were that simple.

Pam knew what he wanted. To be invited in, not for the anticipated good-night kiss, but to continue the conversation she'd refused to have the night before. It was time to stop stalling. Dropping her keys in the blue-and-white bowl on the entry table, she swung the door open wide. "Is it too late to come in for a cup of coffee?"

"Love one." He stepped into the house and peered down the hall to the kitchen and back. "Need some help?"

Did she ever, but not with the coffee. "Nah, make yourself at home. I'll put a pot on and be back in a second."

The first room in the house she'd painted when she'd moved in was the kitchen. A bright yellow. She'd hoped it would make the room feel like sunshine any time of day. At the moment it looked more like an army of lemons had run amok. Maybe she should have stuck with tan like the man at the paint store had suggested.

Taking a deep breath, she willed her body to relax. "Fat chance," she muttered to herself. Not sure if Jeff could hear her, she leaned around the kitchen doorway and glanced down the hall. If he'd heard her talking to herself, he didn't show it.

Sitting in the big old wingback, he flipped through one of the photo albums she kept on the shelf under the coffee table.

"No point in having him think I'm any more loony than he already does." She closed the kitchen door. "So what if I talk to myself while I make coffee." She took another deep breath and opened the cupboard by the coffeepot. "I mean, lots of people talk to themselves or whistle while they work."

After putting a new filter in the basket, she measured out two scoops of coffee and paused, wondering if he'd drink more than one cup. She looked at the pot, over to the door, then back. "If he does, that means he'll have me talking about that night." Her hand fell to the counter. Glancing out the window, she considered what Miss Abigail's daddy had said. *The trick to fixing a skittish filly is lots of patience.* She turned her attention back to the pot and added two more scoops. "I suppose even her daddy might think two years was more than enough patience."

She poured eight cups of water into the coffeemaker, closed the lid, pushed the button, and stepped back. The machine spat and sputtered as small bursts of steam puffed through the top. Her gaze once again focused out the window, she blew out a long breath. "If only Travis hadn't died."

"Maybe that's something we should talk about?"

She hadn't heard the door open, or Jeff walk into the room. The sound of his voice had startled her. Heck, it had probably scared a year off her life. Still she hadn't moved. Hadn't even flinched, never mind jump out of her skin as she'd done most of the day with the slightest provocation. "I didn't hear you come in."

"I didn't think so." He looked at the brewing pot of coffee, and she wondered what he was thinking. There was a focus, an odd sort of concentration, almost as if he expected the coffeepot to speak to him.

When his gazed turned on her, he extended his hand. "That's going to take a few minutes. Let's have a seat in the other room. It's more comfortable."

By the time they reached the living room and sat, it would be time to return for the coffee, but she didn't protest. Her hand accepted his, and she followed him down the hall, his warmth spreading through her like a heated ray of sunshine. It had been a long time since she'd felt such a steady sense of calm. A total lack of fear. She didn't ever want to let go.

Still holding her hand, he sat at the end of the sofa. His back to the armrest, he faced her. She felt the tug of his hand and lowered herself into the seat beside him. Their hands clasped, she stared off down the hall.

The coffeepot still gurgled. He'd been right. The coffee would take longer. But was he right about her? Was she finally ready? His grip on her hand tightened, and she knew it was time to make a decision. It would be her choice. She didn't have to see him to know he watched her, waiting.

Low and gentle, barely above a whisper, like a tender caress, she could feel his voice surround her. "Tell me, Pammy. Tell me what happened."

CHAPTER FIFTEEN

Pam's gaze remained on the kitchen at the end of the hall. She hadn't turned to look at him. Hadn't acknowledged the question. But Jeff found it comforting that she at least hadn't let go of his hand.

Not sure if it would be best to remain quiet or say something to urge her on, his fingers tightened around the small hand still folded in his. The movement seemed to remind her that he was there.

"I've spent so long trying not to remember, I don't know if…if I can."

"I know it's hard, but there's a part of you that needs to remember, to know." His voice still soft and low, he repeated, "Tell me what happened."

She blinked, narrowed her eyes, focused on him, then blinked again. When she turned her attention off into the distance, she pulled free and splayed her hands open on each knee. "I don't know where to start."

Her fingers flexed and tightened until her knuckles gleamed bright white. The grip should have been painful but she didn't loosen the hold. Not sure what else to do, he covered her hand, his thumb casually caressing the top until he felt her grip ease. "You and Travis were driving home."

"It was late. I used to volunteer on Wednesday nights at NICU. Sometimes the best medicine for a sick baby is to be held, and so many little ones didn't have anyone to love on them." Her shoulders relaxed. "Things were going really well with Travis's career. The partnership with Greg was growing. They'd taken on another law clerk. We'd just bought a house. Three bedrooms."

She shifted and looked up at him. The hard edge of fear that had shone in her eyes most of the evening gave way to a soft, gentle glimmer. He could almost see a smile in her eyes. "Travis had a plan." This time her mouth tipped in a wistful grin. "He had it all worked out to the day. When we'd buy the house. Then the station wagon. A dog would be next. When there was enough money in the bank for a rainy day, we'd have our first child. I loved my job, but I knew I'd want to stay home to raise my family. We were young. The plan made sense. We thought we had time."

Her smile faded, and he resisted the urge to slip an arm around her and hold her until the hurt went away. "So on Wednesday nights you'd go to the hospital and hold the babies?"

She nodded. "That night I'd gotten to the hospital early. There was this one little boy. His mom had walked out of the hospital after he was born. Just like that, she walked away." Cocking her head to one side, she stared into his eyes. "How does a mother simply turn her back on her own flesh and blood?"

A long beat passed before he realized she was waiting for him to answer. "I don't know."

"The baby was born with a list of problems too long to detail. Blind and almost totally deaf were the simpler ones. At only a few days old, he underwent heart surgery and would need more surgeries as he grew. He'd been in an incubator for weeks but his lungs didn't want to develop. The neonatologist didn't want to give up, but she didn't hold out much hope. After twelve weeks he seemed to finally make enough progress that I could hold him outside the incubator for a few minutes."

She shifted in her seat, turning far enough that he could see her whole face and not just her profile. "I told myself, even if he survived, children like him don't get adopted. His life would be spent in a system that was overcrowded and underfunded. Somewhere I'd started to think maybe Travis and I could take him. Find a way to make it work. I thought, who needs a station wagon? I'd begun to think of the baby as ours.

"That night everything went wrong. It's mostly a blur. All the babies were so small and frail. Every time we'd lose one, it always hurt…" She pulled her hand back and held it up to her breastbone. "Right here. But when I lost this baby, I felt a bone-deep hurt that burned so hot I thought I'd never feel that much pain ever again. I tried to tell myself it was for the best. He'd be better off in heaven. But I couldn't hold it together."

Tears welled in her eyes, and Jeff wondered if he'd made a mistake in not taking her to a psychologist to tell her story.

"I wasn't any help to anyone, so there was no point in staying for the rest of my shift. I told the head nurse, I'd be okay," Pam continued. "I could drive myself home. But she insisted on calling Travis. The firm had a really huge case coming up for trial. He'd been working until all hours of the night for weeks. It was a make-or-break sort of thing. Had the firm stretched to its financial limits. I hated bothering him."

A tear trickled down her cheek, and she swiped at her face. "He told me to stop apologizing. Said that I would always be more important than a stupid case. Told me we could have our own baby if I wanted. Insisted that winning this case would put us years ahead of schedule. I knew they'd sunk a ton of their own money into it. I'd heard him and Greg talking. They were worried. If things didn't go their way, they could lose everything, but Travis made it sound like the Emerald City was right around the corner."

An unexpected pang of jealousy poked at him. Pam's love for her husband hadn't been a secret, so it shouldn't have surprised Jeff to learn Travis returned his wife's feelings and had treasured her above all else. How could he have expected anything less? Wasn't he doing the same thing now? Didn't he want to take away all her pain and make her world right again?

Pushing aside his own petty jealousies, he focused on Pam. She was all that mattered.

"When we pulled up to the house, nothing seemed out of the ordinary. We had no reason to suspect a thief had been casing the neighborhood. But before Travis had a chance to close the garage door, a man dressed in black walked in."

He felt her stiffen. Her hand grew icy cold, and she blew out a sardonic snort. "I was so naive, it was several minutes before I realized he wasn't an ordinary person lost and looking for directions, or someone with a flat tire needing help with the spare. It never occurred to me we were in danger until the stranger took a step toward me and Travis moved between us."

Pam appeared to focus on a small glass globe on the coffee table. Except for an occasional tear, so far she'd managed to maintain a steady pace retelling the events of that night. Now she stared at the glass sculpture, and Jeff noticed she'd stopped wiping at the tears staining her face.

Alarm bells began to ding in the back of his mind. The blank vacuous look in her eyes scared him. What was she thinking, seeing? He raised his hand to touch her arm, and she jolted back against the sofa. Her tears had dried, and she pierced him with a sharp, angry glare.

"He hit Travis. He must have had something in his hand, something hard, because Travis doubled over and fell to the ground." She grabbed her knees again and focused on the crystal globe. "I remember getting really angry. 'Here's my purse,' I said to the guy and threw it at him. 'Take whatever you want, just leave us alone.' And then I saw it, the look in his eyes, and I knew he wasn't after what was in my purse."

Her fingers balled into a fist, and Jeff could see the vein in her neck beating in time with her quickened pulse. Afraid to touch her, his hands clenched at his sides, his nails biting into his palms. The thought of Pam pawed and violated by a man who was no more than an animal made him want to throw up. He wasn't sure he could sit calmly and listen if she told him that she'd been hurt that way.

"Travis struggled to his feet. I could tell he'd seen it too. And then the creep hit me. Sent me flying against the car. Travis threw himself on the guy. The two of them rolled to the floor. I looked around for something, anything, to use for a weapon."

She loosened her grip and flexed her fingers. Jeff could see her hands shaking. She rubbed her thighs in long broad strokes, remaining silent so long he came close to standing up and ending the whole thing. He couldn't do it. He couldn't put her through this again. And damn it to hell, he'd thought he was prepared for whatever happened, but now, knowing the only thing keeping her from falling apart was staring at a damn piece of glass on the table, he wasn't sure he was ready for the truth.

Still focused on the small globe, she leaned forward and slipped her fingers around the edges of the sofa cushion. "I...I finally spotted a small section of PVC pipe. It wasn't heavy but I thought, maybe, with enough momentum, I could at least slow this guy down. When I turned around, I saw he held a knife to Travis's throat." She closed her eyes and took in a deep breath. "I do remember. I could see what Travis was thinking. The way his eyes darted from me to that creep. He didn't care about his own life, but if he died, there'd be no one left to save me." She opened her eyes and a fresh wave of tears slid down her cheeks. "He wanted me to run. For whatever reason the guy was almost ignoring me, but I couldn't leave."

She lifted a hand and rubbed at her eyes. Her movement swift, jerky, and hard, as though wiping away the tears would erase the memory and change reality. "I'm so sorry, Travis." She sniffled and blinked back fresh tears. "Maybe if I'd run, if I'd gone for help, gone to a neighbor, he'd still be here."

"Don't." Knowing she was finally facing the guilt she'd buried for years, Jeff wanted to tell her she wasn't to blame, not to do that to herself, but she didn't seem to hear him. She was back in that world, in that time, reliving that hell.

"Instead, I swung with everything I had. The goon lost his balance and dropped the knife, but he'd already hurt Travis so badly he couldn't move fast enough to recover. I reached for the knife but the creep was on his feet again. He kicked Travis and backhanded me. If you're hit hard enough, you really do see stars, but I had to stay strong. I couldn't let the blackness win.

"Travis tried to get up once more. The guy had both my hands in one of his and spun around and kicked Travis in the gut like in one of those martial arts movies. I must have screamed because the guy spoke to me. 'Say good-bye.' Then he kicked

Travis in the head, grabbed me by the hair with his other hand, and dragged me to the ground. I remember trying to stomp on his instep, thinking if I could just break loose. But that only made him grin. 'I like feisty women,' he said. And my stomach rolled. I finally realized what I had to do. If I stopped fighting, if I just let him have what he wanted, then he'd go away and leave us alone, and I could get help for Travis.

"Oh, God." She started rocking in place. "So much blood. Travis was bleeding. The last blow to his head had knocked him out cold. I thought, he didn't have to know. I wouldn't tell him what happened. I could do that for him. I could save him."

Jeff prayed the horror of her words didn't show on his face. Not that it mattered. She hadn't looked at him once since she'd returned to that night in the garage, but he couldn't let her see what he felt. And Lord help him, he had to let her finish.

She'd let go of the cushion and grabbed her wrist, running her thumb back and forth. "I begged him not to hurt Travis anymore. Told him he could have anything he wanted. *Anything.* He sneered at me and said he was going to get *everything* he wanted. He pulled out a rope from his pocket and tied my arms behind my back."

She turned her wrist and stroked harder. Jeff had to look away. He couldn't watch her rubbing away the ropes that had bound her.

"I told myself I could do this. It would be okay. He ripped at my shirt. I heard the buttons bounce against the concrete floor." She closed her eyes again. "He cut the straps on my bra. I don't know if it was the same knife he'd held on Travis or a new one. He used the edge of the blade to draw across the top of my breasts. I didn't realize I'd closed my eyes. I guess I thought if I didn't see him, didn't watch, then maybe it would be less real. Maybe I could tell myself it was just a nightmare. Then I felt it."

Jeff clenched his fists. He pictured the scrawny bastard's neck in his hands, and the man falling limp to the ground unable to hurt Pam anymore.

"He'd put the knife to my chin and told me to open my eyes." Her eyes flew open. "One hand pinched my nipple and twisted. I tried not to scream, not to flinch, but it only made him squeeze harder until I winced. I couldn't help myself. But when I saw the glint in his eyes, I swore I wouldn't make another sound. I wouldn't give him the satisfaction of knowing he hurt me."

What Jeff wanted was the satisfaction of making that SOB hurt until Christ came back. If it meant that Jeff suffered in hell for eternity, it would be well worth it.

"When I wouldn't scream, he bit me." She lifted her hand, gently soothing a breast. "That wasn't enough for him. After a while I didn't even feel the punches anymore. I'd gone numb. I'd been numb for a long while. He leered at me long and hard. 'Maybe we should wake hubby up, let him watch?' Part of me wanted to scream, plead, beg him to leave Travis alone, to just get this over with and go away. Another part of me knew if I reacted, then he'd go after Travis again. He'd do whatever gave him the power.

"He unzipped his pants and pulled out...pulled... I thought this was it. He'd finally get it over with. But he turned to Travis and smacked his face. 'Come on, you don't want to miss this.' When Travis didn't respond, he hit him harder. 'Showtime,' he said and hit Travis again.

"I couldn't stand it. I rolled over and screamed, throwing my weight against him . He spun around and pinned me against the floor again. His fingers wrapped around my throat. 'Don't tell me what to do, bitch.' I couldn't breathe."

Pam's hands clutched at her throat like she'd done last night in his mother's kitchen. Bile lurched to his mouth. Dear God, was this what she remembered in her nightmares, felt, saw? A half-naked pervert, torturing her and her husband, and now robbing her of her last breath?

"I felt him shove up my skirt. Couldn't breathe. His fingers, rough and scratchy, brushed against my stomach. I heard my panties rip. Even with only one hand on my throat, the pressure was so strong. I pulled at his arm. Had to breathe. I couldn't breathe."

Closing her eyes, she drew her knees up to her chest and hugged her legs. "That's it. It's gone. I don't see anymore. Don't remember. I guess that's when I passed out."

Pam rocked in place, and he wanted desperately to pull her onto his lap and promise he'd protect her for the rest of her life. But he didn't doubt if he touched her now, she'd shoot through the ceiling. She might not remember the final violation, but she remembered enough.

"I did come to for a few minutes. I remember rolling along on the gurney down what must have been my driveway. Greg, my husband's partner, walked alongside, holding my hand, telling me everything would be fine. I remember a voice telling him that he couldn't ride in the ambulance, that he'd have to meet us at Medical City. Then everything faded to black again." She rested her chin on her knees. "When I woke up, I didn't remember. Jake told me Greg came by to drop off some papers for Travis. He must have gotten there just as I blacked out. The doctors assured me that the creep didn't… I mean there was no evidence he…" She closed her eyes and somehow drew her knees closer to her chest. "Greg said he pulled the creep off me before anything more could happen. But I don't remember Greg showing up or saving me."

"I'd like to meet Greg someday." He hadn't meant to speak. He wanted to let her talk until she didn't have anything else to say. Besides, he wasn't sure of the right thing to say, to do. But right or wrong, for the first time since she'd started talking, she turned and locked her gaze on his.

Tears pooled in her eyes and cascaded over her lower lashes. She didn't blink, didn't unwrap her arms to wipe them away, and didn't seem to care she'd lost the battle to stay the watery reaction. Her gaze lingered a moment longer. "Every time I dream, I let him win. I don't want the bastard to win."

It didn't take much to lean forward and draw her onto his lap. She hadn't let go of her legs. She remained balled up in his arms.

Her head resting on his shoulder, she cried in earnest. Tears gushed, and still she kept her arms wrapped around herself in a protective fetal embrace.

Jeff whispered into her hair. "We won't let him win." He had no idea why he'd said that, but he knew he meant it. Even though he had no idea what triggered the dreams, or what it would take to make them stop, he knew he would not let that bastard win.

***

How many times was she destined to fall apart in this man's arms? She knew she was crying like a baby, but she also knew she couldn't stop. Except for the police, she'd never told anyone else what little she remembered from that night, and not even then did she remember all she'd just shared with Jeff. No stranger to tears, for over two years she'd cried for the man she loved, for the life they'd never share, and the children she wouldn't give him.

But never had she let herself face the terror, the fear. Like a geyser unstopped, a flood of emotions overwhelmed her. The pain, the panic, the horror clawing over each other was too much to control, too hard to suppress. That night she hadn't cried. She wouldn't give her assailant the satisfaction. When she came to from the nightmare, she'd been too numb to cry. Fighting to move on, to survive, she kept her feelings bottled up neatly inside her. And now, Jeff had forced her to uncork the tightly sealed bottle, and she didn't think she would ever stop crying.

"Let it all out," Jeff whispered, drawing slow comforting circles along her back. At the same time, the long nimble fingers of his other hand slowly brushed her hair.

Cocooned in his warmth, she felt the pressure in her chest ease. She wasn't sure exactly when she'd released the strangling lock her hands held around her knees and turned into his chest, gripping his shirt tightly in each fist. Nor did she notice when the heaving sobs weakened to breathless whimpers. Loosening the hold on his shirt, she laid her hands flat against his chest. The rapid rhythm of his heart beat under her fingertips. Heat seeped through the thin cotton of his shirt. How she'd missed the comfort of another human being, a man.

She liked the way Jeff smelled. A raw earthy smell of soap, and leather, and maybe fresh air. If she let herself forget, she could almost see herself staying here forever.

Forever?

Jolted by the shocking implication of her mind's musings, she shot up straight and practically jumped out of his lap.

"It's all right." Jeff cooed her back against his chest, into his arms, his soothing comfort impossible to ignore. Right now, tonight, all she knew was that for the first time in a very long time she felt safe, really safe.

***

Jeff probably should have carried her upstairs and put her to bed, but he needed to hold her as much as she had needed a good cry.

The clock on the mantel said four in the morning. Somewhere around midnight she let go of her legs and let her hands clutch his shirt as she cried. By one o'clock the tears had slowed, and her hands had come to rest gently on his chest. Once she sprang up, her expression painted in fear. By two o'clock she'd fallen sound asleep still in his arms. For the last two hours he'd held her close and stroked her hair. He needed this time, to calm down, to think. But more than anything he needed to know she was safe and protected, and there simply was no way he could let go of her. Not yet. His insides felt raw with pain and anger.

He'd stopped praying for wisdom and instead ran every memory of every psych class he ever took through his mind. Somewhere in the recounting of the night had to be the small detail, the trigger for her nightmares, but what?

His fingers stilled in her blonde hair. It was long and fine, and reminded him of winter wheat. He hated what she'd had to suffer at the hands of that animal, that she'd had to relive it again last night, but his mind kept circling back to the one thing he couldn't grasp. Something he'd heard was the key to the nightmares. Wasn't it?

It had to be. But the more he thought of it, the more he realized any of a million little details could be the answer. The color of her attacker's clothes. Except, she'd see black every day. Maybe the style of his shirt or his shoes? She didn't mention what shoes he wore. Perhaps every time she saw white sneakers or gray cowboy boots, her subconscious remembered that night and taunted her with nightmares. Or it could be the color of his eyes? His hair? The smell of the bastard's breath? Damn!

He'd gone over her story again and again, back and forth, and was no closer now to understanding how to help her than the first day he'd watched her from his mother's kitchen window.

Something had to be done, and he didn't know what. He could see only one option. First thing in the morning, okay, later this morning, he would call his old college roommate. Caleb would be able to tell him how to handle things until Pam could arrange to go to Poplar Springs. Caleb was good at what he did. No, he was great at it. Caleb would be able to unravel the information and find the root of the problem. He had to.

Everything in Jeff screamed the answers were right in front of him. Only where? Which part? Damn it. What wasn't he seeing?

CHAPTER SIXTEEN

Making love in the morning. How she loved making love in the morning. The feel of a man's morning stubble under her lips. Strong hands stroking, caressing, dragging fiery sensations from corners long forgotten. Oh, how she missed this.

Missed?

Pam's eyes shot open. Oh, God. Not only was she sprawled across Jeff's chest, she was gnawing at his chin like a starving kitten lapping up fresh caviar. Oh, God.

Somehow they'd fallen asleep spread out on the narrow sofa. Jeff underneath her, his arm wrapped around her hip holding her in place, his other hand on her shoulder, his fingers barely moving. And good grief, how the heck had she managed to wind her leg around his? Their bodies snuggled close, if she shifted an inch she'd rub against… Oh, God.

She had to move. Slip away. Break free. But how without waking him up? She closed her eyes and took a deep breath. There had to be a way to extricate herself without giving away her currently precarious position. Then she felt it. His fingers froze. His steady breath seized in his chest. Busted.

***

As far as dreams went, this one was spectacular, except, this wasn't a dream. He'd fallen asleep with Pam in his arms, and now she was…kissing him?

Or maybe that part had been the dream and now he was… Oh, Lord, he wasn't? Was he? Yeah, no doubt about this one. He had her trapped against him with one arm and roaming fingers on his other hand had slipped inside the edge of her blouse and were playing a contented tune on a patch of bare shoulder.

If she, heaven forbid, wiggled an inch to the left, there'd be no hiding his morning glory. And from the stiff way she braced herself in his arms, he was pretty sure she'd already come to the same conclusion.

Seminary had failed to teach him the appropriate response to this particular situation. And much to his chagrin, what he really wanted to do was totally out of the question. His only option was to suck it up, not make a big deal, then apologize for the rest of his natural life. Of course getting his hand out of her blouse would probably be a good start.

Releasing his hold on her, and letting his arms fall to his sides, relief swept through him as Pam rolled off the sofa, saving them both any further embarrassment.

"Sorry about that." He sat up, not ready to stand.

"No, I'm sorry. This is all my fault. I…I…thank you."

Thank you? For what? Letting you go instead of kissing your socks off?

She tucked her hair behind her ear and took another step back. "I think I needed a good cry. I really do feel better. Thank you."

Right. The nightmares. Her attack. Get your mind out of your pants and get real, Jefferson Parker. "You know that won't be enough?"

She hugged herself. "Enough?"

"It's good to talk. And to cry. Very cathartic. Only…" He hesitated a moment, wondering if it was too soon to push forward, to mention Caleb. "We still need to find the connection between what happened and your nightmares."

"Just telling someone seems to have lifted a weight I didn't realize I carried. Maybe that's all I needed."

"I doubt it's that easy. As horrible as your dreams are, I don't think they're a way of reliving the trauma. If they were, I would think they would happen with more regularity. I believe there's some unconscious reminder that's triggering them, but what?"

"I don't exactly relive what happened. At least I don't think I do." Touching the arm of the sofa as though about to sit, she took another step and instead sat in a nearby chair. "When I lived in Dallas, the nightmares came every night. If I slept through a night peacefully, it was more the oddity than the norm. Not until I moved home did they almost go away."

"I see." Somehow, moving to Hope's Corner had made a difference. But how? "I wonder if you'd consider sharing with someone else?"

Tucking her chin against her neck, she looked startled at the request. "Sharing?"

"Talk to someone. A professional. Find the trigger, make the connection to what causes the nightmares."

"What causes the nightmares? My husband was murdered, and I survived. Isn't that enough?"

"I think there's more to it than just post-traumatic nightmares. Do you remember me mentioning my friend Caleb from college?"

She nodded and gripped the arm of the chair.

"I think he might be able to help find exactly what happens during the day that brings on the nightmares."

She nodded again, her expression less startled, but wary. He waited, expecting her to say something more, but she remained silent still nodding her head.

"Then I take it you agree with me?"

She continued to nod. He wondered if maybe she was convincing herself more than answering him.

"I've got his number at home. I'll call you with it as soon as I get to the apartment."

Expecting her to keep nodding, it surprised him to see her stop and reach for her purse. Did that mean she didn't want him to give her the number?

"Pam? You do want to see him don't you?"

Flipping open her wallet, she pulled out a folded sheet of stationary. Paper in hand, her gaze shifted to his with such intensity he could feel her determination come across the room in powerful waves.

"I want whatever will make this stop. It has to stop."

***

"Jefferson Davis Parker. Have you lost your mind?" Etta Mae's voice blasted through the receiver with such force, Jeff pulled it away from his ear.

Pam had insisted on making him breakfast before he left her house. Neither mentioned the previous night or awkward awakening. They ate scrambled eggs, bacon, toast, and chatted about his niece, the new baby, the fund-raising proposals, next week's board meeting, Mrs. B's double chocolate chip cookies, and pretty much anything that would keep the mood light and…normal.

About ten minutes ago he'd come in his front door in search of Caleb's phone number. He was about to dial his friend when the phone rang.

"Morning, Ma."

"Don't you *Morning, Ma* me, young man."

Uh-oh. His full name was one thing. *Young man* usually meant time to duck and cover.

"What were you thinking?" she carried on. "The phone hasn't stopped ringing, and it's not even eight o'clock."

"I'm sorry, Ma, but I had a long night. What exactly are you upset about?"

"Oh, Lord, grant me patience."

"Ma."

"You, young man, may have had a long night, but you should at least have had the decency to keep the whole blessed neighborhood from finding out. How could you?"

"What does the neighborhood have to with my…" Oh, crap.

"Mrs. McCarthy must have worn out the battery on her pacemaker running across the street to tell me about my son, the pastor, making whoopee with my young widow neighbor."

"It's not what she thinks, Ma."

"No? Well, Mrs. Jackson down the street, and Mrs. Harper on the other side of Pam are thinking the same thing. By now half of

Hope's Corner is thinking the same thing."

Oh, brother. He hadn't given any thought at all to what people would think of him leaving Pam's house so early in the morning. He'd even waved at Mrs. McCarthy as she kneeled over her begonias pulling weeds. Damn.

"Jefferson?"

"Sorry. Pam has nightmares."

"And *that* is exactly the problem. A man of your position shouldn't know Pamela Sue has nightmares."

"No. I mean her jitters and nerves are caused by nightmares. Last night she told me about them. It was very difficult for her. She cried herself to sleep. I couldn't leave her alone. I never gave a thought—"

"No, you didn't." She paused. "That's all there was to it?" For the first time since he'd answered the phone, her voice lowered to its normal octave.

"I was about to call Caleb. Give him a heads-up about Pam when the phone rang. She needs real help. This is out of my league."

"I see." He could almost hear his mother sit down and nod her head, considering the new possibilities. "I'm glad you were there for her, Jeff, but this does pose a problem."

"Yeah." He sighed. "I know."

***

"So what do you think?" Jeff asked, juggling the phone on his shoulder while searching for a mate to his black sock.

"You're on the right track, but I suspect it's not so much something she told you but something she didn't."

"What do you mean?" Jeff glanced at his watch. Eight fifteen. Pam was probably already settled in her office.

"The mind and body are very good at self-protection. It's not unusual for an accident victim to develop retrograde amnesia. In order for the body to heal, the mind wipes away any memory of impact. Often victims never recover memories of what happened, sometimes for up to hours before the life-threatening situation. It's easier to forget and move on than to have to deal with the resulting emotions."

"How does that relate to Pam? She remembers the night in vivid detail. At least she does now." He sat, pulling on his socks.

"Or so she thinks. My guess is there's something she's blocked out, doesn't remember, and that something is trying to break through."

"I thought you said it was easier for the mind to simply forget the difficult and move on?"

"With a simple accident that's true. But if there's more involved, for instance if the patient feels responsible for the death of another person, say a passenger in the vehicle they were driving, a loved one, the inner battle to atone versus to forget can create unbearable turmoil."

"And that's what you think Pam has?"

"I don't know. But from the little you've told me so far, I wouldn't rule it out."

"Well, it's a start. How soon can you see her?"

"Yeah, well, that may be a problem."

"Why?" Jeff tied his shoes, then looked at his watch again. He really wanted to get to the church. He didn't want Pam alone to deal with gossiping parishioners.

"Remember that second honeymoon I promised Kathy in Europe?"

"You mean a few years ago when you forgot your anniversary?"

"That would be the one."

"What about it?"

"We leave tomorrow morning. You know, like that movie, *If It's Tuesday, This Must Be Belgium*. I think we're doing twelve countries in fourteen days."

Jeff chuckled. "Better not lose Kathy on a bus of Japanese tourists."

"Funny. But seriously, I can recommend someone else to see your friend if she doesn't want to wait."

"No. I'd feel better if you handled it. I suppose if she hasn't dealt with any of this in over two years, she can certainly wait a few more weeks."

***

"Yes, Mrs. Cahill. I'll be sure to tell Pastor Jeff you called. … No, ma'am, I won't forget. … Yes, ma'am." Pam stared at the phone for a split second before putting it back on the cradle.

"Sounds like you're having a busy day." Sandra Quinn had come into the office somewhere between Mrs. Tidwell's and Mrs. Hawkins' phone calls, and sat patiently as Pam explained to Mr. Haskell and now Mrs. Cahill that Jeff hadn't come into work yet.

"This place is always busy, but it doesn't usually start so early." Pam shrugged, not sure if she should make something out of the parade of calls or not. "Yesterday the phone rang off the hook with inquiries on Pastor Harlon, but today, they seem to have forgotten all about him."

"I wouldn't go that far. But I don't think folks are as concerned with the senior pastor as much as they are with you and Jeff."

"Me? Why are they worried about me?"

Sandra glanced around as though making sure no one overheard. "Word seems to have gotten around town about, you know, last night."

"Last night?" What could folks around town possibly know about last night? Talking about the attack had been difficult, but in town thought Travis had died in a car accident. It was a story his mother had started, and one Pam never saw reason to correct. The poor woman had lost so much. All she wanted was for her son to be remembered for the life he had lived, not the way he had died. Pam didn't see any point in upsetting her more by telling the truth. After all, what would it change?

"You know." Sandra glanced away, and if Pam wasn't mistaken, the woman blushed. "Jeff staying over and…all."

Good grief. Did the whole town think she and Jeff had spent the night *together*? "You mean all these people think Jeff and I are…" Pam couldn't say the words.

Sandra nodded.

Hand on her cheek, Pam realized her mouth was hanging open. It took a few more seconds for her to close her mouth and swallow. Wasn't this a pickle?

"I know Pastor Jeff is fond of you."

Pam's jaw fell open again.

"And he is a man after all. I'm sure it's not easy to ignore his needs."

Pam closed her mouth and tried not to gape like a frightened owl. "Oh, boy, are you barking up the wrong tree."

"Excuse me?"

"Jeff and I aren't involved. Not the way the town thinks. And as for his *needs*, well that's certainly none of my business."

Her expression blank, unreadable, Sandra watched Pam for several long seconds. "Don't worry. I happen to think Jeff's one of the good guys. He cares about the people of this town. If the two of you want to keep things secret, I'll go along. You can trust me."

"There's nothing to keep secret. I was simply upset, and Jeff was kind enough to keep me company. If we'd been fooling around, don't you think we would have been more discreet?"

"Your neighbor Mrs. Harper did mention her surprise at seeing Jeff so brazen, waving at Mrs. McCarthy, not trying at all to protect your reputation."

"My reputation doesn't need protecting."

"That's not what people are saying."

How the heck was she going to explain Jeff leaving her house at the crack of dawn to the entire town? "I promise you, the only relationship between Jeff and me is that of pastor and secretary with a little bit of good neighbor thrown in."

For now it was probably best to ignore the morning's somnambular activities. Heaven knows neither she nor Jeff had wanted to mention it.

Sandra shrugged one shoulder. "Whatever the case, you can count on my discretion."

"What I really need is to stop the flow of erroneous information before Jeff hears."

"I'm not sure that's humanly possible." Sandra's mouth twisted into a partial smile. "You grew up here. Do you really think we can stop the grapevine once it takes off?"

"Ugh." Pam groaned.

"Exactly. Look honey, I believe you. Really I do. I'll admit you look pretty upset, but you don't look guilty, and you certainly don't look like a woman who had her bells rung last night."

Bells rung? This couldn't be real. She was in bed, having a crazy dream, and if she opened her eyes, she'd find herself in her own room, laughing at all the absurdity. All she had to do was close her eyes real tight, and tell herself time to wake up.

"Are you okay?" Sandra asked softly.

Pam opened her eyes to find Sandra still sitting in front of her, her expression transformed from curiosity to concern.

"Yeah, sorry."

"Pam." Jeff's voice echoed down the hall. "Are you o—" He skidded to a halt when he spotted Sandra.

"Morning, Pastor." Sandra smiled up at him.

"Oh, good morning, Sandra. How's Mrs. Perkins doing?"

"Great. She's put on almost three pounds."

"That's wonderful news." His eyes darted across the desk to Pam. An easy stance and an attempt at casual conversation did nothing to hide the worry in his eyes. "Were you waiting for me?"

"No. I came in to visit with Pam, but I'd better let you two get back to work." She turned to Pam. "Call me if you need a little moral support."

Pam nodded. "Will do. And thanks for the heads-up."

"Anytime." Tossing another smile in Jeff's direction, Sandra headed out the door.

"What was that all about?" Jeff asked.

"It seems we are the brunt of local gossip this morning."

"Yeah." He sank into the nearest chair. "Euphemia McCarthy called my mother as soon as I left your house."

"Oh, no." Pam dropped her face into her hands, and felt the warmth of Jeff's hand on her shoulder.

"It's not that bad. I told her nothing happened. I sort of told her that you were having a little trouble with nightmares."

Pam's head shot up and her gaze flew to his. "You didn't?"

"I told her just enough so she'd believe me when I explained we're not steaming up the bedroom."

"Oh." With a groan she let her head fall back onto her hands. Her face still buried, she mumbled through her fingers. "The whole town thinks we're sleeping together."

"Maybe not the *whole* town."

That wasn't what she wanted to hear. Turning her head, she glared at him with one eye. "All right then, the whole town except your mother."

"By now Dad probably knows the truth too."

Before Pam could respond, her brother Jake's voice carried loudly down the hall. "Pamela Sue!"

Pam rolled her eyes and moaned like a wounded moose. "This can't be happening."

Jeff pushed to his feet. "I'll talk to him."

"Pammy?" Her sister Valerie called out, the clicking of her heels tapped out a sharp tattoo alongside the thump of heavy male footsteps.

Pam didn't need to look up; she already knew those footsteps belonged to not one but both her brothers. Sure enough, when she found the nerve to raise her head, both her brothers and her sister stood in the doorway. Jake toe-to-toe with Jeff.

Legs spread wide, arms folded, Jake glared at Jeff. "When you agreed to help, this wasn't the sort of help I had in mind."

"Now, don't you listen to them. I think it's wonderful about you and Jeff." Valerie shuffled around her brother's blocklike stance and scurried to her sister's side. "Absolutely wonderful."

The way her sister beamed, Pam didn't know if she wanted to laugh or cry. "There is no me and Jeff," she managed to croak out.

Bo, the leaner of her two brothers, stood silently holding up the wall, hands in his pockets, carefully watching each person as though following a key moment in a dramatic play. Pam knew she could reason with Bo, but Jake she wasn't so sure about. He was known to swing first and ask questions later. A rather awkward habit for a well-respected banker.

Jake's eyes narrowed, and he glowered over Jeff's shoulder at her. She resisted the urge to squirm in her seat. "This is all a waste of time. My virtue is intact."

Jake shifted his attention back to Jeff. "That's not the way I heard it."

"What exactly did you hear?" Jeff asked.

"Redding and Mabel were arguing in the kitchen this morning over at the café. Redding insists you're not trifling with my sister. He bet Mabel a Sunday dinner for any takers that my Pamela Sue will be wearing a wedding ring before Dad can clean his shotgun."

Pam closed her eyes and dropped her head on her desk. *Dear God, please let me be dreaming.*

Jake continued, "Mabel insists Pamela Sue is a grown woman and has the right to *dally* with anyone she wants without being shackled to one man."

"Mabel's right." Valerie settled a hand on Pam's shoulder. "Maybe all Pammy wants is to start having a little fun."

Pam looked up at her sister. "You're not helping." Splaying her palms flat on her desk, she pushed upright then waved her arm from one side of the tiny office to the other. "Everyone out."

Jeff turned to her, surprise on his face.

She stepped around the desk. "I am not chattel, and I am not *out to have some fun.* I told Jeff about *that* night. To say it was upsetting might be a tad of an understatement. Jeff was nice enough to keep me company so I could get some sleep. Though none of you need to be telling that to anyone." She paused and nudged her sister toward the door. "I want all of you to go back to work and stop giving the gossipmongers more to feed on."

She stopped in front of Bo. "And you, go tell Dad to put

away the shotgun."

Bo's eyes twinkled with amusement. Without a word, he smiled at his sister and pivoted on his booted heel.

"And you, Jake Wharton, owe Jeff an apology. How dare you come marching in here and accuse one of your oldest friends, an honorable man, of something so dishonorable?"

"I haven't accused anyone."

"The hell you didn't. You may not have said it in so many words, but any moron can tell what you're thinking. Now wipe that scowl off your face, apologize, and let us get back to work."

Jake stared at Jeff for so long, Pam thought she was going to have a real fight on her hands.

"Did she really tell you what happened?"

Jeff gave a short nod.

"All of it?"

He dipped his chin again in affirmation.

"And?"

"It's complicated. She's agreed to see a friend of mine in Poplar Springs."

Jake nodded, and like his brother, turned on his heel, this time walking softly out the door.

Valerie hesitated in the doorway. "You two really didn't…?"

Pam and Jeff both shook their heads.

"What a waste." Valerie followed her brothers.

Still staring at the glass doors leading to the parking lot, Pam mumbled, "John Haskell called earlier, twice."

Jeff nodded, his gaze somewhere off in the distance.

"We're in trouble up to our eyebrows, aren't we?"

"Not you."

Pam cringed at the sight of John Haskell pulling into the parking lot. "How are we going to fix this?"

Jeff spotted the white SUV. "How did they put Humpty Dumpty back together again?"

CHAPTER SEVENTEEN

From where Jeff stood, John Haskell practically slithered out of the front seat of his car. Quite a feat for a man only five-foot-eight or so and pushing 250 pounds.

"John, what a nice surprise." Jeff held the door for the president of the church's board of directors.

Red faced and huffing, Haskell's blistering disposition cooled to almost gracious when he spotted Pam on the other side of the doorway. "Morning, Pamela Sue."

"Good morning, Mr. Haskell. Lovely day isn't it? Any day now we'll be buried in scorching summer heat."

"Yes, my Wilma is enjoying her garden while the cool weather lasts."

"Shall we go to my office?" Jeff gestured down the hall.

John Haskell nodded.

"I'll bring some coffee." Pam's eyes settled on Jeff's for just a second before she turned into the small kitchen. Maybe if she spiked the coffee, this conversation would go better than he expected, but there probably wasn't enough whiskey in Scotland to make this an easy visit.

He closed the door behind him. "What can I do for you, John?"

"I think you know what this is about, Jeff." Haskell didn't bother to sit. That couldn't be good.

"We've had an emergency board meeting this morning."

Fast work, Jeff thought, even for John Haskell.

"As the leader of our congregation, you're expected to maintain a certain level of respectability, morality."

"Of course." Jeff stood behind his desk, and gestured for Haskell to take a seat, but wasn't surprised when he shook his head.

"We simply can't have our pastor seducing female

parishioners."

"I couldn't agree with you more."

"Then you understand why this can't go on? The church simply can't stand by and let this situation go uncorrected." Haskell dropped his hands flat on the desk, staring up at Jeff. "For heaven's sake, you're a man of God. What will our young people think when they learn their pastor is bedding a woman who is not his wife?"

"And who is going to tell our youth of my alleged indiscretions?"

The question seemed to catch Haskell off guard. From his expression, Jeff was sure the man expected a different response.

"Well, uh," Haskell stammered. "I'm sure it's no one's intention to malign you or Mrs. Dawson's reputations, but this is not the sort of news that is easily kept under wraps."

"Apparently not." Jeff wasn't in any mood to play the game. He'd had enough with Haskell's highbrowed meddling.

"Then you understand why the board feels, until this matter is settled, it is in everyone's best interest for you to step aside?"

"So we've been judged and condemned immoral without facing a single accuser? I must have missed when we removed Mathew Chapter eighteen from our Bible."

Haskell's face flushed a ruddy color reminiscent of a garden gnome. "Yes, well, I'm here in private now, am I not?"

"But first you gathered with more than two or three, not to encourage our repentance as scripture dictates, but to plan the best way for the church to save face."

Jeff glanced at the Bible on his desk. The one his father had given him the day he graduated seminary. His father would have had the wisdom and patience to play the game, to open the book and sway the board with scripture and godly logic. Jeff almost laughed. He wasn't his father, but he knew exactly which scriptures were appropriate. Taking the matter before the congregation, and putting Haskell and the entire board in its place for bypassing church court procedures and jumping on the gossip bandwagon, would be an easy task even for him.

But he didn't want any part of it. Enough was enough. He wasn't the man for this job. Since the day he'd chosen to confront Jenny Buckner's abusive husband, only to have her die at his hands the next day, there'd been no hiding from that simple truth. Now, there was no point in defending a position he no longer deserved. Even if the reason had nothing to do with Pamela Sue. "For the record, I am not in a sexual relationship with Mrs. Dawson, but does anyone on the board want to know what really happened yesterday? Is anyone concerned with the truth? I don't think so."

Haskell's entire face pinched at Jeff's bitter words. "See here, Jeff. If you have some defense that would explain your behavior, which I have previously pointed out, and in private, then of course the board would be more than willing to reconsider our position."

"That won't be necessary. I'm sure the elders will be able to step in until an appropriate replacement can be found." Jeff moved around Haskell and opened his office door in a silent dismissal. There was no point in continuing.

"Yes, well…" Haskell straightened his spine and sputtered like a used car as he walked through the doorway, passed Pam in the hall holding a tray, and practically raced to the front door.

Pam stepped into Jeff's office carrying the coffee. "That didn't go well, did it?"

"It depends on whether you consider requesting my resignation going well."

The coffee cups rattled when Pam set the tray on his desk with a thunk and collapsed into the worn visitor's chair. "This is all my fault."

Jeff shook his head and sank into what was, until recently, his father's chair. "I should have given at least some thought to what neighbors might think if they saw me leaving your house so early in the morning."

"Only guilty people worry about appearances."

"And pastors. My whole life my parents have drummed into

all of us the need to be careful. A pastor's family lives their life under a microscope, and it doesn't take much for something innocent to be misconstrued as inappropriate. I should have known better. I should have protected you."

"Protected me?"

He opened a drawer and removed a bottle of aspirin, then returned it to its corner. Whoever replaced him would definitely need the aspirin. "Most people in town don't care what you and I do or don't do in the privacy of our homes. But there are lots of older, conservative folks in this town. Someone is bound to brand you Hester Prynne."

"That's absurd." Pam jumped to her feet. "This isn't the eighteenth century, and neither you nor I have done anything wrong."

"That's not the point, Pam." He slipped the photo of his brother's children into his briefcase. "This is a small town. Gossip has a way of making people forget the truth."

"Then we'll stop the gossip." Her eyes followed his movements as he emptied a drawer onto his desk.

"And how do you propose we stop a boulder from rolling downhill?"

"By telling people the truth. Let them know why you were at my house."

"That would mean telling everyone how Travis really died." He noticed the pink in her cheeks fade away. He'd have pointed out the obvious, that telling folks of her troubles would bring about new ones. Those few people ready to brand her with a scarlet letter would instead just as happily brand her crazy. On the other hand, he already knew she would be less willing to sacrifice her husband's memory.

"Maybe we wouldn't have to tell the whole truth. After all, lots of people seek grief counseling with their pastors."

"But not all night." He shook his head. "I'm afraid our best hope is that someone else does something more outlandish to keep tongues wagging."

"We can't leave everyone thinking that you, I mean, you and me are involved."

"I made it clear we're not involved in that way. But it won't matter. John Haskell and the board have made up their minds."

"I'd bet a month of Sundays it's more like John Haskell made the board's mind up for them."

"Probably, but John Haskell isn't my problem anymore." Jeff needed to tie up a few loose ends, reschedule some meetings, make clear notes for his temporary replacement. And then he'd need to face his mother and father. At least he was sure his mother believed him. He just hoped this latest twist didn't put his father back in the hospital.

***

"How can I ever face them again?" Pam paced the small room bathed in an earlier century. "They've been so good to me. And now, because of me, their son's been fired. Fired."

Abigail Clarke sat silently in the velvet Victorian chair, her eyes following Pam cut a path across the fanciful bedroom with the intensity of a spectator anticipating the winning point in a tied tennis match.

Pam hadn't meant to come to the charming senior citizens home or to burden Miss Abigail with her troubles. She'd locked up the church at the end of day and gotten into her car with every intention of heading home, curling into bed, and having a good cry. When the car came to a stop, instead of sitting in her driveway on Live Oak Lane, she found herself parked in front of the old Keller place.

Inside the well-preserved nineteenth-century mansion, she'd managed to remain composed for all of five minutes. As soon as Miss Abigail asked how young Jeff was, words tumbled out of Pam's mouth like water off a cliff.

"I don't know what to do. How to handle this." Pam spun around, facing Miss Abigail. "I really, really hate this."

"Do you like pizza, dear?"

"Excuse me?" Of all the things she'd thought her older friend might say, this wasn't one of them.

"Pizza. I don't mind admitting I'm rather fond of pepperoni pizza with extra cheese."

"Oh. Uh, yes, I like pizza."

"We have to order it from town. It's a rare treat for me. Most folks shy away from too much spice or too much cheese. Our digestive systems aren't what they used to be, you know."

"No, I guess not."

"That's what I like about young friends. Not afraid of a little indigestion." Abigail Clarke opened her nightstand drawer, pulled out the menu for Joe's Italian restaurant, and thirty minutes later, Pam found herself sitting on the bed with Ms. Abigail, an open box of pizza between them.

"You know, dear." The woman pulled another slice from the box and slid it onto her plate. "I'm not sure we ever get used to what life throws our way while we're busy making other plans."

Pam chewed on her pizza and nodded. Even though working for the church hadn't been part of her plans, never in a million years would she have expected to find herself in the middle of a church scandal.

"When my Edgar died, I thought never in my life would I ever love another man. Now what a sorry way to spend your days is that?"

Pam choked on a small bite, and briefly wondered if her sister Valerie had been talking to Miss Abigail.

"I lingered in the memory of our love for years. At night I'd read over the notes and letters he'd sent me." She paused and chuckled. "Some of them were mighty sparse. But they were all I had left. I felt safe, alone with my memories, comfortable. Yep, comfortable." She took another bite and grinned, pulling a string of cheese from the corner of her mouth. "Love's a lot like pizza."

Pam glanced up from her plate. She was still dealing with how they'd gone from her getting Jeff fired to Miss Abigail's love life; she wasn't ready to get philosophical about pizza.

"The taste is so pleasing and satisfying, but every once in a while you make a fool of yourself with cheese dripping from your face or sometimes wind up with heartburn. But in the end, you still want your pizza. Some days not so much, other days there's just nothing that will satisfy that yen for a slice of pizza."

"I guess I've never given it much thought." And Pam wasn't sure she wanted to, either. She needed to find a way to get Jeff out of the mess she'd gotten him into. "About Jeff and the gossip…"

"Gossip's always there. Nothing much you can do about it. Back in my day, gossip could bring a man or woman to ruin. Today, bad press makes you rich."

"I don't think that applies to small-town pastors." Pam closed the pizza box.

"Maybe, maybe not. Depends on the small town, and depends on the gossip. If it weren't for the wagging tongues, I might never have married my Percival."

"Married?" Of course. *Mrs.* Abigail Clarke. Pam had been so taken by Abigail's story of her lost love, she'd never given any thought that the old woman must have married later in life.

"I remember the day Percival Clarke moved to Hope's Corner. September 21, 1948. He drove into town in a shiny new dark red Cadillac convertible. Folks came running out onto Main Street as he drove by. Such a fancy car."

She set her pizza on her plate and glanced far off out the window. "I was at Phoebe's Beauty Parlor having my hair done for my birthday. I knew folks would be stopping by the house that evening—that's the way things were done back then. Folks paid you a call on your birthday. I wanted to look my best. Like everyone else, I ran out into the street to see for myself."

"You mean people stopped what they were doing to see a car?"

"Not just a car. The new Cadillac. It was all the rage. First year Cadillacs had fins. Automobile supply houses were selling fins that folks could put on their Fords and Chevys. But Percival had the real thing. I didn't care much about the car, but I'll never forget his face when he drove by. Just as I stepped up to the curb he turned toward me and smiled. My heart fluttered to my throat, and my stomach sank to my shoes. I knew it wasn't me he was smiling at. He was just smiling at folks in general. But I stood there grinning back like a nervous schoolgirl all the same."

Pam's mind wandered back to her interview with Jeff at the church, the way her knees had gone weak at his smile. Not since she'd been six years old and fallen in love with Travis had a man's smile had such an impact on her. She'd quickly shoved any thoughts of Jeff as anything more than a boss far away. Striking smile or not, she'd already had the one love of her life. That was all she'd ever need.

"Percival owned a car lot in Dallas," Abigail continued. "His wife had passed on the year before, and he thought it best to raise his young son outside the big city." Abigail laughed. "Seeing how everything's grown now, it's hard to think of Dallas as having been a big city back then, but compared to Hope's Corner, it might as well have been New York. A month later he opened the town's first car dealership. Right on the north edge of town.

"Percival had bought the Brady house just next door to Papa's. Young David was a sweet little boy. Seven years old and missed his mama so. The Clarke housekeeper was a nice lady, but her German accent was so thick, most of us had a hard time understanding her, and David seemed to have an even harder time warming up to her. Instead of going home after school, he spent most of his afternoons either following my father and watching him work with the horses, or in our kitchen gobbling up whatever baking got done that day. He had a special spot for my shortbread cookies.

"Percival would come by and pick up David every night after work, take him home for supper. We'd visit some, not much. I wasn't interested in anything more than being neighborly. Oh, he still had that handsome smile, but I'd had my Edgar. I'd turned thirty-eight. I was past the homemaking age. Settled into caring for Pa and the ranch. I wasn't interested in him as a man.

"Then a couple of months after they'd moved to town, the

housekeeper's mother got real sick, and her sister in Fredericksburg sent for her to come help. Percival was beside himself looking for help with the house and David and all. We offered to take care of the boy while Percival worked. David already spent so much time at our house, it hardly changed anything. I'd cook enough supper for both families, take David home, and then warm dinner on the stove for him and Percival. I remember that night so clearly. It might as well have been yesterday. I'd forgotten the bread rolls at the house and sent David back to fetch them. Such a silly thing it was."

Pam shifted her legs underneath her. "What was?"

"The eyelash."

"Eyelash?"

"Supper was warming on the stove, and I brushed a strand of hair away from my face. That stupid piece of hair kept falling in my eyes. I set the table and brushed it back again, wishing I'd had another hairpin. Percival walked into the kitchen just as I'd started blinking and tearing. An eyelash."

"Oh, you had an eyelash in your eye?"

"That's right. Percival got all concerned that I was upset over something David or he had done. He was such a thoughtful, nice man, it never occurred to me his concern stemmed from his having feelings for me. In those days, men didn't express themselves like they do now. And they certainly didn't take liberties, at least not the way I see it on television."

"No." Pam smiled at the old woman's bluster. "I would think not."

"Anyway, when I told him an eyelash had fallen in my eye, he stepped up close and blew in my eye to make it tear just as Judith Abernathy, the schoolteacher, came knocking on the door. Well actually the old spinster came waltzing right in. 'Yoo-hoo,' she called. 'Mr. Clarke, David?' Percival had his hand on my cheek and was looking for that eyelash. The way Judith's jaw dropped when she'd walked into the kitchen, you'd have thought she caught us stark naked and coupling on the kitchen table."

Pam swallowed a chuckle.

"She'd brought a peach pie warm from the oven and dropped it splat on the floor. Made one heck of a racket. I nearly jumped out of my skin. Percival took a quick step back too, and I guess that just made us look more guilty in Judith's opinion, 'cause the following day the entire town thought the worst.

"Pa was so angry. I don't know who he was more furious with, Percival for soiling my reputation or the town for believing it. The next day Percival stood on my doorstep, flowers in one hand. No one was more surprised than me when he asked me to marry him. He'd said he would have liked to have had more time to win me over, but he couldn't stand the thought of the whole town looking down on me, thinking the worst.

"He pulled out the prettiest little diamond ring. Told me he'd bought it nearly a month before and would stare at it to give him courage to court me." A pretty pink flush rose in her cheeks. "Took an eyelash and a town of gossips to bring us together."

"So you said yes."

"Not right away. I didn't think I wanted a man in my life. Didn't want to belittle what I had with Edgar. But Percival courted me good and proper, and it wasn't long before I realized old letters and memories weren't the way God meant for a young woman to live her life, so I finally said yes."

"Did you love him?"

Abigail rolled across the bed, lifted a silver framed photo from her nightstand and handed it to Pam. "With all my heart."

Pam stared at the photo. Abigail stood next to a tall burly man with a young boy on her other side. They looked the perfect family.

"David and his wife live in Houston now. I lost my Percival twelve years ago."

Pam watched the peaceful smile spread across Abigail's face. The day Abigail had told her about Edgar, there had been sadness and pain in her eyes. Now, even though she'd lost the man she'd been married to for almost fifty years, there was no sorrow to be found.

Abigail placed the frame back in place and grinned wryly at Pam. "God bless Judith Abernathy."

CHAPTER EIGHTEEN

"**S**o you're just going to give up and move on?"

"Pop." Jeff glanced at the clock on the far wall. He and his father had been going around and around for over thirty minutes. On the bright side, despite the heated debate, his father wasn't showing any signs of a man on the verge of another heart attack. Unfortunately he didn't seem to be running short on energy either. "I told you, I'd already planned to leave once you were back on the job. The board just upped my timetable."

"And what about Pamela Sue? Not defending yourself makes you, and her, look guilty. When you're gone, she's still going to have to hold her head up in this community."

"As Pam herself pointed out, we're in the twenty-first century. I'm the only one this town holds to a higher standard. If anything, I suspect the few old coots who thrive on this sort of gossip will blame me for taking advantage of the young widow."

Jeff didn't think it was possible for his father's jaw to clench any tighter.

"And you're going to just walk away and let the town think the worst of you."

"No, Pop. I have to make sure Pam is taken care of. She's got bigger problems than what a few high-strung neighbors think of her. When I'm sure she's set up with Caleb, I'll move on." He wouldn't mention he planned to stick around in case his replacement needed a little help. The last thing he wanted to give his father was any reason to cling to the hope that this wouldn't be a permanent change.

"Darn it, boy!"

"Harlon Parker." Etta Mae stomped into the room. "You promised me, if I let you and Jeff talk, you'd stay calm."

Jeff resisted the urge to mutter aloud *in what lifetime?*

"He's going to let them push him out."

His mom shot him a didn't-I-teach-you-better glare. At thirty-four the look had the same stomach-churning affect as it had when he was six years old, and she'd caught him cutting his sister's hair while she slept.

"Of course he's not." Etta patted her husband's hand and flashed him her everything-will-be-fine smile. "He's just letting the dust settle. Aren't you, dear?"

A smart man knew when to stand his ground and when to agree with his mother. Lately he seemed to be doing an awful lot of agreeing with his mother, yet he didn't feel all that smart. "I already told Pop I won't be going anywhere until I make sure things are right for Pam."

"See." Etta Mae crossed her arms and grinned so wide he could almost count all her teeth.

"*Hmph*. We'll see," his father grumbled, shook his head at Jeff, then nodded at his mom before walking out of the room. For some reason Jeff had the oddest feeling his mother and father were no longer talking about his job.

***

With daylight lasting well into the late evening, Pam wasn't surprised to see Mrs. McCarthy bending over on all fours working the flower beds. Considering how much time the old woman spent crawling about in the flowers, Pam wondered when weeds had a chance to take root.

This whole mess had started with Jeff waving at Mrs. McCarthy as he'd left Pam's house, which made Mrs. McCarthy as good a place as any for Pam to start her efforts to bring this whole mess to an end.

Hitting the button twice on her key fob to lock the car doors, Pam squared her shoulders, raised her chin, and hoped her smile didn't look as phony as it felt. "Evenin', Mrs. McCarthy."

Weed-pulling fork in hand, her neighbor glanced up from her task and smiled at Pam as though this were any other boring day of the week.

"I wanted to apologize for upsetting you this morning."

Mrs. McCarthy pushed back and sat on her heels. "Upsetting me?"

The woman must have knees of stone.

"Pam, dear?"

"Oh, sorry." Now what? She'd had the bright idea to come over and smooth things out, only she didn't have a clue what to say. "It must have been surprising seeing Pastor Jeff at my house so early this morning."

"I must admit it was a bit of a start." A corner of the older woman's mouth twitched upward hinting at a suppressed smile.

"I imagine it was." Pam squatted and reached for a nearby hand spade. "Mind if I help?"

"Not at all. Sometimes there's nothing quite like getting your hands dirty."

Blades of Bermuda grass had made their way across the lawn edging, and Mrs. McCarthy was carefully digging up the roots. "You know in most places this is considered a weed."

"Really?" Pam picked up a clump of grass, examining it more closely.

"Takes a tough breed to withstand the hard Texas climate."

Something in the old lady's tone made Pam think she wasn't talking about just the lawn. What was it with old people? Did they all talk in riddles and analogies? "I suppose it does."

"While I appreciate the help, I figure you have something on your mind beside my flower beds."

"Yes, well I didn't want you to be under the wrong impression about what you saw."

Euphemia McCarthy lifted her straw hat with one hand and brushed at her forehead with the other, never shifting her gaze from Pam's face.

Pam tried not to fidget under her neighbor's steady gaze. "I can imagine what it must have looked like to you." She hadn't done anything wrong. Nothing inappropriate had happened between her and Jeff, yet because of her, he'd lost his job and probably the respect of a lot of good people. "I was…" What? Troubled? Upset? Teetering on insanity? What the hell was she supposed to say now?

"Lonely?" Euphemia said.

"No!" Pam stabbed the small spade into the dirt. Well, maybe, but now wasn't the time to wander down that path. "I was at the Parkers' house when Pastor Harlon had his attack the other night. Went to the hospital with the family. Since Travis died, I tend to get overly upset when people are hurt or sick." *And I have nightmares.*

Still watching Pam intently, Euphemia fanned herself with her hat.

"I was very upset last night," Pam continued. "Jeff's a good pastor. He listened quietly, and when I fell asleep on the sofa, he chose not to leave me alone and waited till I woke up in the morning to make sure I was better." It was close enough to the truth. Pam just wished it didn't sound so lame.

"Jeff's always had a kind heart." Euphemia McCarthy finally turned her attention back to the flower beds. "He'll make a fine husband, but he deserves a good woman." She slanted a glance in Pam's direction. "Someone who's willing to put him first. Fight for him. There will always be someone in his congregation who will cause him grief. And I've never known a church not to have a high-and-mighty elder breathing down a pastor's neck. Doubt Jeff will escape it any more than Harlon has. Yep, a strong good woman to stand by his side is what that man needs."

A strong good woman? What the heck prompted that? All Pam wanted was to convince her neighbors that nothing happened last night, starting with Mrs. McCarthy. "I'm sure someday he'll meet the right woman, but I don't know how easy it will be for him to find a new job if the church insists on replacing him over this…misunderstanding."

"Replacing him?" Euphemia's gardening utensil froze in the dirt.

"Mr. Haskell came to the church offices this morning. The

board has requested Jeff's resignation."

"I see." The old woman sat back on her heels again. "And you think this is somehow my fault?"

"Oh, no. Not at all." *Liar, liar, pants on fire.*

Euphemia pierced Pam with a glare so sharp she worried the woman could read her thoughts and feelings like an X-ray. "You don't want Jeff to…resign, do you?"

"Of course not." Pam set the gardening spade aside. "Especially since this is *all* my fault. If I hadn't been so upset—"

"Yes, so you mentioned."

"Jeff is an honorable man. He would never… I mean…things aren't like that between us." Just because his smile made her insides tingle had nothing to do with anything.

Euphemia's attention drifted down to where Pam was mindlessly spinning her wedding ring around. "Yes, I can see that."

"Good." Pam pushed to her feet. "Now if I can just convince a few more neighbors and the rest of the town."

"Don't you worry about a thing. Troubles like these always have a way of working themselves out for the best. Most times the simplest solution is right in front of your nose."

"I hope so."

Leaning forward slightly, Mrs. McCarthy sprang to her feet with an ease Pam hadn't expected. The woman not only had knees of stone, but the agility of a ten-year-old.

"Yoga."

"Excuse me?"

"Keeps you limber."

"Oh."

"You should try it." Euphemia peeled off her gloves and tossed them into a nearby bucket. "In the meantime I'll talk to Etta Mae and see what we can do to help. We both want what's best for you and Jeff."

"Thank you." *I think.* Pam feared she already knew what Etta Mae thought best. *Oh, Jeff, how did life get so complicated?*

***

Euphemia McCarthy was true to her word. By the time Pam made it across the street, Euphemia had put away her gardening bucket and was on her way to Etta Mae's.

Pushing open her front door, Pam tripped over Peaches. "And they say dogs are faithful. You know, it's easier for me to actually come into the house if you wait near the door, not in front of it."

With a flick of her tail and a muffled meow, Peaches made her irritation with Pam known and pranced off toward the kitchen.

"Okay, be that way." Besides, she had more important things to worry about than a disgruntled feline. First her neighbors, Mrs. Jackson and Mrs. Harper. Then the board. She'd have to change their minds. One at a time. Away from John Haskell's influence. But who to start with?

One thing at a time. She poured some milk into a bowl. "Better?" she asked.

Peaches nuzzled against Pam's ankles. All was forgiven. If only she could make peace with the board that easily. The sound of the doorbell pulled her away from her thoughts. She wasn't expecting anyone. Not at this hour.

"Jeff."

"I was at Mom's. Mrs. McCarthy came by. She said you spoke to her. She apologized to me for jumping to conclusions."

"I'm glad. One down and half a town to go." Pam waved him inside. "I was just about to make some tea. Care to join me?"

He nodded and followed her into the kitchen. "I spoke with Caleb this morning, but he's leaving town for a couple of weeks."

"Oh." So much for Jeff asking his friend to see her as soon as possible.

"Second honeymoon. Europe."

She reached for the kettle on the stove. "As a kid I dreamed of honeymooning in Europe. Salzburg actually."

"Salzburg?"

"*The Sound of Music* was my favorite movie. I thought it would be romantic to dance in the gazebo."

"Chick flick." Jeff slid into the seat closest to the stove.

"Maybe." She wanted to grin. She'd been tied up in knots all afternoon. Not even her visit with Abigail had eased her mind. The old woman's story had tugged at Pam's heartstrings. Mrs. McCarthy's comment that Pam was lonely should have twisted her already stressed heartstrings more tightly. But the familiar pain that always settled in, when reminded of Travis and all she'd lost, hadn't come. As a matter of fact, after only a few minutes with Jeff, her heart felt light again. "Oh, God."

"What?"

Her hand frozen in midair, holding the empty teakettle, she heard Jeff's chair scrape against the floor seconds before she was struck by the heat of his body beside her.

"Are you okay?" Worry laced his words.

Unable to move, she watched Jeff gently pry the kettle from her tightened grip and set it aside.

With a gentle touch he turned her to face him. "Pam, you're scaring me."

"Jeff," she whispered softly.

Hands on her shoulder, his fingertips moved in a slow soothing motion. "What?"

"No." Hugging her waist, she pulled back. "They're wrong."

He stepped toward her and she stepped back. "Who's wrong?"

"Abigail, Euphemia. They're wrong."

In a frustrated gesture he took a step away and raked a hand through his hair. "I'm sorry, but I'm not following you."

She shook her head. "No, I'm sorry. It's nothing. Really."

"Was it another dream?"

"No." She turned her back to him and squeezed her eyes closed. Her heart pounded against her ribs. Space, distance, her head shouted she needed distance, but her heart craved for him to stay close. Time to think. To understand. Oh, God. How could this happen? How could she want so desperately for him to pull her into his arms, and soothe away all the worries and fears? There was only one man for her. Only one. She turned to face him. "I'm married."

The quirk of his brow told her he was struggling to comprehend. But how could he when she had no idea what to make of the sensations and feelings churning inside her. "I think you should leave."

His puzzled expression morphed into one of sheer panic, and her heart nearly stopped. She didn't want to hurt him. "I'm sorry. I didn't mean… I'm just… I'm sorry."

His body shifted forward and then back, before he finally took a step closer to her. "Something is very wrong. What's the matter?"

Moving with the hesitancy of a large man approaching a frightened child, he took another slow step toward her. By the time he stood so close she could feel his shallow breath on her face, the urge to run away and hide had fled. Chased away by the growing yearning to trust for the second time in her life. "I'm scared."

With the same gentle concern he'd shown her last night, he wrapped her hand in his. "Of what?"

"You."

CHAPTER NINETEEN

Him? His mouth hung open, but words weren't spewing forth. Thoughts tumbled about in his head, but he couldn't seem to settle on which one he should form into a question. How could she be afraid of him? Was it yesterday? His reaction to being close? Was it his touch now? Did she somehow believe the "taking advantage" bull that was racing through town on the ends of wagging tongues? *Good God.*

She pulled away, stepped back, her eyes still locked on his.

His hands raised, about to reach out, to touch, hold her, show her that he couldn't possibly hurt her, when his mind caught up with his actions, and he froze in place. If she's afraid of him, the last thing he should do is try to touch her. But God, how he wanted to hold her, reassure her. Right now he'd sell his soul to have her trust back.

"I wouldn't..." His eyelids fell closed as he searched for words. "Why would you think..." Eyes open again, his gaze settled on hers. The pain and doubt he saw warring inside her stabbed at him, drawing out the words hiding in his heart. "I would never hurt you. Never."

"I know that." Pam swiveled around, took a step, and brushed her palms down the sides of her slacks in a swift jerky motion, before turning back and letting her gaze meet his. "I'm married."

"You said that already."

"I've had the love of a lifetime. I don't need or want another man in my life, a Percival Clarke." Gazes still locked, she took another step back. He lifted a foot to follow. "Please." She raised a hand. "Stay where you are."

If she knew he wouldn't hurt her, then why had she backed away from him until her spine hugged the wall? Why were her eyes growing round with fear as he moved closer?

"I don't understand." Or did he? Waking up in his arms this

morning, kissing him awake. In a hazy dream world she'd thought she was still with her husband. Or had she? "Pam, what exactly are you telling me?"

Slow and steady he moved toward her until he was so close he could feel her ragged breaths blowing sporadically against his collar. When he took her hand in his, her breath hitched, and he felt her pulse skip. The fear he'd seen moments ago in her bright blue eyes faded away. Now, eyes a dark steel blue stared back at him. Eyes filled with hunger, and heaven help him, was that desire?

"I..." Pam blinked, swallowed, and the pulse point in her neck picked up speed. "I shouldn't...but I do."

Feminine logic had never been his strong point, and Pam's gibberish wasn't helping, but there was no denying the look in her eye. He should make sure. Be clear. Leave no room for misunderstandings. He opened his mouth to speak at the same moment her pink-tipped tongue peeked out to moisten tightened lips. All logic, all reason, any sense of decency he might have, flew out the window.

His mouth descended on hers in a rush. Delicate soft lips briefly touched, sparking a need so strong that tongues and teeth clashed in a tangle of heat and desire, threatening to overload his senses. A soft groan filled the air, hers, his, another.

Silky blonde hair sifted through his fingers filling his mind with visions of blankets of blonde hair feathered across his chest, his stomach, his thighs, making his groin ache with need. A feral growl rumbled deep in his chest, and he thrust his tongue harder, faster. Her movements matched his. Hands trailed up and down his back, his arms, fingers twirled along the nape of his neck, raking through his hair, blazing a path down his back again. Teasing at his waist, tugging his shirt. Warm, long fingers dipped along the edge of his slacks drawing slow sensuous swirls on his bare flesh. Firecrackers exploded in his gut.

With every lick, every taste, every groan, he pressed against her. He was hard as a rock and desperate to feel her softness surround him. Shifting his stance, legs spread, hip to hip, she fit with him, man to woman, hard to soft, the way God intended.

God.

On a deep sigh, his head dropped to her shoulder. Hands frozen in tangled blonde curls meekly fell to his sides. Blood pulsing in his veins made a slow, chilling journey north to his brain. What was he thinking?

Once again, he wasn't thinking. At least not with the head on his shoulders. Not since he'd been a randy hormonal guy in college had he thought with the head below his belt.

He lifted his head, dared to look her in the face. Eyes closed, her head leaned back against the wall, her neck extended as though calling for him to take one more taste. One last kiss. But he couldn't, wouldn't. Her chest heaved in labored breaths that matched his own unsteady rhythm.

"Pam…" What? What could he say? I'm sorry? I shouldn't have? And God how he still wanted to. Everything in him screamed to throw out his book of rules and carry this woman upstairs and ravish her until the aching need inside was satisfied. Only he didn't think it possible. "Pam—"

"Feel this." She took his hand, palm open, and pressed it against her chest, holding it in place. An erratic beat thumped, hard, fast, with no sign of slowing down. "I thought it was forever broken."

"Definitely not broken." The urge to lean in, press his lips to hers, and start all over was as strong as his need to breathe. He desperately wanted to show her that her heart wasn't the only thing not broken. But damn it, things were crazy enough. He needed to bring sex into the mix like he needed an entire flock of John Haskells in his life. So far he could still look his father in the eye and say he hadn't broken the laws of God, but if he didn't get a grip and get out of here soon, that "I want you" look in Pam's eye might win. "I think I'd better go home."

Pam nodded, but still held his hand against her heart. He didn't try to move. His feet were rooted to the floor the same way his gaze was glued to hers. What could one last kiss hurt?

***

He did it again. And Lord help her, she didn't want him to stop. His hard muscled body pressed against her. Little fires burned where his fingers touched. Nerves that had lain dormant and dead, now sparked and danced with anticipation. Everything in her yearned for more, needed more, cried for more.

"Yoo-hoo."

Yes. Another touch, another caress. More. So much more.

"Pammy, dear?"

Pammy, dear? What? Who? *Etta Mae*! Pam gasped, mortified her neighbor might catch her pawing at Jeff like a lust-driven teen in the backseat of a Chevy.

"Pammy Sue, hon, is everything all..." Etta Mae Parker and Euphemia McCarthy stood calcified in the kitchen doorway.

Jeff leapt away as though he wore springs instead of shoes.

Pam resisted the urge to smooth her clothes and straighten her hair, and instead stole a glance at the two women.

The expression on Etta's face reminded her of the time her mother had tried to slice a freshly baked loaf of bread with the consistency of a brick. Her mom never did figure out where she'd gone wrong. Next to Etta, still standing stiff as a statue, Euphemia seemed to be swallowing a smile. The tight press of her lips could have been that of an angry woman withholding her wrath, but the laughter in her eyes told Pam that Euphemia was struggling to suppress a broad grin.

Hands in his pockets, Jeff looked tired, rumpled and damn sexy. How were they going to get out of this one?

"We rang the bell," Etta finally said.

"Twice," Euphemia added, still munching on her bottom lip.

"We had an idea." Narrow eyed, Etta stared at her son. "You said you'd be back in a few minutes. I thought..." Her eyes darted to Pam and back. "I thought Pammy here might be more upset than she showed, need some emotional support, but I see you've already taken care of that."

Euphemia snorted and quickly covered her mouth with her hand, the curve of her lips still visible.

"Ma, this isn't what you're thinking."

"Oh, really." Etta folded her arms. "Then by all means, explain to me why you were plastered like wallpaper against Pamela Sue."

"I…" Jeff blew out a breath, as much at a loss for words as Pam.

"It's my fault." Pam pushed away from the wall.

"No. I'm the one who started it." Jeff shook his head.

"I'm not going to let you take the blame for this. If I hadn't flipped out, you wouldn't have tried to comfort me."

"You didn't flip out." His attention focused on Pam, Jeff stepped closer. "Something frightened you."

"I was being silly. It was nothing." She waved him off, hoping he wouldn't make her say it out loud. They were wrong. They had to be wrong. She couldn't fall in love with Jeff. She couldn't. She loved Travis. She would always love Travis.

"Pam." He closed the gap between them, his hands gently resting on her shoulders, his thumbs once again drawing soothing circles. "Tell me what spooked you."

She closed her eyes and tried to ignore the tingling sensations ricocheting through her system, again. "We'd be here all day. Haven't you learned? I spook easy."

"Damn." Wrapping his arms around her, Jeff pulled her into a tight embrace. Her face snuggled into his shoulder. His chin rested on her head. The swirling motions of his hands meant to soothe not to arouse. "I don't want you spooked. What are Abigail and Euphemia wrong about?"

"Me?" The glint in Euphemia's eyes faded away.

Pam had forgotten the two women were still standing in the doorway. From the way Jeff held her close, he seemed to have forgotten about the two house invaders as well.

"I haven't said a word," Euphemia sputtered, "And who is Abigail?"

"I think he means Abigail Clarke." Arms still crossed, Etta kept her gaze on her son.

"At the old Keller place? That woman has a good twenty years on me." She turned rather ruffled to Jeff. "I barely know of Abigail Clarke."

"It was nothing." Pam pulled away from the safe circle of Jeff's arms and turned the fire on under the kettle. "Would anyone like some tea?"

"Tea?" Euphemia flipped her attention from Pam to Jeff to Etta and back.

Etta finally spoke. "I think I'd better get back and check on Harlon. I don't like leaving him alone for long in his condition. He's liable to raid the pantry and eat all the doughnuts." Without waiting for anyone to agree or join her, she turned and made her way down the hall and out the door, leaving Euphemia gaping openmouthed in the kitchen doorway.

"Well." Euphemia glanced at the kitchen table, seemed to consider her options, nodded her head, and took a seat.

"Jefferson, dear. Why don't you go check on your mother? I think she's rather upset."

"I'm sure Dad—"

"I'll keep an eye on Pam. You run on now." Euphemia pushed back her chair and stepped up beside Pam. "We'll be just fine, won't we, dear?"

This wasn't what Pam wanted. She didn't want to talk to Euphemia, or Abigail, or Etta Mae, or anyone. All she wanted was to be left alone to sort out this mess. *Oh, Jeff.*

She didn't dare look at him. Didn't want to see the hurt and worry in his eyes. "We'll be fine. Miss Euphemia's right. You'd better go check on your mom. She looked to be pretty upset."

Clutching a teacup in each hand, tight enough to shatter them, Pam waited for him to agree, to move away, and hoped he wouldn't come close. A single touch and she'd fall into his arms again like a broken doll. But she wasn't broken. Just confused. Confused by the ramblings of a couple of old ladies and the physical yearning for the touch of a man.

That's all it was. Of course. It was bound to happen. She'd been alone for a long time. Her sister had told her over and over that she was young, too young to be alone. That's all this was. Natural sexual drive. That's all.

Setting the teacups on the counter, she found the strength to turn and face Jeff. She'd be okay now. A visit with Euphemia McCarthy would be nice. Pleasant. With Jeff out of the room, her nerves would settle. She'd be fine.

He hadn't said a word to her. Hadn't agreed or argued. His gaze had remained steady on her back. She'd felt it, known it without a doubt, but turned to face him nonetheless.

All the air in her lungs lodged in her throat. Sea-green eyes filled with worry, hurt, and, dear God, love burned through her like lasers.

Her mind begged, please don't come close, please don't touch me, just go.

With a short nod, as though he'd actually read her thoughts, understood her pleas, he took a short step toward the hall. "I'll be back as soon as I make sure Mom understands."

Words weren't coming. She nodded, sure if she opened her mouth, she'd beg him to stay, not to leave her. Rooted to the floor she watched his back go down the hall and out the door.

The latch clicked shut, the teakettle whistled, piercing the thick silence. Euphemia reached for the shrilling kettle, and Pam shoved the urge to run after him down deep as far as she could. Just sexual tension. Nothing more.

And if she could convince anyone else of that, she might as well sell lakeside property in Vegas.

***

Every ounce of blood in his veins hummed with need, want, and desire. This wasn't supposed to happen. Or was it? He'd known for some time now how he felt about Pam. His need to protect her, care for her, save her, ran much deeper than the concern of a pastor for his parishioner or neighbor. He'd admitted to himself already that he was in love with her. Wanted her. Needed her. But he couldn't be anyone's savior.

Besides, she was still in love with her husband. Or was she? She certainly hadn't kissed him like a woman in love with another man. The look, no, the longing in her eyes seemed to be so much more than that of a woman looking for a little sexual diversion.

Her heart. The feel of the frantic thrum still lingered on his fingertips. *I thought it was forever broken.* Pam's words bounced around in his head like a child in a carnival air tent. What did she mean? Was she ready to let him in? To make room for another man? For him? Or had she already?

"Oh, God, what a mess." He pushed open the door to his parents' house.

"That might fall under the category of understatement." Etta Mae stood in the hall with her arms crossed. "Did you lie to me?"

He shook his head. "No. Where's Pop?"

"Asleep."

His gaze drifted down the hall to where his father slept in his room. His father would never have let this happen.

"He's not perfect, you know."

His attention snapped back to his mother. She hadn't moved. Not an inch. But he realized now her stiff stance had little to do with anger or even reproof. All he saw in her steady gaze was the loving concern of a mother.

Etta Mae pointed to the living room. "I think it's time you and I sat down, and had a chat."

"Ma, not now. I just came by to check on you, I mean on Dad. Well, on both of you." He sighed. "I should get back. I know this all seems crazy, but something's wrong with Pam. She's upset. I need to—"

"Sit. There are some things you need to learn, and it has nothing to do with teaching Joshua Meechum how to play baseball. Though that might not be such a bad idea."

"What?"

"Your father wants you to teach young Joshua how to play

ball. He thinks that will show you once and for all you've got a strong calling, and you can't let the devil scare you off."

"Ma—"

"What you need is to be told the truth."

CHAPTER TWENTY

uphemia McCarthy stirred sugar into a teacup. "What do you want to discuss first, what I'm wrong about, how nothing is going on between you and young Jeff, or that Etta Mae and I came up with a plan?"

"A plan?"

Pam's older neighbor nodded her head. "Thought you might go there first. We made a list."

"A list?"

"Of folks in town Harlon has spent the night with. Sometimes several nights."

"Excuse me?" Maybe soon Pam would be able to come up with more than two-word sentences, but at the moment her nerve endings were still reeling from Jeff's kiss, and her brain was frantically trying to make sense of her jumbled feelings. Keeping up with Euphemia's rambling wasn't going well.

"A couple of years ago Betty Ferguson's husband was flown to a military hospital in Germany after an explosion in Iraq. Did you hear about that?"

Pam shook her head, reaching for the teacup Euphemia slid across the table to her.

"Harlon spent two days, unchaperoned, with poor Betty. The woman was inconsolable. According to Etta Mae, Betty was convinced her husband was dead, and the army didn't want to tell her."

"Oh, dear."

"Then there was Alice Healey, the time her husband and boy went missing for two days in the woods. Things didn't look so good when the search party found little J.J.'s backpack washed ashore down river. And remember Heather Goodstein? The way that woman carried on when her calico was run over by Wilma Haskell, you'd think it had been her firstborn. And if that wasn't enough for Harlon to deal with, poor Wilma felt guiltier than if she *had* run over a child. Harlon wanted to split himself in two."

"Did Jeff's dad have to spend the night with Wilma Haskell also?"

"Two. His high-and-mightiness John Haskell was at a business conference in Chicago. Etta and I figure Harlon earned extra crowns in heaven for that one."

"How many people are on your list?"

"Actually there are two lists. I'm supposed to call the folks on my list, and Etta Mae is going to phone the names on hers. Between us, we've got four of the seven members of the church board of directors. Five if you count Mrs. John Haskell."

"I don't understand how this helps anything."

"Ever heard the old story about casting stones and glass houses?"

"But those people had nothing to do with Jeff."

"Those people were counting on the support and reassurance of their pastor."

"Their married pastor. It's not the same. Jeff's a single man."

"What? Don't you think married men still have peckers?"

Pam felt the heat rise up her neck and settle in the tips of her ears. Of all the things she'd expected her sweet old-fashioned neighbor to say, *that* wasn't one of them.

"Oh, put your eyes back in your head. By the time Etta and I get through, most of the town won't be willing to point a finger at you or young Jeff for fear of seeing three fingers pointing back at them or a dearly loved relative. This town can't afford to lose Jeff."

"No, they can't. Thank you."

"Good, now that we've settled that, I want to know if nothing is goin' on between you and young Jeff, why did his mama and I find the two of you plastered together like a grilled cheese sandwich without the cheese?"

***

"Mom!"

"Kenny?" Etta Mae pushed to her feet and pivoted toward the front hall. Within seconds her youngest son had her scooped into his arms.

"How is he?"

"Your father is fine. He's taking a nap." Etta released her grip on her baby and patted his chest as she stepped back. "I told you not to leave school."

"It'll be okay, Mom." Kenny kissed his mother's cheek then turned to his big brother for a backslapping hug. "How's everyone else holding up?"

Now wasn't that a loaded question? "Just fine, little brother. But Ma's right. Pop's not going to be happy you're missing class on his account."

"Not missing anything. I only have one class on Fridays, and the professor canceled to go to some conference. I figure it was a sign from heaven and took off the minute my last class ended. I've got two whole days with the family before I have to drive back Sunday."

Jeff gave his brother another hug, only this time he squeezed him good and hard. "Glad to have you home."

"Yeah," Kenny added. "Me too."

"You must be hungry." Etta patted her young son's arm and, without waiting for a reply, headed to the kitchen. "Probably haven't had a decent meal since you left home."

Jeff leaned into his brother and whispered, "That would certainly explain why you look a bit thick in the middle." A smile filled his face for the first time in hours. His kid brother was about two inches taller than him and had the shoulders of a middle linebacker. They shared the same green eyes and famous Parker smile that for generations could supposedly charm a schoolmarm out of her virtue. But anyone could see Kenny did not look like a starving student. "So how many pounds have you put on?"

"Seven, but don't tell, Mom."

"Your secret is safe with me." *Secret*. Jeff needed to get back next door. This was turning into one hell of a day. God knows what would have happened with Pam if his mother hadn't walked in. He needed to get to the bottom of what he'd done to spook Pam, again. And making things worse, his mother was in überprotector mode. He should have stuck with banking; then all he'd have to worry about was a national economic crisis. "Listen, Kenny, I'd love to stick around, but I've got a situation to deal with."

"No problem, man. You know where to find me." Kenny slapped his brother on the back and followed the path his mom had taken to the kitchen.

Jeff cut across the lawn to Pam's and took the porch steps two at a time. He both knocked and rang the bell. By the time he considered that might have been overkill, Pam stood beside the open door.

"Hi."

"Yeah, hi." Great. He'd reverted to the verbal skills of a lovesick fourteen-year-old. "May I come in?"

"Oh, of course." Pam moved back and pulled the door open wider. "Mrs. McCarthy and I are in the kitchen."

"Actually"—Euphemia McCarthy walked up beside Jeff—"Mrs. McCarthy was just leaving. But if you ask me, which I know you won't, so I'm gonna tell you anyhow. You two need to stop kidding yourselves, because you're not fooling anyone else. Just put a ring on her finger and marry the girl. Easiest answer is always the one right in front of you."

The woman gave a quick nod and walked out the door. Pam flushed pink, and Jeff was sure he'd almost swallowed his tongue. Marry?

"Apparently we fit like a grilled cheese sandwich without the cheese." Pam pushed the door shut and turned into the living room. She flopped onto the nearest sofa as though she carried a thousand-pound weight.

"Excuse me?"

"I just spent the last few minutes explaining, without much success I might add, why what she and your mom saw wasn't really what they thought they saw, since it wasn't really anything, because I'm a married woman, and you're my pastor, and I don't need a Percival Clarke or a Judith Abernathy in my life."

"I see." Slowly he moved through the room and took a seat across from her. Leaning forward, he rested his elbows on his knees, his hands clasped together almost as if in prayer. He decided, sometimes, the best thing to say was nothing at all. So he waited.

***

The silence was excruciating. All fifteen seconds of it. "I loved Travis with all my heart." Pam spoke in a near whisper. "All I ever wanted from the time I was six years old was to be his wife."

Jeff nodded.

"I didn't even care about the dress, the party, the church. All the trappings most girls dream of for years. I just wanted to be Mrs. Travis Dawson."

Again Jeff gave a slow steady nod.

"Mom used to say things like, 'Being married is hard work, missy,' or 'The real world isn't a fairy tale.' Sure Travis and I had our disagreements, like anyone I suppose, but it wasn't hard work. I was happy."

"Are you happy now?"

"Happier than I've been in a long time."

"Why?"

You. The reply popped into her head so fast she barely had enough time to stop herself from saying it out loud. She studied his face. To a casual acquaintance his expression appeared calm, relaxed. The steady pastor any parishioner would be comfortable trusting. But those closest to him would know better. She could see the concern in his eyes. The way his fingers linked together, and his thumbs tapped out his silent battle. Her heart nearly stopped. When had she gone from casual acquaintance to the ranks of those who knew better?

His thumbs stilled. Everything in the room was so quiet. *Oh,*

Jeff. What do you want from me?

Jeff? Not Travis. Her head tilted up, she focused on the ceiling. When had she stopped? "I…I don't talk to him anymore."

"Him?"

"Travis." She waited for the pained look of restrained impatience that always came over her family's face when she mentioned talking to Travis. It never came. No reproach. No pity. "I don't understand what's happening to me." She dropped her head in her hands. "Abigail is right. Only I don't have a Judith Abernathy. I have a Euphemia McCarthy."

***

Finally she'd circled back to her ramblings about Abigail and Euphemia. But who was Judith Abernathy? Jeff barely had enough time to formulate his first question when the phone rang, drawing Pam into the kitchen.

"Greg! Hi."

He watched a thin smile slowly grow wider.

"Your voice sounds really good right now."

From where he sat he couldn't be sure, but it looked like she was blinking back tears.

"I'm good… Really I am… Just one bad dream…" Her smile slipped. "Would I lie to you? … Oh, I don't know. Let's see. The day you called to tell me about winning that big landfill case. It was a crazy night. The pastor next door had to be rushed to the hospital… Hmm, well, let me think. Four days ago? … Probably triggered by the hospital and all that."

An odd sensation in his gut told Jeff to move closer to the kitchen. Pay more attention to the conversation. He couldn't place what was bothering him, but he'd had this feeling enough to know he was missing something. Something important.

The phone trapped between Pam's ear and shoulder, her left hand holding a sponge, her right hand scrubbing away at what to him looked like already clean kitchen counters, Pam reminded him of a woman franticly preparing for an onslaught of houseguests. If only the nervous energy could be blamed on something so innocent.

Turning a fraction to work on another section of counter space, Pam spotted him propped against the kitchen doorway, watching, listening. One corner of her mouth lifted in a halfhearted attempt to smile. Eyes quickly lowered, she hurriedly tossed the sponge into the little rubber holder at the side of the sink. The phone now gripped firmly in one hand, she straightened to her full height. "Listen, now's not a good time. I have company. I'll call you in a few days and see how Southern Fancy does." Pam nodded agreement to words he couldn't hear, mumbled a quiet bye and disconnected the call.

"Southern Fancy?" Jeff slid his hands into his pockets. They were safer there.

"A racehorse." Pam set the receiver into the base unit and leaned back against the sink. "Greg was Travis' partner. You remember me telling you the firm was running low on funds during a particularly long and expensive case?"

"Mmm." Jeff nodded.

"Well, Greg got the idea to invest in a racehorse. At first Travis ranted like the father of the bride at a shotgun wedding. The frivolousness of it all. I mean who spends all their savings on a racehorse? Especially when money was so tight. But it wasn't the firm's money, so Travis had to hold his tongue."

"How'd that work?"

"Not so good."

"What happened?"

"Nothing in particular. But the tension was growing."

Jeff's stomach flipped. That earlier odd sensation nearly had him gripped by the throat. What was he missing? "Wasn't this Greg the guy who saved you?"

Pam nodded, dropped her gaze to the floor, and took a deep breath. "I can't go there. Not now."

"Sorry." He pulled his hands from his pockets, stepped to the side and waved an arm toward the living room. When Pam brushed passed him, the urge to reach out, grab her, and pull her against him shot through him like a rocket. Quickly, he shoved his hands back in his pockets. If he dared touch her, he'd have to kiss her, and he knew as sure as his name was Jefferson Davis Parker that if he did that, this time he wouldn't stop.

Halfway to the sofa, the doorbell rang. From over Pam's shoulder he could see the tall good-looking kid. Well, at twenty-two Kenny probably couldn't be called a kid anymore.

"May I help you?" Pam asked.

"You must be Pammy Sue. I'm Kenny Parker. My mother gave me this to bring over. Said you two needed real food." Holding a covered casserole, Kenny stuck both arms straight out passing the dish off to Pam, then turned to his brother and flashed the Parker smile. "I'm not even going to ask why I've been given strict instructions not to leave this house until you do. But out of curiosity, would it have anything to do with why Mrs. McCarthy is at our kitchen table talking wedding plans with Mom?"

***

Kenny wasn't sure whose mouth came closest to hitting the floor. "Do you two need to sit?"

Pammy Sue seemed to struggle to snap her jaw shut before offering a weak nod. Jeff on the other hand looked ready to swoop Pammy Sue off her feet and carry her away to heaven-knows-where. Though the bedroom struck him as a pretty strong contender.

Hands in his pocket, Jeff followed Pam to the sofa, started to sit beside her when, halfway to the cushion, he straightened and moved over a place. *Interesting.*

Kenny took the seat opposite the sofa. "Let me take a stab at this. Are we talking shotgun wedding?"

"No!" Two voices echoed.

"It's not what you're thinking." Jeff let out a heavy sigh. "It's all a misunderstanding."

Pammy Sue whipped her head around, gaze locking onto his brother Jeff.

How could this man be so much older than him and such an

idiot?

"I made an error in judgment, and the church board has asked for my resignation."

"Ooh." Ken winced. "I'll take the short version, please."

By the time Jeff and Pammy Sue finished recounting the last twenty-four hours, Kenny thought he had a pretty good picture of what was going on. "I know as the youngest Parker my opinion doesn't count for much, but I gotta admit, I'm with Mrs. McCarthy on this one. If you announce your plans to tie the knot, then there's no fuel for the gossip. Besides, any moron can see you two are crazy about each other."

"I'm married," Pammy Sue muttered. And Kenny thought he could see a piece of his brother's heart break off and whither.

"You mean *were* married?" Kenny asked.

Pam looked flustered—or was it startled? If he didn't know better, the way her eyes momentarily rounded before her brow creased to form a perfect V, he'd swear he'd just told the woman something she didn't know.

"It doesn't matter." Jeff sprang up from his seat, his hand rubbing the back of his neck. "I'm leaving the church anyway. Going back to the climbing the corporate ladder."

"You can't!" Pammy Sue bolted to his side.

"You don't understand."

"Try me."

"This town needs my Dad, not me."

"Mrs. McCarthy doesn't think so. She and your mom concocted a plan to change the board's mind."

"They what?"

"They came up with a plan for a few well-placed phone calls. That's what they came over to tell us."

Jeff's face pinched as though he'd swallowed a mouthful of sour milk. "I'll talk to them. I know how mom can be on a crusade."

Kenny knew exactly what his brother was talking about. Their mom on a mission was worse than a pit bull on a steak bone, but his dear big brother was missing the point here. Though he had little doubt Mom and Dad both would face their worst fears to save Jeff's job at the church, Kenny was willing to bet his degree that his mother's primary mission involved a church wedding, not a church office.

"Jeff." Pam's hand rested on Jeff's forearm.

"I'm sorry." Jeff closed his eyes a fraction longer than a blink. "I don't know how to fix this."

"Get married." Kenny leaned back and crossed his arms. "Seems to make sense to everyone except you two."

Pam and Jeff shot him a stunned glare that screamed *What planet are you from?*

"Hear me out." He raised his hand to silence the impending argument. "And feel free to correct me, if I get anything wrong. There are several reasons why people get married, and most often there are a completely different set of reasons people stay married."

Jeff didn't flinch; Pam gave a weak nod.

"We'll start with love, desire, sex, security, friendship, and probably another dose of sex and desire."

"Little brother—"

"I said hear me out. Then you have trust, friendship, love, respect, comfort, companionship, did I mention love?"

Pam nodded; Jeff glared.

"Feel free to tell me which one of those does not apply to you. Because from where I'm standing, you have the flash fire to get you to the altar and the steady flame to keep you there."

"You don't understand," Jeff took a step back, away from Pam's touch.

"No." Kenny waved an arm at his brother. "Don't pull away. Stand next to her. Take her hand in yours. Better yet, hold her in your arms, then look me in the eye and tell me you don't want this woman in the rest of your life."

"My life is going to change. I'll be starting over in a new career. An inexperienced old man competing with bright young minds. Somewhere far enough away where people don't think of me as the wayward pastor." Jeff turned his attention to his brother. "Pam came home to Hope's Corner looking for peace and to be close to her family. She needs that safe harbor and help, professional help, to finally put her past behind her. Not more upheaval. I'm not the man she needs. Not now."

"I didn't hear you don't want her." Kenny quirked an eyebrow at his big brother.

"Of course he wants me. He's a man. What man doesn't want sex?" Pam sank onto the nearby sofa.

"Is that what all of this is about?" Kenny directed his question to Pam.

Her cheeks turned pink, and her gaze dropped, but she didn't respond.

Jeff shifted in her direction before stopping in place. "I told you, Kenny. It's just a blown-out-of-proportion misunderstanding."

"Is that it?" Kenny kept his gaze on Pam.

"Just a misunderstanding," she repeated.

Their mom made it look so easy. One well-placed lecture and all shifted as it should be. He doubted a lead pipe could knock any sense into these two. Maybe he should just go home and let nature have a shot at them? "Well, if that's all there is to it, then I guess there's no reason I can't go home."

"You should go with him." Pam stood and smiled at Jeff. "I wouldn't want to give Etta Mae anything else to worry about."

"What about you? Are you okay?" Jeff took a half step, then stopped short, again, and shoved his hands in his pockets, again.

"I'm good. Really I am. I'm sure by tomorrow everyone will come to their senses."

And pigs will fly. Kenny resisted the urge to roll his eyes.

Jeff hitched a shoulder, hands still in his pockets. "If you're sure?"

"Positive." Pam nodded and smiled a little brighter.

"I'll check on you tomorrow then?"

"Sure."

"Okay, then. Tomorrow."

"Tomorrow."

Good heavens, this could go on all night. How old was his big brother? "We'd better get going before Mom and Mrs. McCarthy reserve the church."

"God, don't remind me." Jeff spun around and moved toward the door at a quick clip. Pulling open the door, he paused to glance back at Pam. "Lock the door behind me."

This time her smile seemed more genuine. "Good night."

On the front porch Jeff turned to his brother. "How bad is it?"

"Is what?"

"Mom and Mrs. McCarthy?"

"That depends."

"On what?"

"Do you believe in long or short honeymoons?"

CHAPTER TWENTY-ONE

Abigail Clarke was laughing so hard, Pam feared the woman might burst a blood vessel. "I fail to see what's so funny."

"Grilled cheese without the cheese. I'd like to meet this Euphemia McCarthy."

Pam smiled. "I suppose, if she weren't talking about me, I might find some humor in the analogy."

"That's my girl. Laugh lines show a life well lived. Worry lines mean too much of life was wasted. You shouldn't fret so."

"I can't help it. This whole mess is all my fault." Pam dipped her French fry in ketchup and took a bite.

"I suppose trouble, like beauty, is in the eye of the beholder. Some folks see trouble coming and think only of the challenges. Others see the opportunities. Though I suppose in some ways, it does feel like learning to drive."

"Excuse me?"

"Getting married. When you learn to drive, you find yourself behind the wheel of this big ominous machine with no idea how to operate it. There's a long road ahead of you, yet you have no idea where it's taking you. But you know if you ride the clutch or grind the gears, or any other number of mistakes, you can do serious damage. Same with marriage. The future is open to you, yet any number of mistakes along the way can leave people hurt. Lots to worry about if you let yourself dwell on the unknowns."

"I never worried about marrying Travis." She swallowed the last fry and shoved the crumpled wrappings from her lunchtime burger into the paper bag.

"Children don't think ahead. You were barely more than a child the first time you got married."

First time? The only time. There was only one man for Pam. One love of her life.

"Honey, you're thinking too hard." Abigail brushed her thumb across Pam's brow until she felt her forehead relax. "My Edgar was a strong handsome man. I loved him with every fiber of my being. When Percival came courting after the incident with Judith Abernathy, I was horrified. No woman wants to marry a man to appease town gossip. But worse still, to betray the love of Edgar. I couldn't do that."

"But you did marry Percival."

Abigail smiled. "I did. But I didn't make it easy on the poor man. Daddy was furious with the entire situation. Being a man of his times, he thought it only right a girl should marry. Percival had asked for my hand, and Daddy was more than happy to get the wedding over with sooner than later. Didn't make no never mind to him if the groom was only proposing out of a misplaced sense of duty. But it mattered to me."

"I thought you said Percival had been working up the nerve to court you anyway?

"Oh, he said he was, but I didn't believe him. I thought he was just being noble. Though I wouldn't face it at the time, I'd already developed feelings for the man. I knew how good, and kind, and dear he was. It would have been just like him to put a woman's reputation and honor before his own feelings and happiness. Yes, I knew he was a good man even then."

Abigail smiled and for a few seconds Pam knew the older woman had gone off to someplace only she and Percival had ever been.

"Anyway." Abigail rubbed her hands across her thighs and pushed to her feet. "Daddy and I reached a compromise. I'd let Percival court me proper, and Daddy would put away the shotgun. Every night Percival and David would have supper at our house. Then Daddy or one of my brothers would take David off to watch the horses, or some other chore they'd come up with, while Percival and I sat on the front porch. Sometimes we'd go into town to see the new picture show. Those nights were a big hoo-ha. Dinner out and all.

"As each week passed, something inside shifted. I knew it, felt it, but I refused to accept it. Loving Percival, giving him my all, could only mean that my love for Edgar wasn't everything I'd believed it to be. A lie. I couldn't live with that."

The words sliced through Pam. A lie? She'd promised to love Travis for the rest of her life. She'd loved him with all her heart. That wasn't a lie. It couldn't be.

Taking a seat on the edge of the bed, Abigail held the silver-framed photo of her family. "I'd always wanted children. As my heart filled with more love for Percival, I thought maybe Edgar would forgive me if I married to have children. After all, Edgar loved me. He'd want to give me whatever made me happy. He'd want me to have children. I was starting to look for any justification I could. I hadn't admitted it to myself yet, but deep down, I wanted to marry Percival. I wanted to be his wife in every way."

"So you married him to have children?"

Abigail's grin grew. "I married him because of children, but not to have children."

"I don't understand."

"Sally Cooper."

Pam waited, hands in her lap, her right hand twirling the gold band on her left ring finger.

"Sally and Benjamin Cooper were blessed with fertility. Nine young'uns in all. Right about the time Percival and I were courting, Sally'd given birth to number seven. Or was it eight? No matter. They were a good Christian family. Benjamin was a hard worker but feeding a family that size wore hard on a man. Those of us who had life a little easier would stop by and bring things to help out. Daddy had done some butchering. He gave me a side of pork to take over with a trinket for the new baby. Sally, being prideful and all, gave the expected objections, but in the end, she'd agreed that my Daddy had butchered more meat than our family could eat or store, and taking the extra food off our hands would save it from spoiling."

"Your dad did that on purpose?"

"Daddy was as good a man as they came. He set the standard for the men in my life." Abigail set the photo she'd been holding back in its place. "That baby was the cutest Cooper yet. They were all picture-perfect. Curly gold locks, big blue eyes, chubby cheeks, and grins that could win over the devil. I remember that day so clearly. The older children were at school. Most of the younger ones were napping in the other room. Little Becky came around the corner, her steps slow and minced. I guess you could call it a three-year-old's version of tiptoeing. Her gaze shifted back and forth from her mama to the new baby. Sally didn't say anything, but I knew she'd seen Becky sneaking up on her. When Becky finally stood beside the bed, Sally handed me the baby and patted her lap for Becky to climb up.

"That child's face lit up like the afternoon sun. Sally held Becky tight in her arms and softly said, 'Who do I love more than all the stars in the sky?' Becky scrunched her face and almost whispered her response. 'Me?' Sally squeezed her little girl and smiled. 'I love you more than all the stars in the sky forever and ever.'

"I didn't think a grin could grow any brighter, but it did. Becky kissed her mama's cheek, said, 'I love you forever and ever too,' and then scurried off to play. Sally watched me holding the baby for a long moment before she finally said, 'With every child my heart is so full of love, I wonder how can I possibly have any love left for another? But the heart is an amazing thing. It can hold more love than anybody can give.' That's when I realized the truth."

"The truth?"

"I didn't have to stop loving Edgar to let myself love Percival. There'd be no dishonor in moving on. Little Becky and her mom helped me to see that Edgar would always be alive in his corner of my heart."

His corner of my heart. His corner. Travis's corner of her heart. It would always be his. Always.

"I have to go!" Pam shot up, gave Abigail a quick peck on the cheek, and flew out the door. She had to talk to Jeff, before he did something stupid.

***

Jeff sat at the farthest table in the back corner of the Last Chance Café. After spending the better part of the night tossing and turning and beating up on his pillow, he'd given up on the idea of getting any rest and decided a gallon of coffee at a neutral location was required. He wasn't sure why he'd grabbed his Bible on his way out the door, but he had.

Instead of working through his next plan of action, he found himself sipping coffee and reading through the first book of Romans. If any of the folks coming and going had thought to stop and say something to him, spotting him nose deep in the Good Book had given them reason to walk by without so much as a nod. Halfway through lunchtime and the book of Ephesians, the place was humming with activity. He dared glance up just in time to see Alice Healey pulling out a chair at the table beside him. Their eyes met for only a fraction of a second, but it was long enough for her to drop her purse on the seat and turn, walking in his direction. He should never have looked up.

Steeling himself for what would no doubt be the first onslaught of public reprimands he would have to endure until the scandal passed by, Jeff closed his Bible and forced a pleased-to-see-you smile. His chair scraped against the floor as he stood. "Mrs. Healey."

"Don't you be getting up on my account." Alice waved him off. "I don't want to interrupt, but I wouldn't forgive myself if I didn't take at least a few moments to let you know how much I hope you change your mind."

"Excuse me?"

"About moving on to pastor another church. Mabel was just telling me that she'd heard you were planning on moving on. Leaving us." Alice paused to wave at her sister-in-law taking a seat across the room.

Fortunately for Jeff, the other woman was accompanied by the Friday Afternoon Garden Club, or he'd have no doubt had Alice and her sister-in-law at his side. Though the longer he chatted with Alice, the possibility of being surrounded by the entire garden club loomed more heavily.

"It would be a crying shame if you ask me."

"Yes, well, that's not totally—"

"Oh, I know this isn't a very exciting place for such a handsome young man as yourself," she interrupted, "but I just love seeing how the younger folks have been filling the pews on Sundays."

"I don't know that I can take—"

"Why just last week, Sarah Gibson told me how much she appreciated your sermon from the book of Proverbs. The one you did about a month or so ago. Said the moment she'd gotten home, she pulled out her Bible and started reading. Prattled on about grabbin' a mad dog by the ears, and how she'd never realized how much could be learned about raising children by really reading the Bible. That's why she and her boys have been at church every Sunday since. I love your daddy to death, and I'll never be able to thank him and your mama enough, for how he stood by me and kept me grounded when my little J.J. went missing down river. But we all have so been looking forward to the day we'll be blessed with the gifts of both Pastors Parker. It just seems a shame to me, if having your daddy back means losing you. Just a shame."

Jeff didn't get to say another word. He couldn't explain he wasn't leaving for another church; he was leaving the church altogether. Or that any spurt in attendance was more likely coincidence than his doing. No, Alice Healey had already turned about, grabbed her husband by the arm, still mumbling about what a shame and meeting up with the garden club. The deep breath her husband blew out told Jeff that he was resigned to being the sole man at a tableful of gabbing gardeners. Jeff was almost tempted to throw Earl Healey a lifesaver and invite the poor man to join him. Almost.

"She's right, you know." Redding Foster slid a plate of Mabel's beef stew on Jeff's table. "I know folks have been talking. And I don't claim to understand what happened with you and Pammy Sue, but I'd like to think I know you well enough to know it ain't what some folks have been saying."

It took Jeff a few moments to realize his old baseball coach was waiting for an answer. "Thank you. Your support means a lot to me."

"Then I'm right, ain't I? You ain't been dipping your toe in those waters?"

Jeff had to laugh. Not loud enough to gather attention but just enough to feel a little better. "No, sir. I haven't been dipping my toe in any waters. Things aren't always the way they look."

"Good. Now that we've straightened that out, are you at least thinking about it?"

Jeff felt surprise widen his eyes. "You *want* me to…" He couldn't bring himself to say *dip his toe in the waters* again, and he certainly couldn't bring himself to say *have sex with*.

"Did I say that?" Praise God, Redding didn't make Jeff finish his sentence.

Jeff nodded. When the café owner's eyes narrowed, Jeff changed his mind and shook his head.

"I said *think*. You can do a lot worse than Pammy Sue. That's a woman who could keep a man happy for a lifetime. A married lifetime. Like Ms. Healey said, right here in Hope's Corner. You think on that." Again Jeff didn't get a chance to reply, before Redding had turned on his heel and made his way to the kitchen.

Back in his seat, his Bible open again to Ephesians Chapter three, Jeff found his mind wandering away from the words on the page. What Alice Healey had said played over in his mind. *Younger folks filling the pews.* Even his sister-in-law Terri had said something about his sermons and the younger generation. With everything on his mind, Jenny Buckner, Pam's nightmares, not letting his dad down, and then putting him in the hospital, Jeff hadn't really paid much attention to church attendance. Could these women be right? Was he really making a difference? Dear God, did that mean his father was right? This has always been Jeff's true calling?

On the page before him, Ephesians 3:20 seemed to shout at him. *He who is able to do exceedingly abundantly above all you ask or think.* That's what he'd always been taught to think. To expect from God. Exceedingly, abundantly, above. Jeff raised his eyes to the ceiling. Maybe he did still believe God answered prayers. *Okay, Father, I'm asking. Is my dad right? Am I making a mistake walking away without a fight?*

"Mind a little company?" Pam rested her hands on the top of the seat across from him.

"Of course not." He stood and pulled out the chair for her. "Decided not to brown bag it today?"

Pam smiled. "Egg salad sandwich and carrot sticks are in a brown bag in the fridge at church."

The way she hesitated, stared at him, almost as though she were seeing him for the first time, made him want to check if he had stew broth on his chin.

"You really do know me well, don't you?" she finally continued.

"Because I know you usually bring your lunch to work?"

"That's part of it." She closed her eyes, blew out a soft slow breath, and lifted her gaze to meet his. "I had lunch with Abigail today. Didn't get much sleep last night—"

"Me either," he cut in.

"Well, actually, I guess I didn't get any sleep at all."

"Me either." He took a sip of his cold coffee.

"We need to talk."

He leaned back and set his clasped hands on the table. "Okay."

"No. I don't mean here." Her gaze darted quickly about, scanning the room. Then she leaned forward and lowered her voice. "I want to talk about…" She glanced around the room again, as though ready to share government secrets. "Before you make any decisions, I want to talk about…us."

***

The time had come to face facts. As much as Pam hated admitting her sister might be right about anything, she had to admit Valerie was right about at least one thing. Pam was too young to spend the rest of her life living in the past, mourning a future she'd never have.

Which meant taking all the subtle and not-so-subtle advice from Abigail, Euphemia, and even Etta Mae seriously. It was time for Pam to leave Travis in his corner of her heart and move on. And unless she wanted to keep lying to herself, moving on meant giving herself a chance to love Jeff. All right. If she wasn't going to lie to herself any more, than facing facts meant accepting she was already in love with Jefferson Davis Parker. The question now was, would he be willing to give them a chance, after she'd behaved like a near-raving lunatic the last few days? "I have to get back to work. Come to the church with me?"

"Probably not a good idea."

"It's not like I'm going to be able to get a lick of work done with everything going on. Besides, the church is private and neutral. I don't think rumors will start flying as easily if we're together at church, than if you come to my place alone for say…dinner."

That easy Parker smile spread across Jeff's face. "Is that an invitation?"

"Yes, if you still want to accept after we talk."

The charming grin slipped, an expressionless curtain descended in its place. "Fair enough. Let me settle up here, and I'll meet you at the church."

All the way through town, Pam had rehearsed what she'd say when she found Jeff. What she hadn't expected was to find him someplace as public as the café. It made sense to invite him back to the church. With only an hour for lunch, and having spent most of it with Miss Abigail, it wasn't like she had a whole lot of options left where they could go. Pulling into the church parking lot, she wondered if maybe this had not been one of her best ideas. Sitting alone at her desk for almost ten minutes, she'd gone from doubtful, to confident, back toward confused, and then right on down the road to she'd-completely-lost-her-mind.

When the main glass door to the administration area of the church squeaked open, she stiffened in her seat. "Don't lose your nerve now," she whispered to herself.

"Sorry it took so long. I ran into Heather Goodstein on my way out of the café. She felt obligated to tell me I could count on her full support." Jeff paused by Pam's desk.

"This town loves you."

"Mmm." He glanced out the window at the near empty parking lot. "I wonder."

"What?"

"I'm thinking maybe, just maybe, Mom and Euphemia have been working the phones this morning."

"And what if they have? It doesn't change the basic facts. You are a fundamental part of this church and this town, and you can't let pompous John Haskell run you out of town on a rail."

"Don't forget tarred and feathered, too."

She shot him her best don't-push-your-luck glare.

"Sorry, but I'm doing no such thing."

"Then what do you call it?"

"Facing facts."

"Malarkey." Pam sprang from her seat and jabbed a finger in Jeff's chest. "How many people have to tell you we need you before you believe us?"

"We?" Jeff's tone softened. An unexpected heat flared in his gaze to match the sizzle that shot up her arm when he gently brushed his hand against her. "Who is we? Who needs me, Pam?"

"The…the town does. We all do." She swallowed hard, every nerve tingling where his fingers caressed the sides of her arms. "I do."

At first she thought maybe she'd said the words too softly for him to hear, because he said nothing, just stared at her. She'd opened her mouth to say it again when his lips descended on hers, and the sizzle ignited into a flame. Her arms wound around him, pulling him closer. She needed this man now, today, tomorrow, for always.

His hands dropped to her backside, his fingers drew slow lazy circles across her hips before drawing her more tightly against him. She could feel every inch of him, the strength of him, the wanting. In a matter of seconds she found herself backed up against her desk. Something heavy dropped from the desktop to the floor with a thud. It didn't matter. Papers fluttered to the ground, when Jeff spun about and lifted her onto his lap. One of them moaned, or both of them, she wasn't sure. She didn't care.

His lips pulled away from hers, and she nearly whimpered at the loss. Her fingers ran a frantic path through his hair, guiding him back to her starving mouth, only he had a different plan, trailing soft moist kisses along her jaw, settling on the sweetest spot behind her ear. Another thud sounded nearby followed by the muted clunk of something scraping against the floor.

She felt Jeff's fingers stiffen and stop seconds before registering the recent sounds as the door bumping against the wall and the trash can skidding out of place. Before she could catch her breath, Jeff managed to set her on her feet and spin her behind him just in time to see Sandra Quinn standing wide-eyed and slack jawed beside the open office door and tipped-over wastebasket.

Not sure who was more shocked at the discovery of her and Jeff doing an encore of their grilled-cheeseless-sandwich impression, Pam tried to find something sensible to say.

Sandra found her voice first. "I see the rumors are true?"

Jeff cleared his throat, whether needing air or time, Pam wasn't sure. "Despite how this looks, I can assure you most of what you've heard is probably not true."

"Could've fooled me." Sandra turned to Pam. "You seemed so sincere when you said there was nothing romantic going on between you and the preacher. When I heard the latest, I thought the least I could do was rush right over here to let you know it's all over town the two of you are getting married." She turned back to Jeff. "Now I don't know who to believe."

"Married?" the two echoed. Apparently Etta Mae worked faster than Pam gave her credit for. Searching for how to respond, Pam wished she'd had time to talk to Jeff first privately. The front door of the church squeaked open once more, and John Haskell marched into the office stopping abruptly beside Sandra.

"Why, Miss Quinn." The old goat nodded in polite recognition. "What a pleasant surprise running into you here. I've been meaning to thank you on behalf of the church board for your devoted service to our elderly shut-ins."

Sandra's gaze shifted briefly to Jeff before settling on Mr. Haskell. All the air in Pam's lungs lurched to her throat and clogged any ability to breathe. She'd done it again. Caught devouring Jeff's tonsils by a parishioner, she'd thrust more problems on a man she only wanted to help.

"You're quite welcome, Mr. Haskell." Sandra lifted her chin. "But I assure you our pastor has already expressed the church's appreciation. Not that it's necessary. I'm only doing my Christian service." Sandra flashed John Haskell a stiff smile, hefted her handbag onto her shoulder, and offered Pam a more natural grin. "Call me if you find you need any help."

Nodding at Sandra like a bobble-head doll, Pam took in a relieved breath. Sandra hadn't said anything to fuel John Haskell's mission to replace Jeff as pastor. With Sandra out the door, Pam turned her attention to the man intent on single-handedly ridding Hope's Corner of immorality, and Jefferson Parker, only by the time she'd cast her attention on John Haskell, she realized he was pumping Jeff's arm as though drilling for oil.

"I can't tell you how happy we are to hear the good news." The head of the church board of directors now had a double-handed hold on Jeff and a grin to outdo the Cheshire cat. "Such wonderful news. Of course the little misunderstanding is behind us. Yes. Wonderful news."

He finally let go of Jeff and spun around, reaching for Pam.

Somehow the broad grin seemed more predatory than congratulatory, and she took a quick sidestep away from John Haskell and closer to Jeff.

"Yes, yes." The old man beamed. "My wife is always right. Just this morning over coffee, we discussed what an asset you've both been to the church. Yes, yes. The announcement came as no surprise. All is well and good."

Before either of them could edge in a response, John Haskell barreled out the door as briskly as he'd entered, still muttering, "All is well and good."

Jeff stared through the glass doorway at the man's departing back. "Why do I feel I've just fallen down a rabbit hole?"

"Do you suppose this is how Alice felt?" Pam slid her fingers into Jeff's grip.

"Maybe." Still looking into the empty parking lot, he continued, "I asked God if it was a mistake to walk away without a fight. I wonder if taking away the fight is His way of answering yes?"

"Does this mean you're thinking of staying on? Not leaving the church? Not leaving Hope's Corner?"

"That depends." He turned his gaze on her.

"On what?"

Jeff squeezed her hand, his eyes focused so intently on her that she thought for maybe a moment he could see her soul. Her heart skipped a beat.

"On whether or not the rumors are true."

CHAPTER TWENTY-TWO

"It's time." Etta Mae Parker leaned over her husband's favorite recliner. "Euphemia and I have done all we can do. The rest is up to you."

Bundled under the blanket Etta had crocheted for Harlon while he was in the hospital for bypass surgery, her husband seemed too old, too frail. The last few days—since her son had announced his intentions to leave the church and rejoin the corporate world—had aged her husband ten years. She'd fought the fear of what this change would do to her family, if she couldn't help her son see the light, so to speak. But she refused to lose what was left of the man she loved. She wanted her husband back, all of him.

Harlon took a slow sip of his hot chocolate. "Little marshmallows are the best. Whipped cream is for sissies."

"Harlon Parker."

"I know, Etta, dear. I know it's time. Every father wants to remain a Superman in his son's eyes. Perhaps my eagerness to remain his hero has cost us both more than I ever imagined."

"Honest to heavens, I don't know which of the two of you is worse. There's no sin in what happened to you anymore than what happened to our son with Jenny Buckner. Y'all are men of God, not God. You can only do so much."

Senior Pastor Harlon Parker blew out a staggered sigh. "I'll call him now." Harlon reached for the nearby telephone, flashing the famous Parker smile at his wife. "Maybe some of your blueberry pie will make the telling easier."

Nearly forty years of marriage and that grin still held the same power over her. Standing to go warm the pie she'd baked earlier in the day, Etta Mae hoped Jeff answered his phone. If her calculations were correct, and things had progressed as planned, the happy news should be reaching Jeff anytime now, and once he blew in here to confront her, there'd be no listening to anything else.

***

Jeff didn't need to hold his breath. He was fairly sure anticipation had stopped his lungs from functioning altogether. As a matter of fact, his heart was none too steady at the moment either. "You said you needed me."

Pam nodded.

"Was that true?"

She nodded, just once, but affirmation nonetheless.

"The whole town thinks we're engaged."

Her chin dipped in agreement once again.

"Most likely my mother's doing."

Again, she nodded. Jeff wasn't sure if he should be concerned Pam wasn't speaking or delighted she wasn't disagreeing.

"I know this isn't very traditional, and it's certainly not what you deserve, but—"

"I'll Fly Away" burst loudly into play from Jeff's cell phone tucked away in his breast pocket. Silently cursing the poor timing, he whipped out the phone and glanced at the caller ID. "It's my dad," he told Pam. "Are you all right? … Yes… Right now? Can't it… Yes, Dad, I'm sure it is, but it's not… Yes. I have a few things I'd like to discuss with Mom anyway… Yeah, I know she does… Okay, I'll be there in a few minutes."

Disconnecting the call, he slipped the phone into his pocket. "Dad needs to talk to me. I suspect it's more of the same, but he sounded a little agitated. I'd make my parents wait, but right now—"

"Your father has to come first. You should go."

"Is the offer for dinner still open?"

"Absolutely."

"Then I promise we'll take this up where we left off." The twinkle in her eyes told him, if he kissed her, she wouldn't object, but the fire inside him shouted, if he kissed her now, he wouldn't stop.

***

"Where's Pop?" Jeff kissed his mom on the cheek.

"Waiting for you in his study."

"Don't think you're getting off easy." He tapped his mother on the nose with his finger. "You and I are going to have a very long talk when I'm done with your husband."

"Of course, dear. I love chatting with all my children." His mom winked and led the way carrying two plates with freshly sliced blueberry pie. Though he doubted the pie would make his upcoming conversation any easier, it certainly couldn't hurt.

Turning the corner at the end of the hall, he could see his dad tucked away under the bright blanket his mom had made. The sight reminded him of an invalid in an old black and white movie. Where a man far too young was portrayed as older than Methuselah.

"Ah, you made it." His father stood, giving him a strong bear hug that belied the fragile appearance from a moment ago, then sat, once again becoming the picture of aged frailty.

"You said this couldn't wait."

"Yes. Yes I did." Harlon Parker nodded to his wife as she set the two plates on the desk. "Thank you, dear. If you don't mind, please close the door on your way out."

She smiled at her son, shot her husband that remember-what-I-told-you look, and backed out of the room pulling the door closed behind her.

"Thank God." His father tossed the blanket to one side. Took a long slow breath. Did a deep knee bend. Handed his son a dish with warm pie, then walked around his desk and sat. "I love your mother beyond reason, but some things are best kept to yourself."

Jeff wasn't sure if he wanted to scold his father for overdoing or sing the "Hallelujah Chorus" that his father appeared strong and healthy.

"Might as well make yourself comfortable." His father waved toward the recliner.

No one was ever allowed to sit in his father's favorite chair, never mind invited. Clearly this was more serious than Jeff had expected. "What's wrong? Just tell me straight out."

"Nothing is wrong." Harlon forked a piece of pie, then stopped halfway to his mouth. "Since you were a small boy, your mother and I have known you had a special calling. A special way with people. A gift."

"Pop…"

Harlon held up his hand. "Hear me out." He dropped his fork back to the plate without taking a bite. "For years your mother insisted I should do more to prepare you. Share some of what I'd learned. Spare you from learning all your lessons the hard way as I did, but I felt it wasn't my place to impose my ministry on you."

Harlon hesitated, toying with the fork and pie. "I suppose in some way I feared having you think I was less than perfect. I'm sorry."

"Pop—"

"Please, Jefferson."

Jeff leaned back into the chair that felt way too big for him and nodded his agreement to let his father finish.

"They say history repeats itself. You'd think, by now, we'd all have learned why that expression never dies, yet we always fail to think it applies to us. When your mother and I were first married, I was offered an associate pastorship not far from her hometown. We thought it a wonderful opportunity. The congregation was large enough to need an associate pastor, but not so large that we didn't feel at home."

His father paused, and Jeff interjected, "I remember the stories. Hudsonville, wasn't it?"

Harlon nodded. "There was a family, the Bensons. Lovely people. Judy Benson was an exemplary member of the church. On the telephone prayer team, the new mother's meal committee, the new member welcome group. I could go on. The father worked two jobs but always found the time to come to church with his family on Sundays. The oldest daughter had a bit of a wild streak.

The police brought her home liquored up more than once. By the time she was seventeen, her parents had discovered she'd made an appointment at a clinic over in Tyler. For an abortion. Of course, it was the counsel of the pastor to have the baby. Her parents were willing to take on the responsibility. The daughter, Angela, fought them constantly at first, but then she seemed to straighten up. Her parents were thrilled to see the positive changes in their daughter's behavior."

The expression on his father's face shifted. Until now his father was merely a man retelling a story. The memory of what he was about to say clearly weighed heavily. The natural sparkle in his dad's eye faded. A muscle along his jaw flickered with tension.

"Shortly after the birth of the baby girl, Angela seemed to have found wilder ways. She'd sneak out of the house in the middle of the night and disappear for days. Sometimes the police would find her wandering the streets high on her drug of the day. When Bill and Judy Benson realized their baby girl was hooked on heroin, for the first time in my life, I could truly see a broken heart. The girl was in and out of rehab programs over the next year or so. Finally she seemed to turn a corner. It had been decided by my superiors that someone younger, closer to her age, would be a better counsel. We'd worked together for over a year, when I saw the signs she'd turned the corner. She'd gotten a job, paid more attention to the baby, the Bensons were so happy to have put the horrible past behind them."

Though Jeff wouldn't have thought it possible, the sadness in his father's eyes deepened. His shoulders dropped, and he finally stopped all pretense of eating pie, letting his fork fall to his plate with a clank.

"Her parents came to me worried. Something wasn't right. Angela was going through all the motions, a steady job, a small apartment for her and her daughter, a night class at the community college, but Judy was convinced something was amiss. I visited with Angela one evening at the Dairy Queen where she'd been working. I didn't see it. Didn't notice the way her eyes never met mine. Didn't give any thought to the back booth full of boys who were there before me and yet never ordered any food. Judy called me several times a week convinced her daughter was pulling away, hiding something. By then your mama and I had been blessed with you going through teething. I'd assured Judy that working and raising a little girl was exhausting work, that Angela was learning independence.

"Then it happened. One day Angela didn't drop off the child with Judy before going off to work. When Judy called her daughter and no one answered, she rushed over to the apartment. Angela was gone. I was still convinced Judy was overreacting. Angela and her daughter had probably spent the night with friends and simply forgot to call her mom. I reassured her Angela would be calling in anytime now. Two days later the Dallas police called. A concerned neighbor called on the toddler who seemed to be wandering in her yard unsupervised, and no one would answer the front door. Angela had been dead for two days. A heroin overdose.

"Every pastor at some point in his life has an Angela Benson. The ones we want to help and can't. I've learned never to dismiss a mother's instinct. Not to accept the easiest answer because it's what you'd like it to be. And especially, all I can do is my best. Unlike Angela Benson, Jenny Buckner didn't die because of your ignorance or mistakes. She died at the hands of an animal because you cannot will people to do what you want. You couldn't make Jenny leave her husband any more than I could take away Angela's cravings for the stronger faster high. Don't set an impossible standard for yourself."

It took a few minutes for Jeff to register his father had said all he intended to say. "What did you do?"

"I fought with God for days. Why? Why her? Why me? Why didn't I know? Why couldn't I do more? And then one day a calm settled over me, and I understood, I knew. I'd received my answer. I can only show people the way, but I can't force them to follow any more than God can force His will upon us. Every person is responsible for his own decisions and his alone."

Jeff leaned forward, his hands clasped, forearms resting on his knees, his gaze caught on a distant speck of lint on the carpet. "Every time I thought I'd convinced Jenny to leave her husband, he'd promise to change, and she'd believe him. The last time the battered women's shelter had even arranged for a safe place for her to stay. If only she'd… I thought confronting him was the answer. Instead he snapped as Jenny had always feared."

"Son." Harlon moved next to Jeff and placed a hand on his shoulder. "You can't blame yourself for what Frank Buckner did. But there are more Jenny Buckners and Angela Bensons out there. If you walk away now, you may not be there for the one who *will* follow. The one who will fail if you're not there for them."

"I can't stop thinking, I should have known better, should have done something…different."

"We live in an imperfect world. Frank Buckner was a stick of dynamite ready to explode. You did everything humanly possible to save Jenny, but your mother is right. We're not God. You have a gift. This community needs you. You can't walk away now."

"Well, it does seem my resignation is being ignored." Jeff looked up at his father. "John Haskell thinks Pamela Sue and I are engaged."

Harlon's eyes grew wide.

"Marriage to Pam seems to be the Holy Grail that wipes clean all my sins."

Harlon scratched his head, looked over his son's shoulder at the closed door, then silently walked around the large wooden desk before slowly sinking into the leather chair. "I didn't see that coming."

"Mom didn't tell you?"

One eyebrow shot up. "Tell me what?"

"I'm not sure, but I know she and Euphemia McCarthy are behind this. Kenny mentioned it briefly last night. I thought he was exaggerating."

"And now?"

"I don't know."

His father leaned back in his chair and steepled his fingers together. "What precisely are we talking about?"

Jeff let out a heavy sigh. "I suppose everything."

***

At exactly four minutes to five Pam was more than ready to call it a day. A very long day. After fielding three phone calls within ten minutes from happy parishioners dousing her in well wishes and congratulations, Pam opted for screening the rest of the day's calls with voice mail, including the one from Jeff letting her know he'd be at his parents' house until she got home from work. Apparently he and his father were having a long overdue heart-to-heart.

She'd avoided the four calls on her cell from her sister. Until she knew what to say to these people, there was no point in answering the phone. While earlier in the day she'd struggled over what to say to Jeff when she found him, this afternoon a blanket of calm had settled over her, and now she knew in her heart it didn't matter what she said. Whatever happened, they'd be in it together.

By five-thirty she'd pulled into her driveway with a roasted chicken and quart of macaroni and cheese from Kroger's supermarket in hand. She'd promised Jeff dinner, but at no time did she say she'd be the one to cook it.

As she stood by her door, key in the lock, a warm baritone voice floated up to her. "Do you need some help?"

Unlike the first time she'd heard that molten voice, this time the words filled her with warmth and a yearning she thought she'd never feel again. "You bet."

Jeff eased the bag out of her arms. "Smells good."

Pam unlocked the door. "Gotta love Kroger's in a pinch."

"Don't tell Mom. She thinks takeout is sacrilege."

"I bet!" Pam laughed, loud and deep. It felt wonderful.

While Jeff emptied the grocery bag, she set the kitchen table. Aside from Jeff mumbling, "I'm starved," and Pam agreeing, neither had much to say. Not about the parental heart-to-heart, not about the engagement rumors, and especially not about making out like randy teenagers on her office desk.

Jeff sliced some chicken breast for her, and Pam wondered, when had he learned she preferred white meat? From the fridge she pulled out a pitcher of sweet tea and poured two glasses. Setting them on the table, she paused to ask, "Would you rather have something else to drink?" It didn't surprise her when he replied, "Tea is perfect." The man drank more iced tea than anyone she knew, and she did know. The same way she knew he'd have one cup of coffee after dinner with half-and-half, not milk, and no sugar.

"I can throw a salad together, if you'd like?" She placed a serving spoon in the tub of macaroni and cheese.

"No need."

"Okay," Pam managed to say through a yawn. "Excuse me."

"I know how you feel." Jeff pulled her chair out for her. His mama had certainly taught him right. "It's been a long day and not getting much sleep last night isn't helping."

"Try no sleep. I know I closed my eyes, but it was a complete waste of time." She yawned again.

"Just don't fall asleep in your food."

"As far as I know, I haven't done that since I was a toddler."

"Fall asleep in your food?"

"Mmm." She forked a mouthful of macaroni and cheese. "My baby books are filled with photographs of me in my high chair, gripping a spoon or fork in one hand and leaning over, sound asleep, in my dinner."

Jeff swallowed fast, almost choking on his chicken from laughter. "Those I want to see."

Pam waved a forked piece of chicken in the air. "We might be able to work something out."

It wasn't until dinner was finished and the two stood side by side at the sink rinsing plates that the subject of the engagement rumors came up.

"Mom insists she can't be held responsible for other people jumping to conclusions." Jeff slid two dinner plates onto the bottom rack of the dishwasher.

"Well, what did she expect?" Pam handed him some silverware. "You can't very well call your local printer, ask how much it would cost to print two hundred wedding invitations, and not expect her to think you're planning a wedding."

"Believe me, I said pretty much the exact same thing to her, but she merely shrugged a shoulder and went back to rolling dough for more pie crust. According to Kenny, Mom called the Promenade Print shop at 10:00 a.m. and thirty seconds. The thirty seconds was probably to allow Gladys time to put away her keys. Apparently that and two hours was all it took for the entire town to put two and two together and marry us off."

"You know, you gotta give your mom some kudos for a well-conceived plan. She knew darn well, if she called that early, it would only add a sense of urgency to the situation. Folks would jump to the expected conclusion, and without your mom actually coming out and saying there's a wedding, marriage rumors would spread like wildfire."

"Oh, yeah. As far as we can deduce, within the first hour, Gladys had notified her bridge club, the head of the PTA, the church board, the city council, and every single person on her prayer chain."

"Busy woman." Pam closed the dishwasher and hit the buttons for the short cycle. "And the best part of it is, no one can accuse your mother of making this up to protect you. Gladys and half the town took care of that for her. Coffee?"

"Sure."

Before Pam could grab the carafe, Jeff was filling the glass pitcher with just enough water for two cups. One for each of them. She reached across to scoop the coffee grounds into the filter and nearly gasped when her chest brushed against his arm. An innocent contact and yet every sensory nerve had now gone on high alert. Her insides clenched in fiery anticipation of the next touch. In self-defense, she abandoned the search for the coffee can, and settled instead for moving away from him and retrieving the half-and-half from the fridge.

Jeff hit the coffeemaker's on button and spun around, arms and ankles crossed, to face Pam. "We're going to have to stop the rumors. And soon."

"Before or after coffee?"

The trivial question brought the desired effect. Jeff dropped his hands to his sides and flashed a broad smile. "I suppose after will work."

Pam stifled another yawn. "That's assuming I don't fall asleep standing up."

A deep crease formed a sharp V at the bridge of his nose. "Maybe it's better if I leave and let you get some sleep. We can talk about this tomorrow. Another twelve hours won't make much of a difference either way."

"No. I'm not really that tired. A cup of coffee will do the trick."

"Are you sure?" His hand moved forward slightly, before he snatched it back to his side.

He was certainly right about that much. The slightest of touches from Jeff at this point would send all their good intentions to hell and back. All her common sense seemed to have leaked out her ears in the last few days. Who knows what she'd be capable of with no one to interrupt them this time? "Yeah, I'm sure. All I need is a quick dose of caffeine."

"In that case, you go rest in the living room. I'll bring the coffee."

Though the hostess-with-the-mostest in her wanted to argue the point, the too-pooped-to-pop woman in her was more than happy to wait for her after-dinner coffee on the comfy overstuffed living room sofa. Most definitely.

Grabbing the remote from the coffee table, Pam collapsed onto the sofa, and chose an old Barbara Stanwyck film on the classic movie channel.

Two cups of coffee in hand, Jeff found Pam curled up in a corner of the couch sound asleep, her head resting on a large pillow, her arms folded around it. All he could do was stare. Had he ever felt like this about anyone in his life? She looked so delicate, so vulnerable, and so damn beautiful.

While he had no intention of allowing more fuel for rumors to stir around them by remaining all night just to watch her sleep, staying to drink his coffee shouldn't pose a problem. When he finished, he'd nudge her toward her room. Though he'd much rather crawl in bed beside her, even if only to hold her close, he had enough of the sense God gave him to know that would be a really bad idea.

Resisting the urge to be near her, he opted to sit on the smaller sofa across from her. Remote in hand, he flipped through the channels. Three-quarters of the way done with his drink, he was watching the sports news when he heard Pam whimper. A quick glance in her direction, a furrowed brow followed by her mouth curling into a painful grimace, and he knew she was slipping into one of her nightmares. "Damn."

With no idea if waking a person from a nightmare had any repercussions like waking a sleepwalker, he had no intention of letting her fall deeper into the painful darkness he knew her nightmares to be. "Pam." He nudged her shoulder gently.

"No," she mumbled.

"Pammy." He shook her shoulder more forcefully.

"No, not you. Not you."

It took Jeff a few seconds to realize she was talking to someone in her dreams, not him. "Pam!" This time he pulled gently, tapped her cheek. "Please, Pam, honey. Wake up."

"No!" she bolted upright, screaming. Her eyes flew open, and she stared at him. The reflection of sheer terror hit him as hard as a clenched fist in the gut.

Afraid to move, unsure if it was him or someone else that she was seeing, Jeff waited. Within seconds the horror in her gaze shifted to a softer sense of sadness, and then her eyes filled with moisture. Throwing herself against him, draping her arms around him, she burst into sobbing tears.

"Shh," he whispered in her ear. "It's okay. It's okay."

She shook her head in his shoulder and seemed to cry harder. Warm tears penetrated his shirt bathing his cold skin in sorrow. He had no idea what to do; so he held her, let her cry, and waited.

Whether Pam had been crying for twenty minutes or two hours, Jeff didn't know, but when her sobs finally eased to the occasionally hiccup, he braced himself for what might come.

"I saw him." Still snuggled in the crook of his shoulder, she hadn't lifted her head or let go of his arms.

Jeff waited, wondered. The silence seemed to drag on for another twenty minutes or two hours.

"I can't believe it. I just can't believe it."

Her last words came out in a long whimper that started the tears flowing again. Not sure what to say, whether to push or wait, Jeff wondered what time it was in Italy or Belgium and if Caleb's cell phone had international calling.

"If it's not true, why did I dream it?" Still clinging to him, Pam lifted her head just enough to look into his eyes.

Taking in a deep breath, Jeff prayed for the wisdom not to screw this up. "You're going to have to tell me what you dreamed."

"The same as always. Shadows, pools of wine that turn to blood, pressure on my chest, my throat, so I can't breathe. But this time, all the faces were so clear. Not just Travis but the attacker too. I could see the green of his eyes and the little scar on his right cheek."

The hairs on the back of Jeff's neck prickled. Now more than ever he wished he had Caleb here to help. "Do you remember it well enough to talk to the police again?"

She nodded. "Yeah, I do, if what I saw was real."

"You don't think it was real?"

"Oh, God, I hope not." Her head dropped back against his shoulder. "I saw someone else too." She drew in a ragged breath. "It was Greg."

This time Jeff pulled back to look at her face. "Greg? Your

husband's business partner?"

She nodded.

"The one who I hear you talking to every so often?"

She nodded again, and this made the wheels of his mind work overtime. Something had always nagged him about the conversations he'd overheard, but he could never quite put his finger on it. Now, if what she dreamed was in fact a reality, and Greg was somehow involved in her husband's death, the lack of memory and the nightmares were starting to make sense.

"Didn't the police say he saved you? Is that what you're remembering?"

She shook her head, tightening the hold on his arms. "I felt the weight, the pressure, lift off. There was mumbling, fuzzy sounds, but I could make out Greg's voice. He said, 'You crazy bastard,' and mumbled something else I couldn't make out or maybe I passed out because everything was dark and black. Next thing I could understand was something about 'Kill only the man and not the woman,' then the other voice said I was a bonus surprise, and he wouldn't charge extra. I tried to open my eyes, but they felt so heavy. A smacking sound echoed loudly in the garage. I'm guessing Greg must have hit the attacker."

Jeff thought of interjecting, making a few comments to paint Greg in a better light. To point out, in order to subdue the attacker, it would only make sense to fight him, but he realized whatever was truth or fiction, Pam probably needed to do this her own way at her own pace.

"There was a shuffling sound. I wondered what was happening. Was he helping Travis? Travis needed help. I had to help. I managed to open my eyes, barely. My lids still felt so heavy. Everything felt so heavy, so numb." Pulling away from Jeff, eyes closed, she leaned her head against the sofa back. "I saw it. Greg handed the man in black an envelope. 'Unmarked bills,' he said. 'You'll get the balance, when I'm sure he's dead.' That's when I woke up."

It all made sense now. If her husband's best friend had

anything to do with the attack, to be betrayed by his best friend, their best friend, was more than she could take. Jeff thought back to when he'd witnessed her nightmares. To the earlier phone calls from the dear friend. Greg had to be the trigger. What her mind couldn't handle and wouldn't quite let her forget. Good God, now what?

CHAPTER TWENTY-THREE

"Why are you answering your phone on vacation?"

"I've got a better question." Caleb's voice sounded raspy from sleep. At least Jeff hoped it was from sleep. "Why are you calling me at…five o'clock in the morning?"

"Sorry, man. I know this is your second honeymoon and all, but I have to say, I'm really glad you didn't turn off your cell phone."

Caleb hesitated long enough for Jeff to wonder if he'd fallen back asleep before he muttered, "Using it for an alarm." The silence carried on for a few more seconds. "Okay, I'm out of the bedroom now. What's so important you had to call me halfway around the world?"

It didn't take long for Jeff to recap the events of the evening. Emotionally exhausted, Pam had dozed off on the sofa half an hour ago. Convinced she was sleeping soundly, Jeff had taken a chance and called his old friend. "So what do you think?"

"I think you have one hell of a way of waking a guy up in the morning."

"Come on, Caleb. I'm floundering here."

"I know. I'm sorry, really. But dreams are a tricky business. Not everyone agrees on their application or importance. The mind is even more complex. But honestly, I believe your initial assessment has merit. Without talking to Pamela myself, it does seem this dream is likely a breakthrough memory. It would certainly explain why, if she was not sexually assaulted, her mind shut off recall. And if you're correct that the nightmares followed phone calls from this friend, then it makes sense he's the trigger."

"I can't be sure. But she mentioned while working with her husband's business partner, she had the nightmares daily. Once she moved home, they eased up. His occasional calls have to be the trigger."

"Could be."

"So what do you suggest I do?"

"Call the Dallas police. See if her family, someone, knows the name of the detective in charge of the original investigation. Let the man know that Pam might be able to give them a visual of the attacker, but more importantly, convince him to investigate this Greg person. I don't work with the police very often, but when I do, money is usually at the root of all the trouble. Have the police thoroughly check this character's finances at the time of the murder. See if he needed a little help from a big insurance policy. If they're lawyers, odds are they were smart enough to carry whoppers on each other."

"Yeah. That's what I was thinking." Jeff peeked into the living room to check if Pam was still sleeping then stepped back into the kitchen. "One thing I don't get."

"What?"

"Why now? What made today any different than yesterday?"

"To remember?"

"Yeah."

"Simple. She's ready to move on."

Jeff wondered.

Caleb continued, "What about you?"

"What about me?"

"Are you ready to move on? Have you figured out you can't save the world?"

"Have you been talking to my mother?"

Caleb laughed. "Don't have to. I have my own degree."

"I'm thinking on it still."

"Well, don't think too hard. I wouldn't want your brain to explode."

"Comedian. Where'd you say you got that PhD? Doctorateonline.com?"

"Dot Net." Caleb yawned. "Seriously, this is going to be tough on your friend. This could be only the beginning. There could be more memories locked away ready to be brought into the light of day. Let her move at her own pace. Just listen, see what she wants to share, and be with her if she needs you. But the police should be your next step. Murder is a nasty business."

"Yeah, especially if you're the only living witness to the crime."

***

"We've waited all day." Jake Wharton stood from the table. Enough was enough. He'd held his tongue all through dinner with the family.

Valerie Wharton patted her brother's arm. "Look, this isn't the first time we've believed the gossip mill. We've made fools of ourselves the last two times. If there was any truth in what's happening, Pammy would have called one of us."

"Give me a good reason for her not to return any of your…how many phone calls?"

Val hitched a shoulder. "Four."

"Exactly. I say we go over."

Bo had kept silent through most of his brother's ranting. "I agree with Val. Pammy's a big girl. Besides…" He grinned. "I like Jeff. Always have."

And that was part of the problem. Jake liked Jeff too. A lot. He couldn't have picked a nicer guy for his sister, but none of this was going down easy. The gossip, the rumors, all of it was creating bedlam in the family. "I'm worried about her. Is there anything wrong with wanting to take care of my kid sister?"

Bo smiled at his older brother. "I'd be more likely to think something was wrong with you if you didn't, but there's a difference between taking care of Pammy and not trusting her. This time we need to wait her out."

"Besides," Val cut in. "Ten o'clock at night is no time to pay your sister a visit."

Jake checked the clock on the wall. They'd been arguing back and forth for nearly an hour since their dad had gone to bed. "Ten's not too late. If she's alone, she'll be waiting to watch

Leno."

"And if she's not alone?" Bo asked.

There was no time to respond. Jake's phone rang. "Who the he... Well, my, my."

"Who is it?" Val asked.

"The devil himself." Jake punched at the keypad. "It's about time I heard from one of you—"

"It's been a crazy day," Jeff said. "We've had a breakthrough."

"What? How to spread gossip faster than wildfire?"

"Your sister remembered the face of the man who attacked her."

Jake sat down heavily in the nearest chair. "She did?"

"Yeah. It was a shock. She's fallen asleep from sheer exhaustion."

"But she's okay?"

At those words Bo leaned forward; Valerie jumped from her seat to stand over her brother.

"So far," Jeff answered. "But I need to know if any of you have the name of the police detective who worked the case?"

"I remember the man's name as well as my own. Hannigan, Leo Hannigan. I can get you his number."

"No. His name's good enough. If Pam's up to it in the morning, I thought I'd give him a call."

"You planning on staying with her all night...again?"

"Actually, I'm concerned she might remember more and don't want her waking up alone. I was thinking of asking Valerie to come stay with her. Do you think it's too late to call?"

"No. Val's standing right here." Jake handed his cell to his youngest sister.

"Jeff, what's wrong?" Valerie's tone dripped with worry.

"Nothing. We may have a lead on who killed Travis. It was pretty rough on Pam reliving it all again. She's sleeping now, but I don't think she should be left alone tonight."

"I agree. She shouldn't be left alone. You go on back to my

sister, and I'll explain to the boys here that Pammy will be in your good hands."

"No!" Jeff called out loud enough for both Bo and Jake to hear. "I thought you could come stay with her. I mean, under the current circumstances and all."

"Exactly. Under the current circumstances and all, you might as well stay. It's not like you can make things any worse. Just do whatever comes naturally."

Bo covered his mouth to hold back a laugh, and Jake almost choked on his own spit before reaching out to grab the phone back from his sister.

"Listen, Jeff." Val turned away. "Jake here needs some medical attention. Just remember women can be very needy when under emotional stress, if you know what I mean. I gotta run. I'm trusting you to take care of my sister. Night." Val hit the disconnect button and handed her brother his phone. "Relax, big brother. If all goes well, you might just get that wedding you've been wanting."

***

Jeff stared at the dead connection. Maybe he should just call his mother to come over.

"You're still here." Eyes foggy from sleep, Pam stood in the kitchen doorway.

The first thing to come to mind was to wrap his arms around her and do as Val had said, what comes naturally. Staying put seemed to be the safer response. "Did I wake you?"

"Not really." Pam wiped the sleep from her eyes, then stretched like a lazy cat who'd had her fill of cream. "I can't believe I slept so long."

"It's been a long day. You needed the break."

She plopped in the seat across from him. "So what do we do now?"

"Calling the detective in charge of Travis' case would be the first move. Tell him what you remember. See if they have a mug shot, or whatever they call it, that resembles this guy. Then..." He reached over the table and took her hand in his. "Just in case there's any truth to your last dream, you have to tell the police we suspect Greg may be more involved. Knew the attacker, his plan."

She sprang from the table. "I can't."

He didn't dare go to her. The last few days had his control frayed to a single thread and ready to snap. He needed to keep his distance. "Pam."

"Don't." She squeezed her eyes closed and wrapped her arms around herself. "It has to mean something else. It just has to. He couldn't have known. Not Greg."

"Okay." He eased back his chair and pushed to his feet. "I spoke with Caleb."

"I thought he was going to be gone for two weeks."

"He is. Wherever they are, it's seven hours ahead of us, and his phone works."

Frustration bloomed in her expression. "You didn't?"

"Well. We've been friends a long time and sleep is overrated. Besides, this is important."

She nodded, letting her arms fall by her side. "What did he say?"

"The mind's a tricky thing." He folded his hand around hers and led the way back to the living room. "He's not placing any bets on what this new revelation means, but he's not discarding it's an actual memory."

Pam sank heavily onto the sofa beside him. "Caleb said that?"

"He thinks the police should take a look at Greg's finances at the time of the…incident." Somehow the word *murder* simply wouldn't roll off his tongue.

Her face pinched with regret and sadness set deep in her eyes. "All right. But if this is just some Freudian-Jungian psychobabble, and Greg turns out to be completely innocent, I'm going to hate myself for even considering otherwise."

"Agreed. But you will live easier having no room for doubts of his innocence."

"Yes. Yes I suppose I will. Thank you." Already perched on the edge of the sofa, only inches away from him, Pam easily leaned over to give Jeff a quick kiss on the cheek. A kiss that lingered a fraction longer than it probably should have.

She held her gaze steady with his. He wasn't sure if she was talking herself into something or out of something, but before he could make up his own mind, her lips found his.

Soft, delicate, she tasted of coffee, cinnamon, and sweet Pam. Whatever control he'd hoped to hang on to slipped away at the feel of her arms snaking around his neck, her fingers swirling through his hair. Heat poured through his veins like freshly spewed lava.

All reason and common sense seemed to tumble out of his brain. If any words were left, he couldn't find them. He could only feel how much he wanted this woman now licking and kissing the edges of his lips and working a slow, tingling path along his chin and across his jaw, the tip of her tantalizing tongue teasing the edge of his ear, dipping. "Oh, God."

Jeff grabbed her shoulders in each hand. He had to put something between them, even if only an inch of air. "You have no idea what you're doing to me."

A smile warmed her face. "I think I do."

"Pam." He didn't move, didn't let go of her. Drawing in a deep breath, he gathered what was left of his wits, waited for his heart to steady, his pulse to slow. With Pam pressed so closely against him, he could feel the rapid beat of her heart. A dunking in the Siberian Sea wouldn't cool his hyperready libido. "Pam," he repeated, his scrambled senses unable to find words.

"I thought... I mean the way you, we... It just seemed...time." She pulled back. "I'm sorry."

The flash of pained rejection in her eyes was more than his restraint could handle. "I'm the one who's sorry. You're right. This is right. But I'm not making love to you on a cramped couch like a horny teenager." In a move that would have been worthy of a major motion picture, he drew her fully onto his lap and pushed to his feet in one dramatic swoop.

As Pam nipped and kissed his chin, his throat, any bare spot within reach of her talented lips, his need spiraled off the charts. At the top of the stairs he almost tripped when her tongue ran a slow path along the edge of his ear. Thankful to find her bedroom door open, his long strides crossed the room quickly. Without letting go, he deposited his precious cargo on the bed, rolling with her until she lay flat on her back, her long blonde hair feathered across the pillow with the exquisite precision of a Renaissance painting. "God, you're so beautiful."

God. A pang of guilt kicked at his heart. Then his eyes settled on Pam; her gaze a reflection of everything he felt for this amazing woman. Nothing could be more right. "I love you."

The words said, his mouth took hers with a ravenous hunger he'd kept banked too long. Tongues clashed, battled, then settled into a slow dance of desire and love. Impatient to feel every inch of her, but determined to go slow and easy, his fingers worked to undo each button of her blouse, resisting the urge to rip off the garment and toss it away, never to be found again.

Intent on his goal, he hadn't realized Pam's fingers had steadfastly worked to undo his buttons. When she pushed him up to shrug out of the shirt and raked her fingers down his front, stopping to draw swirls in the vee of hair at his pant line, all the air rushed from his lungs.

"Let me help you." With one hand she undid the snap on his jeans and ran her finger along the edge of his hip.

A groan strangled in his throat. "I don't know if I can do slow."

"I guess we'll have to find out." Just yesterday the thought of ever being with another man seemed as foreign as a Japanese car. At this moment Pam couldn't think of anything more right than making love to Jefferson Davis Parker. She tugged on his jeans.

Before she could get a good hold on the fabric, Jeff had toed off his shoes, kicked out of the pants and dropped his briefs. Slow would have to wait for another day. Seeing him stand before her in all his naked glory, she sucked in a deep breath. On her knees, she inched her way to the edge of the bed and reached out to wrap her hand around him.

"No, ma'am." He pulled her up until she clung to him, her legs wrapped around his waist. In a single move, his fingers adeptly unsnapped her bra.

"Smooth," she whispered.

A soft smile spread across his face, a mischievous twinkle gleamed in his eyes. "Like riding a bike. Some things you never forget."

Still holding her in his arms, ducking his head, he latched onto one breast and gently tugged. Like a wanton woman, she thrust her chest forward, silently pleading for more. The sensations shooting from the tips of her nipples to the apex of her thighs had her back arching with the ease of a contented cat.

One knee on the bed, Jeff lifted his head and caught her gaze, a huge grin breaking across his face. "You like that."

"Mmm," she cooed, mourning the lost sensations.

"There's lots more where that came from." Placing her gently on the bed, his mouth settled on her breast again, one hand softly kneading the neglected breast. His other hand eased her sweatpants down her legs, pausing along the way to brush her delicate skin, toy with her soft curls.

The flashes of fire burning everywhere he touched had her gasping for air. Needs snapped to life, sweeter, hotter, darker than anything she'd ever known. Enough was enough.

She rolled out from under him, slung a leg around his hip, and shoved him down against the bed until he lay flat on his back, her breasts dangling in his face. Before he could make a move, she slid down over him. Taking him in, inch by tantalizing inch, she watched the agonizing pleasure take over his face. His hands grabbed for her hips, lifting her and setting her down, faster, harder. A perfect rhythm. Bursts of heat exploded in every nerve. Waves of pleasure washed over her until bones turned to gelatin could no longer hold her upright.

Still inside her, Jeff rolled them over. Propped up on his

elbows, he brushed a gentle kiss against her lips. "Not to sound corny, but I could stay with you this way forever."

Pam lifted her hips playfully. "Sounds like a plan."

His gaze lingered on hers for a long moment. "The whole town thinks we're getting married."

She nodded.

"Public opinion is a terrible reason for two people to marry."

She nibbled on her lower lip and nodded again.

"Would you consider marrying me for love?"

Tears welled up in her eyes. She waited for the doubt, the hesitation, the sensation she was somehow cheating on her vows to Travis.

Calm slipped from Jeff's face. His brow curled with concern. "Am I wrong? Did I misunderstand what just happened?"

"No. You're not wrong." She'd made love. No doubts, no guilt. "I love you."

Tense lips spread into a broad grin. "Then marry me now. Today."

***

"You can certainly wait one month." Abigail Clarke patted Pam on the cheek.

"Right now a month seems like forever. Texas only requires three days."

"Sweetie, in ninety-seven years, if there's one thing I've learned, it's that patience has its rewards. Both you and young Jeff have to finish your course before you start a new race."

Pam pondered her friend's words. She hadn't really considered marrying Jeff a race.

Abigail took a seat beside Pam on the old Victorian sofa. "Tell me more about your memories. What did the detective say when you called?"

"He asked me to come in and work with a sketch artist. Apparently Dallas has a pretty good one. Detective Hannigan doesn't want my memory influenced by photos." Pam leaned back and blew out a heavy sigh. "I don't know. It doesn't sound like he believes I've actually remembered the face of my attacker."

"What about the other part?" Abigail set her hand on Pam's.

"He said they'd checked out Greg the first time. But the man he saw at the accident scene wasn't faking. Greg was distraught and fawning over me like I'd been his wife and not the wife of his best friend."

"And…" Abigail coaxed.

"And Detective Hannigan agreed to take another look just to put my mind at ease." Deep down she wondered if nightmares weren't better than facing what she hoped to God wasn't the truth. "Jeff will be picking me up here to leave for Dallas."

"And I'll be darn pleased to see that young man. Thursdays haven't been the same the last few weeks without him."

"He's missed coming, but now that he's not working, I'm sure he'll have more time to visit."

"Being stubborn is he?" Abigail pressed her lips in a tight clench and set her foot tapping. "We'll have to see about that."

Pam wasn't sure what the old woman had in mind, but she almost felt sorry for Jeff. If there's one thing she'd learned since moving home, it was to stay out of the way of smart old ladies with a plan.

***

"Are you sure you want to go through with this?" Jeff sat at the table for four at the Three Italians' Restaurant in Uptown and wondered how he'd let Pam talk him into this.

"You heard what Detective Hannigan said. After this much time the odds of my dreams being very accurate are slim."

"But not impossible."

"And no reason not to have dinner with the man who Travis trusted to take care of me."

There wasn't much he could do or say. While he still didn't think meeting Greg face-to-face was the best thing for Pam at the moment, he couldn't deny he was looking forward to meeting the son of a bitch in person. Despite Pam's doubts, with every passing moment, Jeff was more convinced Greg was the key.

"Here he is." Pam's smile seemed strained but genuine.

"Why, if it isn't the prettiest woman in North Texas." Greg Johnston took Pam's hand in both of his before pulling her into a good old Texas bear hug. "Man, you're a sight for sore eyes."

Jeff watched. The guy was good. Real good. He could probably steal the shirt off a man's back and then sell it back to him.

"And you must be the good news?" Greg offered his hand to Jeff, his eyes clearly summing Jeff up.

"Jefferson Parker." Jeff extended his hand.

"Greg Johnston."

Good firm handshake. The guy never blinked. The message loud and clear: Greg Johnston was not giving up his claim on Pam.

"Okay, gentlemen." Pam's smile shifted into a soft chuckle. "Everyone to your respective corner."

"Now, Pam." Greg reached over to pull out Pam's chair. Jeff beat him to it by a finger.

"Thank you." She glanced over her shoulder at Jeff.

The sheer adoration in her eyes was enough to make Jeff forget all about Greg, the nightmares, the police, and anything else under the sun.

"Okay. I see the way the wind blows."

Jeff took his seat. "And that would be?"

"A blind man would be able to see the sparks flying between you two." Greg shifted to face Jeff. "Let's get this on the table and over with. Travis was my best friend."

The man said the words with such conviction and sincerity he almost made Jeff doubt the dream, but the nauseous flip of his stomach reminded him the man was as smooth as snake skin.

"Though he never outright asked me to, I've taken it upon myself to see to it that his wife is well cared for, not lacking for anything." Greg paused, cast a glance at Pam, then returned his attention to Jeff. "I can tell you'll do the same."

A hell of a lot better than you did. Jeff practically had to bite his tongue to keep from speaking his mind.

"But be warned," Greg continued. "If anything goes wrong, if you hurt her in any way, you'll be sorry you were ever born."

"Greg." Pam rolled her eyes. "He's a pastor."

"He could be the pope for all I care." He turned to Jeff again. "Are we clear?"

"Perfectly." Jeff forced a smile.

"And for the record, Pammy, I know Travis is real pleased to see you this happy. So am I."

Pam slipped her hand over Greg's. "I appreciate that."

"Why don't you tell him why we're in Dallas?" Jeff picked up the menu.

"There's more good news?" Greg asked.

Pam set aside her menu. "I think so."

Jeff pretended to be reading his dinner options, keeping an eye on Greg over the top of the menu.

"I recently remembered something." She flicked open her napkin and set it on her lap. "The face of the man who attacked me."

Jeff had to give the man credit. Except for a quick blink, Greg's expression remained neutral. The guy was probably one hell of a poker player.

Greg took a sip of water before asking, "How is that?"

"My dreams. They're becoming less fragmented, more clear. That's why we're here in Dallas. We just left the police department."

And there it was. The momentary flash of panic followed by a quick curtain of calm. The bastard was guilty as sin.

"Then you remembered what he did to you?"

This time Jeff saw a deep-set pain in the man's eyes. Whatever his crimes, Jeff had to admit the guy really did care about Pam.

"Some. But this was just about the time you arrived to save me. I saw him clear as day."

"But you were unconscious when I arrived." Gripping his glass of water, Greg's knuckles turned white.

"Mostly."

"Mostly?" The flash of panic in Greg's eyes had now taken permanent residence. The man was running scared.

"I seem to have been semiconscious, when you pulled him off me. I think I remember you hitting him."

"Should have killed him," Greg mumbled.

Pam reached across the table and patted Greg's hand. "It's okay." She blew out a breath. "That must be when I blacked out for real."

"What happens now?" Greg took another sip of water and flagged down the waiter for a refill.

"The police have a sketch, but after all this time the detective didn't seem very hopeful."

For the first time since Greg had walked into the restaurant, his shoulders deflated with ease.

The conversation soon shifted to horse races and wedding plans. Under any other circumstances, Jeff would probably have liked Greg. Especially his heartfelt concern for Pam, but all Jeff could see was a snake in the grass.

"Well, I hate to cut this short." Greg rose from the table. "I've got a late business meeting in twenty minutes."

"Is she blonde or brunette?"

"Paying client." Greg grinned. "Honest. Mario'll put this on my tab."

"That won't be—" Jeff started.

Greg held up his hand. "Call it an engagement gift."

Though it grated at him to say, Jeff had no choice. "Thank you," he and Pam echoed.

"Be happy. That's all the thanks I need."

They watched him walk through the restaurant and out the door.

"I have to be wrong. I just have to."

Jeff didn't say a word. There was no winning in a situation like this. The two of them might have spent the rest of the evening staring after Greg, if Pam's phone hadn't rung.

"Hello… Oh, yes… Oh." Pam's brow curled. "Yes. Mmm-hmm." All the color drained from her face, and she flipped the phone shut without even saying good-bye.

Jeff reached out and covered her hand. It had turned as cold as ice. "Who was that? What happened?"

"Detective Hannigan. His partner just came into the precinct. Thought something about the picture looked familiar. On a hunch he looked through his files. They think they know who my guy is." Pam stared down at her phone. "He wants me to go back. Look at some photos."

Twenty minutes later Pam sat in the wooden seat, resisting the growing urge to bolt and run. One by one, a Dallas police officer who bore a surprising resemblance to a granite statue held the photo of a potential suspect in front of her. With each new face her heart beat a little faster, and her breath seemed a little shorter.

"Tell me if anyone seems familiar." The officer held photo number four.

Her racing heart stopped. Even in a passport-sized photograph she recognized the vicious gleam in the eyes of a monster. Scenes from her own private hell flashed before her. She didn't need to see suspects five and six.

"Mrs. Dawson. Do any of these men seem familiar?"

She nodded but couldn't make a sound.

Jeff tightened his hold on her hand. "Pam?"

Blinking in a vain effort to stop the memories, Pam forced the words from her mouth. "Number four."

The officer placed the photo in front her again. "You're sure this is him?"

No need to look down. She was sure. "Yes."

Within minutes Detective Hannigan slid into the chair across from her. "His name was Michael Shraeder. Not much of a rap sheet. Mostly petty stuff. Couple of assaults. We found him dead in an alley less than a week after your attack." He slid a sheet of paper in front of Pam. "My partner collared him a few times, had to testify. He remembered this scum always had the same lawyer get him off. Normally I wouldn't have this information, but..." His finger fell on the name at the bottom of the page. "The lawyer was Gregory Johnston."

CHAPTER TWENTY-FOUR

"**E**veryone is just buzzing with excitement." Etta Mae poured a cup of chamomile tea for her husband.

Harlon smiled. "I had John Haskell on the phone for over half an hour gushing about how the smartest move he ever made was naming Jeff as my fill-in."

"Why that arrogant…" Etta dropped her hands on her hips, elbows flaring. "Everyone knows George Beauchamp made the recommendation and Theresa Cahill seconded. John Haskell sputtered and huffed to have been outvoted."

"Apparently he doesn't remember it that way." Harlon's satisfied smile remained firmly in place.

"And what may I ask are you grinning about?"

"Our boy is accepted. The town rallied around him." Harlon set down his teacup and cocked his head toward his wife. "With a little help from his mother."

"Nonsense. Jeff made his own way."

"Yes." Harlon nodded. "Yes he did."

"You're worried though. That he's still thinking of walking away."

"Not nearly as much as a few days ago, but yes, it's still a concern. I wish—"

Both Harlon and Etta turned to the sound of the front door squeaking open.

"Now who might that be?" Etta pushed to her feet as her son and new fiancée walked into the kitchen. It took only a few seconds for Etta's words of welcome to freeze in her throat. Pam looked as though she'd lost her best friend and seen his ghostly apparition in the same instant. Jeff didn't look much better. "I'll put on a fresh pot of water for tea."

That's what Etta did best. Mother and fuss in a moment of crisis. And Jeff knew he wouldn't have to say a word for both his parents to realize this was the case. "Thanks, Ma."

"Would you like some pie too?"

Pam cleared her throat. "Just tea for me, please."

Harlon looked at his son. "Is there anything I can do?"

"Thanks, Pop. Not this time. I was wondering if Pam could stay in Carol's old room?"

Pam's eyes widened into button-round circles. "Oh, that won't be necessary."

Jeff put his hand over hers. "You shouldn't be alone, and I can't keep staying at your place, engaged or not."

"If you haven't noticed, I'm a big girl. I don't need watching over."

"I know you can take care of yourself, but I won't get any rest worrying if you're sleeping or having trouble with more dreams."

"I can call Valerie."

"I tried that last night. She has other ideas." Jeff squeezed her hand. "If nothing else, do this for me?"

"Then Jake. He loves playing protective big brother."

"Protective?" Harlon cut in. "What's happened?"

Having placed cups in front of everyone at the table, standing over the kettle that wouldn't boil, Etta Mae shot her husband an oh-Lord-now-what look. One of the many subtle communications his parents had perfected probably before he could walk.

Pam eyed Jeff, then barely nodded for him to tell the story. "We went to the Dallas police station today. Pam remembered the face of the man who killed Travis."

"That's wonderful news." Etta rushed over to give Pam a full-press motherly hug. "You'll rest better once justice has been served."

"It already has." Pam took in a deep breath. "He was found dead in an alley shortly after the…after that night. He had a record. The police didn't have any real clues. Chalked it up to a drug deal gone bad. He had a history of petty theft and assault. It seems he finally met his match."

"You reap what you sow." Etta pushed away at the sound of the whistling kettle.

"Your mother's right." Harlon nodded. "Play in the devil's backyard and you're bound to get burned."

"There's more." Jeff hesitated while Etta Mae poured water into his mug. "Travis's partner was the last attorney to defend the guy."

Neither Harlon nor Etta showed any expression. Harlon waited. Etta poured the last cup then carried the kettle back to the stove.

Pam wrapped her hands around the warm mug to still the tremble. "It's looking like Greg might have had something to do with what happened to us that night."

Etta gasped, her hand quickly clapped against her still-open mouth.

Harlon looked to his son. "The nightmares?"

Jeff nodded.

"Then it's settled." Etta Mae stiffened her shoulders. The pastor's wife was once again at the table prepared to do nurture or battle, whichever the situation called for. "Jeff is right. You'll stay here with us."

"But—"

"No buts. Why don't you run home and put an overnight bag together. I'll go put clean sheets on the bed in Carol Ann's old room."

Pam stood to follow Etta Mae. "At least let me do that."

Etta turned to Pam, and gave her the look that had usually been reserved only for her children.

Pam retracted immediately. The same as Etta's children would. "Yes, ma'am. I'll go put a few things in a bag. I'll be back shortly."

"Do you want company?" Jeff asked.

Pam sighed. "I think I can handle this much alone."

She made quick business of scurrying across the yard and in the front door. The entire evening had left her nerves on end, and now an eerie sensation of being watched hung over her. Taking her time, moving from bedroom to bathroom and back again, she tried taking deep breaths and thinking good thoughts. No matter how much she shifted her thoughts to Jeff and their future, along with all the other fears and doubts battling about inside her, she couldn't shake the feeling someone was out there watching—no matter how absurd.

Her carry-on bag in hand, Pam flipped off the light switch. Cloaked in darkness she inched her way to the window. Nothing. A peaceful suburban neighborhood in small-town East Texas spread out before her. Minutes ticked by while she stood in the dark waiting. But for what?

"Oh, Jeff. Here I am being silly again." She shook off her ill-ease, slipped out the back door, and turned the lock. As if she didn't have enough working against her, now she had to learn to deal with paranoia.

At midnight, wearing her favorite pink terry cloth robe, the one her mom had given her for Christmas the year before she'd passed away, and snuggled in Jeff's arms, Pam watched the flickering light from the Parkers' fireplace.

Jeff had promised his mother that he wouldn't go home until the fire had completely burned out. Judging from the few remaining flames and fading orange embers, it wouldn't be long now. By the time she'd left her house, that odd sensation had lifted, and she'd decided there was no point in telling Jeff. The last thing he needed was one more thing to worry over her about. Now looking into the fire, she wondered why she had let her mind wander in absurd directions and was glad she hadn't told Jeff.

Jeff gave her a peck on the cheek. "Maybe I could stay here tonight?"

"If you were going to stay, we could have done that at my place."

"At your place I wouldn't get any sleep." For the first time all day his smile reached his eyes.

She pulled out of his arms and sat up on the sofa. "The fire is almost out."

Jeff's expression morphed into the perfect three-year-old pout.

"Not that fire." She smacked him lightly on the arm, a heartfelt grin on her face. "You should head home. As soon as this is out, I'll head up to bed. Then we'll both get a good night's sleep."

"I could probably make the sacrifice and stay until the embers burn out."

"I love you too much to put you through that." It was fun to feel light enough to tease.

Jeff pulled her into his arms again. "Say that again."

She grinned. "The part about you heading home or the one about a good night's sleep?"

"The part about I love you too much."

"I love you too much," she whispered just before his lips met hers.

Tender, soft, like the caress of a fresh rose petal, she loved Jeff's kisses. Just another minute and she'd be logical and send him home.

Pulling back, resting his forehead against hers, without opening his eyes, he blew out a slow ragged breath. "The next month is going to kill me."

"I think you'll live."

"Maybe." Jeff loosened his hold, slowly pushing to his feet. "Lock the door behind me."

"Yes, sir, Captain." She saluted.

Jeff rolled his eyes, leaned down, and kissed her cheek. "I'm out of here. I'll be by for breakfast."

Pam nodded, nudged him through the door, then shut it behind him. There was no point in arguing. She suspected he would be hovering closely for the next few days, and to her surprise, she didn't mind one bit.

Halfway to the sofa, she nearly jumped out of her skin at the sudden banging on the front door.

"Pam!"

Tripping awkwardly over her dangling belt, she tumbled to the door, swinging it open with such force it bounced off the wall. "What's wrong?"

"Your house is on fire." He shoved his cell phone into her hand. "I've already dialed 911. Tell them where you are."

In a flash he'd turned on his heel and galloped down the porch, tearing across the yard at full speed.

"Peaches!" she screamed.

"Stay put! I'll find her," Jeff yelled from across the lawn.

Tears in her eyes, she followed Jeff's shadow until he disappeared into the backyard. "Be safe. Both of you."

Everything seemed to pass in hurried slow motion. By the time the blaring sirens of the first fire truck's arrival could be heard, Harlon and Etta Mae had come dashing down the stairs. Draping her arm around Pam to keep her close, Etta Mae and her future daughter-in-law followed Harlon out the door. Pam's neighbor on the other side sprayed her home with his garden hose while his wife stood uneasily on the curb with all the other neighbors occasionally calling out *Be careful*. Even Euphemia had coupled hoses together and dragged them across the street to be used in the wetting down of Pam's roof.

By morning, despite the efforts of most neighbors and the Hope's Corner Fire Department, not much was left of Pam's home.

"A faulty panel box did that?" Jeff pointed to the charred structure beside them.

"Most likely. The company that made the box went out of business years ago. Breakers are known to simply not work. I can't tell you how many house fires we're called on because of a short in a failed circuit breaker."

"Hmm," Jeff mumbled.

Pam stared at the black and charcoaled outline of her home. "When can I see if anything can be salvaged?"

"I'd let it cool another day."

"Thank you." She waved her arm in the direction of the men wrapping up hoses and loading equipment onto the large red truck. "All of you."

"The inspectors will have an official cause of fire for you in a few days." With a brief nod and a wave, the chief scurried off to give his men a hand.

No matter how many sweaters she wore, there was no escaping the bone-deep chill coursing through her body. Too much had happened. Too much heartache in only a few hours. Despite the darkness she'd uncovered in the last day, the deceit of a trusted friend, her mind wandered to all her belongings. Not the sofa or jewelry, but her memories. The afghans her mother had made. The albums filled with photos of her family, her mother. "Mom's favorite rolling pin."

"What?" Jeff asked.

"Do you think it survived?"

"Did what survive?"

"Mom's favorite rolling pin."

"I thought your mother didn't bake?"

"She baked. All the time. It was just never edible." The memory of the doorstop loaf of bread made Pam smile.

Jeff slung an arm around her and pulled her close. "The important thing is you're safe."

"The chief said if I'd been home, I'd have been trapped upstairs."

"Don't think about that. You and Peaches are alive and well. Most everything else can be replaced. You can't." His gaze drifted back, surveying the damage.

"But you're still worried?"

One corner of his mouth inched up in a sly smile. "Reading my mind like an old married woman already?"

"Maybe. What is it?"

Lips pressed together, Jeff focused a long moment at the smoking ashes before speaking. "I can't help but wonder if this has anything to do with Greg. He knows you're starting to remember, and if he's guilty"—Jeff raised his hand to cut her off before she could interrupt—"If he's guilty, you are the only living witness of his supposed crimes."

She spun in his arms and dropped her head on his shoulder. "I won't believe that."

"I know, but just in case…"

"I'll call Detective Hannigan," she mumbled into his shirt. "But I won't like it."

***

"Have they found him yet?" Etta Mae set a glass of sweet tea in front of her son.

"Not yet." For over a week since the house fire, the Dallas police had been unable to locate and speak with Greg Johnston. He was out of cell phone range. Camping. Not that the police were buying his secretary's lame excuses. A judge had issued a warrant for all of Greg's financial records, something Jeff was surprised to find hadn't been done when Travis had died. So far the lawyer was smelling anything but rosy.

"I didn't want to ask Pammy. She seems to be settling, accepting the loss. If she's not thinking about him, I certainly don't want to drag her mind in that direction."

"Salvaging some of her mom's things helped."

"It was definitely the grace of God how that one room seemed to have so little damage when the rest of the house was left in ashes."

Jeff circled his mother in his arms and kissed the top of her head. "Yes, Ma, it was, and, no, I haven't made up my mind yet."

"Was I asking?" Etta smiled coyly.

"I'm just saying."

"Saying what?" Harlon walked into the room.

"The police are still looking for that louse of a friend," Etta offered before Jeff could mention leaving the church. Jeff knew his mom didn't want to let anything upset his father, and bringing up Jeff's resignation was a surefire way to raise his dad's blood pressure.

"They'll find him. You'll see."

"They already have." Pam walked into the room. "I just got off the phone with Detective Hannigan. It seems Greg thought he could easily get lost among the tourists in Tulum."

"Tulum?" Etta asked.

"Mexico." Pam dropped into a kitchen chair. "Greg got a little tipsy and admitted everything to a local…" She hesitated a moment looking at Harlon, then shrugged. "Working girl. Apparently he'd been embezzling funds from the firm for years. That's where he'd gotten the money to buy the horses. He'd hoped a big win would put it all back. But the expenses mounted and with the costs of fighting their big case reaching crippling proportions, Greg feared Travis might have reason to look more closely at the books and why money was so tight. So, he hired that goon to kill Travis. He told the woman that he'd killed the…" She glanced at Harlon again.

"It's all right." Harlon nodded. "Sometimes you have to call a spade a spade."

"Well, Greg killed the…spade." She grinned feebly at Harlon. "When the creep tried to blackmail him. But Greg's big mistake was mentioning to the woman in Mexico that he'd cashed in the two-million-dollar life insurance policy the firm had on the partners. She saw reward dollars in her head and called the authorities. The sad thing is, Greg's first racing win was only days after Travis died. It would have set all the finances straight."

Shaking her head, Etta sat down beside Pam. "Are they bringing him home?"

"Yeah. I doubt he's stupid enough to defend himself, but according to Detective Hannigan, with the evidence they have, Clarence Darrow couldn't get him off."

"Are you okay?" Jeff rested his hand gently on her shoulder.

"You know, oddly enough, I am. I thought it would hurt more knowing the truth, but somehow, all I feel is relieved."

"The Good Book always explains things best." Etta Mae smiled at Pam and patted her son on the arm. "The truth will set you free."

***

"This will be perfect." Pam held her paint sample along the newly hung sheetrock in the kitchen. "I can't believe how much has been done so soon. I mean, don't things like this take months?"

"When your landlord decides to deed you his burnt out property, and every contractor in town wants to work on rebuilding the house for a wedding gift, amazing things can happen." Jeff kissed her cheek. "By the time we're back from our honeymoon, it will all be done. At least enough to live here."

"Hey, Coach." Joshua Meechum pranced into the empty room. "Mrs. Parker said it would be okay to come over here and find you."

"Yep, almost ready to go." Jeff ruffled the ten-year-old's scraggly blond hair. "I thought you were getting a haircut? Can't play ball with hair in your eyes. Not to mention when it's 110 degrees in the summer, you're going to want it all off."

Josh rolled his eyes. "Tim Lincecum has long hair."

"When you can pitch ninety-eight-miles-an-hour, we'll discuss it again."

Eyes down, Josh scuffed a toe along the plywood floor and nodded. The belittling gesture tore at Jeff's heart. "Got your glove? Tryouts are in less than an hour."

The boy's face lit up as any self-doubt seemed to slip away. "In my bag on the porch."

"Okay, then. Let's go." Jeff kissed Pam gently on the lips and mumbled, "Only six more days."

Pam giggled like a schoolgirl and pushed him off with her hand. "You'd better go. Don't want to keep Coach Redding waiting."

She couldn't be happier. Just six more days till their wedding. The builders had accomplished an amazing feat in only three weeks and promised most of the work would be done in three more when they returned from their honeymoon cruise. She supposed if a TV show could build a house in a week, small-town builders could do it in six.

"Talk about a cute pair." Sandra Quinn stood at the back door.

"Oh, hi! Yeah they are, aren't they? I'm so glad Harlon asked Jeff to help Josh. It's doing Jeff a world of good to be involved. I think he's having as much fun as Josh."

"I heard he's also helping Redding from the café with the boys baseball league."

"Hmm." Pam slipped the paint samples into her bag and pulled out the stain chips for the cabinets. "He has more time on his hands now."

Sandra stepped closer, looking over Pam's shoulder at the chips. "The town's worried he won't stay."

Pam blew out a deep breath. "So am I."

"Antique white." Sandra stepped impossibly closer, grabbing Pam's hand holding the samples. "If it were my house, I'd keep it light and bright. Jeff would like that."

Feeling Sandra's breath on the back of her neck, a chill suddenly crept up Pam's spine. Something was off. She shifted away but Sandra's grip tightened, keeping her close.

"This would have been so much easier, if you'd just died in the fire like you were supposed to." Sandra pulled at Pam's hand so the tall nurse now had a hold around Pam's waist, pinning one arm at her side, still gripping the other so Pam couldn't move.

"You? You started the fire?"

Sandra shrugged a shoulder. "It was easy. Did you know I used to date an electrician?"

Pam had no idea what to say, what to do. Stunned didn't begin to cover the way she felt at Sandra's admission. Now what? Standing in an empty unfinished room left no weapons for self-defense.

"He was looking at me. Etta Mae was looking to me. Then you came along. I wouldn't have let scandal fall on him. I'd have taken care of him. He belongs here. In the church. With me."

Panic already licking at Pam's insides now flared to the surface as the glint of a metal blade shone in her face. "If you hurt me, you can't be with him."

Sandra held the blade closer to Pam's face. "No one will ever know. I'll be here to console Jeff in his devastation. He'll remember who I am. We'll be happy."

"What he'll remember is seeing you come up to the house when he and Josh left."

A loud hysterical laugh pierced the tense silence. "You think I'm stupid? I waited until he and that snot-nosed little kid drove away. No one knows I'm here."

"Your car…"

"Is at the mechanics." She smiled.

For the first time in her life, Pam understood what it was like to see true madness in someone's eyes. "Still…" She looked around the room again. There had to be something. An old paint bucket stuffed with tools sat in the corner. The end of a caulk gun stuck up high. Not much she could do with that. Maybe a trowel? A hammer. A screwdriver would be asking too much.

"We're going to go for a little ride." Sandra held tight.

"But you said your car was at the mechanics."

"I borrowed my uncle's."

"Uncle? I thought Etta told me it was just you and your mom?" Maybe if Pam could get Sandra talking, distracted, she could figure a way out of this mess.

"He's not really my uncle. Teddy just liked me to call him that when he'd been drinking. Since he and my mom spent more time liquored up than sober, the name stuck. No one will ever connect the old goat's car with me or your disappearance."

Well at least she hadn't said *murder*. That offered Pam a fragment of hope. "And how are we going to get to your uncle's car without the neighbors seeing you hold me at knifepoint?"

A look of sheer confusion flashed across Sandra's face. "I guess I'll have to change the plan. Shall we see if the plumbers installed the bathtub upstairs?"

"No." Pam steadied herself. "I mean, no, there are no fixtures in the house yet."

The eerie quiet ruptured with a bang when the back door burst open, startling the two women.

Joshua Meechum flew into the room. "Sorry, Jeff forgot his…" The boy skidded to a halt, his eyes grew wide with surprise for only an instant before he spun on his heels and ran out of the house yelling for help.

Sandra spun Pam around, twisting one arm behind her back. With the knife pressed against Pam's neck, Sandra pushed and shoved Pam out the kitchen and down the hall.

"Where are we going?" Pam spoke through the fear.

"Upstairs. You're going to have an accident."

"Accident?" She stumbled over a box of flooring in the hall and ignored the prick of the blade. "Joshua saw you with a knife."

Sandra scowled, then quickly shook her head. "Don't distract me. He's a little boy. No one will believe him. You're distraught. Upset. Guilty. You can't live with yourself after what you've done. I tried to save you."

They'd barely reached the newel post at the bottom of the stairs when the front door eased open. At first Sandra slowed and tightened her hold on Pam. When Peaches sauntered through the doorway exposing an empty porch, Sandra eased her grip, her attention on the cat preening at Pam's feet.

"You stupid animal." Sandra kicked at the intruding feline, the words barely past her lips, when Pam felt Sandra's arm swing away and a heavy weight shove her backward.

Within seconds Sandra stood halfway up the stairs wielding the steel blade at thin air with Jeff standing between Pam and a crazy woman.

Jeff took a step back and waved Pam toward the door. "Joshua's calling 911. Go to him."

When she didn't move, he flicked a sideways glance at her. "Go!"

Pam inched her way closer to the doorway. From where she

stood, she could see Jeff's family and half the neighbors standing on the sidewalk, silently gesturing for her to come out. There was no way she would leave the man she loved with a madwoman with a knife. Never again.

***

Jeff stood at the bottom step for a long minute before he finally spoke. "How is Mrs. Perkins doing with her thyroid?"

Sandra blinked, then furrowed her brow, staring at Jeff.

"I hear she's feeling like her old self again. I can't tell you how much I appreciate what you did for her." Moving softly, without a sound, Jeff took a step closer.

Still holding what looked to be a nine-inch carving knife, Sandra relaxed her stance. "I like helping you."

"And you do. I don't know what I would have done without you. You're so gifted, Sandra. Helping Mrs. Perkins and then my mother at the hospital. And your voice. You've done miracles for the choir." Jeff eased his way closer, up one step. "Do you know my favorite song?"

A full-blown smile spread across Sandra's face. "'I Can Only Imagine.'"

Nodding, he smiled back at her, moving up another step. "That's right. By MercyMe."

Sandra began to hum the popular tune. From the corner of his eye, Jeff could see Pam working her way across the front porch carrying a tire iron. He was just a little more than an arm's reach away from Sandra. He'd have to move fast before Sandra spotted Pam too.

"Can you sing it for me? Please?" He practically purred.

That was all Jeff needed. The pretty brunette closed her eyes and belted out the first line, "I can only imagine, what it will be like when I walk by your side…" In a single leap, Jeff bolted up the last two steps between them. Stretching out one hand, he snatched the knife away from the singing woman, and with the other pulled her into the circle of his arms. She kept singing.

***

The sirens had long ago slipped into silence. Wrapped in a blanket provided by the sheriff, Pam lingered in the warmth of Jeff's arms. "I still can't believe it."

Jeff nodded. "It isn't every day a woman I think is perfectly sane and normal turns out to be a psychopath."

"All I can think of is thank God you were here to save me. Who knows what she could have done by the time the sheriff got here." Pam shivered at the possibilities.

"Save you," Jeff mumbled softly, his arms folding more tightly around her.

Etta Mae set a tray with four steaming mugs on the table. "Once I got to know her better, I knew she wasn't right for my boy. Something didn't sit right, something I couldn't put my finger on, but I didn't expect this." She handed Pam a cup. "You could have been killed."

"Would have," Pam corrected. "There was no way out, and the situation was slipping from dangerous to desperate until Josh and Jeff showed up."

Etta Mae dropped her hand to her heart. "And praise God nothing happened to that young boy."

Pam nodded. "Most kids would have been overcome with fear. Josh took all of five seconds to recognize the danger and hightailed it out of there. I'm still amazed."

"And I'm thankful," Jeff added.

"Amen to that." Etta sat beside her husband.

Harlon patted his wife's knee. "I'm proud of you, son. You knew exactly how to handle that woman. I don't know if I'd have been able to do the same, if it was your mother's life at stake."

"Thanks, that means a lot to me." Jeff kissed Pam's cheek and leaned forward to pick up a mug of tea. "After this morning, I can't help but wonder if there's anyone else out there who needs us?"

"Us?" his father asked.

Jeff smiled, and leaned back against the sofa. "Us. You, me, and the church."

Etta sat up straight, grinning like a kid at his first carnival. Harlon reached for his wife's hand and squeezed.

"I get it, Pop. I can't help everyone, but if I walk away, I help no one."

EPILOGUE

Abigail Clarke sat near the back of the church. This day had been a long time coming. "First day I met Pamela Sue, I knew she was the right woman for young Jeff."

The music started and Dan Parker's little boy walked down the aisle with a cute little blonde beside him dropping rose petals. "I wonder if that's Beullah Gath's kin? Spitting image of Beullah as a girl."

Valerie came down the aisle next. The girl shone in her midnight blue gown. Maybe she'd be next to come down the aisle in white. "It's time that girl stopped flittering and settled down."

Valerie was halfway up the aisle when the traditional bridal march sounded, and Abigail shifted her gaze to the front of the church. Jefferson Davis Parker stood proud and tall, and not a lick of nervousness on his face. On the other hand, best man Jake Wharton fidgeted like a two-year-old. There was another one who should be settling down.

Shaking her head, she spotted the bride approaching. In a floor-length ivory gown with a small chapel train, Pam looked like a vision. Focused and determined, the pretty blonde made her way up the aisle to her future husband. "Yep, these two are gonna get it right. Sometimes you gotta help these young'uns to understand their past so they can find their future."

As Harlon Parker spoke to the congregation, everyone's eyes on the handsome couple, Abigail cast her gaze about the room. Poor little Kenny Parker, he still looked the little boy unhappy to be wearing a suit on Sunday. "Oh, Percival." She sighed. "So much work to do and so little time."

Champagne Sisterhood

Prologue

Flashing lights grew brighter as more emergency vehicles arrived on the scene. One squad car, then another, two fire engines, the sirens of additional ambulances could be heard in the distance. At the beginning of the early morning rush hour, the chaos created by the mangled vehicles already had traffic backed up for miles.

A police sergeant stepped out of his vehicle catching faint smells of burning rubber and gasoline. His gaze fell on the black Lexus sedan. The passenger side had completely crumpled like aluminum foil from the impact of another vehicle. The front end of the SUV across the way bore a strong resemblance to an accordion. "Idiot must have been flying," he mumbled, slipping under the yellow tape closing off the area.

Reaching the lead police officer on the scene, he tipped his head in the direction of the metallic mess. "What have you got so far?"

"The driver of the SUV is on his way to the drunk tank." The officer pointed with disgust to the police vehicle driving away. "Struck first on the passenger side by the SUV, the Lexus spun around and was struck again in the rear by the oncoming pickup, sending the Lexus straight into that pole."

The sergeant's gaze traveled down the length of the utility pole now lying horizontally across the roofs of the two vehicles and most of the street. Telephone and electric wires dangled loosely across both sides of the pavement.

"The Lexus took the brunt of the impacts." The reporting officer glanced at the black clump of metal, and let out a small sigh. "It's going to take a while before they can get those two out of there. The passenger is DOA but we can't get close enough to the driver to determine status."

The roar from the Jaws of Life filled the air as rescue workers slowly peeled the car open like a tin can. Not far from the mangled car, an EMT whose face showed he'd seen one too many accidents like this, and his younger, more anxious female partner, waited for the signal. Both ready to spring into action. When the sound of cutting metal finally ground to a halt, with a nod from the fireman they raced to the vehicle, creating a new flurry of activity.

Silence hung heavily as everyone waited for news, knowing it wouldn't likely be good.

Finally, the older EMT shouted from the torn vehicle to the rescue workers standing by, "She's alive. Barely." He scrambled to save the driver's life as his young partner worked to extricate the deceased passenger for transport to the morgue. A soft thumping sound caught their attention. His partner gasped and all color drained from her face. He shifted, straining to see, his gaze finally settling on the rear seat. Leaning back he yelled over his shoulder to the cop standing nearby, "We've got a baby in here!"

Chapter One

"You can run, but you can't hide. Not from me," Anna Bartiglioni muttered into the receiver at the Italian version of Musak. Juggling the phone on her shoulder and ignoring the rumbling in her stomach, she flipped through several sheets of paper, meticulously highlighting every discrepancy between the ordered merchandise and the first received shipment. She'd taken her last antacid an hour ago.

The oversized corner office she'd sweated blood and tears for offered postcard views of Central Park and the famed Plaza Hotel. Neither did much to brighten her day. This blasted deal was going to be the death of her. Junior had gone behind her back, signed on the dotted line and committed the House of Nobel's new *Madam Nobel* spring line to be produced entirely by a new factory outside of Rome.

Nobel's had been an anchor on Fifth Avenue's avant-garde shopping scene since the doors opened in 1889. Except now, thanks to Junior, she had a boatload of garbage in her warehouse that wouldn't be fit to distribute at Bernie's Bargain Basement. If she didn't straighten this mess out and fast, she might as well kiss her job goodbye and start peddling Gucci knock-offs on Canal Street.

"Damn that irritating little..." Anna yanked her desk drawer open, rummaging for the third time in search of another bottle of antacids when a sharp edge pricked her finger. "Ow!" Sucking on the throbbing fingertip, with her other hand she pulled the offending object out into the light. The silver-framed photo made her smile.

She'd almost forgotten. Her first day in the shiny new office. Babs had arranged for Kat and Erin to fly in and surprise her. When Anna walked into the office at seven forty-five that sunny Monday morning as the youngest Division Merchandise Manager in Nobel's history, she'd been walking on air. When her best friends in the world stood waiting, arms raised, holding glasses of green champagne, Anna almost fell off her new Prada heels from laughing so hard. Her assistant, Liz, stood by, camera in hand, waiting to capture the moment. Before the day was over the photograph of the four friends laughing had been beautifully framed and meticulously placed on her desk.

It hadn't been long before the only personal object in the office was put aside to make room for another project. Now, not a speck of desktop was visible. Every inch was covered with files, drawings, swatches, samples, and one of the new factory's deplorable creations.

The phone still trapped between her ear and shoulder, Anna stared wistfully at the framed photo. Babs' normally curly red hair was pinned up in a simple French twist. A touch of sophistication that came so easily to her. On the other hand, Kat's long blonde hair hung over her shoulders nearly to her waist, making her look more like a California hippie than a Miami Latina. And Erin, named after the Emerald Isle itself, with her dark hair in a ponytail could easily pass for one of her students rather than the high school teacher she'd become. They all looked so happy.

As soon as this latest snafu was behind her, assuming she still had her job, no matter how impossible the timing seemed, she was determined to make time for a vacation and visit her friends. Maybe they could meet up on a cruise again. Babs had talked them all into a group cruise after their ten year class reunion. Babs' Scottish heritage showed in more than her fiery red hair and brilliant green eyes. When it came to keeping her clan together, she was almost tyrannical in her insistence that nothing get in the way of the four of them escaping to have a little fun. Hard to believe over a year had gone by since their last outing. Not that they didn't talk on the phone regularly, but it wasn't the same.

"Anna?" Liz peeked into the office.

"It's okay. I'm on hold. Still." She turned her wrist to see her watch. At this rate she could probably catch a flight to Rome before anyone at the other end actually took her call. She hated that saving her job might come to that. She didn't have time for a jaunt to Italy.

"I've got a Mark Lambert from San Francisco on the other line."

Mark from San Francisco? "Oh, yeah, Tom and Babs' friend. If I hang up now, Italy will hand me some malarkey about the switchboards closing. Get his number and tell him I'll call back in a few."

"I already told him you were on an overseas call and couldn't be disturbed. He insisted it's urgent. He said to tell you it's about Barbara Preston."

* * *

"I've only got about five minutes between classes." Standing in the teachers' lounge at East Dallas Senior High School, Erin glanced down at her watch.

Kat Valdez chuckled into the phone. "Let me guess, you got to class this morning and found all the chairs facing the back wall again, and now you need to vent before you lynch the little darlings?"

"Thanks for bringing that up, again. No, the chairs and my

class are just fine, but I've got one of those feelings. I tossed and turned all night. No matter how much chamomile tea I drink, it won't go away. I just know something's wrong, very wrong, and I don't have a lot of time."

"Sorry, but it's not me. Except for a leaky toilet and a somewhat irate roommate over the cancellation of his favorite TV show, I'm fine."

"I tried calling Anna before my last class. With her job I figured if any of us were likely to have something going wrong it would be Anna."

"She did go a little ballistic the time that freighter caught fire in the middle of the Atlantic and had to be towed, with her new fall line, back to Europe."

"Her assistant said she was on an important call and couldn't be disturbed. If she's fixin' to skin some foreign polecat..."

"Liz told you that?"

"Not quite in those words, but I got the picture. Anyhow, I figure if Anna's well enough to do what Anna does best, then it can't be her, and I didn't want to call Babs at seven o'clock in the morning. Since you're on East Coast time, you're next on my list."

"Gee, you always make me feel so loved." The grin in Kat's tone softened the sarcastic edge of her words.

"Yeah, yeah. I guess I can scratch you off my list."

"I'm sure Babs is fine too. She's probably got that new-mommy-not-getting-enough-sleep syndrome."

"I don't know. This one's just so strong it's scaring me. I haven't been able to eat a thing this morning. Derrick Keaton even brought me a creme-filled chocolate covered donut, and I haven't been able to touch it."

"The kid with the rubber bayonet?"

Erin laughed. "That's the one. I think he's catching onto the concept that scaring the hell out of a gal isn't likely to win her heart." She glanced down at her watch at the same moment the shrill of the bell for the start of class sounded overhead. "Blast, I gotta run. No time to call Babs now."

"Want me to call?"

"No, I should wait a little while. If you're right and there's nothing seriously wrong, I don't want to make Babs' day any worse by calling too early. I'll call after this next class."

"Let me know if it turns out to be anything more than a hangnail."

"Will do. Catch ya later."

Kat hung up the phone. Sitting at the kitchen table, her fingers back in place on the keyboard, she stared blankly at the screen unable to bring her thoughts back to her article about "Visiting St. Augustine Florida on a Budget".

A single file line of fuzzy yellow ducklings waddling across the patio caught her attention. Slowly, a fist-sized knot clenched in her stomach. If Erin was upset, anything could be wrong. One of Erin's feelings could run the gamut from something as simple as knowing a loved one had been burglarized and was alone and upset, or something as serious as needing to rush someone to emergency surgery.

Kat leaned back, remembering the burglary as clearly as though it had happened yesterday and not five years ago. She'd been alone in her trashed apartment, freaking out at the thought of a stranger's fingers touching her stuff. When the phone rang, she nearly shot through the ceiling.

"Are you okay?" Erin had asked in a rush, sounding more frazzled than Kat felt.

After chatting with her intuitive friend for an hour and a half, Kat had felt a little less violated. By the time Erin had spread the word to Anna, Kat had almost forgotten anything bad had happened. When she'd gotten off the phone with Babs, she was packing for a much-needed girls' weekend in San Francisco.

Erin might be the second-sighted of the group, intuitively aware of whatever mischief abounded in their lives, and Anna the fighter ready to march into battle for those she loved, but Babs was the mother hen, making sure the family always found the time to come home. If Erin was right, and Kat didn't doubt she was, whatever was happening, it was happening to Babs.

Still staring out the window, Kat watched as mama duck dipped her webbed toe into the edge of the water before gliding across the small man-made lake. Like good little ducklings, the fuzzy little balls of yellow feathers followed mama's lead, swimming away. She'd never tell her friend, but Kat had named the mama duck Babs.

* * *

"You all right, Miss O'Hanlon?"

Erin glanced up at the young man in front of her. "I'm sorry. Did you say something?"

"You look a little...upset." The handsome kid in baggy jeans that hung low on his hips leaned his book on Erin's desk.

"Just distracted." She lifted a shoulder and shook her head. Jason was a quiet boy. It usually worried her when her students didn't seem to have many friends, but Jason appeared to be content in his solitude. It shouldn't have surprised her that he'd be the one to notice her mood. Touched by his still furrowed brow, she smiled despite the unease stirring inside her and watched him take his usual seat at the back of the room.

"Y'all have ten minutes to go over your review sheets before I pass out today's quiz." The simultaneous groans that rumbled through the room would have been amusing if Erin weren't so preoccupied. Something simply wasn't right.

Her grandmother always said the women in the family had a way of knowing when they were needed, some more so than others. Her mother always got the urge to telephone someone at just the right moment to offer comfort, support, or a ride to the hospital. Her grandmother was much the same, though she also often knew days before anyone else when someone in the family was about to pass on. Whatever this sight was, it seemed to have dwindled with her generation.

All Erin knew was that she'd get a sick feeling in the pit of her stomach telling her something wasn't right with someone she cared about. Didn't matter if it was an irritating hangnail as Kat had teased, or a bellyache that struck at two in the morning like Babs' appendix had done their sophomore year of college. Unlike her mom who knew straight away who to call and bypassed the nervous Nellies, Erin could spend an entire day, or longer, figuring out who and what had her all worked up.

At least her friends didn't think she was nuts, despite having given her the nickname Taisch. Once during a visit to Dallas the summer after freshman year, her grandmother had told Erin's friends the Irish had a name for those with second sight. Even though Erin's premonitions were more a feeling than an actual seeing of the future, they'd begun to call her by the Gaelic word after Erin had awakened in a cold sweat an hour before Babs curled into a ball, screaming from the pain of a burst appendix. Her friends had quickly learned to respect whenever one of those feelings struck. She wished this one wasn't scaring her so.

In thirty minutes the class would be over and she could call California. Who knows, maybe Kat was right and it really was just a hangnail. The vise in her gut tightened. She looked past the kids' grimaces to the clock on the wall. Twenty-eight more minutes.

* * *

Barbara Preston - Babs. The phone slipped from Anna's ear and landed in her lap. Her mind ran in a million directions. Anna remembered the last time her friend had seen fit to interrupt an important meeting. Babs had called to say the flight her parents were on had fallen off the radar somewhere over the Rockies. *Oh God.*

With her heart racing at mach one, she retrieved the receiver from her lap and waved it at her assistant. "Take over the call to Italy for me, then patch Mr. Lambert through. And find me some Tums."

"Right away." Liz stepped back, pulling the door closed.

Placing her overseas call on hold, Anna took a deep breath, straightened her shoulders then pressed the button with the green flashing light. "Anna Bartiglioni."

"Hi, Anna. This is Mark Lambert."

"Yes, Tom's friend. How are you?" She tried to inject a calm to her tone that she didn't feel.

"I wasn't sure you'd remember."

She thought he sounded a little shaky and wondered if he was making the same effort to sound under control that she was. "Of course, I remember you. Scotch, neat, and you balance a mean lampshade. What has you calling at seven in the morning? Or are you in New York?" New York. Maybe that was it. He was in New York. But that wouldn't be considered urgent. Or was he so arrogant he thought she'd consider his visiting New York an urgent matter?

"It's not good news. I had a flat tire this morning. Easy enough to change but I was already running late and the tire only made it worse. I needed to let Tom know he might have to take over for me at a company meeting scheduled for first thing this morning. Since I knew he wouldn't have had time to get to work yet, I called him on his cell."

Anna took another deep breath, wishing he'd skip the details and get to the point.

"A Burlingame police officer answered." Every ounce of oxygen she'd breathed in whooshed out in a dizzying rush.

"All he would tell me is there'd been an accident and the victims were being flown to San Francisco Memorial."

Victims? Flown? Anna's fingers tightened their grip on the phone. For a short instant she'd felt a guilty relief that Tom was the one in trouble and Babs would merely be in need of emotional support. Just as quickly, relief transformed itself into anguish at the thought of Babs losing Tom *and* the baby. It would kill her. "He wasn't alone?"

"No. I called San Francisco Memorial. All they would tell me was that Mrs. Barbara Preston was in surgery."

Anna didn't hear another word. The chair seemed to wobble beneath her, threatening to slip out from under her with the rest of her world. Her heart and lungs had stopped, and her mind had gone blank except for one thought. Babs was hurt. Badly. "I'm on my way."

"I thought you'd want to know. I don't know how to reach--"
"I'll call them," she interrupted. "I should be on the next flight.
See you there." Without waiting for a response Anna hung up the
phone, opened her desk drawer, grabbed her oversized
pocketbook, stuffed the framed photo inside and pushed away
from the desk with such force, the chair flew back and crashed into
the wall. Shoving her office door open with a bang, she turned to
Liz without stopping. "Walk with me."

"I'm still on hold."

"They can go to hell. Call old man Peterson. Tell him I've
got a family emergency. Let his precious Junior figure out this
mess." If she didn't get the right designs, have them up to Nobel
standards, and in store by the debut date, her name would be mud.
If anything happened to Babs and she wasn't there to help, her
name wouldn't mean a damn thing to her anyway.

She was nearly to the elevator when she realized Liz was
scurrying to keep up, a small bottle of antacids in hand. "Book me
a one-way ticket to San Francisco."

"Coach or business?"

"You can put me on the damn wing if you want. Just make
sure when that plane takes off, I'm on it." She dropped the pills
into her pocketbook and stabbed impatiently at the elevator
buttons. "Arrange for a car at the airport- no, wait, an SUV. I'll
have my cell phone. If I'm able to work from San Francisco, I'll
notify you what to send me."

Liz was hurriedly taking notes. "Shall I notify anyone else?"

"You'd better warn all the buyers. If this turns out to be as
bad as I think it is, God help us, Junior will be in charge."

MEET CHRIS

USA TODAY Bestselling Author of several contemporary novels, including the award winning *Champagne Sisterhood*, Chris Keniston lives in suburban Dallas with her husband, two human children, and two canine children. Though she loves her puppies equally, she admits being especially attached to her German Shepherd rescue. After all, even dogs deserve a happily ever after.

More on Chris and her books can be found at
www.chriskeniston.com

Follow Chris on Facebook at ChrisKenistonAuthor
or on Twitter @ckenistonauthor

Questions? Comments?
I would love to hear from you.
You can reach me at chris@chriskeniston.com